JUMANA

JUMANA

Clive F Sorrell

AuthorHouse™ UK Ltd.
1663 Liberty Drive
Bloomington, IN 47403 USA
www.authorhouse.co.uk
Phone: 0800.197.4150

© *2013 by Clive F Sorrell. All rights reserved.*

No part of this book may be reproduced, stored in a retrieval system, or transmitted by any means without the written permission of the author.

Clive Frederick Sorrell has asserted his right under the Copyright, Designs and Patents Act, 1988 to be identified as the author of this work

This novel is a work of fiction. Names and characters are the product of the author's imagination and any resemblance to actual persons, living or dead, is entirely coincidental.

Published by AuthorHouse 09/20/2013

ISBN: 978-1-4918-7870-5 (sc)
ISBN: 978-1-4918-7871-2 (hc)
ISBN: 978-1-4918-7872-9 (e)

Any people depicted in stock imagery provided by Thinkstock are models, and such images are being used for illustrative purposes only. Certain stock imagery © Thinkstock.

This book is printed on acid-free paper.

Because of the dynamic nature of the Internet, any web addresses or links contained in this book may have changed since publication and may no longer be valid. The views expressed in this work are solely those of the author and do not necessarily reflect the views of the publisher, and the publisher hereby disclaims any responsibility for them.

JUMANA

For Sophia
in appreciation of her
support whilst editing
my work.

BOOKS BY THIS AUTHOR - PUBLISHED BY AUTHORHOUSE

SIDDIQUI
KAWTHAR
JUMANA
Stories for Dark and Stormy Nights

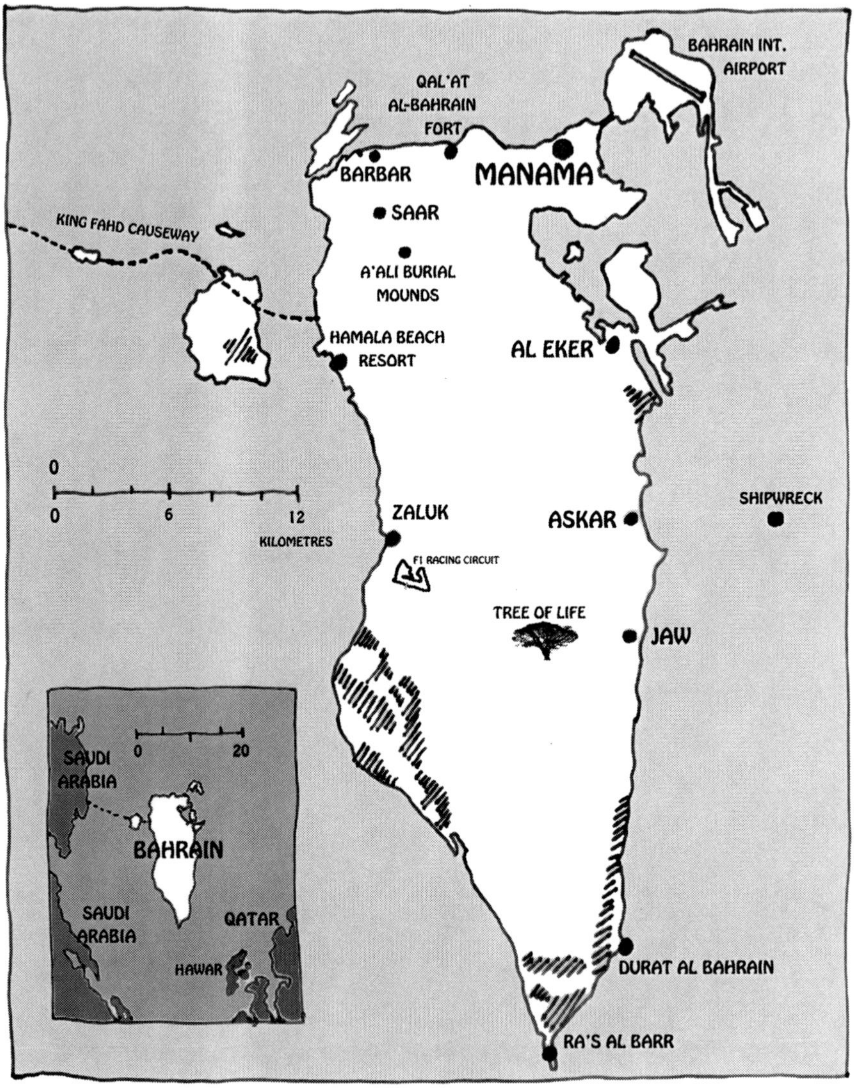
BAHRAIN INT. AIRPORT
QAL'AT AL-BAHRAIN FORT
BARBAR
MANAMA
SAAR
KING FAHD CAUSEWAY
A'ALI BURIAL MOUNDS
HAMALA BEACH RESORT
AL EKER
0
0
6
12
KILOMETRES
ZALUK
ASKAR
SHIPWRECK
F1 RACING CIRCUIT
TREE OF LIFE
JAW
0
20
SAUDI ARABIA
BAHRAIN
SAUDI ARABIA
QATAR
HAWAR
DURAT AL BAHRAIN
RA'S AL BARR

1

The stream of air bubbles rose like inverted summer rain to the calm surface of the Persian Gulf that shimmered beneath the blistering sun. Stuart looked down through the distorting column of bubbles to watch the progress of his dive buddy who was slowly moving along the encrusted hull of the *Fifi*. This had once been a hard-working tugboat that had mysteriously caught fire in 1980 and sunk, fortunately without loss of life. Goldrim butterfly fish and curious cleaner wrasse followed Alan as his fins disturbed the marine growth clinging to the open ironwork of the small ship. Stuart kicked vigorously with his own fins and glided down through his friend's bubbles to swim alongside him. A large stingray suddenly rose from beneath the sand that had partially covered it and gracefully swam away from the men who at first had been startled by the sudden upheaval of the sand beneath them. Stuart gave the universal thumbs up and Alan nodded as they followed the ray's progress with appreciative eyes.

As Stuart reached the skeletal stern of the *Fifi* he disturbed a pair of adult dugongs that had been cruising around the wreck. He signalled to Alan who joined him and they followed the two timid mammals. The three-metre-long herbivores used their paddle-like forelimbs and fluked tails to glide over the sandy seabed. Occasionally they paused to uproot a tuft of seagrass and both men slowed their forward motion until the pair had moved on and the sand clouds had settled sufficiently to restore reasonable clarity to the water.

Briefly glancing towards the surface Stuart noticed that the shimmering shafts of light that penetrated the water were no longer vertical but at a slight angle and he held his dive watch up to his mask. Over an hour had elapsed since they had begun their dive and he realized that they had wandered too far from the dive boat to be within normal safety limits. He had ten years of open-water diving experience and he knew that they were cutting it fine. He checked the pressure gauge and then tapped Alan on the shoulder to draw attention to their situation. Stuart's vision momentarily blurred and the face of the gauge became impossible to read. They had inadvertently swum into an upwelling of fresh water that was spewing towards the surface from an aquifer hundreds of metres below the seabed. These inexhaustible sources of spring water had existed beneath and around the islands for millions of years. Ancient mariners had paused in their voyages to take on vital water, which was why the ancient Dilmun people and the various Arab tribes who followed them named the archipelago *Bahrain*, the land of two seas.

After passing through the dividing curtain that separated the salt water from the fresh the vision of both divers swiftly returned to normal. The first thing they noticed was that the dugongs had completely disappeared and that they were now moving through an almost lifeless zone. Stuart slowed until he could stand upright on the seabed and waited for Alan to catch up.

His friend stopped beside him and jerked his thumb questioningly towards the surface. Stuart nodded but as he prepared to return to the boat he noticed something dark and angular breaking the tan monotony of the seabed. He swam towards the strange object and scraped away some of the marine growth to expose the rim of a large wooden box. Scooping some of the sand away from one side and allowing the grains to settle he could see that it was an old iron-bound chest with corroded hinges and a barely recognizable faceplate. Stuart beckoned to Alan and together they struggled to release the chest from the remorseless grip of the sand. After five minutes of concerted effort that used far too much of the precious oxygen remaining in their tanks they managed to raise the chest a mere fifteen centimetres. Once again Stuart checked his watch and then rapidly jerked his thumb upward and the two men quickly rose together, travelling within their own amassed air bubbles to the surface.

'What the heck was that?' Alan asked after they had surfacd and then spluttered in pleasant surprise as a wavelet of sweet, fresh water filled his mouth.

'By the look of it, a very old sea-chest,' Stuart said as he used his fins to rise higher in the water to look around, 'which will be of very little interest to us if we don't locate our dive boat soon, very soon.'

Knowing that they were a good three kilometres from the coast Alan followed his friend's example and kicking hard rose high out of the water. In this tried and trusted way the friends repeatedly rose up, twisted around and sank down again as they searched their limited horizon for sight of the small dive boat that they had hired. It was Stuart who spotted the gleaming white hull anchored more than four hundred metres from their position.

He removed the mask from his face and as he rose with the slight sea swell he raised his arm and aimed the large area of toughened glass at the sun. Alan followed suit until they saw the tiny silhouette on the deck respond to their signals with wildly waving arms. The two men discussed the strange find on the seabed as they waited patiently for the dive boat to reach them.

It did not take long for the sleek, ten-metre Dubai Marine craft to cover the distance. It slowly pulled alongside the two men as they rose and fell in the gentle swell and with an expert hand on the throttle it stopped dead in the water. The round, cheerful face of Captain Rishikesh briefly beamed over the side at the two divers and then disappeared from their low viewpoint. The salt-stained steel ladder unfolded over the bulwark and swung down into the water.

'Welcome back, gentlemen,' the captain said. 'You have had good diving, yes?'

'Very good, Captain,' Stuart replied, removing his long fins before attempting to climb aboard. He gripped the rails and with the captain tugging on his straps he hauled himself up as the heavy air tanks threatened to topple him back into the water.

'Please drop the anchor, Captain. We want to dive here as soon as we've refilled these tanks,' Stuart said as he in turn helped to pull Alan over the side.

A puzzled expression lined the old seaman's face. 'But there is nothing down there that can be of interest, Mr Taylor. A sea without salt gives very little life.'

'That sounds like tommyrot to me,' Alan teased.

'I do not know this Mr Tommy Rot of whom you speak, sir, but I do know that there are more groupers, dolphins and hammerhead sharks in the real ocean than in these freak waters,' the captain said. 'I have sailed these waters for more than fifty years, I should know.'

'We don't wish to question your invaluable knowledge, Captain, but I don't want to dive here just to see fish but to recover something that we found on the bottom,' Stuart explained. The captain shrugged at that and shuffled to the stern to lower the recently raised anchor, arresting any further drifting with the tide.

'What would that something be, darling?' a lilting voice asked sweetly. Stuart turned and gave a broad smile to the woman who was in the process of smoothing yet another layer of high factor sun cream onto her lightly tanned arms. Dr Helen Taylor, MD, raised herself up and rested on one elbow to look down at her husband. She was lying on a thick beach towel that protected her from the splintered raised deck at the prow of the boat.

'We found a very old chest buried in the sand which I believe warrants closer inspection,' Stuart answered as he slipped the straps of his tanks from his broad shoulders and dropped them onto the deck.

'It appears to have come from a far older boat than the *Fifi*, possibly a merchantman or the type of fast, manoeuvrable caravel favoured for exploring the African coast in the fifteenth century,' Alan added.

'Or if we're really lucky we may have found the site of a carrack, or nau,' Stuart said as he opened up the valves on both tanks to expel what little air compression remained.

'And what's a carrack?'

'It was a three- or four-masted Portuguese ship that usually carried highly prized cargoes from India to Hormuz Island and Bahrain in the sixteenth century. A well-preserved Portuguese stone castle still exists on the island today.'

'Hardly worth a visit, though,' Alan muttered.

'However, if we have found a carrack then it means that we may have found something of archaeological value.' While he had been talking Stuart had walked along the deck and climbed the four steps to where Helen lay sunbathing. With eyes closed against the sun's glare she was reclining sleepily when he leant over her and dripped relatively cool water drops from his undried hair onto her warm skin. She instantly rolled away and leapt to her feet with a playful squeal and began flicking the droplets off her bare midriff in mock irritation.

Stuart ran his adoring eyes over the shapely woman in the blood-red bikini. Wagging a finger in his face, her auburn hair glowing in the afternoon sun she warned, 'Do that again, Stuart, and I'll throw you over the side.'

He accepted the unspoken challenge and rapidly advanced upon her. Nimble as she was Helen wasn't quite quick enough and he effortlessly scooped her up into his arms and carried her to the side of the boat.

'Don't you dare, Stuart,' she said breathlessly as she struggled to be free. 'Let me go, now,' she demanded.

'Your word is my command, darling,' Stuart replied while holding her over the side. Helen had time for one more squeal of fright before she plunged into the warm sea and briefly disappeared in a foaming cloud of bubbles before bobbing back to the surface.

'You'll pay dearly for that, Stuart,' she spluttered as she wiped wet strands of hair from her eyes before energetically breaststroking to the boarding ladder. Alan bellowed with laughter as he watched the grinning woman climb aboard and quickly dodged the spray of water from her vigorously shaken head. He returned to the task of connecting the last freshly filled pair of tanks to a regulator. Stuart blew a kiss to his wife before kneeling on the deck beside Alan to begin double-checking the pressures of the diving sets.

'Have you got time for a sandwich before you dive again?' Helen inquired as she draped a length of terry towelling over her glistening shoulders.

'If you can get something together in an hour it would be appreciated,' Stuart said. 'We'll eat whatever you have concocted after we've brought the chest up.'

Helen nodded and went below decks to dry herself and to begin preparing the meal. The captain had been content to remain at the stern during the playful episode of the three foreigners and was now totally absorbed in washing his face and hands in a small copper bowl in preparation for the *asr* afternoon prayer.

Alan took a long coiled length of rope from his backpack and securely fastened one end to the railing. He dropped the coil onto the deck and proceeded to tie a two-hundred-dollar ice axe to the other end. He then casually tossed it over the side.

'I would never have guessed that my expensive mountain-climbing gear would be so useful in a place that's no higher than one hundred and twenty-two metres,' Alan said ruefully as he watched the rope speedily uncoil behind his descending Grivel Matrix ice axe on its way to the seabed.

Stuart fastened his BCD and hoisted the twin tanks onto his back in readiness for the dive. After the two buddies had checked each other's equipment they both sat on the bulwark and holding their face masks in place with one hand they toppled backward and plunged into the sea.

They followed the line down until they reached the ice axe that was partially buried in the silt and then they both slowly turned to search the desolate terrain. Alan nudged Stuart and pointed to a dark smudge that could vaguely be seen rising above the seabed forty metres to their right. He retrieved his ice axe and with smooth strokes of their long fins they were soon hovering over the chest.

It took their combined strength and a further thirty-five minutes to overcome the reluctant grip of the sand and free the chest. The climbing rope was then threaded through the small iron rings at the ends of the chest before being firmly tied off with a clove hitch. Satisfied with their handiwork Alan gave a quick scissor kick that sent him soaring towards the shadow of the diveboat floating twenty metres above their heads.

After placing a small weighted flag on the seabed Stuart followed his friend to the surface where Helen's smiling face was beaming down at them. She had a bottle of ice-cold lager in each hand. Although it was illegal to purchase alcohol anywhere in the archipelago Captain Rishikesh could magically conjure a dozen bottles every time they hired his boat. After shedding their dive gear they took the condensation-streaked bottles and downed the entire contents without pausing for breath.

'Food will be ready in ten minutes and I expect you to spend a little more time appreciating the cook than you did the brewers,' Helen said as the men returned the empty bottles. She descended to the galley muttering to herself about the ungracious drinking habits of men. The men grinned at each other and after running the rope over the top of a hoist they began pulling and raising the chest bit by bit until it broke the surface dripping seawater and draped in seagrass. Curiosity overcame the captain and he left his favourite seat beneath the awning that covered the stern and went to where the two men were engrossed in turning the hoist to swing the chest inboard.

'This thing is old, yes?' he asked.

'It is at least four hundred years old,' Alan panted as they lowered it carefully onto the deck.

'Treasure?' the old man queried with averted eyes to conceal his rising excitement and avaricious interest.

'Quite possible, Captain Rishikesh, but highly unlikely,' Stuart said as he fingered the keyhole in the corroded but visibly engraved faceplate. 'It most probably contains old clothing that has rotted into a fibrous pulp.'

'Or, the treasure of Edward Teach, old Blackbeard himself,' Alan teased and he laughed out loud when he saw a wave of disappointment cross the captain's weathered face. Captain Rishikesh turned away, feigning disinterest and spat into the sea as Stuart began to tackle the iron platelock.

Stuart had selected a thin screwdriver from the messy toolbox he had found in the wheelhouse and pushed it into the keyhole to clear away the marine growth. Taking great care he lightly tapped the end of the tool against the unseen bedplate inside the lock and to his surprise it immediately detached itself from the primitive funnel-shaped escutcheon, completely freeing the lock's action.

'That seemed easy enough,' he said as he tentatively tried to lift the lid. 'I hope I haven't damaged it too much. I read somewhere that even old locks have a very high value in the antique market.'

Once more Stuart rummaged in the toolbox to find a reasonably sharp wood chisel. He inserted the flat blade into the thin gap nearest to the lock and attempted to lever the lid up. Years of marine encrustation refused to yield and Alan, who was kneeling on the other side of the chest, reached over and grasped the edge of the lid in an effort to apply extra leverage.

Captain Rishikesh looked over his shoulder and sniffed disdainfully at the two men straining to remove the five-hundred-year-old growth that covered the seam running around the chest. He picked up a crumpled copy of the *Gulf Daily News* and had just begun reading about the latest rioting in Nuwaidrat when a loud metallic screech made him jump. The seal had been broken and with a teeth-setting sound the lid was slowly dragged upright.

Sweating profusely Stuart sank back onto his haunches to stare at the sodden contents. 'Clothing,' he muttered, 'just as I suspected.'

Alan carefully lifted out what appeared to be folded pieces of clothing that instantly shredded into smaller pieces despite the care he took in placing them on the decking. 'Looks like a uniform jacket,' he said as he lightly fingered what may have been decorative frogging down the front. 'Could have belonged to one of the ship's officers. The Bahrain National Museum may be interested but with the material in this poor condition they might well tell us to sling our hooks.'

Stuart nodded as he lifted out further items of clothing until he revealed a dark-brown block. 'I think we have something a little more interesting here,' he said holding up one of the heavy objects. 'It feels like wax or at least something very similar.'

The captain shuffled closer to study the object in Stuart's hand. 'You must open it now,' he insisted. 'It may contain something very valuable.'

Stuart shook his head. 'Sorry, Captain, but this will have to be taken back to Manama just as it is. If we try to open it we may destroy something very precious that might have added a new page to the history books on the region.' Stuart pushed against the old lid and with great effort managed to close the chest. The captain stomped away and went into the wheelhouse where he muttered angrily in Arabic.

Stuart and Alan both shrugged their shoulders at the captain's bad-tempered reaction and looked around as Helen emerged from below deck carrying a steaming plate of upside-down chicken *maqlooba*, a Palestinian dish she had perfected during the time she had spent practising medicine in a Dubai hospital. All thoughts of treasure were pushed to the back of their minds as the two men eagerly took plates and helped themselves to generous portions of the heavily spiced dish. They ladled chilled yoghurt onto their plates and the mingled aromas of cumin, cardamom, coriander and cinnamon couldn't be resisted and the captain emerged from the tiny wheelhouse to join the feast. Fifteen minutes later four fully replete diners were sprawled in their seats and the men slipped thumbs under their waistbands to ease their discomfort.

'As usual, you've excelled yourself, darling,' Stuart said as he uncomfortably leant forward to soak up the last few drops of gravy with a folded piece of flat unleavened bread.

'I can always tell when you've been hungry,' Helen said with a knowing smile.

He raised an eyebrow.

'I don't need to use the dishwasher.'

'And he always undoes the top button of his jeans,' Alan added.

Helen laughed lightly and took the licked-clean plate from Stuart who then turned to face the old fisherman. 'I think it is time for us to return to Askar, Captain.'

The captain nodded and reluctantly rose to his feet, his eyes flicking to the chest that was still leaking seawater. 'We should be back in time for *maghrib* prayer, *insh'allah*,' he mumbled as he climbed the steps to the open bridge and flopped heavily into the cracked leather chair. The small instrument panel and stainless-steel wheel seemed incongruous set against the rest of the tired, sun-bleached fishing boat. He turned his head to look down at Alan as he inserted the ignition key. 'Would you be so kind as to raise the anchor, *min fadlak*,' he asked politely.

Alan gave a mock salute and in no time at all he had the small anchor raised and neatly stowed. The boat was soon powering across the calm sea towards the small coastal town that lay six kilometres to the west. Stuart and Alan used the time to shower and dress themselves in lightweight cotton shirts and shorts before joining Helen who was sitting in the stern, hypnotized by the silvery wake spreading out behind them like a dove's tail. As Stuart sat beside her and placed his arm around her slender waist she dropped her head onto his shoulder and he luxuriated in the fresh natural perfume of her auburn hair that had been burnished gold by the sun.

Alan busied himself with packing their dive equipment into four canvas bags and stacking them with the eight empty air tanks that they would refill when they arrived in Manama. As he worked he caught the captain occasionally looking down at the old chest standing darkly and mysteriously on a deck that was so different to the one it had stood upon many centuries before.

A beach stretching from one side of the horizon to the other gradually materialized and it wasn't long before the boat was slowly motoring towards its normal berth on a very short jetty constructed with timbers that had rotted with age. Captain Rishikesh throttled back and then briefly slipped into reverse to stop and deftly drift the boat in against the battered car tyres that acted as fenders.

The captain hailed a couple of passing fishermen and they caught the mooring lines he tossed to them. With a couple of expert twists of their wrists the craft was tied to the crude bollards and they continued walking along the beach without a pause in their animated conversation.

The friends quickly unloaded all the tanks and bags and carried them to a tired-looking Jeep that had been parked on the coastal road. As the two men returned to the boat for the sea-chest they saw Captain Rishikesh talking to a scrawny-looking man in patched jeans and a stained shirt. Stuart could tell he was of Iranian origin by the Qatari dome-shaped cap of red felt he was wearing.

'Who's your friend, Captain?' Stuart called out as they drew nearer to the two men who were engaged in deep discussion about something that necessitated a lot of hand gestures and angry looks. Captain Rishikesh looked round with a startled expression as though he had been caught red-handed. His unkempt companion simply looked down, partly hiding his face in shadow before scurrying away across the beach without saying a word.

'He claims his name is Ahmed and that he is an out-of-work fisherman and needing a job,' the captain said unconvincingly as he turned away to avoid direct eye contact with either of them and hurried back to his boat.

The two friends followed the captain on board and the old man promptly disappeared below deck, once more muttering to himself in Arabic. Stuart shrugged and helped by Alan he lifted the chest and carried it ashore. As they staggered across the sand in the debilitating heat they were unaware that the Iranian whose real name was Behrouz, was watching them from behind a beached fishing boat. Captain Rishikesh had hinted at treasure and the man's glittering eyes were firmly fixed upon the iron-bound chest.

Stuart opened the back of the Jeep, relishing the release of the cool air, and with a final burst of energy that taxed their remaining strength they hoisted the heavy chest into the vehicle.

He returned briefly to the dive boat to settle the hire fee and to bid farewell to Captain Rishikesh who, in contrast to his normal behaviour, accepted the money without any attempt to barter. The old man guiltily muttered his thanks, nervously glanced along the beach and once more disappeared below deck.

Stuart took his seat beside Helen and as Alan pulled away to accelerate along the Harwar Highway towards Manama the swarthy little man with the red felt cap took a cellphone from his pocket and dialled a city number that he had committed to memory for fear it would fall into the wrong hands.

Behrouz was contacting Changeez, an Iranian like himself, and a man who was greatly feared for he was the major drugs distributor in the region. Changeez had the responsibility of ensuring that large quantities of heroin flowed uninterrupted from Tehran into Bahrain and then along the twenty-seven-kilometre King Fahd Causeway and into Saudi Arabia. He was the middleman for Saudi addicts, from shop assistants to high-born princes, who relied on him to satisfy their uncontrollable habits.

Behrouz knew that if the slightest hiccup occurred in the smooth running of this multi-million-dollar operation it would be the little men, such as himself, who would pay the ultimate price of imprisonment or even capital punishment. Powerful people like Changeez would simply fade away like the dense fog that frequently swirled in from the sea, and only reappear when the coast was clear to resume their deadly business.

'Speak,' Changeez brusquely demanded.

'Sir, I have just watched three Westerners return from a diving trip and unload a very old chest that the captain of the dive boat told me could contain something of great value,' Behrouz whispered.

'Speak up, idiot. What chest? Where did they find it?'

'On the bottom of the sea close to the old *Fifi* shipwreck,' Behrouz explained as he bit down hard on a fingernail. 'The captain said that they had opened it and found clothing that was hundreds of years old and a strange, hard packet that they couldn't open. The captain swore it must be some kind of treasure because he overheard the two men discussing taking the chest and the packet to the Bahrain National Museum.'

'Follow them and let me know where they go and what they are doing the moment they do it,' Changeez coldly instructed and then abruptly broke the connection.

Behrouz held the humming phone to his ear for a moment before dropping it back into his pocket and sprinting across the road to where he had parked his Toyota pick-up. Excessive peeling of the brown paint gave the vehicle a camouflaged appearance that had proved highly useful in the past in evading the competition in the desert. The engine coughed, spluttered and then broke into an uneven rhythm and Behrouz pulled away and put his foot down hard.

He knew he had to catch up with the Jeep or suffer the wrath of Changeez.

2

Alan braked to a standstill outside the Bahrain National Museum and the lack of any traffic or pedestrians immediately alerted the trio that the complex was closed for the afternoon. Stuart left the Jeep and hurried across to the administration building and found the doors securely locked.

'Let's go home,' Helen suggested, stifling a yawn as the day's physical activities began to take effect on her and Stuart climbed back in and sat beside her. 'I feel a little tired and could do with a nap before we decide what to do next,' she added as she leant her head against his shoulder and unavoidably closed her eyes.

Stuart nodded his agreement and he leant forward slightly in order to tap Alan on the shoulder. 'How about polishing off the last of the beers back at our place?' he said invitingly.

Alan slipped the Jeep into gear and accelerated out of the museum's service road and into light traffic. 'Sounds right by me, mate. I'll have us there in a jiffy.' He filtered onto Al Fatih Highway and they soon covered the three kilometres to the Juffair district where many of the Western expatriates chose to live. Alan drove down the steep ramp into the underground car park beneath the high-rise apartment building and neatly parked in one of the two bays reserved for Stuart and Helen. The other was already occupied by a little Honda Jazz that was used by Helen to travel to and from the hospital. The men carefully removed the chest from the Jeep and walked slowly to the lift followed by Helen who had slung their sports bags over her shoulders and carried the small coolbox containing the remains of their lunch and the lagers. They speedily ascended to the second floor and were soon making themselves comfortable in the chilled apartment. Alan flung himself onto the couch in front of the giant plasma screen and reached for the remote control on the coffee table. Helen sank into one of the two high-backed armchairs with a deep sigh as Stuart headed for the kitchen to fetch the much-needed drinks.

'You're not going to watch football, are you, Alan?' Helen scolded as she stared at the chest standing on their Ardabil kilim in the middle of the room. 'Surely we've got something much better to look at.'

'Such as?' Stuart asked entering the room with three tall glasses of chilled lager on a small wooden tray. He offered one to his wife and followed her gaze to the object that was now beginning to reek of decaying marine life.

Alan looked away from the Manchester United and Chelsea match. 'Can anything be better than this?' he gestured at the big screen just as Wayne Rooney powered a long ball to pass over the crossbar by mere millimetres.

'That particular match is a week old, Alan, and anyway, you already know the final score and I can assure you that it isn't going to change with each replaying,' Helen said. Then she pointed at the chest, 'But this is five hundred years old and we know nothing about it at all. I don't know about you guys but I'm curious.'

'She's right, Alan, what are we going to do about it?' Stuart added as he raised the lid and removed the mystery package. 'I'm really impatient to know what's inside this.'

'Then go ahead and break it open,' Alan said before downing half the contents of his glass. 'I don't think the original owner would object if you did.'

'I would most definitely find that an act of wilful vandalism and so would thousands of archaeologists,' Helen said in a strong voice as she took the packet from Stuart and cradled it protectively against her chest, as a mother would her child. 'This is history sealed against the ravages of time and you just want to tear it open, willy-nilly, and possibly destroy all the knowledge that it could pass on to us.'

Alan held his hands up defensively and grinned. 'Okay, Helen, don't shoot me, you've made your point. We'll wait until the museum opens tomorrow morning.'

'Or we could take a peek tonight,' Stuart murmured with a devilish twinkle in his eyes as he reached across and scratched at the dark-brown surface with a fingernail. A little of the substance gathered under his nail and after tentatively sniffing it Stuart smiled.

'Would you believe it, the whole thing is solid beeswax,' he declared. 'It must have hardened over the years which means we only have to heat it to melt the outer covering.'

'Any heat may possibly damage the contents, mate,' Alan observed.

Stuart sank into deep thought for a minute before excitedly leaping to his feet. 'I know how we can check the contents without even touching the bloody thing,' he exclaimed. 'And we can do it right now. Tonight.'

Little creases appeared between Helen's eyebrows. 'How on earth are we going to be able to do that? We're not magicians.'

'It's very simple, actually, but you'll have to do a little night shift work,' Stuart said, suppressing a grin.

There was a stunned silence before Alan, who was slumped on the settee, suddenly jerked upright, spilling beer down the front of his shirt. 'But of course! Helen can use the X-ray machine at the hospital! Right?' and he gave Stuart the thumbs-up sign. Helen looked at her husband who was now beaming broadly.

'You've got it in one, Alan. We'll all go to the hospital and Helen can use her medical pass and slip unnoticed into Radiology, do a quick scan and then nip out with the processed film without anyone realizing that she had been there.'

'And if I get caught?'

'You won't be caught, darling, because as a doctor you won't be asked your motive for being in that department and using a machine,' he said confidently. 'Just shrug off any questions by saying that you are doing a little medical research.'

'And if I'm questioned by another doctor?'

'You'll think of something, Helen. You're a very clever lady,' Alan added enthusiastically. 'Let's go now and see what we've found.'

'Helen?' Stuart said with one eyebrow raised as he held out his hand to his wife.

The young doctor looked up at his eager expression and she felt her resistance crumble under the onslaught of the boyish charm that had originally stolen her heart. 'Very well, Stuart, but I'm telling you, we may not find it as easy as you make it out to be,' she said and put the heavy waxy package in Stuart's outstretched hand.

They left the apartment and as Helen drove past the Al Fateh Grand Mosque with its stunning floodlit minarets a vehicle pulled out of a side road and began to follow them. There was hardly any traffic as they smoothly cruised along Awal Avenue and passed the California Hotel before finally driving through the gates of the Bahrain Specialist Hospital where Helen worked as a general practitioner for ladies only. Fortunately Helen's ID badge on the windscreen enabled Stuart to park the Toyota in a bay reserved for doctors close by the covered walkway to the main entrance.

The car that had been following halted at the hospital entrance and then drove on into the general car park where it stopped and doused its lights. Behrouz locked his car and hurried into the large reception area where he immediately spotted Stuart and Alan sitting together in the waiting section. He circled the two friends and sat at the back where he could observe the men without being easily noticed.

Helen left the reception desk and crossed the large lobby to where Stuart was sitting. 'I have just checked and it seems nobody is booked for radiology for another hour. If I'm going to do it I should do it now.'

Stuart was reaching into the small sports bag to take the package out when Alan placed a hand on his wrist to stop him. 'Let Helen take the bag otherwise security may be a little concerned at spotting a strange object being passed from hand to hand in a public area.' He flicked his eyes upward towards the slowly rotating cameras that hung from the high ceiling. 'There are some crazy protesters who might justify bombing a hospital as the perfect way to gain international attention for their fight for a democratic government.'

Stuart grunted his agreement and handed the whole bag to Helen who was stifling a yawn. 'Try to do it quickly, darling, and I'll have you home and in bed before you can say, "Take me, I'm yours".'

'I'll be as quick as I can but don't hold your breath on the latter.' Helen laughed softly and then strode away. She gave a cheery wave to the uniformed receptionist as she disappeared through the set of swing-doors leading to the departments marked Gynaecology and Radiology.

Behrouz saw the young woman depart with the sports bag and keeping his eyes fixed on the two men he sidled around the huge lobby until he was able to slip through the same swing-doors. He was mystified. Why did the three Westerners need to visit the hospital and what was in the sports bag that the woman had taken from her husband?

The corridor was long and starkly lit by fluorescent tubes and Behrouz began to search for the woman by opening the first door which revealed a janitor's closet. He eyed the long white dust jacket that hung on the back of the door and quickly slipped it on over his shirt before checking if the name badge on the breast pocket would be acceptable to any cursory glance.

The next door had a doctor's name stencilled on it and proved to be an unoccupied examination room, as were the next four rooms. When he came to the last door Behrouz heard a low humming noise and on peering inside he saw Helen place a dark block on a stainless-steel examination table at the far end of the room. Suddenly a gleaming piece of scanning equipment began to move slowly into posititon and Behrouz understood what she was trying to do. Helen was too preoccupied in preparing the X-ray to notice the Iranian as he slipped into the room, closed the door quietly behind him and concealed himself behind a row of high filing cabinets.

As he waited he heard a quick burst of clicks followed by a long period of silence and he guessed that the scanning equipment had been switched off and that the doctor was now processing the film. Then he heard the door open and close and the lights in the ceiling went out leaving him in total darkness. Behrouz rose to his feet and went to the door to locate the switch and the room was once again brightly lit. He crossed the room and opened the door to the small room where the film had been processed. There were odd sheets of clear film lying on a stainless-steel table standing against the wall and he casually ran his fingers over them, sliding sheet over sheet until he found an exposed film. He picked it up and placed it on the lightbox that the radiologists used to check exposure quality. At first he was unable to read the negative fuzzy images but then individual shapes began to be recognizable. They were the contents of the large brick-shaped package that had been standing on the examination table and he now knew for certain that they were extremely valuable and would be of great interest to Changeez.

Behrouz quickly tucked the film inside his shirt and checking both ways at the main door he slipped out into the corridor. He sprinted to the swing-doors where he stopped and cautiously peered through one of the small porthole windows while removing the dust jacket and dropping it on the floor. It was now getting very late and there were only a couple of elderly people in the large reception and the woman behind the counter was dozing in her chair. Behrouz pushed through the doors with an air of confidence that was lost on the sleeping receptionist and the elderly couple who had been waiting an hour for their doctor to arrive. He strode across the marble-floored lobby and out through the main doors.

Half an hour later Behrouz had arrived back in his shabby apartment and was faxing a copy of the X-ray film to a nondescript villa in Saar. Changeez liked to be close to the King Fahd Causeway as that was his main pipeline into the Saudi market. Within five minutes the old Bakelite landline telephone on Behrouz's kitchen table rang and he picked up the receiver with a shaking hand.

'Meet me in the middle of the Misan Gardens at 11 pm precisely. I wish to see the original film,' a voice demanded and hung up. Behrouz checked his watch: he only had ten minutes to reach the suburb of Saar on the other side of the city and he snatched the X-ray film from the table and dashed from the apartment. The high humidity of the evening brought beads of perspiration out on his forehead as he ran down the two flights of stairs and leapt into the old Toyota pick-up parked by the entrance.

It took Behrouz fifteen minutes to drive sixteen kilometres and he was sweating more from fear than exertion. He arrived at the park seven minutes late and found his employer standing by a small dolphin-shaped fountain. This had stopped spouting water on the day the street rioting had started.

'My apologies, Mr Changeez, but the traffic delayed me,' Behrouz lamented.

'The X-ray,' his employer snapped, his voice rendered hoarse from habitual *shisha* smoking. He extended a slender, well-manicured hand imperiously and Behrouz gave him the sheet of film. The X-ray was snatched so fast that the thin edge of the polymer inflicted a stinging cut across the palm of his hand.

'Consider that punishment for your delay,' Changeez said as he watched Behrouz lick a trickle of blood from his grimy palm. 'Now point this towards the X-ray,' he demanded as he tossed a flashlight at the aggrieved man. Behrouz clumsily caught it, switched it on and pointed it at his employer. Changeez held the X-ray up and moved it around until the images became clear to see. 'Oh, yes,' he declared softly. 'This is of great interest to me, Behrouz, and I expect you to get it for me. I don't care how you do it but make sure it is in my hands by this time tomorrow.'

The ominous tone of voice sent a cold shiver down Behrouz's spine and he could only nod his mute compliance.

Changeez took a pure white handkerchief from the top pocket of his Armani jacket and meticulously wiped the edges of the film that he had touched before passing it back to Behrouz who took it with his bloodied hand. 'Make me an A4 positive print of this so that I can fax it and remember, be here tomorrow night at 11 with the actual item and the photocopy or be ready to accept the consequence of failure.' Changeez turned on his heel and swiftly strode away to leave the frightened man standing alone in the silence of the park.

As Behrouz was scurrying back to his pick-up Helen and Alan were gazing at a similar X-ray film that Stuart was holding up against the shade of an anglepoise lamp on the dining table.

'That definitely looks like a double strand of pearls,' Helen whispered.

'Large ones, too, and that must be a couple of large ladies' rings,' Alan said as he pointed at two distinctly recognizable objects.

'Everything appears to be wrapped in some kind of dense material,' Helen said as she expertly interpreted the nuances of the X-ray. 'I would hazard a guess that it's animal hide.'

'So, whoever it was, wrapped the goodies in damp leather, possibly calf or goat skin, to maintain essential humidity and ensure the lustre of the pearls would not be compromised and then cast the whole package in beeswax to provide a protective airtight seal,' Stuart summarized as he picked up the block of wax. 'Ingenious.'

'I studied a little of the Persian Gulf history when I first arrived in Manama and I remember that a Portuguese captain called Alfonso De Albuquerque tried to capture Hormuz Island with twenty-seven ships. If my memory serves me right he had about 1,500 Portuguese soldiers and a few hundred Malbarese soldiers,' Alan said thoughtfully.

'Who were the Malbarese soldiers?' Helen asked.

'They were an ethno-religious group that came originally from Kerala in India. The Syrian Malabar Nasrani people followed any church that practised the Saint Thomas Christian tradition.'

'Was Alfonso successful?' Helen inquired.

'More to the point, what's the whole relevance of this history lesson?' Stuart added cocking an eyebrow.

'Firstly, he was very successful.' Alan turned to Stuart. 'And secondly, it was rumoured that one of the ships totally disappeared during the battle and it was assumed that its captain and his crew deserted, taking all the booty they had captured in the recently fought campaign in Bahrain. They were all subsequently judged by a military court in absentia for desertion and sentenced to be garrotted.'

'Which never happened . . .'

'Because the ship must have foundered on a reef or in a storm and sunk,' Alan completed.

'That also went into the records?' Helen asked.

'No, it's simply that the ship and its crew were never seen again and in my opinion that's the ship we discovered,' Alan said holding up the X-ray.

'So you think that the captain or one of his crew most probably wanted to protect the pearls for a lengthy voyage of one or two years and ended up lying beside them for five hundred years,' Helen murmured. 'I wonder what condition they are in. I read somewhere that pearls can survive for something like two thousand years.'

'There was an archaeological dig at Susa where a Syrian necklace was found in the sarcophagus of a very rich person, possibly a queen,' Stuart said with eyes closed as he racked his memory for more details. 'It was supposedly dated two centuries before Christ but the necklace was found to be in a terribly deteriorated condition as many of the pearls simply crumbled at the slightest touch.'

'Not much hope for these little beauties then,' Alan replied as he picked up the television remote control.

'But these are only five hundred years old and have been stored in a way to prevent oxidization whereas the Susa pearls were exposed to dehumidified air in an ancient tomb in the desert. Judging by the X-ray image these all appear quite clearly defined around the edges which could mean that they have retained some of their hardness and lustre,' Helen countered.

'It's also far too late for football,' Stuart said with a mock yawn aimed at Alan; this wasn't far from the truth as the prolonged diving was now affecting him.

Alan grinned at his friend as he put the remote down and turned to address the young doctor. 'Sorry, Helen, you must be really tired. I'll be on my way but maybe we can rendezvous at the museum tomorrow for our big donation to the world of archaeology.'

'That'll be perfect, Alan. Shall we make it one o'clock, lunchtime, at the main entrance?' Stuart said, wrapping the beeswax block in a tea towel and putting it back in the small sports bag. Helen dropped the X-ray into the bag with it before Stuart ran the zip around to close it.

With a cheery wave Alan left the couple and the apartment, closing the front door quietly behind him.

'Don't wake me until nine o'clock, darling,' Helen called over her shoulder as she went into the bedroom. Stuart wearily followed her and called out, 'That's fine by me, darling, but make my morning call ten o'clock.'

They both awoke to the sound of the amplified muezzin calling the faithful to morning prayer and after a very brief breakfast they went their separate ways to their places of work.

Stuart took no notice of the battered pick-up that was parked in the street outside their building as he drove past. Helen, following one minute later, glanced briefly at the vehicle only to check that it wasn't about to drive away from the kerb and present her with a problem. She turned right and settled down for the short drive to the hospital.

Behrouz watched both vehicles depart with a satisfied smirk on his face and waited until they were both out of sight before leaving his Toyota and going into the lobby of the residence. The uniformed security guard sitting behind his desk looked up with a weary expression as the Iranian approached him.

'*Es salaam alykhum*, how can I help you, sir?' he asked politely as he stood up and smiled at the stranger.

'*Alykhum es salaam*, I have an appointment to see Mr and Mrs Taylor at nine o'clock and I cannot afford to be late.' Behrouz looked at his wristwatch, making a grand show of checking his punctuality.'

'Second floor. Apartment 203, sir,' the security man said with a broad smile that multiplied his lines of age as he pointed to the lift bank at the end of the lobby. He then turned the visitors' book around and held out a cheap ballpoint pen for Behrouz to use. The Iranian wrote a false name and address with an exaggerated flourish before returning the pen and striding away to the lifts. The guard watched him enter the first open lift before returning to his copy of the Qur'an. After studying the same *hadith* for a few minutes he casually swept his gaze over the group of monitors beneath the reception counter and was struck by something that he wasn't quite able to put his finger on. He shrugged and was about to return to the holy book when it clicked in his brain. He leant forward and studied the particular monitor screen that showed a wide-angle view of the car park and instantly saw that the two bays reserved for the doctor and her husband were empty. Both cars were missing which could only mean that they had left the building and weren't upstairs waiting for 'Mr Ramzi' to keep his nine o'clock appointment with them.

As the guard left his desk and trotted to the lifts Behrouz was already picking the lock to enter Apartment 203. With a final click the door swung inward and Behrouz hurried inside and closed it behind him. He strode along the hall and into the living room where he instantly spotted and recognized the old chest which stood on what appeared to be an expensive kilim.

Behrouz eagerly opened the top and fine linen tore beneath his scrabbling fingers as he searched for the weird block that had been X-rayed. After scattering the last of the precious items on the floor all around him and emptying the chest he realized that the package had to be hidden elsewhere and his eyes flickered around the room.

As Behrouz noisily swept his arm along shelving, scattering books upon the floor and shattering Helen's precious collection of porcelain figurines the security guard entered the living room. He looked around in horror at the damage being wreaked and quickly withdrew the short wooden baton from his trouser pocket.

Arthritic knees slowed the guard's ability to approach the wildly muttering vandal silently and a stab of pain caused him to stumble over the edge of the carpet just as he was preparing to strike.

Behrouz caught sight of the upraised arm in his peripheral vision and spun away as the old man ineffectually made a swing at his head. He took a few steps back and withdrew a wicked-looking knife from the camel-skin sheath he wore beneath his shirt. Seeing the long blade the guard hesitated for one brief moment but then bravely advanced towards the burglar who simply waited for the right moment.

The old Bahraini made the fatal error of swinging his baton at the arm holding the weapon, hoping to disarm the man, but Behrouz simply swayed to one side and with one smooth movement of his arm ran the razor edge across the wrinkled face. Blood spurted and with startled eyes the wounded man clamped a hand to his cheek and staggered backwards. Behrouz advanced on the guard who tripped and fell awkwardly onto the sea-chest. There was a loud crack as the old man's neck struck the brass-bound wood and he rolled over to end up kneeling against the chest. The liver-spotted hand released its grip on the baton and his head flopped down lifelessly.

Behrouz coldly watched the man die and noticed that at the point of death, when the head fell forward, the man appeared to be praying.

Rather appropriate timing, he thought with a sardonic smile and turned away to continue his search for the artefact. He was eventually attracted to the red-and-white sports bag standing on the dining-room table. He quickly unzipped it and gave a grunt of triumph on finding the dark-brown block that was waxy to the touch. He closed the bag and swept the room with one final appraising glance before snatching a gold cigarette lighter from the small side-table and leaving the apartment. The lift seemed to be taking forever and when it finally stopped and the doors opened Behrouz was confronted by a uniformed policeman. The officer had come in response to the silent alarm that the security guard had the presence of mind to activate and noticing the scrawled note left on the reception counter he was now hurrying to Apartment 203.

'Excuse me,' Behrouz said as he brushed past the officer and walked across the lobby to the main entrance.

'Stop, sir!' the officer called out and Behrouz paused midstride. 'I would like to have a word with you before you go.'

Behrouz looked through the thick plate at the police cruiser parked outside and saw that there was another officer behind the wheel who, if alerted by his partner, could prevent any attempt to escape. The killer turned and returned to the lift wearing a broad smile. 'How can I help you, officer?' he simpered.

'There has been a breach of security at this building and I cannot let anyone leave until it has been fully investigated.'

'I have a very urgent appointment in the city, officer, and I'm sure I cannot help you,' Behrouz said as he began to turn away until a hand gripped his left arm to restrain him.

'I'm sorry, sir, but until I've spoken to security I must ask you to remain in the building,' the officer said with an apologetic smile that in an instant was transformed into a grimace of agony as Behrouz plunged his knife into the man's stomach, hurriedly hustling the man into the waiting lift. As the officer doubled over, fumbling with the flap of his pistol holster, Behrouz twisted the knife once more. The Iranian stepped out of the lift after pushing the top button. As the doors closed on the swiftly dying man he casually sauntered out of the building and across the street to his pick-up, broadly smiling while giving the police cruiser a casual wave.

3

Behrouz checked his cheap wristwatch and decided that he had time for a leisurely coffee and to summon Dabir, his servant, before the appointment with Changeez. To avoid the banner-waving protesters in the city centre he took the Sheikh Khalifa Bin Salman Highway until he reached the turning for the Seef Mall. His pick-up was soon well-hidden amongst a thousand other parked vehicles beneath the shopping centre. He took the lift to the second floor and went directly to his favourite coffee shop where he chose a seat that gave him a good view of the entrance before putting the sports bag under the table and signalling to the *barista* to bring him a double espresso; he then settled back into the soft cushions to await Dabir.

Behrouz was on his second espresso when a man who was almost as broad as he was tall briefly blocked out the light on entering the café. He wore tight black jeans and a black sleeveless T-shirt that displayed elaborate tattoos on a living canvas of solid muscle that he had developed during countless exercise periods in prison.

After his escape in the back of a laundry van from Kahrizak Detention Centre in Iran the man had changed his name to that of Dabir, a wrestling hero who had been the Iranian gold medallist at the 2000 Olympic games in Australia.

The pseudo Dabir left the country using false papers that he had purchased on the black market. When he arrived in Manama, Behrouz was the only person willing to offer a man of his dubious character somewhere to live and since then Dabir's loyalty lay with his new employer and he faithfully carried out every dirty task assigned to him.

'*Es salaam alykhum,*' Dabir grunted as he sank heavily into the chair opposite his compatriot. Behrouz jerked upright when Dabir's outstretched leg loudly struck the sports bag beneath the table.

'Careful, you bloody idiot, what's in that bag is worth a fortune,' Behrouz hissed as he bent to check the contents for any damage. Dabir raised his bushy eyebrows in silent recognition of his employer's sentiment.

'If the boss doesn't have it by eleven o'clock we'll be in deep trouble and I mean up to our necks in a shit load of trouble, so be careful.'

'What is it?'

'Seems to be jewellery from a very old shipwreck,' Behrouz muttered, shifting the bag away from the outsized sandalled feet. 'We must take this to Mr Changeez in the Misan Gardens at precisely eleven o'clock; no earlier and no later.' He reached across the table and grabbed the big man by the wrist and twisted it so that he could synchronize Dabir's time with his own. 'You are precisely ten minutes late, correct it now,' Behrouz snarled, holding out his wrist to expose the yellowing face of his ancient Rolex. He watched with growing impatience as the big man fumbled with the tiny knurled knob until the hands showed the correct time.

'Is it okay now, Behrouz?' he whimpered, holding his arm out for inspection with the crumpled expression of a scolded puppy.

Behrouz grunted, withdrew his arm and finished his espresso as Dabir raised his arm to get the attention of the *batista*.

'You didn't listen to me, Dabir, we've no time for coffee; it's fifteen minutes to eleven and we have to go now,' Behrouz said as he rose and threw a couple of greasy notes onto the table and strode from the café. Dabir sighed and hauled himself up out of the comfortable seat and lumbered out to catch up with the comparatively slender man.

Ten minutes later the two men walked around the swimming pool and headed for the tennis courts in the centre of Misan Park. They cautiously approached the drug smuggler who was already waiting, leaning against the chain-link fence around one of the courts. He raised an eyebrow when he saw Dabir but Behrouz quickly assured him that he was trustworthy and unlikely to cause any trouble.

A man emerged from the darkness and walked towards the trio who watched him approach with guarded eyes. He held a taut leash in one hand to restrain a Labrador and a filled plastic bag distastefully in the other. He passed the suspicious men with hardly a glance and disappeared in the darkness of the park, being towed home to a bowl of dried biscuits and a well-chewed slipper.

Changeez waited, staring at Dabir for a few moments until the dog walker had completely vanished and then he shrugged, took the bag from Behrouz and inspected the beeswax block and the photocopies of the X-ray.

'These will be adequate for faxing to Tehran,' he said grudgingly and then to the disappointment of both men he held up the block and added, 'I'll open this at home.'

Changeez thrust the block back into the bag and zipped it shut. 'I will telephone with new instructions later,' he said before turning and walking away without saying anything further. His subordinates watched him until he disappeared amongst the hedges and then they both returned to the pick-up.

Back at his villa Changeez could no longer keep his excitement contained and taking the wax block into the kitchen he selected a knife and began to chip away at the age-hardened wax with the tip of the blade. It took two hours before the inner wrapping of goatskin was exposed. Carefully prying at the skin he managed to lift one end completely and slowly unrolled it until it lay flat upon the marble worktop and the contents were displayed.

Small parcels of fine muslin material were tightly packed together and Changeez reverently unfolded one to reveal a heavy gold band set with small rubies circling a single diamond of immense size. It was an old single-cut design that became popular during the early part of the sixteenth century.

'The stone has to be at least fifteen carats,' he whispered aloud as he slipped the ring onto his fourth finger and turned it, creating a dazzling display. He placed it to one side and then took the longer parcel and placed it on the cool marble. With fingers that hadn't stopped trembling since uncovering the ring he unrolled the muslin cloth to expose a double strand of pearls strung on fine gold wire. He ran a fingernail over the surface of one of the many pearls and found that it was slightly rough and yet hard, the signs of a natural pearl. Taking the necklace by its intricately worked gold clasp he lifted it up to the light and his heart raced as the lustre of the dozens of pearls revealed their real beauty in the lamp light.

Changeez knew little about Persian Gulf pearls but instinctively guessed that he was holding the very finest in his hands. The transparency, smoothness and overall thickness of the nacre had produced the deepest lustre he had ever seen on a pearl and he assessed that apart from its historical value the necklace he now held had an estimated worth of two to three million dollars on the American market.

He carefully laid the flawless necklace on the muslin and checked the contents of the remaining parcels which all contained rings and gold chains of the finest sixteenth-century workmanship; all in perfect condititon. Even without the double strand of pearls they were collectively worth a small fortune.

Changeez sat down and poured a stiff whisky to steady his hands. The fiery liquid that he had bought on the black market burned and clarified his thinking as he considered his next steps. He realized that Jahandar Saad, his boss in Tehran, would claim all the items and as Changeez had been instructed to fax copies of the X-ray he would be unable to misappropriate one or two rings for himself. He simply had to reveal all and rely on Jahandar's generosity for any share of the treasure; he went to the machine and quickly faxed the photocopy to an unlisted Tehran number.

Changeez finished his whisky at leisure while staring fixedly at the jewellery until the computer voice sexily breathed 'You have mail'. With the hypnotic spell of the jewellery broken he walked across the room to the computer and opened the mailbox. The message briefly stated:

From: J.S.
Subject: X-rays
To: C.
Arriving Manama 09.00—Caspian Airlines—make plans to acquire more of same. I expect results.

Changeez winced at the commanding tone and began racking his brains. How could he force the expatriates to dive for more blocks of beeswax and, further more, compel them to give all the recovered items to him. Changeez picked up the landline phone and dialled a local number.

'Yes,' a voice answered gruffly.

'Behrouz, I need you to come to my villa right now. I have an urgent task at Saar that may require your friend's particular skills.'

Behrouz was excited at the prospect of some action and agreed to collect Dabir and meet Changeez at the Saar burial mounds. Changeez then dialled Stuart Taylor's number, impatiently tapping a pencil on the desktop.

Stuart returned to the apartment at lunchtime to pick up the sports bag they had planned to take to the Bahrain National Museum and found scores of police swarming around his building like angry bees around a disturbed hive. A junior officer waved at him to drive on but Stuart persisted and turned onto the down ramp to the car park. The officer stormed over to the creeping car and rapped on the glass with his baton. Stuart powered the window down and told the angry-looking officer that he lived in the building. A senior officer was promptly beckoned over and Stuart had to explain all over again that he was a tenant before he was grudgingly permitted to enter.

Stuart parked in his usual bay near the bank of lifts. Finding they were roped off and obviously out of service he was forced to use the stairs. Arriving at the lobby he was stopped again, this time by a different officer, who eventually waved him up the stairs away from where a number of policemen and other officious-looking people in all-white coveralls crowded at one of the lifts.

'What's happened?' Stuart asked.

'A man has been murdered.' The policeman was in no mood to continue any conversation. The distraught man only felt like striking out at someone, anyone, for the killing of a brother officer. Stuart decided on the wisest course and without saying a further word he climbed the stairs to get as far away as possible from the angry hubbub of Arabic voices that followed him up the stairwell.

He was perspiring heavily when he reached his floor and welcomed the prospect of a nice cool shower. He entered the apartment and began stripping off his jacket and tie as he made his way to the bathroom. As he passed the open door to the living room he glanced in to see a man kneeling before the old chest. Stuart froze before slowly advancing on the motionless man until he was standing right behind him. It was as Stuart bent to tap the man on the shoulder that he realized he was either unconscious or dead. He quickly stepped round and stared into the old man's lifeless eyes.

'Hello, darling, are you there?' Helen's voice called down the passage and Stuart rushed to prevent his wife from entering the room.

'Did you see all the pandemonium downstairs,' she said hurrying towards her husband. 'They said that a man had been killed,' she went on, giving a wide smile on seeing Stuart walking towards her with outstretched arms to greet her. She allowed him to enclose her in his welcoming embrace and then gave a small cry of surprise as he spun her around to face back the way she had come.

'Darling, you can't go into the living room. There's a dead man in the middle of the room and I think it's our security guard.'

Helen pulled away and said, a trifle sarcastically, that he should be aware that as a doctor she had seen many dead people before.

'This one has died from either an accident or something else and I think his neck is broken,' Stuart said as he picked up the phone and called reception. A policeman answered and while Stuart explained that they had yet another corpse on their hands Helen wandered into the living room and examined the praying man out of curiosity.

When Stuart joined her she made the sign of a finger across the throat. 'His neck was broken, transecting the spinal cord and causing a massive drop in the blood supply to his heart. The poor chap died within seconds but only after someone had cut his cheek with something very sharp.'

Stuart was about to answer when the phone rang and Helen being nearest picked up the handset.

'Doctor Helen Taylor, who's calling,' she asked.

'Can I speak to Mr Taylor, if you please.'

Helen waved to get Stuart's attention and he took the receiver from her. 'Hello, who is this?'

'You don't know me, Mr Taylor, but I know of the chest that you found in the Gulf and in light of its contents I would like to know a little more about the dive you made. Maybe we should meet at the Saar burial mounds. I suggest that you be there at three this afternoon to discuss this matter further. Just be sure you will be there.' There was a sharp click and the connection was broken before Stuart could say anything.

Stuart went to join Helen in the kitchen with a puzzled expression on his face. 'I don't know who the hell that was but he knew that we had raised something from the sea bottom and he seemed a little too familiar with the contents.'

'Ergo, he must have had something to do with the burglary?'

'What burglary?'

'Ours. The sports bag containing the beeswax block and the X-rays that we left on the dining-room table are missing and I wouldn't mind placing a bet that this has something to do with the murder downstairs.'

'My God, you're most probably right, darling. That means it's not just a bungled burglary but a deliberate killing,' Stuart exclaimed, pointing towards the living room. At that precise moment an authoritative pounding began on the front door; the police had arrived and wished to be admitted.

For four hours Stuart and Helen were interrogated, first separately and then together. They were allowed one short break after telling Major Mohammad Kazemi, the case officer, about the weird telephone call. Major Kazemi turned away from them to rattle off a string of orders in Arabic to the four officers who had grouped around him. It was then back to more repetitive questioning while two men dressed in white forensic coveralls thoroughly inspected the chest and its contents and dusted the room for fingerprints. Eventually the police tired of chasing their tails and left the exhausted couple after instructing them to be at the police station the following day to give their written statements. The coroner and his team then replaced the police as they moved in to remove the praying man.

As the front door slammed behind the last official Stuart looked around the room. 'How do we explain this to the landlord? You know how sensitive they are to any scandal.'

'We don't, darling. We let the police give all the explanations,' Helen said. 'And right now, I'm going to pack a few things for us both and then we're going to leave this charnel house and get a room at the Ramada Palace Hotel until all the police have left.'

Stuart nodded, his stomach churning at the thought of the poor guard's homicide. 'I'll just let Alan know what has happened and where we'll be staying,' he said as he picked up the telephone.

'And tell him to be on his guard. This maniac may try again.' Helen hurried into the bedroom and began to grab some essential clothing and toiletries that would be adequate for a few days' absence from the apartment.

It took Stuart a few minutes to reassure Alan that they were both okay, pass on Helen's warning to be on guard and to arrange a rendezvous at the Ramada for a breakfast council of war. As he hung up the phone Helen appeared from the bedroom with an expertly packed suitcase and her familiar medical case.

'What about the man waiting at the Saar burial mounds?' Stuart said pensively.

'Forget him, Stuart, it's far too dangerous. We'll leave that sort of thing to the police to sort out.'

'Can't we just go and see who they catch?'

'No, let them deal with it,' she said and strode to the front door, her light cotton dress dancing around her long elegant legs. They walked down the stairs to the car park and after a brief pause at the police cordon to show their identity cards they drove out into the heat of the day and away from the ill-fated apartment building.

Behrouz collected Dabir and drove the pick-up past the Hamad Town roundabout until he reached the east side of the burial mounds. He left the engine running to keep the air-conditioning going and then both men slumped down out of sight to await the arrival of Changeez. Hundreds of breast-shaped mounds were scattered across the scrubland and fading from view in the hazy distance. Some were of medium height while others seemed to soar twenty-five metres into the sky. This amazing landscape began right beside their parked car yet it had little effect on the two waiting men who only stirred occasionally to ease the stiffness in their joints.

'Changeez isn't coming, is he?' Dabir muttered, raising his head to look around.

'I trust him to know what to do,' Behrouz hissed between clenched teeth, 'and you'd better, too, if you want to remain employed.' A black Hummer with smoky windows turned into the road where they were parked and slowly cruised past the pick-up without stopping. The two men were unable to see through the glass and they had to be satisfied with just watching it pull into the driveway of a large villa forty-five metres further on.

Behrouz relaxed his shoulders and sank back into the soft leather but then sat upright again as a second Hummer appeared and approached them from behind.

'Get ready, it looks like we've got trouble,' he whispered while retrieving an Uzi sub-machine gun from under his seat. Dabir reached beneath his shirt and extracted a 9mm Beretta from the chamois leather holster under his armpit. He pulled the slide back to feed the first round into the chamber while Behrouz slammed a full clip into his Israeli weapon before reaching up and tilting the mirror to see the car behind. As he did so the doors opened and six officers in full SWAT gear leapt out. Behrouz immediately released the handbrake and hit the throttle. Seeing a second group in full body armour pour out of the driveway where the first Hummer had disappeared to Dabir powered the windows down. The SWAT team scattered across the road and aimed their weapons at the accelerating pick-up but they were immediately instructed to hold their fire to avoid accidentally hitting the group of officers running behind the pick-up.

Behrouz swept past the officers who then turned and fired their automatic weapons after the rapidly departing vehicle. Both men ducked and were showered with glass as the rear window and the windscreen disintegrated into thousands of flying splinters. Behrouz steered the pick-up round the next corner and the shooting ceased. All they could hear was the sound of their own engine and that of distant Hummers being slammed through the gears.

Jahandar Saad felt naked travelling without his favourite weapons but the decision to leave the small 357-magnum revolver and his favourite stiletto on his desk in Tehran ensured that he passed through customs and immigration without any embarrassing delays.

Impeccably dressed in a white linen suit he emerged into the arrivals hall with a rolling gait and began waddling across the concourse while he searched the throng of meeters and greeters for his regional distributor. In spite of the extreme humidity two men wearing long black coats and dark sunglasses followed closely behind, pushing luggage trolleys.

Changeez shuddered slightly when he saw the trio before raising his hand to attract their attention.

'Where is my car?' Jahandar demanded, his high-pitched voice grating. 'I trust you have secured the items I wish to see, Changeez.'

'Yes sir, I have obtained the jewellery and it is at my villa,' Changeez replied with a slight tremor in his voice. 'Your car is right outside the terminal.' Despite the absence of any form of greeting or politeness from his master Changeez still managed to create an ingratiating smile and with a broad sweep of his arm indicated the main entrance. 'This way, sir.'

Jahandar's corpulent body and the two attaché cases that accompanied him wherever he went fully occupied the rear seats and after loading the suitcases into the trunk Changeez and the two minders squeezed themselves into the front seats. As he started the engine the car began to reek of expensive Arabic attar that Jahandar always used and Changeez surreptitiously turned the air-conditioning up.

The journey to the villa was tedious as it was constantly being slowed by frequent police action against protesters who were congregating at all the main road junctions. Rocks, cast-iron railings, rubber bullets and spent shotgun cartridges littered the highway, showing the ammunition of choice by the opposing factions. With cold dispassionate eyes Jahandar watched a group of men carrying a badly wounded comrade with bloodied features away from the scene of the latest conflict.

'The fools waste their time,' he sneered. 'They cannot possibly effect a totally democratic government when military and political power are in the hands of those who have had control of the nation's wealth for so many generations.'

'It happened in Cairo,' Changeez said lamely.

'The Egyptians weren't protesting about a dynastic family ruling over them but a corruptly elected government consisting of self-interested politicians. Here in Bahrain the more they protest the more violent the sheikh will become to put them in their place.'

Changeez knew not to pursue the conversation and lapsed into a long silence while focusing on his driving. As the car left the main road the gates to the villa were opened by Behrouz who scowled at Changeez as the large car swept past.

'Your servants don't seem at all happy to see you,' Jahandar observed as Dabir opened the rear door with a sullen expression and without a word disappeared into the building.

'They didn't like the warm reception they received at an appointment I was unable to attend while meeting you at the airport,'

Changeez said with a cold smile. 'I wished to arrange a further investigation of the seabed where the chest was discovered but the people who found it had other ideas and informed the police.'

Jahandar swayed up the steps to the main entrance with a minder supporting each elbow. 'I trust you will eventually be able to change their minds?' he said silkily.

Changeez nodded vigorously as he watched the drug lord enter the villa and then he turned and instructed Behrouz to take the luggage to the guest suite that had already been prepared.

Notwithstanding his deep-rooted fear of Changeez, Behrouz seized his employer's arm in a tight grasp. 'Where were you, why did you not come to the burial mounds? I was almost killed in a police trap.'

Changeez shook himself free and a knife mysteriously appeared at Behrouz's throat. 'Touch me again and I'll slit you from crotch to gullet,' he hissed. 'I was unable to go to Saar because Jahandar's flight was early and I had to collect him.'

'You must have known that Taylor would tell the police about the meeting. Did you want the police to catch me?' Behrouz muttered as he followed Changeez into the villa.

'If I had wanted that it would have happened months ago,' Changeez said as he arranged his face into a smile before entering the main *majlis*. 'Enough Behrouz, let it be said that I knew you could fool the stupid police of this country,' he whispered and then walked across the meeting room and sat facing his guest on a hand-embroidered silk cushion that ran along one wall. Jahandar was already seated cross-legged on a similar cushion opposite while his minders remained standing by each of the two arched entrances to the room.

Changeez rang a small brass bell and a surly faced Arab retainer entered with a tray containing a coffee pot, small handleless cups and a porcelain bowl filled with sweet Nadiya dates.

'The prophet Mohammed, peace be upon him, said that in a house without dates the inhabitants go hungry,' Jahandar murmured, taking a filled cup and greedily helping himself to the contents of the bowl. 'However, I hunger for more than fruit; show me what I flew all this way for and you had better not be wasting my time.'

Changeez turned to a small bundle of silk that had been lying beside him on the cushion. He went to kneel before Jahandar where he slowly unrolled the silk until the glitter of precious stones and the rich lustre of pearls were revealed in all their glory.

Jahandar put his cup to one side and leant forward with eyes narrowing as he assessed the value of the jewels. Pudgy fingers gently probed at the glittering stones before selecting the necklace and lifting it up to inspect it more closely. Without a word he put the strands down and picked up one of the rings that briefly dazzled him as he turned it beneath the strong spotlight set in the high ceiling.

'I am pleased to say that you have not disappointed me,' he said cheerfully and then looked deep into Changeez's eyes. 'You can guarantee me that there will be more?'

Changeez returned to his place against the opposite wall before speaking. 'I will make sure that the men who found those will be only too willing to find more for me by the time I have finished with them,' he snarled.

'You can promise to make them dive again for me?' Jahandar said softly, underlining his question with raised eyebrows.

'They'll dive again, even if I have to kill to make them do it.'

Jahandar slowly nodded his approval.

4

Stuart opened the door a few inches to confirm that it was Alan who had knocked before flinging it wide open and pulling his friend into the hotel room. He waved a welcoming hand towards one of the chairs beside a small coffee table as he relocked the door.

'Good morning, Alan, I hope you slept well,' Helen said from beneath a fluffy pink towel while emerging from the bathroom, vigorously drying her hair. 'We've been up most of the night trying to work out what we should do next and so you must excuse my appearance.'

'You'll always look good to me, Helen. I don't understand why you stay with this unappreciative chauvinist,' Alan said as he turned to admire his friend's wife.

Helen beamed as she tossed the towel onto the unmade bed. She shook her long auburn hair down and then theatrically smoothed her hands down curves that refused to be hidden by a plain cotton dress. 'Well, I doo dee-clair, sir. You say the nicest things to turn a poor girl's head,' she murmured, parodying Vivien Leigh in *Gone with the Wind*.

'Enough of that you two, let's get a little more serious about the whole situation,' Stuart said as Helen plonked herself down onto his lap. 'What are your thoughts, Alan?'

'Well, mate, apart from a few precious items in the chest, you appear to have told the police everything. So, there isn't much we can do now until the bastards have been caught.'

'That's very true but I can't just sit on my hands and do nothing.'

'We could have a word with the captain of our boat,' Helen said, moving to one of the small armchairs beside the bed and picking up a hairbrush to style her hair. 'We saw him talking to that stranger and he could have been telling him about the chest we found.'

'It was a small chap wearing what seemed to be an Iranian hat,' Alan added thoughtfully.

'Called Ahmed, according to the captain,' Helen said.

'He was lying and we need his real name. Only then can we get any ideas about who perpetrated the killings,' Stuart said. 'I think I'll go and have a chat with our loyal captain while you escort Helen to work.'

Alan nodded as he unwound his long legs and rose to his feet. 'I'll let the projects manager at the office know that you've been kept from the test site by an urgent personal matter.'

Stuart nodded as Helen finished brushing her hair before taking her handbag from the coffee table. Alan opened the door and checked the corridor before beckoning to the couple. The trio went to the lift bank and descended to the hotel's underground car park where they went their separate ways.

After a short drive Stuart reached the small wooden jetty at Askar and spotted the same dive boat moored there. Captain Rishikesh was nowhere to be seen and Stuart parked as close to the jetty as possible. A small group of fishermen were sitting on the sand repairing storm-damaged lobster pots and they briefly looked up from their labours and smiled broadly as Stuart passed by. He didn't recognize any of them despite their smiles and climbed onto the jetty and walked purposefully to where the familiar dive boat was skilfully moored fore and aft.

'Hello, Captain Rishikesh, are you aboard? Rishikesh, hello,' Stuart called out but there was no response. Only the light rhythmic slapping of small waves against the hull and the distant murmur of Arabic voices could be heard. He called a couple of times more before jumping on board and making his way to the wheelhouse.

Stuart entered the small chart room but it was deserted and he went out on deck and descended to the scruffy saloon. Dirty clothing lay scattered over the small divan and the remains of the last meal was still congealing on plates that had been left on the fold-down table. More unwashed crockery filled the sink in a galley area that ran along the starboard side of the saloon.

Stuart stumbled through all the clutter and ducked his head to enter the small cabin at the stern that the captain used as his sleeping quarters.

A rumpled heap of grubby sheeting covered the bunk bed but the most noticeable sight was the amount of blood soaking through the material. The sharp smell of death assailed Stuart's senses and he involuntarily recoiled before stepping forward to pull the damp sheets to one side: a totally naked Captain Rishikesh was lying on his back. The unfortunate man had been disembowelled and his intestine spilled between his legs. The slender, long-bladed weapon that had performed the surgery had been arrogantly left impaled in the captain's right eye.

Stuart clamped a hand over his mouth as he gagged and stumbled backwards out of the cabin and into the relative fresh air of the saloon. He sank down onto the divan and put his head between his knees while breathing deeply until the bile had cleared from his throat.

The sudden sound of the old Arabic lullaby *Yalla Tnam Rima,* drew Stuart's attention to a cellular phone that lay under a discarded tissue. It had obviously belonged to Captain Rishikesh and without thinking he picked it up and opened it to connect with the caller.

'I imagine I am speaking to Mr Stuart Taylor who is married to a charming lady doctor called Helen,' a voice hissed and Stuart felt the hairs on the back of his neck rise. He said nothing and waited for the mystery voice to continue.

'You have witnessed what happens to those who disappoint me, yes? And your action in notifying the police about our little meeting at the Saar burial mounds deeply disappointed me, Mr Taylor.'

'Who are you, what do you want?' Stuart said. 'You have what we found in the sea and killed two innocent men to get it, what more can you want from me?'

'I would like a little more of what you found. Or else . . .'

The threat was left unfinished and Stuart went cold. 'Or else what?' he asked in an unsteady voice knowing full well what the answer would be.

'Or else you will become a widower by the same kind of accident that the late captain experienced.'

'Harm a single hair on my wife's head and you'll wish for a quick death,' Stuart shouted, clenching the phone until the plastic case creaked under the pressure.

'Nothing will happen to the beautiful Helen if you do as you are instructed,' the voice continued calmly. 'I simply ask that you take my friends and me to the place where you found the old sea-chest. That's not much to ask in return for your woman's life, is it?'

'Very well, but as you already know, the place is eight kilometres offshore and I have no guarantee that you won't kill me as soon as we get there.'

'You are quite right, you have no guarantee, Mr Taylor, but I can assure you that I will end your wife's life painfully if you don't do as I ask!'

'Very well, I will take you but I will need to get my diving gear first,' Stuart insisted as he stood up and began to climb the steps leading out of the saloon.

There was a long silence before the man spoke again. 'I have all the gear you can possibly need, Mr Stuart, and therefore I expect you to go directly to the blue fishing boat that lies in the small anchorage at the southern end of this beach. If you attempt to call the police again I wish to inform you that I have two men awaiting a call from me. Their task is to demonstrate my disappointment in a very violent fashion.'

Stuart sucked in his breath and said nothing.

'You do understand, don't you, Mr Stuart?' the voice snapped.

'Yes, I understand perfectly you bastard and I will come to your boat now,' Stuart snapped back and with shaking hands closed the phone to cut the connection. Pausing on deck he dialled Alan's mobile and as soon as he was connected he quickly put his friend in the picture.

'For God's sake, Stuart, let me come with you or at least let me contact the police and arrange an ambush at sea while I guard Helen,' Alan pleaded.

'It's no good, Alan. Firstly, they would kill you as soon as you appeared and secondly, it will only take a phone call to put Helen's assassination into operation and you and Helen wouldn't stand a chance against hired killers.'

'What can I do, mate. What can I bloody well do then?' Alan said helplessly.

'Just collect Helen from the hospital where she works, take her back to the hotel and stay by her side until I return,' Stuart said. 'Do you promise to do that for me, Alan?'

'Too true, mate. You know you can count on me to guard her with my own bloody life.'

'I know I can, my friend. See you later.' Stuart closed the phone and as he stepped back onto the jetty he dropped the mobile into the sea. He walked back past the group of fishermen who murmured to each other while furtively eyeing the foreigner. For some reason the gleaming white smiles no longer seemed genuine and Stuart could distinctly feel a cold draught running down his spine.

It only took five minutes to drive along Hawar Highway to where a small promontory of land marked the end of the long beach and the small island that was the Shrine of Shaikh Ibrahim could be seen in the distance. Stuart drove the car off the road and across the sand to stop opposite a moored fishing boat that was painted green.

A man wearing an Iranian Qajari hat and crudely patched jeans was waiting on the shoreline by a small inflatable. Behrouz signalled to Stuart to come to him before sliding the boat into the water. The geologist was forced to wade into the sea in order to climb into the fragile craft and join the scrawny fisherman. Without a word Behrouz retrieved a paddle from the bottom of the inflatable and skilfully propelled them towards the fishing boat.

Two men waited by a salt-stained steel ladder that had been folded over the bulwark and Stuart immediately recognized the leader by his immaculate charcoal-coloured suit. Standing beside him was a round boulder of a man.

'Come aboard, Mr Taylor,' Changeez beckoned with a perfectly manicured forefinger. 'We have to get going before your friends decide to do something foolish. You have undoubtedly been in communication with your wife and your colleague.'

Stuart swung a leg over the side, ignoring the offer of help from a heavily tattooed hand. The man let it drop to his side with an uncaring shrug of his powerful shoulders as he automatically assessed the strength of the slightly older man coming aboard.

'I can assure you, whoever you are, that my friend is far from foolish.'

'That has yet to be proved,' Changeez said with a sardonic smile. 'Shall we go below and check that we have all the diving equipment that you and Dabir will be needing once we get to the wreck of *Fifi*.'

'You want me to dive with him?' Stuart said looking more closely at the big man. 'Is there a wetsuit capable of fitting him?'

'He is a very capable open-water SCUBA diver and will be armed with a very efficient speargun should it enter your mind to try to escape,' Changeez said while descending the companionway. Dabir nodded at Stuart, clearly indicating that he should follow his boss. Stuart went below, closely followed by the big man to find himself in a comfortable, well-appointed lounge.

Changeez was waiting with a glass of white wine in his hand. 'A delightful white Burgundy that I trust will please your palate, Mr Taylor.'

Stuart took the chilled glass and as he sipped the crisp wine he felt the boat shiver—the engine had started. Ignoring Stuart, Changeez began to write with a pencil in a small notebook. Without being invited Stuart sat down on the semi-circular divan as the fishing boat pulled away from the shore. With thick legs spread to steady himself against the boat's movement Dabir stomped across the large cabin to sit on the opposite side, his eyes constantly fixed on Stuart and every move made.

'Dabir is a highly dangerous man, Mr Taylor,' Changeez said without looking up from what he was writing. 'He wouldn't hesitate to snap your neck like a twig if I asked him to. Or, if you try anything silly when I'm not around he won't wait for any orders,' and Changeez snapped the pencil in half and tossed the two pieces out of an open porthole.

Stuart smiled and remained silent as he studied the man who had issued the deadly threat in such a casual manner. He had high cheek bones and heavily hooded eyes of dark brown, bordering on black. A hooked nose above thin lips completed the appearance of a formidable predator. Stuart noted the man's taste in expensive clothing from the Issey Miyake suit down to the Berluti shoes.

'It seems that kidnapping and theft pay good money, yes?' Stuart said as he pointed an accusing finger at the man's clothing.

'I like to dress well, Mr Taylor, and I am fortunate enough to be in a business that enables me to afford the very best,' Changeez said with an arrogant sneer before turning his back on Stuart and climbing the companionway. Stuart could hear muffled voices on the deck above, especially the deeper-sounding voice that Stuart could only assume was the captain's. He was unable to make any sense of what was being said for both men were talking Persian.

Stuart checked that the equipment was suitable and the remaining six kilometres passed slowly during which time Dabir never stopped staring at Stuart, constantly flexing the stubby, nail-bitten fingers on both hands as though imagining what it would be like to grip Stuart's throat.

Just when Stuart felt that his patience was at breaking point the captain closed the throttles and brought the boat to a standstill over the wreck of the *Fifi*. A small anchor was dropped over the side and while the fishing boat rose and fell with the calm swell of the sea Dabir stood and waved at Stuart to go up the steps.

Emerging into the blinding glare of the midday sun Stuart saw that Changeez was standing in the small wheelhouse with the captain and that Behrouz had gone below and was passing the SCUBA gear up to Dabir.

When everything was spread out on the deck Changeez stopped talking to the captain and ordered Stuart and Dabir to get ready. Picking up the smaller of the two wetsuits Stuart soon slipped it on and zipped up at the back. While he assembled the first- and second-stage regulators from the heap of gear on the deck he watched Dabir out of the corner of his eyes with some amusement as the big man struggled to put his wetsuit on.

Dabir was sweating profusely and his chubby features were an uncomfortable shade of red as he finished dressing himself, by which time Stuart had put on his BCD, strapped on a weight belt, slung the tank into position and tested his regulator. He picked up the more professional facemask as Dabir finished his preparations and fastened his fins.

'You are ready, Mr Taylor?' Changeez asked as he lit a cheroot and expelled a small cloud of blue-tinged smoke into the humid atmosphere. Stuart nodded briefly and the Iranian pointed to the steel ladder: 'Then find me another fortune and remember . . .' he paused as he passed a wicked-looking Cressi pneumatic speargun to Dabir, ' . . . any tricks and your wife will pay and you'll be fish food.'

Dabir took the weapon that could fire a barbed shaft of nearly a metre with extreme accuracy and a wicked gleam appeared in his eyes. He waved Stuart on to precede him down the ladder. Ignoring the instruction Stuart sat on the side of the boat, gripped the mask tight to his face with both hands and rolled over backwards into the calm sea. As he plunged into the bath-warm water and descended in a cloud of bubbles he began to give his buoyancy compensator short shots of air to arrest his descent and achieve negative flotation.

He came to a stop and hung perfectly still while Dabir tumbled past him still fighting to compensate for the extra weights he had ill-advisedly attached to his belt. He slowed and stopped six metres beneath Stuart who leisurely swam down to join the armed man. He gave the universal 'okay' sign that was immediately returned and Stuart checked his bearings on the wrist compass before moving off with strong strokes of his fins through the clear water. As they drew closer to the site of the ancient shipwreck both men occasionally glimpsed unidentifiable shapes in the distance that mysteriously glided by before disappearing into the darker green of deeper water.

Stuart noticed that Dabir had slipped the safety switch to the fire position on the pneumatic speargun and he subtly changed direction so that he was swimming slightly to one side and not directly in front of the thug. The familiar blurring of his vision heralded that they were passing into the upwelling of fresh water that he and Alan had previously experienced and Stuart knew that they were getting near to their destination. The entry into the 'dead' zone and the sudden lack of small fish created a chill that physically overcame the warming effect of his wetsuit.

Stuart soon spotted the site marker with a large orange balloon suspended six metres above it and pointed to it. Dabir gave the 'okay' sign and began to search the area for any signs of the shipwreck, slowly drifting across the divide and back into salt water.

Stuart watched the man swimming back and forth for a few moments before beginning his own search in the fresh water. He swam close to the sandy floor, trailing his hands in the fine sand in the vain hope of touching something that could lead them to the ship. Dabir had noticed how Stuart used his hands and he adopted the same technique when crossing back into salt water. He had swum for another five minutes when something sharp hit his hand and a stinging sensation made him jerk it free from the sand. A tiny spot of blood spread like a drop of ink in a water pot and the man watched as an infant stingray flurried itself out of the sand and indignantly 'flew' away. The big man held his finger close to his face mask and shrugged on finding only the tiniest of marks that had already ceased to bleed. Dabir knew that the sting of the juvenile fish now fading from sight would only be equivalent to that of a bee and therefore of no great danger to him. He continued searching, unaware of the dark shape that had glided past when he had been preoccupied with his bleeding finger.

A movement in his peripheral vision alerted Stuart and he saw Dabir snatching his hand from the sand. He caught sight of the flat-bodied baby with its adolescent tail fleeing from Dabir and then he spotted a bigger predator: a full-grown hammerhead shark that had been attracted to the tiny drop of blood.

As Stuart quickly swam towards the Iranian to warn him the hammerhead appeared again and this time Dabir also saw the creature. In panic he raised the Cressi speargun and jerked on the trigger. The spear sped through the water followed by a cloud of minute bubbles and impaled the shark in the dorsal fin. The giant fish veered away from the man, trailing a thin line of blood, and Dabir busied himself reloading the weapon with a fresh shaft. As he pushed the spear into the barrel his hand slipped and the barb sliced across the palm of his hand. The water around Dabir's arm was instantly stained with a dense red mist and Stuart quickly looked around to see the wounded shark only fifteen metres away and rapidly closing in on Dabir. As he kept his eyes fixed on the most efficient eating machine in the sea rushing towards Dabir he caught sight of another and then another shark that were also approaching fast. Stuart turned and keeping as close to the seabed as possible he swam away from the spreading scarlet veil.

With his hand clenched to slow the flow of blood Dabir turned to see Stuart retreating and knew that the only thing that would save him was to enter the fresh-water upwell. He had just begun to kick furiously when the first shark struck. The sheer impetus of the strike tore a large chunk of flesh and wetsuit from the big man's side and the water turned red, instantly reducing visibility as blood flowed freely from the gaping wound.

A circling hammerhead that had strayed into the fresh water streaked over Stuart as though he didn't exist to return to the comfort of seawater and the offering of a meal. As Stuart continued to move away from the condemned man and the dense scarlet shroud that hung in the clear water he watched the shark's jaws gape wide and then clamp down on the Iranian's arm before tearing it off completely. As Dabir's body was spun around by the impact he faced Stuart, revealing his terror and excruciating agony as more sharks darted in to tear away piece after piece until finally the man's head flopped and Stuart knew that he was dead.

This onset of death didn't deter the feeding frenzy and despite the unlikelihood of any shark willingly entering the upwelling of fresh water Stuart remained lying flat on the seabed. He wished that the stream of bubbles from his regulator didn't make so much noise when escaping; looking down at the gauge he saw that he only had ten minutes of air left. Although every part of his body willed him to rush to the surface his brain stayed calm and Stuart remained perfectly still even though he was forced to watch the sharks rapidly devour Dabir until only dive equipment lay scattered on the seabed. Small fish were now beginning to fill the water with their iridescent colours as they began the task of removing any evidence of the man's existence.

As the hammerheads began to disappear into the deeper waters to search for their wounded companion Stuart began to rise slowly, the dappled surface above him beckoning and promising him safety from full-bellied predators and empty air tanks. He paused for as long as he dared at six metres to help with decompression and surfaced with the last few gulps of air remaining. He tore the mouthpiece from between his teeth and breathed in deeply, relishing the long draughts of hot yet fresh air that filled his lungs. Stuart checked his compass and then turned slowly until he had the right bearing before beginning to swim back to the relative safety of the fishing boat; he kept his fin movement below the surface to minimize the splashing that can so easily attract predators.

After a quarter of an hour there was still no sign of the boat and Stuart discarded the tank on his back and kicked hard to rise up as high above the water as he could, turning as he rose but the sea was completely empty; he was alone.

Weariness was beginning to take its toll but Stuart swam on for another ten minutes to check if he could see the boat but he remained alone apart from a solitary seagull that had settled on the surface not more than eight metres away.

Stuart stopped swimming and to save energy he used minimum movements of the long fins to stay afloat while he thought about the eight kilometres he had to swim. Then he considered the most critical factor: in which direction should he swim?

5

Alan arrived at the hospital and asked the receptionist to page Dr Taylor. As he waited his mind turned over all that Stuart had told him and he soon came to the conclusion that if his friend did find the wreck and more treasure then his life wouldn't be worth wombat's piss. He had begun to outline a rescue plan in his head when he saw Helen crossing the hospital lobby with a smile of recognition that soon became a frown on seeing Alan's expression.

'What is it, Alan. Is it Stuart, has something happened to him?'

Alan raised both hands, palms forward. 'Hold it, Helen, don't panic. Stuart's not in any danger yet. However, I think we'll have to do something otherwise he may soon be in very hot water; no pun intended.'

Helen gripped Alan's arm. 'What do you mean?' she said, visibly alarmed.

Alan told her what had happened and where Stuart had gone. Then he put forward the plan he had been working on. 'I suggest that we beg, borrow or steal a boat and head back out to where we were yesterday and confront the guy who telephoned Stuart. When he knows that we have his number he'll back off and if Stuart is diving when we get there he can swim to our boat and we'll return to shore.' Helen stopped short and turned to the stocky Australian.

'That sounds very risky to me, Alan,' Helen said nervously as she twisted a handkerchief between her fingers. 'They sound like men who would be armed and prepared to shoot first and not bother to ask questions later.'

'Ah, not so, my clever doc, for I can borrow a shotgun from a skeet-shooting colleague at the office who owes me one for the two bottles of whisky I gave him at Christmas.' They left the hospital and walked towards the car park.

'Using a weapon some eight kilometres out to sea sounds far too risky when there's a good chance they'll shoot Stuart and then shoot us. Why don't we simply notify the police and let them send a patrol boat out to the *Fifi* wreck? No matter who they are they wouldn't dare shoot at the police. Let's use my car.'

'We tell the cops? That would be a big mistake, Helen, because there is a very good chance that they will first spend hours questioning us before going in with all guns blazing and possibly hitting Stuart in a wild firefight.'

'What if I ask a very clever Saudi policeman for his advice?'

Alan stopped and looked at Helen over the roof of her car. 'Get advice from a Saudi Arabian cop?' Alan said incredulously. 'He would be more likely to claim we were the terrorists and send in a SWAT team to take *us* out.'

'No, that's not what Walid would think. If you recall I once told you that he's the good friend who went through thick and thin to save our lives. He'll know what to do in a situation such as this.'

They got into her Honda Jazz and after Helen had driven through the hospital gates she turned onto the road that led back to the hotel. As she drove she recalled the good-natured police captain who had become a very close friend of Stuart's when they both were living in Saudi Arabia and Dubai. His charming smile disguising a fanatical determination to fight any form of injustice also found a place in Helen's heart and she knew that they could never have a more resolute friend. In both countries when they had been exposed to the darker underbelly of society Walid had battled to save all their lives and now Helen was asking that history be repeated.

She went straight to the telephone as soon as they entered the hotel room at the Ramada Hotel and after flicking through a tiny notebook began dialling a rather lengthy number. As she stood waiting for her call to be answered Alan switched on the electric kettle and dropped a teabag into each of the two cups.

'Hello, is that Captain Safa?' Helen asked while pressing the phone hard against her ear. 'Captain Walid Safa,' she repeated and then smiled broadly. She pushed the speaker button and replaced the handset.

'Major Safa speaking, who is this?' a deep, bass voice rumbled.

'You've been promoted, Walid, how wonderful,' Helen exclaimed.

'Helen, is that you?' the surprised man asked.

'Yes it is and we're in trouble again and I need your advice.'

'Tell me what it is.'

It only took Helen five minutes to relate the unfortunate circumstances, from finding the old chest to Stuart's abduction, omitting no details, at the end of which she was completely out of breath.

'What should we do, Walid?' she gasped.

'You will do nothing until I get to where you are now,' Walid said calmly. 'Do not tell anyone anything or go anywhere, do you understand me, Helen?'

'It'll be hours before you can get a flight to Bahrain, mate,' Alan interrupted.

'Who is that, Helen?'

'Alan is a colleague and a very good friend of Stuart's,' Helen answered.

'Then I can tell you both that I will be with you in sixty minutes.'

'But you're in Jeddah, on the other side of the Arabian pensinsular,' Helen said. 'You can't possibly make it in an hour.'

'Surprise, surprise, Helen, I'm currently based in Al Khubar and only eight kilometres from the King Fahd Causeway to Bahrain. I still control the anti-terrorist division within the Saudi Security Force and I'm currently observing the civil unrest in Bahrain and how the local police and military force is handling the situation. That, fortunately, is why I am so close to where you are and should be able to cross the causeway and reach Manama in under forty-five minutes. Now what is your hotel and room number?'

After giving the major directions to the hotel Helen hung up and for the first time that day Alan saw a slight smile on her face.

'This Major Whatsit is good, is he?' he asked casually as he handed her a mug of scalding hot tea.

'Walid is very good, Alan. Very good in every sense of the word and I have faith that he will have the right solution to get Stuart out of the mess he is in,' she said and then cautiously sipped from the steaming mug. The two friends sat down to begin what seemed a long wait for Walid's arrival.

Major Walid Safa dismissed his driver for the day and took charge of the vehicle. He immediately drove to the temporary barracks where his elite group was billeted and sought out Sergeant Shehhi, the toughest member in D-Team. The 40-year-old bewhiskered veteran had distinguished himself in the liberation of Kuwait and had served under Walid for a number of years. Walid found the small man sitting quietly by himself reading a book of *hadith* while idly running his fingers through his full beard. Walid waited patiently until the sergeant had finished the *hadith* entitled *al-Faraaid*, Laws of Inheritance, and looked up at the major. Walid instructed him to authorize and collect side arms for them both at the armoury and to meet him at the guardroom.

The S-Class Mercedes hummed quietly to itself as it devoured the kilometres to the 22-metre-wide, four-lane causeway that ran out into the shimmering Gulf. The official Saudi Security Forces badge on the windscreen gained top priority at the Saudi Border Station checkpoint, Naran Island on the Causeway and at Al-Jasra on the main island of Bahrain. The flashing blue lights behind the radiator grill promptly moved military barricades to one side and cleared all traffic ahead. Occasionally it attracted stones and tin cans thrown by angry protesters but the bulletproof windows and resealing tyres ensured the limousine's smooth progress through the city and within fifty minutes from starting the journey Sergeant Shehhi was parking the car at the main entrance to the Ramada Hotel. Ignoring the baleful looks of the doorman he left the locked vehicle at the foot of the steps and brushed past the uniformed man to follow the major. They both entered the hotel foyer and rapidly strode to the bank of lifts.

The imitation of a giant blowfly in a jam jar alerted the waiting couple and Alan looked through the spyhole. 'Stocky build, black hair, bushy moustache and a round face,' he reported with his cheek pressed against the wood panel.

'That's Walid, let him in Alan,' Helen called out.

'He has someone with him, a short burly man in an ill-fitting suit and surly expression.'

'If he's with Walid it's okay.'

Alan released the chain-lock and opened the door. 'Welcome to a lot of trouble, Major. I'm Alan.' The two men shook hands warmly and Walid studied the dark-brown eyes, scarred face and unruly black hair pulled back in a ponytail and promptly decided that he liked the man with the Australian accent.

'Just call me Walid, Alan,' he replied and immediately his face lit up on seeing Helen over the big man's shoulder. He released the big paw and brushed past Alan to greet Helen with outstretched arms and the widest grin revealing perfect white teeth.

'Helen,' he exclaimed gruffly. 'It is so nice to see you again, and looking so healthy, too.'

'You aren't looking too bad yourself, Walid, apart from a few pizzas that seem reluctant to desert your waist,' Helen laughed, allowing herself to be drawn into an affectionate bear hug.

'My apology, this is Sergeant Shehhi, a battle-scarred warrior from the Najd region and my right hand in times of crisis,' Waid said over Helen's shoulder.

Alan shook Shehhi's hand and was surprised at the strength in the man's grip. '*Es salaam alykhum*, Sergeant, my name is Alan.'

Shehhi smiled. '*Alykhum es salaam*, Alan. You find my English adequate, yes?'

'Too true, mate,' Alan said with a laugh and sensing a kindred spirit led the tough commando across the room to the side table where beverages could be prepared. As the two men worked together to make the welcome coffee Walid followed Helen across the room and they sat facing each other.

'It has been a long time since our little adventure in Ras Al Khaimah in the UAE and as if that wasn't enough you seem to have got yourself involved in yet another spot of trouble,' Walid said.

The two men drifted across the room to the chairs grouped around the coffee table as Helen took the coffee pot that Shehhi had prepared and began pouring. 'You're right about being in real danger, Walid. I think this could be worse than the last time and I'm scared about what those men may be doing to Stuart.'

'Who are they, do you have any idea?' Walid asked as he took the tiny handleless coffee cup being offered to him.

'It appears one of the kidnappers could be an itinerant fisherman and from the brief glimpse we had of him on the beach he seems to be Iranian,' Alan said. 'He wore very scruffy Western-styled clothes and a national hat; he had a long, vicious-looking face.'

'That's not very helpful,' Shehhi observed, nodding to Helen as he reached to take the traditional cardamom-flavoured coffee. 'That could be any one of the many unemployed fishermen who live along this stretch of the coast.'

'Sorry we can't be more specific,' Alan said with a glum expression.

'As we have no links to anyone on the island we will be forced to go to sea and search for these men who are holding Stuart,' Walid said, slapping his knee decisively.

'That could be a huge risk to Stuart,' Helen said with a frown.

'Not if we boldly approach them flying an official military flag and then clearly demonstrate that we are heavily armed and not to be trifled with. Is that how you say it in English?' Walid said as he placed his inverted coffee cup on the small metal tray as a sign of having had sufficient.

'We could use one of the Bahraini Fairey Marine patrol boats, sir. And with a reasonable rationale, such as apprehending drug smugglers, we might convince them to let us have the one with the Oerlikon 20mm cannon on the foredeck,' Shehhi said with the gleam of impending battle in his eyes.

'That sounds like a bloody good idea to me,' Alan said and gave Shehhi an appreciative nod. As the two men looked around to gauge Walid's reaction they found that he was already using his cellphone. As all three stared expectantly at the major he made his connection.

'Commander? This is Major Safa. We met at the anti-terrorist conference last week.' There was a long pause while Walid listened to the high-ranking Bahraini officer launching into a rehash of the conference. 'Sorry to interrupt you, sir, but my main reason for calling is that I have reason to suspect that there is a shipment of drugs coming ashore later today and I need to apprehend the smugglers while they are still at sea. Do you have an armed patrol boat that I can use for an hour or two?'

There was a long silence broken only by Walid scribbling furiously in the little notepad he habitually carried in his top pocket.

'Thank you very much, Commander. I and Sergeant Shehhi, plus one civilian undercover agent, who can only be known as Mr Alan, will be at the docks to take command of BN103 in fifteen minutes.'

Walid closed the connection. 'And that's that, gentlemen. We are now the possessors of a twenty-metre naval vessel with the firepower to sink any fishing boat in seconds.'

Helen looked at Walid with thoughtful eyes and as she poured herself another coffee she quietly asked the major why a commander of the Royal Bahraini Naval Force could so easily be convinced to hand over one of his precious patrol boats to a Saudi Security Force major who was only in the commander's country to observe crowd control.

'I am here to do a lot more than study methods of handling protesters, Helen. My undercover remit in this region is to identify and apprehend those people who are running hard drugs into the kingdom by using Bahrain as a distribution centre.'

'Wow. No wonder the commander was so eager to help you,' Alan said. 'He obviously doesn't want his country to be held responsible for the drugs that are now flooding across the Arabian Peninsular.'

'Well put, and in a very small nutshell, I believe,' Shehhi laughed, unaware of the prophetic nature of his words.

'You understand my language more than you would lead me to believe you do,' Alan growled good-humouredly.

'Sergeant, we must hurry,' Walid said authoritatively and the three men stood and began filing from the room.

'And what do I do in the meantime, just twiddle my thumbs?' Helen asked angrily.

Walid turned back and took the doctor firmly by the shoulders. He looked deep into her grey-blue eyes that sparked accusingly and spoke softly. 'Helen, we will return with Stuart or die in the attempt. Of that you can be sure. But, I will only be able to concentrate fully on this task if I know that you are safely locked in this hotel room, well away from any harm. Promise me you will be patient and stay here and that you will not answer the door to anyone other than myself, Alan or Stuart.'

The brief surge of frustrated anger faded and Helen's face became calm and untroubled. 'I promise, Walid. But you must also promise to return soon and safely.' She rose up onto her tiptoes and, with his bristly moustache tickling her face, she lightly kissed Walid's cheek.

Walid looked round and into the broadly smiling features of Shehhi and felt colour rush to his cheeks. 'Helen is like one of my daughters, Sergeant, so stop smirking and get a move on. *Yallah, yallah.*'

The three men hurried from the Ramada Hotel and were soon leaving the Juffair area and speeding along Al Fatih Highway to reach Guraifa. They raced past the ship registration office and at Mina Salman they crossed a short causeway to enter the naval dockyard. Walid showed his ID at the heavily armed gate and on being given permission Shehhi drove along the dockside until the distinctive silhouette of a Fairey Marine Tracker II patrol boat caused him to brake violently.

'Just look at that,' Shehhi whispered, his eyes lustfully fixed on the large weapon that dominated the foredeck. The single barrel of the 20mm cannon was pointing skyward in a position of repose.

Walid approached the duty officer at the gangway and showed his identification and murmured something that the other two couldn't hear. The officer snapped to attention and gave Walid a salute worthy of a lieutenant commander.

'I guess this must be the right boat, Shehhi,' Alan said and the Saudi tipped his head forward to laugh quietly into his black beard.

The duty officer nodded politely to each man as they boarded and then with a final salute to Walid he instructed ratings to remove the gangway. Apart from the captain, his helmsman and one deck rating there was only one other Bahraini naval man aboard and he was below tending to his beloved twin engines.

When they entered the wheelhouse Captain Mahmood coolly welcomed the intruders into his domain and nodded when asked if he was familiar with the location of the *Fifi*.

'If I didn't know the whereabouts of the *Fifi* after fifteen years in these waters then I wouldn't be worthy to command a rowing boat, Major Safa,' he replied with a humorous twinkle in his eyes. He instructed the deck rating to cast off and signalled 'slow ahead' to the engineer below. The boat slipped away from the landing stage and slowly turned towards the open sea. As soon as the bow was lined with the dock opening the signal was made and the quietly burbling engines burst into a throaty roar. The water at the stern became a white maelstrom and then transformd into twin plumes that marked their passage as the patrol boat rapidly accelerated into the sun.

Sergeant Shehhi lost no time in talking the deck rating into instructing him on the use of the heavy weapon and Walid watched the enthusiasm of his sergeant bubble over as he settled into the shoulder pads and test-fired short bursts over two kilometres out to sea. The cannon was capable of firing 450 rounds per minute at a muzzle velocity capable of ripping the heart out of a small vessel. Walid smiled to himself as a parent might over a child's wilful behaviour.

The captain signalled full power and the bow of the patrol boat rose higher as their speed increased and very soon they saw a small dark smudge on the horizon. It was a clear indication that they were not alone on the smooth sea that shone like a smoked mirror beneath the washed-out sky.

Walid picked up a spare pair of binoculars and joined the captain in studying the distant vessel. It sprang into sharp focus and both men could see figures scurrying about on deck and the occasional flash of glass as someone turned their binoculars on them.

'They appear to be in a bit of a hurry to get away,' the captain muttered without lowering his glasses. 'Do we intercept?'

'Yes, and if they refuse to heave to we will stop them with extreme force,' Walid said through clenched teeth.

'And Stuart, what about Stuart, Walid?' Alan asked as he laid his hand on the major's tense forearm.

6

In 1964 as Ayatollah Khomeini left Tehran and flew into exile a baby boy was born in a poverty-stricken district of Tehran. He was soon abandoned by his mother who fled the brothel she was working in and was raised in the establishment to become an aggressive bully. He was appropriately given the name Jahandar which means 'owner of the world'.

After the Pahlavi dynasty collapsed in 1979 and while guerillas were overwhelming loyal troops in street battles the 15-year-old adolescent was already running a small but successful protection racket in the Vali-e-Asr district of Tehran. He more than held his own in the frequent street fights when broken bottles, knives and pistols proved to be the only way to successfully settle a score.

Apart from smuggling and robbery, drug dealing was the prime occupation of many inhabitants in the district, including the youth. It wasn't long after the Shah had fled the country that Jahandar also discovered the financial rewards that could be had from drugs and very soon he was selling opium to interested parties who could process the more desirable heroin.

The first murder he actively participated in was that of a minor drug runner who had attempted to keep a small share of Jahandar's opium product for himself. Jahandar ordered one of his men to cut the man's throat and leave his body in an open drain as a reminder to others. After this had been done Jahandar found that he had a taste for absolute power that could control the lives or deaths of others.

During the six years that the Iraq-Iran war raged Jahandar avoided becoming canon fodder by ensuring that all his identity records and those of his right-hand men that were kept in the local government offices were conveniently mislaid.

His business in drugs flourished, as did his first venture into prostitution, due to the increased demand for any kind of escape from the war weary, including the badly maimed victims who begged on the streets.

After the two nations had signed the truce Jahandar was able to acquire a large supply of medium to heavy weaponry that he sold on to customers on the African continent. This money was then reinvested into the development of his own heroin production facilities.

The new millennium issued a new challenge for Jahandar for although he now employed more than two thousand people and marketed his drugs throughout the Middle East, he constantly looked for a safe way of entering the highly lucrative markets across Europe and America.

It was his passion for nibbling Fandoghi pistachio nuts while at meetings that provided him with the solution. Jahandar had e-mailed a few of his top chemists to set up a brain-storming session to be held at his head office.

During a discussion on raising the number of heroin bags they exported one of the junior chemists suddenly joked: 'If we could export the same number of bags as the bags of pistachios Jahandar ate we could buy the whole country.'

A deathly silence descended on the smoke-filled room and all eyes swivelled as one to study Jahandar's reaction while the young man, realizing his moment of disrespect, froze.

'He's right, gentlemen, I do get through a lot of these and it is beginning to show,' Jahandar said softly as he patted his rotund form before daintily choosing another large Fandoghi from the bowl set before him. He removed the nut and was about to discard the two halves of the shell when he paused.

'You have also given me a brilliant solution to our problem, young man,' Jahandar shouted triumphantly. His bloated belly shook like blancmange beneath the hand-tailored silk shirt. 'Meeting adjourned, gentlemen.'

It was fast approaching midwinter when Jahandar took complete control of one of Iran's biggest pistachio farms. Of the many businesses growing a total of fifty-nine-thousand tons of nuts each year Jahandar had selected this particular farm because of its convenient location close to his other interests in the city of Sirjan. He also selected it because it regularly harvested the largest round-shaped Fandoghi nuts in the world.

He completed a successful buyout for the highly profitable farm by offering the owner a financial pittance plus the promise that his younger daughter who was learning to play the piano wouldn't lose any fingers.

Under the strict control of Jahandar's hand-picked management team the company continued to harvest and market a variety of pistachio types including the Fandoghi. However, Jahandar's plans didn't stop there and on taking over the company he immediately set up a separate operation in a remote compound with the tightest security.

Production took place in over-heated iron shacks that were isolated from the outside world by razor wire and patrolling armed guards. Within each of the four prefabricated shacks dozens of poorly paid workers removed the Fandoghi nuts from their half-opened shells and replaced them with micropolythene sachets filled with the purest heroin. The pistachio shells were then sealed shut with a touch of superglue and these were finally packed in twenty-five-kilogram bags ready for export to Jahandar's select clients.

The hermetically sealed sachets inside the closed shells and a further layer of thick polythene provided perfect protection against the most sensitive sniffer dogs and yet only required a deft blow with a small ball-pein hammer to deliver the yellow brick road to dreaming addicts.

As he had done for many years Jahandar sourced all his opium in Afghanistan and this was subsequently processed in the unfriendly mountain district of Ana Dara. The extracted morphine was then mule-trained across the skin-blistering Dagh-e-Tondi Depression to cross the border undetected into Iran.

Diamorphine was then produced from this base drug and the resultant heroin was packed into the tiny sachets by a customized machine, the engineer of which had mysteriously disappeared shortly after the first successful test run. The electric packer had then been carefully hidden in an old farmhouse that lay eighty kilometres north of the pistachio farm. The previous owner had abandoned the property during the horrific violence of the Iran-Iraq War in '86. The widespread destruction during those futile years had subsequently led to the complete dereliction of the building.

Closed vans with security service markings were used to transport the end product on the first day of each month. These were only permitted to pass through the heavily fortified gates of the experimental unit in the dead of night. If local residents noticed and commented on this activity the deliveries would always be attributed to security precautions for the farm staff payroll.

Whenever one of Jahandar's customers placed an order for fresh supplies the required number of twenty-five-kilogram bags would be transported to Tehran airport and checked in for dispatch by one of the highly respected courier services. The graphics on the clear plastic bags had been designed in Tehran by a reputable advertising agency. Professional copywriters had also penned the product descriptions and the short flowery blurb giving an imaginary heritage to the farm.

The simplicity of Jahandar's idea would undoubtedly be its Achilles heel if any word leaked out and therefore secrecy had to be strictly maintained and the slightest indiscretion by staff was punishable by instant dismissal with a 9mm in the back of the neck. The pistachio bags were blatantly branded with Jahandar's name, which added credence to the legitimacy of his export business.

While the beautiful, pale-green nuts that begin to open on ripening were generally consumed for their excellent flavour and energy-giving goodness, closed pistachios were sold to industry to be used in the manufacture of products such as ice cream and cakes.

An English slogan printed on the front of all the 'special' bags read: 'For the Nuttiest Fruitcakes', and this identified the drug-carrying bags to clients who on the whole were unaware of the real meaning of the phrase. The outer plastic bag also gave customs officials a clear view of the contents and consequently all the consignments passed random inspections by men as well as dogs.

The latest delivery of drugs were scheduled to arrive in Bahrain at midday on the Airbus direct from Tehran and although Jahandar never liked to be associated with the end product when it was in transit he nevertheless instructed his bodyguards to make the collection and to bring the shipment directly to him at Changeez's villa.

When they received the order Jahandar's men left the villa and were soon driving onto the short Sheikh Isa Bin Salman causeway, leaving the main island of Bahrain and heading for the international airport. Within ten minutes they had crossed the smaller island and parked at the courier company's logistics office at the airport.

The white Toyota pick-up that they had stolen from a street close to the villa rolled to a halt at the courier off-loading bay and the two men entered the refreshingly cool environment. The quiet efficiency of the desk clerk and one quick signature that matched the one in the forged Iranian passport they presented ensured that the bodyguards were soon speeding back to their boss with four large cartons stacked in the back of the pick-up, each containing sixteen bags of the 'special' pistachios.

The giant toad of a man sat crossed-legged on the hand-embroidered silk cushions with his customary bowl of pistachios beside him as one of the large cartons was placed before him. Taking the razor-edged stiletto that Changeez had drawn from the scabbard at his waist Jahandar slit the sealing tape. He removed one of the colourful bags and lightly ran the tip of the knife across the top edge. Pistachios spilled from the open bag and he placed some in his cupped palm and slowly closed his hand, crushing the shells against each other until he felt something give under the pressure. On opening his hand he removed the shell that had been crushed and prising the two halves apart, removed the small sachet containing the white powder.

'Another successful delivery, gentlemen; we are almost ready to control every addict in the world,' Jahandar gloated as he rubbed the polythene between a fat forefinger and the ball of his thumb. 'You may celebrate tonight, Javid, with my blessing,' he added as he threw the tiny sachet to one of the waiting men. The bodyguard, whose name ironically meant 'long lived', threw out a greedy hand to catch the reward and his partner gave him a pitying look.

Jahandar looked at the other man through dark eyes that were almost hidden by rolls of fat. 'I want you to deliver this shipment to the usual place of storage and then to pick up a little insurance for me regarding the treasure.'

'Insurance, sir, what kind of insurance?' the bodyguard asked, removing his dark glasses to reveal his puzzlement.

'Changeez may fail in getting the geologist to do as he is told but I will not,' the man hissed. 'You will bring the wife of the man called Stuart Taylor to me and she will be my guarantee that the man will do as he is told. According to the spies Changeez employs they have now reported that she moved from her apartment and is staying at the

Ramada Hotel. She also works at the Bahrain Specialist Hospital as a doctor.' He handed a large glossy photograph to the bodyguard.

'One of Changeez's men took this picture of the woman as she was leaving the fishing boat at Askar.' The man studied the picture briefly, nodded and began to leave the room. 'Alive and in one piece, Shayhar. She must not be harmed in any way, do you understand?'

'Understood, sir,' the man replied, slightly bowing and touching his forehead with his fingertips. He left the room and instructed one of the household servants to bring the four cartons of pistachios to the waiting pick-up before going to his room to choose the tools he would require to abduct the expatriate doctor.

The door to Javid's room was wide open and he looked in to see his partner binding his upper arm and squeezing a rubber ball in preparation for the needle.

'I will need you for an important job in ten minutes, are you sure you'll be ready?' Shayhar asked as he watched the man insert the needle into the raised vein and depress the plunger with the same concentration on his face as a lover might have when entering his sweetheart. Javid grunted as the drug flowed through his system and then ecstatically sighed that he would be ready for anything. Shayhar left and went to his own room to finalize preparations.

Jahandar summoned a shisha water pipe and sat drawing on the cool, apple-flavoured tobacco as he contemplated his next moves. He was reluctant to stay on the island for longer than was necessary; whenever he was outside Iranian borders he felt at risk and instantly longed for the security of his heavily defended lifestyle in Iran where he had the back-up of police, judges and his own assassins on his payroll.

It was time for the afternoon prayer when Shayhar returned to Javid's room to find him sleeping peacefully. He shook the man's shoulder until his eyelids opened, revealing black pinpoint pupils. Javid struggled to sit upright and began scratching his body furiously. Shayhar slapped his face hard with his open hand. 'Are you with me, Javid?' he shouted.

The addict raised his hand to strike back but his moving wrist was arrested by the strong grip of his partner. 'Okay, you're ready,' Shayhar said in a satisfied tone. 'Let's go. We have a lot of work to do before the sun sets,' and he squeezed Javid's wrist hard before releasing it.

Both men left the villa and following the written instructions Shayhar drove to the storage centre Changeez used for the drugs. They checked that they were unobserved before unloading the cartons and then drove on to the centre of Manama where they abandoned the pick-up by the side of the road.

'This will have been reported stolen and no doubt there's an APB out on it already,' Shayhar said. 'We need fresh transport,' he added as he studied the parked vehicles. 'Something not too obvious and possibly a little like that one,' and he nodded his head at a five-year-old Chrysler with rust beginning to stain the edges of the chrome fender.

Javid grinned, revealing large teeth that had yellowed from excessive use of Turkish cigarettes. He left Shayhar and hurried across the road to get a closer look at the car. A quick test of the door handle revealed that it had been left unlocked by a very trusting owner and he nodded subtly to his partner. Shayhar crossed the road as Javid climbed into the vehicle and began working on the ignition lock.

The Chrysler pulled into the Ramada Hotel car park and drove to the far side to park partially shielded between two large 4x4s. The two men replaced their dark sunglasses and made their way to the rear of the hotel where they were able to enter the pool area. The smattering of guests reclining on loungers beneath the searing sun was too preoccupied in conversation to pay any attention to the two men. They sauntered casually round the perimeter of the sparkling water and entered the hotel reception area where they chose a comfortable settee and ordered espresso coffees from an attentive Filipino waiter.

One hour and two more espressos later their patience was rewarded as Helen strode through the lounge and sat in a corner were she could survey every part of the room. She ordered coffee and a Danish pastry before settling down to read a technical book on the subject of arterial gases.

Shayhar went to stand by Helen's table. 'Excuse me, are you Mrs Barbara Williamson? I had arranged to meet Mrs Williamson here but I do not know what she looks like,' he said in a voice as smooth as silk.

'I'm sorry but I cannot help you,' Helen replied as she glanced up from her book and into the anonymous black sunglasses hiding the man's face but reflecting her own. She put the book down on the table beside her coffee cup and the man picked it up to read the dust jacket.

'This doesn't appear to be light reading for a vacation,' he said and as Helen reached to take the book back she felt a slight stinging sensation in her hand.

'I'm not here on holiday. I'm a doctor working at the hospital,' she answered as she turned her hand to seek the source of the pain.

'My apologies for disturbing you, madam, I will see if I can find Mrs Williamson in Le Jardin restaurant,' Shayhar murmured as he straightened up and prepared to move away.

Helen tilted her head in farewell to the stranger who watched with more than a little interest as she raised the small coffee cup to her lips. Helen followed the man's progress as he walked to sit down beside another man wearing similar sunglasses; as she watched she realized that her lips had gone numb. They felt as though her dentist had just administered Novacaine and she tried to raise a hand to feel them but her arm failed to respond. She tried to rise to her feet but was unable to move and could only watch as the men in black suits and dark glasses walked to her table and sat down on either side of her.

'Do not worry, Mrs Taylor. The paralysis is only temporary and my friend and I will help you out into the fresh air to recover from the effects of the curare. It was only a small pinprick,' he added as he turned his hand to show the small needle protruding from the ring on his finger. 'We will now need to administer artificial respiration in our car before your lungs finally stop working but, being a doctor, you will know the effects of curare.'

Helen watched, unblinking, as together they lifted her to her feet. She tried to cry out but couldn't say anything, her tongue remained immobile and her mouth firmly closed even though every breath was becoming more and more difficult.

The Filipino waiter hurried across the room to render some assistance when he saw the men half-carrying Helen to the door.

'Our friend has been taken ill and we are going to take her to the nearest hospital,' Shayhar explained as the three shuffled across the coffee shop and out into the pool area. 'If you could help us get her to the car it would be very much appreciated.'

The waiter nodded his head vigorously. 'The Bahrain Specialist Hospital is the nearest, just turn left when you drive out of the gates,' he said as he helped the men carry Helen to the Chrysler. When they reached the car they laid her on the back seat and covered her with a light travelling blanket. As Javid got into the driver's seat Shayhar tried to tip the waiter but the young man was far too distraught about a hotel guest taking ill to consider accepting any gratuity.

The waiter stood in the path of two other cars that were planning to leave and waved the Chrysler out of the car park. As he watched the car speed away he was briefly puzzled that it chose to turn right and go in the opposite direction to where the hospital was located. With a deep sigh the relieved waiter watched a potentially embarrassing problem for the hotel disappear down the road and he went back to his lounge duties without mentioning the incident to anyone.

In the fast-moving Chrysler Shayhar slid a lubricated tube down Helen's windpipe and placed a respirator mask over her face before preparing the hypodermic with the anti-cholinesterase antidote. The needle plunged into her upper arm and when the syringe had been emptied it was thrown from the car to be lost in the debris of the latest demonstration that littered the intersection.

'The antidote will take effect in roughly five minutes by which time we will have arrived at our destination,' Shayhar said as he powered the window up to give the air-conditioning unit a chance to cool the interior.

Helen wheezed heavily in the mask in time to the pumping action of the portable respirator standing on the floor. She was incapable of any movement and remained like that for the rest of the journey.

As the Chrysler drove through the entrance and up to the villa the wrought-iron gates electronically closed behind them and Shayhar pulled a white bag over Helen's head before pulling her up into a sitting position. The car was driven round the building and it stopped by a side entrance. The men leapt out and between them they carried the doctor and the respirator into the villa and up one flight of stairs to a windowless bedroom. Helen was carelessly thrown onto the large bed and the oxygen cylinder placed beside her before the two men left the room.

The portable respirator unit stood by the bed hissing for ten minutes before Helen was able to move the toes of her left foot. Soon after she regained the ability to move her fingers and hands and to breathe unaided. She slowly withdrew the breathing tube without gagging and then began a series of physical exercises while lying down to loosen the muscles and regain full mobility of her body. With a certain amount of stiffness Helen got to her feet and slowly walked to the heavy door. It was locked on the outside. She was a prisoner.

Shayhar reported his successful abduction to Jahandar who simply nodded contentedly and slid a thick envelope over the table to his bodyguard. 'That's your bonus and there are instructions in there as to what I wish you to do with the woman. I want you to do it now,' Jahandar murmured, his beady little eyes fixed on the tall man. Shayhar nodded as he glanced inside the envelope at the bundle of currency and the single sheet of white paper. Two of the miniature sachets were dismissively tossed to Javid who grinned inanely and slipped them into his jacket pocket before following Shayhar out of the room.

After a futile struggle Helen had her hands bound and the bag replaced over her head before being manhandled downstairs and into the big limousine. Shayhar quickly read the instructions and drove through Manama to a remote part of the coast where the ruins of the ancient Islamic fort at Qal'at al-Bahrain had for centuries stood guard by the sea. Javid followed in the battered Chrysler until they were halfway to the fort before abandoning the car to join the others in the limousine. For the remainder of the journey he watched the young doctor with an unblinking black-eyed stare not unlike a circling tiger shark before it strikes.

They left the main highway at Meqsha and meandered through dusty backstreets that were lined with baked mud houses boasting clean, brilliantly coloured clothes waving listlessly from rooftop washing lines. Soon the surroundings gave way to hectares of crumbling stonework that comprised the ancient ruins of the Qal'at al-Bahrain. Shayhar avoided the normal parking area where a small tourist coach and a couple of cars had stopped and continued on round the historic site to the far side of the ruins bordering the coastline.

The limousine was stopped out of sight of all habitation and any guide-led tourists. Helen was bundled out of the vehicle and down a long flight of steps that had been worn to a glass-like finish by the passing feet of many generations. The Iranians produced mini Maglites and after descending fifty steps they arrived at a corroded iron gate with a shiny stainless-steel padlock. Shayhar removed the bag from Helen's head while Javid took a key from his trouser pocket and unlocked the gate. With a loud, teeth-setting shriek the door was pushed open and Shayhar urged Helen on with occasional thrusts of his torch against her neck. Javid relocked the padlock to deter curious explorers from coming any further down the passage and then hurried to catch up with them.

Apart from the dancing pools of light to guide them the narrow passageway was completely dark and became even more so after they had descended a further forty steps. Finally, a heavy iron-bound oak door that Helen roughly estimated as being eight centimetres thick was revealed as the final formidable barrier. Javid produced a larger key and after a hard twist was able to stir the rusty mechanism and unlock the door. Using all his strength he thrust it open so they could squeeze through into the small vaulted room that lay beyond.

'The old dungeon, Mrs Taylor,' Shayhar said with a tone of triumph as he swung his torch round to illuminate their dismal surroundings. 'Thieves and murderers, whether men, women or children, were chained here for months, even years, until it was time for their execution. Many never saw sunlight again unless it was to be briefly introduced to the executioner's sword.'

The man laughed as he passed a piece of rusting chain between Helen's handcuffed wrists and padlocked the ends to a large iron ring set in the wall. He then placed a litre bottle of mineral water within reach and backed away from the fettered woman until she was an indistinguishable shape in the dim interior.

'We will be back to release you tomorrow but only if your husband complies with my master's wishes,' Shayhar said as he shone the torch into Helen's eyes.

'There is no point in shouting for help, either,' Javid added. 'These walls are three metres thick. Nobody ever comes to this side of the fort because it's too far from the souvenir shop and the tourists don't like to get too hot.' His harsh laughter was like a dog's snarl and Helen shivered involuntarily.

'Goodbye, Mrs Taylor. Pray that your husband does as he is told or that water may be the last thing to pass your lips.'

The two men left the cell and with a dull, forbidding thud the heavy door slammed shut, cutting off the faint glimmer of light from the torches and entombing Helen in darkness and silence with only her own imagination to keep her company.

With unseeing eyes wide open Helen lowered herself to sit upon the rough stone floor before carefully groping around in the black until her fingers brushed against the water bottle. She picked it up and held it against her body to try and draw some comfort from the cool plastic cylinder against her skin. 'Take care, Robert,' she whispered as she hugged the bottle.

7

The captain spun the wheel and pushed the throttles forward as far as they would go. 'We must leave now,' he shouted above the increased engine clatter from below the deck. 'That's a navy boat and I don't want trouble with the authorities.'

'You're leaving Dabir behind,' Behrouz said as he stepped forward to confront the fisherman.

Changeez grabbed the Iranian by the arm. 'We can't spend time looking for Dabir in the water. If we do that we run the risk that Taylor will tell the navy that we were forcing him to dive by threatening to harm his wife.'

'He wouldn't dare take the chance.'

'And nor will I. We keep heading back to shore.'

The captain turned briefly, nodded and then turned his attention back to navigating his boat safely back to Askar. The official patrol boat began to close the distance and Changeez studied the approaching vessel through his binoculars—an officer was standing in the wheelhouse with two civilians, his binoculars trained on the fishing boat.

Changeez lowered the glasses and turning to the captain he snarled, 'Get this wreck moving Captain before we have to answer some very awkward questions.'

'The first being, why are we running away from a navy patrol boat?' Behrouz said with a sarcastic curl of his lip. 'I suggest that we slow down and pretend we are tourists who have chartered the boat for the day to do a little fishing. Do you have rods?' he shouted to the captain and the older man nodded and pointed down below. Changeez looked at Behrouz with a little more respect and agreed with the idea before both men hurried down to find sufficient fishing tackle to justify their presence. They emerged back on deck to the roar of powerful diesel engines as the patrol boat rapidly overhauled the fishing vessel.

'This is the Royal Bahrain Navy Force,' an amplified voice boomed across the intervening water. 'Heave to now and wait to be boarded,' the authoritative voice continued.

The captain pulled the throttles back and the fishing boat immediately slowed until it was wallowing in the sea swell. The much larger vessel continued to race ahead, leaving the fishing boat rocking and rolling in its high wake. As it slowed and turned the large Oerlikon gun swivelled to remain trained on the old vessel's wheelhouse.

'Lucky we did stop, that little popgun means business,' Behrouz muttered.

'Keep your mouth shut and leave all the talking to me,' Changeez replied. 'And that means you too, Captain.'

The captain shrugged and checked his boat for drift while waiting for the naval boat to come alongside. When only a metre separated the vessels a naval rating jumped aboard the fishing boat with a line that was professionally tied to a deck cleat to keep the boat's distance fixed. Captain Mahmood and Major Safa immediately followed him. They ignored the two men self-consciously holding fishing rods and went straight to the wheelhouse to confront the captain.

'I am Captain Mahmood of the Royal Bahrain Naval Force and this is Major Safa,' he said briskly. 'Would you please state your business, where you have been and where you are going?'

The old man turned a weathered face to stare unblinking into Mahmood's eyes. *'Es salaam alykhum*, Captain. I am Ismail, the owner of this boat and our last mooring was over the old *Fifi* shipwreck to let my customers do some fishing and now we are heading for Askar.' Mahmood nodded and looked at Walid for some help.

'You had a successful trip?' Walid said looking around as though searching for something.

'It was good for my customers.'

'I don't see many fish, where do you keep them?'

While the two officers were questioning the old captain Changeez had moved into the wheelhouse in time to catch the last question.

'We are humane gentlemen, Major. We don't catch fish to eat but simply for the sport. As soon as we have caught anything, whether it be a small puffer fish or a hammerhead shark, we release it so that it may live another day.'

'Very honourable I'm sure, Mr . . .'

'Changeez and this is my servant, Behrouz.'

'However, the real reason we stopped you is that we are seeking a Western geologist who goes by the name of Stuart Taylor—have you seen him?' Walid suddenly added with keen eyes studying the body language of all three men. The slight stiffening of the man called Behrouz who was leaning casually against a stanchion did not escape his attention; nor the sudden glance at Changeez by the boat's captain.

'I'm sorry your time has been wasted but we know of nobody by that name,' Changeez coolly replied as he began to remove the Artica fixed-spool reel from the rod he was holding.

Captain Mahmood quickly noticed the clumsy way in which Changeez was releasing the retaining rings. 'You are a novice fisherman, Mr Changeez?' he nonchalantly observed. 'Strange that you should choose to fish so far from land.'

'The captain suggested the place as ideal for catching shark,' Behrouz interrupted and then immediately regretted his words.

'You're a novice and yet you want to take on a powerful fish like a hammerhead shark. That's very brave of you, Mr Changeez, but it is also very foolish,' Walid said, smiling falsely. 'We shall leave you to your foolishness unless you wish to add anything further.'

'I do not think we can help you with anything more, Major,' Changeez said with a feeling of triumph as he watched the two officers leap back onto the patrol boat while the rating unhitched the bow line and jumped after them.

The two boats slowly drifted apart and when only five metres lay between the two rising and falling vessels the patrol boat surged forward with a terrifying roar of its engines and was soon moving seaward at high speed. Ismail restarted his engine and pushing the throttles forward he let the fishing boat ride with the tide towards Askar.

By the time they entered the wheelhouse of the patrol boat Walid was seething with rage. 'They were lying through their teeth,' he shouted. 'He may not be there now but he was on board earlier which means they have either murdered him and disposed of his body or simply left him to drown far from land.

Sergeant Shehhi put a hand on his arm. 'Slow down, sir, I suggest we head towards the old *Fifi* wreck and see if we can find any evidence that Mr Taylor had been on their boat.'

'We'd better do it soon otherwise the light will be gone and if he is still alive you can safely bet that he won't be by tomorrow morning,' Alan called from the back of the wheelhouse with an edge of rising panic.

Captain Mahmood nodded and with a violent gesture of his hand the seaman at the wheel immediately asked for full engine speed. The patrol boat seemed to spring forward as the twin diesels turned the sea behind them into a white maelstrom and the men held on to the nearest grab rails to keep their balance.

'Wow,' Alan whooped. 'What do you use for engines, Saturn V booster rockets?"

'Just the best from General Motors plus a little mechanical genius from our navy's finest marine engineer,' Mahmood grinned as the vessel sliced through the sea with its bow riding high.

In a matter of minutes they were in the vicinity of the *Fifi* and Captain Mahmood cut the patrol boat's speed until they hardly made any headway while the four men used binoculars to sweep the surface of the sea. The polarized lenses softened the sun's effect but the men's eyes soon tired from its reflected glare as they studied every square metre of the glassy surface.

The sun rapidly began to sink towards the horizon and the sea was slowly flooded with an eye-watering rosy pink that made the search even more difficult. After twenty passes over the sunken *Fifi* the captain answered a call from the engine room and he shrugged his frustration. 'I'm sorry, gentlemen, but we are running very low on fuel and will have to head back to port.'

'A few more minutes, please Captain,' Alan pleaded as he steadfastly held the glasses to his eyes.

'Not much to ask for,' Walid added as he swept a section of sea to the west.

'I know what it must mean to you but unless we get a move on now we will be stuck at sea ourselves,' Mahmood said holding his hands out in a helpless gesture.

Walid nodded slowly. 'You have responsibilities that you cannot neglect, Captain. I fully understand.'

Mahmood gave Walid a brief look of thanks and then spoke quietly to the seaman who rang down the captain's instructions. The patrol boat increased its speed and was soon cleaving the blood-red surface on a heading that led to the naval dockyard. As the sun's rim touched the horizon Alan went out onto the aft deck and continued to scan the empty sea as the light slowly faded.

'In half an hour it will be pitch black and we'll be unable to see anything but the stars above,' Walid murmured as he joined Alan in his futile search. Alan didn't reply but simply went on sweeping the sea from east to west. The sun had half set and was now visibly sinking fast when Alan gave a small cry of astonishment.

'There, there,' he cried. 'There's something flashing over there,' and he lowered his glasses to point excitedly to a part of sea that he had been studying.

Walid swung round and trained his glasses in the same direction and instantly caught a glint of light in the darkening waves. He adjusted the focus ring and waited for a few seconds until the light flashed once more. Walid ran into the wheelhouse and grabbed Mahmood by the arm.

'Over there, on the right, check it but I think we have something we need to investigate,' he said handing his glasses to the surprised captain.

Mahmood rested his elbows on the compass binnacle to steady himself and on seeing the same flash of light he barked out his orders. The patrol boat accelerated and peeled off to starboard before straightening and heading straight for the pinprick of light that was occasionally flashing midway between them and the horizon.

'What ever it is, it's about nine hundred metres distant,' Mahmood said as he kept his eyes fixed on the point of the last flash.

The captain's estimate was very accurate for they had travelled only eight hundred metres when they were able to identify the dark shape as being that of a man holding his face mask above his head.

As the boat throttled back to edge closer Stuart's tired but beaming face looked up at his two friends. Alan shouted his delight while Walid just breathed out a deep sigh of relief and rushed to help the seaman pull his old friend out of the sea.

Stuart reached for the boat hook and was swiftly pulled in close enough for Walid and Alan to grab an arm each and to haul the exhausted man aboard. Stuart lay on the deck breathing heavily as his friends squatted down on either side.

'Planning to swim home to Scotland, mate?' Alan said. He laughed briefly in a futile attempt to disguise his enormous sense of relief as he busied himself by removing the large swim fins from his friend's feet.

'No, just waiting for a lift, mate. Thanks for stopping,' Stuart wheezed as he unzipped the wetsuit.

'Let's get you below and get something warm inside you,' Captain Mahmood said as he appeared carrying a large towel that he wrapped around Stuart's shoulders. 'Then you can tell us what happened. I have to make my report very soon and a few details would be handy.'

Stuart nodded and wearily climbed to his feet. The four went below deck while the vessel sped on to the naval dockyard with the fuel gauge needle edging into the red zone.

As they entered the wardroom they found the chief engineer waiting with a large, chipped mug of hot chocolate. Stuart took the steaming mug with a grateful smile and sipped until a warm glow permeated his whole body. He then told them what had happened, from the threat about Helen's health on the telephone to Dabir's horrible death. Captain Mahmood finished writing in his notebook and hurried up the gangway. 'I'll notify the port authorities about the fishing boat we stopped and the three men we spoke with,' he shouted over his shoulder as he climbed.

'And I'll call the police and put out an APB on Changeez and Behrouz,' Walid said while he speed-dialled headquarters.

Stuart asked Alan for the use of his phone and called Helen at the apartment. When she didn't answer he tried her cellphone but again no response. 'I don't like this Alan, she's not answering.'

'Could be she's gone to work and is with a patient,' Alan said reassuringly. 'You know she has to switch her phone off in the sensitive parts of the hospital dealing with pacemakers.'

'It's not switched off. It just rings and rings,' Stuart returned the cellphone to his friend with a worried expression. Sergeant Shehhi had been standing to one side watching the two friends and noticing Stuart's distress he quickly used his phone. He muttered rapidly in Arabic and although Stuart could speak a little of the language the sergeant was talking far too fast for him to understand anything except for the mention of his wife's name before the sergeant closed his phone.

'Who were you talking to, Sergeant?' Stuart asked.

'I was asking a colleague of mine who works near the hospital if he could go and make inquiries about Doctor Helen. He will call back as soon as he has spoken to her,' Shehhi said quietly and Stuart smiled his appreciation.

'That's very kind of you, Sergeant,' he said and then jerked upright when he heard the ringtones of Alan's cellphone. The Australian flipped his phone open and listened for a few seconds before passing it to Stuart with an angry look.

'*Es salaam alykhum*, Mr Taylor,' a voice murmured. 'So nice to learn that you survived being left in the ocean by that terrible Mr Changeez.'

'Who the hell are you, what do you want?' Stuart barked and Walid, returning from the wheelhouse, gave Stuart a puzzled look.

'It must be one of them,' Alan growled.

Stuart fell silent as he listened and the blood drained from his face as Jahandar continued speaking in a deadpan, emotionless voice.

'I have your wife sealed in a room that she cannot possibly escape from and she is provided with a single litre of water. With careful rationing it should last two or three days after which your wife will rapidly dehydrate and eventually die of thirst. I don't believe it's a painful way to die but what would I know about that?'

Hearing Stuart's sharp intake of breath Jahandar shouted, 'Do not say anything, Mr Taylor, if you want to see your wife again. Listen to what I have to say. You will not notify the police or try to find your wife for that is an impossible task. However, what you will do is hire another boat and return to the site of the shipwreck. There you will recover as many of the precious jewels as you can and await my next call. Is that clear?'

'Yes, you've made everything very clear,' Stuart growled and the line went dead. Stuart returned the phone to Alan and related what Jahandar had done and what he now demanded. The three men were horrified by the news and immediately Walid began dialling a number.

'He said no police, Walid,' Stuart reminded the major.

'This man has now added kidnapping to murder and attempted murder, Stuart, and I have to act on this fast otherwise you may never see your Helen again,' Walid said, making clear the harsh fact that kidnappers rarely let their victims live. Stuart nodded wearily and watched with hopelessly blank eyes as Walid made his call.

Captain Mahmood descended into the wardroom and was given the latest news. 'I would gladly change course and chase the swine into Askar but for the fact that the engines are running on fumes and we may not even get to the village,' he said, combing his fingers through his hair in frustration.

To conserve as much fuel as possible Captain Mahmood nursed the patrol boat at half-throttle towards the naval port. In the meantime Changeez and Behrouz arrived at Askar and hurried to the large limousine that had been waiting for them.

'Hurry, we must leave this village as quickly as possible,' the man in dark sunglasses snarled as the two men approached. As soon as the doors slammed shut the wheels spun on the loose shale and the heavy car raced towards the city.

'Mr Jahandar is displeased with the way you handled things, Changeez. He fully expected Mr Taylor to have recovered the items from the bottom of the sea and for them to be in his possession by now. He did not expect you to be questioned by naval authorities; men who now know what you look like and have issued descriptions to every cop on the island.'

'Mr Jahandar does not know the facts of the situation,' Behrouz snapped irritably before his head was jerked back by the hard slap of a large calloused hand.

'Mr Jahandar knows everything he needs to know about you. I believe he is too generous and you should consider yourselves lucky that he hasn't asked me to slit your throats,' the bodyguard hissed as he raised his hand again. Behrouz cringed back in his seat and watched the man through half-closed eyes.

'What does he want us to do,' Changeez asked meekly.

'You will lie low until Mr Jahandar needs your services.'

'Bahrain is a very small island, where can we go to remain reasonably safe?'

'That's easily solved. You will leave the island immediately by chartered boat under these assumed names,' and he handed Changeez two passports. 'You will go to Hawar Island close to Qatar and abandon the boat on the deserted part of the coast indicated on that.' He pointed to the passports and Changeez slid out a small white slip of paper sandwiched between them and studied a crude sketch of a coastline. 'A car, driven by a man called Yahya will be waiting to take you to the Tulip Inn Hawar Beach where bookings have been made under the names in the passports.'

'And Mr Jahandar?' Behrouz asked suspiciously.

'He will join you there later and give you your new instructions.'

'Our first problem is to find a boat to charter while the police are looking for us,' Changeez said.

'This is not a problem; one has already been hired and is waiting for you at the Bahrain Yacht Club marina,' the man answered before turning away to ignore both men and concentrate on the road ahead with his partner.

After a few minutes of absolute silence the car turned off the highway and into desolate coastal terrain to follow a minor road for three kilometres to the marina. Scores of moored yachts greeted them with the constant clatter of halyards being whipped against the alloy masts by the offshore breeze.

The limousine cruised past the tennis courts until it reached the Al Bander Resort and parked at the end of the harbour. Changeez and Behrouz were told to get out and go to the Beneteau Swift Trawler that was moored alongside the limousine.

As the last rays of the sun briefly coloured the thin cloud strata Changeez stepped across the gap to board the vessel with Behrouz close behind. A middle-aged and heavily bearded Bahraini appeared from below to greet them with a dazzling white smile.

'You are Mr Abdulkarim and his man servant?' he asked, holding out a hand that Changeez briefly took.

'We're in a great hurry to reach Hawar Island before evening prayer, so how soon before you'll be under way?' Changeez enquired as he watched the limousine quietly pull away and drive towards the distant city.

'I can clear the marina within ten minutes,' the man replied and he hurried away to begin his checks before starting the big 300 hp engines. Changeez shrugged and entered the luxurious saloon where cool drinks and sandwiches had been laid out on the table. Both men immediately set to and satisfied their intense hunger, devouring every morsel and washing it all down with bottles of non-alcoholic beer.

They had just loosened their belts, given deep belches of satisfaction and settled back into their comfortable seats when a large hatch at their feet lifted. They instinctively reached for weapons under their jackets as a figure in a boiler suit emerged from the engine room and turned to face them while the hatch automatically lowered with a faint hydraulic hiss.

'Good evening, gentlemen,' said a young man who was undoubtedly the boat owner's son. 'We are now ready to depart and I anticipate that our 40-kilometre crossing to Hawar will be roughly seventy minutes.'

Changeez grunted and took a bottle of whisky from the drinks cabinet. 'If you can cut that time down there'll be a bonus in it for you both,' he said as he poured a stiff measure into a cut-glass tumbler. The young man nodded and left the saloon to release the moorings and swing the fenders inboard. He then climbed to where his father had just turned the ignition key to fire up the engines and told him about the offer of a bonus. The Swift Trawler pulled away from the quay and quietly purred its way out of the marina to head into the growing darkness with its navigation lights reassuringly lit.

Behrouz flopped back on the settee in the saloon and as his chin dropped into his chest he sank into a light sleep. Changeez watched him for a while with distaste wrinkling his nose before rising to explore the interior of the luxury cruiser. He admired the stainless-steel of the galley that swept round to where steps descended to the two single cabins and the owner's master bedroom. He sat on the huge bed and sank into the soft mattress. He removed the automatic pistol from the holster beneath his armpit and removed the magazine to check that it was fully loaded before ramming it back into place and pulling back the slide to cock the weapon. He placed it under the pillow and lay down to wait for the moment when they would be within sight of the lights on Hawar Island. Even though a shallow channel of two kilometres in width separated the tiny island from the Qatari nation, Hawar remained sovereign territory of Bahrain and had become a very popular tourist destination for both countries.

After forty minutes had elapsed Changeez arose and left the cabin to wake Behrouz. He was irritated at being woken so soon but seeing the expression on Changeez's face he smiled grimly and loosened the long knife in its scabbard before following his employer onto the rear deck and up the steel ladder to the Portuguese flying bridge.

Father and son were bent over the illuminated control panel, checking the compass heading and briefly checking the dark sea ahead for any sign of white breakers that indicated a sand bar or coral reef.

They had done the trip so often that everything came naturally and the distant flash from the lighthouse on Hawar was only a bonus as they navigated through the treacherous waters.

The son became aware of the two men behind them and turned with a smile. 'Welcome to the bridge, gentlemen,' he said. 'Hawar is now only five kilometres dead ahead and we no longer have bad currents or shallows to contend with.'

'Perfect, then I think we can take over now,' Changeez said with a cold, tight-lipped smile. In a smooth rapid motion he took the automatic from behind his back, placed the barrel to the youth's forehead and pulled the trigger. The heavy report of the nine-millimetre weapon crashed out across the sea. The young man, thrown back by the impact, hit the edge of the bridge coping, toppled over and crashed onto the deck below.

The father, his hands suddenly frozen to the wheel in extreme shock, had only begun to turn towards Changeez when Behrouz grabbed him by the hair and jerked his head back. One quick flicker of steel across the exposed throat and the instrument console turned crimson. The two men worked swiftly to cut both bodies randomly with their knives before tossing them overboard. The dark slick spreading on the moonlit surface would soon attract sharks to dispose efficiently of the bodies.

Changeez returned to the flying bridge and took the slip of paper from his pocket in readiness for when they could begin to identify any coastal features. Behrouz used buckets of seawater to rinse away all traces of blood.

It was not long before Changeez saw a light in the dark smudge of a building and he referred to the crude map. 'We go left for approximately four hundred metres,' he muttered to himself as he spun the wheel. The cruiser gracefully turned in the moonlight, leaving a blue phosphorescent arc on the surface of the sea. Changeez throttled back until they were barely making any headway against the light offshore current and stared at the pale wavy line of the beach that was fifty metres to starboard.

'This should be about right, now,' he muttered and then exhaled noisily in reaction to the brief flash of headlights on the land. Changeez spun the wheel once more and blipped the throttle to send the cruiser in towards the beach. A sudden jerk almost threw both men off their feet and a harsh grating noise broadcast the crossing of a small sand bar. Both men held onto the bridge coaming as the cruiser dodged a few mangrove stumps to run into and slightly up the mud flats. The craft came to an abrupt halt with its screws still ineffectually spinning and Changeez throttled back and turned the ignition off. The sudden silence that was broken only by the regular, gentle swish of the sea was deafening and both men peered into the darkness, half expecting a crowd of people to come and investigate the strange behaviour of their cruiser.

'Switch off the navigation lights, fool,' Changeez whispered and Behrouz ran to the binnacle to obey. 'Let's go ashore and find the car that flashed its lights.'

They went to the rear of the boat and stepped off the diving platform into warm water that was still shimmering from bioluminescent algae. It only reached mid-calf and they waded ashore and onto the mud flat with the slight wind already beginning to dry their trousers. When they breasted the first small sand dune a bright light flashed across their faces to dazzle them.

'You are Changeez?' a voice inquired in a loud whisper.

'Put that light out or I'll have my man cut your throat,' Changeez snarled and the light went out. As their night vision returned they could see an old man who appeared to be so thin that his clothes hung like untidy washing on a line.

'I'm Yahya. I have been expecting you,' he said and then bent double with a paroxysm of coughing.

'When you're ready you are to take us to the Tulip Inn,' Behrouz said. Realizing how unnecessary his instruction had been he added lamely, 'as soon as you can, *yallah*.'

The man simply grunted, spat and waved at them to follow him. They trudged through sand and salt-marsh grass until they stumbled onto a crude dirt track where an Oldsmobile that was almost as decrepit as its owner was parked. The man opened the door for Changeez but ignored Behrouz. Climbing into the driver's seat he managed to start the car after a series of explosive backfires and with nerve-grating gear changes they drove from the beached vessel and sped along the rough surface until they reached the tarred road leading to the Tulip Inn.

8

The Fairey Marine Tracker II limped into port with both engines misfiring on the last few drops of fuel before cutting out at the mooring. The captain wiped mock sweat from his brow and smiled at Stuart and the police officers. 'I wouldn't like to cut it that fine again,' he said and the others laughed. 'It's a court-martial offence to lose a naval ship over something as trivial as not checking fuel gauges.'

'Well, we made it back to dry land and it's all thanks to you, Captain,' Stuart said gratefully.

'We also have a good idea of whom we're up against,' Walid added as he gripped the naval officer's hand and shook it vigorously.

The three friends bid farewell to the crew and followed by Sergeant Shehhi went ashore to join in the search for Helen. A police cruiser was waiting on the quay and they drove to Stuart's apartment where he and Alan were dropped off; Walid and Shehhi were taken on to police headquarters to follow up on the progress of the search.

Major Mohammad Kazemi nodded a greeting to Walid as he strode into his office and then continued reading the sheet of paper that he had just taken from his in-tray. There was another small desk on the far side of the office at which sat a junior officer who was undoubtedly the major's secretary.

'Any sightings reported, Major Kazemi?' Walid asked as he dropped into the uncomfortable fibreglass chair that faced the major's desk.

The Bahraini didn't immediately answer but continued to read until he reached the end of the message. 'Unfortunately, none matching the descriptions you gave me on the phone have been spotted and I believe that we'll need to create photo-composites if we are to get any further with this seemingly impossible task.'

Walid nodded. 'I'd be happy to sit with your artist at any time and would suggest now as the matter is urgent.' He handed a glossy print that he had taken from a silver frame in Stuart's apartment to Major Kazemi. 'In the meantime this is a fairly recent picture of Doctor Helen Taylor. I would suggest that this goes out on the news channels tonight.'

The major took the photograph and studied the picture with growing appreciation of her beauty. Helen was dressed in a white shirt and skirt and was holding a tennis racket as she laughed into the lens of the camera. 'A very nice-looking woman; it would be a pity to find her dead,' he said in an off-hand manner as he signalled to his secretary to take the photograph.

'That'll not be the case. I'll make sure of that,' Walid murmured as he watched the young policeman briefly speak into the phone on his desk before hurrying out of the office with the photograph.

After discussing a few more details of the operation with the major and then spending an hour with the photo-composite artist until he was quite satisfied that he had created good likenesses of both Changeez and Behrouz, Walid telephoned Stuart at the apartment.

'No news, Stuart,' he reported. 'Helen's picture will be on tonight's news broadcast so we are hopeful that this will produce some results. Can we three get together and discuss this further?'

The friends agreed to meet for an evening meal at Zoe's restaurant, a very popular eating destination that had loft-style architecture and a relaxed atmosphere heightened by retro music and superb Middle Eastern and Western cuisine.

The three men settled on starting with a mini mezza of hummus, tabbouleh and muttabel to be followed by beef carpaccio. Conversation was put on hold until they had downed their first cold beers.

Then Walid opened with a question intended to distract Stuart from any thoughts about Helen and her situation. 'Tell me, Stuart, how did you and Alan meet?'

Stuart stopped staring at the damask tablecloth and looked up, surprised by the question. 'When I arrived in Bahrain Alan was already working for the company and test drilling in the southern part of the island. We were initially thown together when I joined him on the same project.'

'Not that I needed any help, you understand,' Alan added with a laugh before continuing to help himself to the muttabel with great relish.

'True, but we became a good team and we've had a lot of laughs together.'

'Can't deny that, mate.'

'And you Alan, how did you come to be working in the Middle East?' Walid asked as the main dish was served.

'Long story, mate,' Alan said thoughtfully. 'I'm the second son of a Northern Territories cattle farmer. I had it real good, hunting roo with a crossbow and swilling beer with my mates at the pub. I then went to university and graduated with honours which prompted my father to declare that I had to support myself and find my own source of income. I soon learnt that life isn't all that easy or as much fun without cash. I had gained a first in geology but in spite of the bloody size of our country I was still unable to get a job with any of the mining companies. So, to make a crust and stop my ribs from tickling my backbone I began looking elsewhere and ended up leaving the land of beer and barbies. I travelled quite a bit until what little cash my dad did give me ran out and I ended up in Peru. Fortunately I managed to get a job there with a small company, boring for water, but after a couple of years I ended up in a fight with one of the natives who decided he wanted to decorate my body with his bloody long knife.' Alan smiled pensively. 'He thought I'd been making out with one of his sheilas.'

'And had you?' Walid asked with a grin.

The stocky man rubbed a hand across his shiny pate and smiled, increasing the depth of the permanent laughter lines radiating from the corners of his mouth. 'Well, not so involved that you'd think that I was going to marry the girl. It was just a bit of Saturday-night fun, not something you'd think would make an ordinary, skinny little whippet of a bloke whip out a knife and a machete and start trying to separate my highly-valued head from my shoulders.' Heads turned in the restaurant as Stuart and Walid laughed out loud.

'Anyway, I thought it best to practise my skills in a country as far away as possible from Peru.'

'And in what field would those skills be, geology or biology?' Stuart asked in an innocent voice.

'Very amusing, mate,' Alan said flicking an olive at his friend. 'Anyway, that's how I ended up coming here and spending my precious time baking to a crisp in this bloody big kiddies' sandpit for a pittance of a salary.'

'Which happens to be tax free and twice what you'd earn in Australia,' Stuart finished and the three men chuckled while they finished their carpaccio.

'I'm going out of my head worrying, Walid,' Stuart said suddenly through gritted teeth as he ignored the small dessert dishes being assembled before them. 'This waiting for news is killing me.'

'Me too, mate,' Alan added. 'We need to do something, anything other than sitting and twiddling our thumbs.'

Walid sampled the *hunayni* date concoction appreciatively. 'Why don't you both do as the kidnapper ordered and return to the site of the *Fifi* to see if there's anything new there.' He signalled for another helping. 'At the very least it would be a productive way to take your minds off what we are doing.'

'That's the best idea you've had for a long time, Walid,' Alan teased and then laughed as a broad smile crossed Stuart's face for the first time since learning of Helen's kidnap.

'Okay, we'll do that but you must promise, Walid, that you'll contact us the second you have any news,' Stuart said with eyebrows raised questioningly.

The major reached across the table and placed his hand over Stuart's. 'You have my guarantee that you'll be the first to know,' he said.

The friends finished their meal and separated at the door to go their own ways. Stuart arranged a time to meet Alan in the morning and then went back into the restaurant to settle the bill.

Arriving back in the lonely apartment Stuart switched on the television to check the newscast and was immediately shocked to see Helen's laughing face looking back at him. It wasn't until the camera pulled back that he remembered the photograph he had given to Walid. It was being accompanied by a dispassionate voice requesting any information regarding the sighting of 'this person' and the telephone number to call. He switched the set off and went to the drinks cabinet to prepare a stiff drink to help him get through the night.

Throughout that night the police interviewed scores of people who claimed to have seen either Helen or the two men. Many were discounted as nutcases or limelight seekers until a fisherman dressed in a stained and rather smelly dishdasha walked into the police station in the Manama district of Sitrah and announced that he had recognized one of the men as a casual fisherman called Behrouz. An instant cross-check with immigration and the Department of Labour produced a photograph of the suspect which was immediately given to the press and the Bahraini TV station.

A SWAT team was despatched to the last address that Behrouz had listed for his sponsoring employer. The team entered an empty two-room apartment; judging by the rotten food in the refrigerator and the thick layer of dust on the filthy bedding it had clearly not been used for many months. Their suspect had moved on without notifying the authorities.

It was mid-morning when another caller gave the police a vital lead. A reader of the *Gulf Daily News* had seen the man in the Misan Gardens late one night. He had been walking his dog around the tennis courts when he saw the man called Behrouz talking with another man whom he addressed as Changeez.

Once more the police accessed the immigration records to find an Iranian of the same name living in the district of Mugaba. The same SWAT team rushed to enter the villa but Mr Changeez had left and his guest and two servants had also departed shortly after without giving any explanations to the staff.

A thorough forensic study was implemented and to the satisfaction of all, including Walid, some of the fingerprints that had been lifted in the villa matched those on the fishing boat they had tracked down in Askar. The crime scene investigators also found a large number of ordinary pistachio shells scattered amongst the cushions in the *majlis* sitting room. Then a more significant discovery was made in one of the guest bedrooms. To the surprise of all involved they found that the discarded shells of two pistachio nuts on the bedside table had a minute quantity of white powder in them. As this was being analysed a keen-eyed Sergeant Shehhi carefully lifted two tiny sachets from the waste-paper basket with a gloved hand and showed them to the major.

'This is fortunate indeed, Sergeant,' Walid muttered to himself.

'Why is that, sir?'

'I think we may have stumbled on the drug runners we've been chasing for the last two years.' Walid slipped on a glove and taking one of the sachets he held it up to the light streaming through the latticed window. In the bright beam he was able to detect a few fine grains of white powder within the plastic envelope as well as the small incision that had been made along one edge to release the contents.

'This is incredible, Sergeant,' Walid exclaimed triumphantly, 'These ingenious little sachets are how they import the heroin into Bahrain. It's then removed and transported into our country.'

With building excitement he hurried into the living room and cornered the officer in charge of the evidence bags containing the pistachio shells. 'Excuse me, Lieutenant, but could I have a closer look at one of the shells?'

'Certainly, Major.'

Walid held the bag up to study the small half shells and immediately noticed the thin residue of adhesive coating on the edges of each shell. Walid grunted in appreciation of the ingenuity of the drug runners and gave the bag back to the mystified officer.

'I don't know who's behind this, Sergeant, but his identity will have to be our next priority and we'll have to tread carefully because whoever it is will prove to be extremely dangerous. He has developed a very clever piece of engineering that can produce hundreds of thousands of heroin mini-bags to fit inside empty pistachio shells,' Walid said. 'This man is not just clever but a true genius.'

'And this so-called genius is killing thousands of innocent addicts with his product as he rakes in his millions,' Shehhi interjected coldly, returning the major back to reality with a resounding thump.

'You're quite right, Shehhi, and we're going to get the bastard if it's the last thing we do as police officers,' Walid replied vehemently and he turned and walked across the room to accost one of the fingerprint experts.

'Would you please liaise with every authority in the region as well as Interpol and post every fingerprint that you find in these living quarters on their websites; do not bother with the servant's quarters, it's the visitors that I'm interested in.'

With the pictures of both men regularly being shown in the media Jahandar knew that it was only a matter of time before the Tulip Inn staff recognized Changeez and Behrouz. Jahandar told Shayhar and Javid to place their bags in the limousine and without a single backward glance the visitors left the villa and drove through Manama and down the coastal road to Askar.

As they slowly cruised along the minor road and passed through Askar they spotted police cruisers in the vicinity of the old fishing boat and Jahandar told Shayhar to keep on driving. They continued on to a small development of villas called Jaw. Changeez had once informed Jahandar that it had a small mooring for the powerboats of the rich expatriates. After six tedious kilometres of dusty desert driving they rapidly approached the large roundabout that Jahandar vaguely recalled.

'I believe Changeez said straight on for another two hundred metres before turning left,' Jahandar instructed. 'He had better be right or I'll make sure he doesn't forget anything ever again.'

Both bodyguards laughed and Javid instinctively touched the knife in its sheath. As they left the crude road for an even rougher track they could see a line of moorings in the distance, many with medium-sized motor cruisers tied up and waiting for their owners to arrive at the weekend.

'We must look as though we know where our boat is so before we get any closer let's select the right one that can get us to Hawar Island in comfort and without too much trouble,' Jahandar snapped and both men peered through the tinted glass at the long line of craft as they drew closer.

'Second from the left,' Shayhar stated confidentally. 'It looks like an eleven-metre Sea Ray Venture with twin inboard engines. Better still, I cannot see anyone at that end of the mooring.'

'Then we'll use that boat,' Jahandar said as he noisily cracked another handful of pistachios.

The limousine bounced on the rutted track until it slid to an abrupt halt opposite the chosen vessel. Shayhar leapt out and retrieved some of the bags from the trunk before being joined by Javid who lifted out the last two and slammed it shut. The two bodyguards, loaded down with the luggage, strode to the gangplank leading to the deck of the smartly raked craft. An awkwardly shuffling Jahandar, sweating profusely and cursing beneath his breath, followed them more slowly. Shayhar boarded first and one by one the bags were handed down by Javid while Jahandar stood waiting impatiently.

As Jahandar sprawled in the comfortably padded saloon Shayhar checked the control panel and deftly shorted the ignition wires while Javid released the mooring lines. Both engines misfired with a belch of white smoke and then caught with a throaty roar as Shayhar thrust open the throttles to let the powerful Mercury Verados have their head.

The vessel sped away from the moorings and Jahandar called out but his words were muffled by the noise of the engines. Javid went inside to hear what the drug lord had said and reappeared with a puzzled look. Putting his mouth close to Shayhar's ear he shouted, 'He wants you to rig the boat to explode on a signal from his cellphone.'

Shayhar nodded and grinned, his malicious smile curling the corners of his mouth as he indicated that Javid should take over the controls. He went to the aft deck and selected one of the soft sports bags to retrieve two small grey packets of C4 and two IED detonators that he waved in Javid's surprised face.

'It's the only way to clear up those annoying loose ends, my friend,' and he raised a bushy eyebrow in a knowing manner; Javid grinned back nervously, his eyes fixed on the innocuous-looking grey packets. Shayhar reached across the control panel and pressed the switch to open the engine compartment. As the large panel in front of their feet automatically lifted it exposed the powerful Mercury 300 CXL engines that deafened them with their raw power. Shayhar squatted down and began placing the packets of C4 in strategic places before inserting the detonators and wiring them together. With a grunt of satisfaction he straightened his legs to ease the cramp that had begun and clicked his fingers under Javid's nose.

'Phone, cellphone,' he demanded, snapping his fingers and Javid fumbled in his pocket for his old Nokia. Shayhar took it and stripped the cover off in order to attach the wires. 'If this is switched on just pray that nobody calls you right now, Javid.'

It's off, I think it's off,' Javid screamed in panic as he stared down at the cellphone carcass being taped to the top of the engine.

'Relax, fool, I checked,' Shayhar sneered. 'Do you think I'm as big a fool as you?' He stretched languidly before tripping the switch to automatically close the engine bay. 'I'll set the phone just before we go ashore at Hawar. Does Jahandar have the number of that phone?'

Javid nodded, eyes mirroring his rancour, and relinquished control of the boat to Shayhar. He went down to join Jahandar and as he entered the luxury saloon he saw that the drug lord had gone into the forward cabin and had fallen asleep on the double bed. Without disturbing the man Javid switched on the gas stove and selected a large spoon from the drawer beneath. He then took two mini sachets from his pocket and using the tip of his long knife transferred the contents to the spoon. It only took him minutes to prepare the needle and the addict was soon slumped on the settee with rapidly contracting pupils.

The sun was touching the black silhouette of the low-lying island when the Sea Ray Venture approached Hawar Island. Shayhar went below to warn Jahandar and discovered that Javid had also fallen asleep. He kicked the legs of his partner hard as he went past him and entered the bow cabin to wake his employer. He gently rocked the fat man by the shoulder and watched with a curling lip as the huge stomach undulated beneath the unbuttoned silk shirt.

'Wha . . . whas up?' Jahandar mumbled as he slowly regained consciousness and struggled to sit upright.

'We're just entering the marina at Hawar Island,' Shayhar said and returned to the unmanned wheel to begin guiding the craft into the harbour. The Venture rose and fell with the gentle incoming swell and then steadied to remain level as it moved behind the sheltering breakwater. Shayhar throttled back even further and although he could see no officials on the quayside he steered to the far end of the row of unused moorings where he slid into a vacant space and stopped the vessel. He then opened the engine compartment and switched the phone on. Javid who had been stretching his arms in the stern went into action and tied the lines.

Jahandar waddled out of the cabin and into the pale rosy light of the setting sun. 'We must get to the Tulip Inn as quickly as possible. Leave the key in the ignition for Changeez.' He watched two marina attendants hurry towards the Venture and picking up one of the smaller cases he went ashore. After loading themselves with the remaining bags Shayhar and Javid quickly followed and with certain misgivings they watched the two officials intercept Jahandar.

'Excuse me sir, do you have a permit to moor for the night?' the shorter, tubbier man said haughtily.

'Certainly,' Jahandar snapped as he held out a $50 bill. 'Is this permit in order?' he asked with a curl of his lip. 'Can we go to our hotel now?'

The man looked at his colleague and then down at the crisp note in Jahandar's hand. 'I do believe that your permit is appropriate, sir, but I must warn you that you must depart before nine in the morning as you are in a resident's space and we are expecting him to arrive at ten o'clock.' He snatched the bill and quickly stuffed it into his pocket.

'The boat will have disappeared by then, of that you can be sure,' Shayhar said as he strode past the man and followed Jahandar who was walking along the quay to the distant cab rank.

The sun had long gone when the three men arrived at the hotel. They entered the spacious foyer and after presenting passports at the reception desk they were ushered to the two suites that Jahandar had booked earlier that same day. 'Shall I find Changeez?' Javid asked with a glint of eagerness in his eyes.

'Do it now and give him this message,' Jahandar said, handing a plain white envelope to Javid who immediately strode into the adjoining bedroom to use the landline phone on the bedside table.

He returned two minutes later with a twisted smile on his face and tugging at his black goatee. 'They are in their room. I will go to them straight away,' he said and left the suite.

Behrouz opened the door and Javid strode across to where Changeez sat to hand him the envelope. He tore it open avidly and read the brief message. 'We are to return to Manama and check on the woman he is holding in Qal'at al-Bahrain.' Changeez turned to Javid with a puzzled look. 'And why would he want us to do that?' he asked. 'He knows the Bahraini police are looking for us.'

'I never question Jahandar's orders,' Javid hissed as he slipped a hand beneath his jacket.

The subtle action did not go unobserved and Changeez quickly smiled and held up his hands in a gesture of protest. 'Don't misunderstand me, we will certainly do as Jahandar asks. I only wondered whether you knew why we had to do this for him.'

'How would I know,' Javid snarled and he left, slamming the door behind him.

Changeez read the note again and then rose to his feet with a mystified shrug. 'According to Jahandar's note we must leave immediately,' he muttered, shaking his head as the two men went into the bedroom and began packing their bags.

It was pitch dark when the two men finally arrived at the marina and made their way to the Venture at the far end. They boarded the boat and Changeez saw that the key was still in the ignition. After Behrouz had cast off the lines he switched on and was rewarded by the throaty roar of the twin engines bursting into life. When sufficient clear water separated them from the mooring he pushed on both throttles until they were burbling towards the sea entrance. Having cleared the breakwater the boat began to rise and fall with the incoming waves and Changeez gave the Venture its head and the craft bit into the waves before rising on the planes and roaring seaward.

Behrouz stepped up beside Changeez and studied the binnacle. 'How do you know if we're going the right way?' he asked as the compass floated lightly from side to side as they rode the waves.

'GPS, global positioning system, fool,' Changeez snapped impatiently as he pointed to the illuminated screen set to one side of the control binnacle. 'I've set the signal for Askar and we only have to follow the direction indicated there.' He pointed at the dayglo line that ran erratically across the screen.

'Why isn't it a straight line?' Behrouz said.

'We have to avoid reefs, shallows and rising coral heads. I think it's time you took over the controls. All you have to do is keep the little diagram of the boat, which is us, on the line and maintain the same speed and we'll be in Askar in approximately sixty minutes.' Changeez descended to the lower cabin to take an ice-cold bottle of beer from the cool box that they had brought with them.

As Behrouz gripped the wheel and ran his eyes over the control panel he became aware of a switch that didn't have a legend printed below it like the others and it only took two minutes before curiosity overcame common sense.

He flicked it down and was startled as a large cover rose by his feet and an onslaught of engine noise physically struck him. 'Wow,' he thought as he dropped to his knees and peered down into the illuminated area packed with deafening machinery. He was about to rise to his feet when the strange sight of a broken cellphone stopped him. It appeared to have been taped to the engine and had wires leading from it to some small grey packets. Behrouz knew in an instant what they were and who they were intended for.

He stood up and looked back at the peaceful sprinkling of residential and harbour lights tracing the black silhouette of the receding coastline and then peered down into the cabin where Changeez was well into his second bottle. Behrouz flicked the switch to close the engine cover and as soon as the noise was muted he climbed over the side coaming and carefully walked along the Venture until he had reached the bowsprit rail. The bow of the vessel glistened as it sliced through the calm sea and the sight of two porpoises racing the Venture momentarily hypnotized him. He suddenly realized that to avoid the screws it would be a lot safer jumping off the stern. Steadying himself against the odd wave that made the craft lurch sideways he went to the rear seating area and stepped onto the swim platform. The white maelstrom created by the twin screws stretched away, becoming one phosphorescent wake all the way back to the island.

Over the boiling rush of the water and the roar of the engines Behrouz vaguely heard Changeez shouting, 'What the hell are you doing?'

Owing nothing to anybody but himself Behrouz ignored the voice and stepped off the Venture and into the boiling water to disappear from sight. The raging sea twisted and tumbled his scrawny frame until everything suddenly became calm and he bobbed to the surface, coughing up the brine he had inadvertently swallowed. Slipping off his jacket and shoes Behrouz trod water and turned to watch the Venture racing away. The backlit figure of his employer standing at the stern was shaking an empty bottle in amazement as he watched his servant rapidly disappear.

The boat had travelled another hundred metres before Changeez scrambled back to the steering wheel to change course and return to Behrouz when the vessel disappeared in a rising ball of brilliant flames. The sound that followed crashed into Behrouz's head and he quickly sank below the surface to soothe that first painful impact. As he surfaced he was struck by the heatwave from the vaporizing craft and once more he choked on a mouthful of seawater. Spluttering helplessly he tried to dodge the falling debris while treading water and when the flaming deluge finally ended he slowly swam back to Hawar Island.

Behrouz limited his actions to a gentle breaststroke in order to conserve his strength for the long swim back to shore. He prayed that night predators would ignore him as his survival instinct drove him on, one stroke after the other. The only thought that went through his head over and over again was to exact revenge on the person who had tried to kill him. He was determined to terminate Jahandar in the cruellest and most painful way he could devise.

9

Jahander stood on the hotel balcony and watched the distant fireball expand and then quickly diminish in size until it was only a pinprick of light near the horizon. The sound of the detonation moved swiftly over the surface of the sea, fading in volume as it raced towards the Tulip Inn until it was just a muffled thud in the ears of the three watching men. With a brief nod of satisfaction Jahandar tossed his cellphone onto the sunlounger and returned to sipping his iced cranberry juice through a straw. A few foolhardy, romantic couples who were strolling in the oppressively humid night air pointed out to sea and their excited chattering filtered up to the listening men. Jahandar noticed that nobody ran to raise the alarm and he only saw the occasional shrugs of baffled witnesses who had convinced each other that it must be a big firework display on the main island.

'Everything will have quietened down by tomorrow and we'll return to Manama to ensure that the main consignment is ready for despatch. We'll also check that the Taylors are doing as they were told while I find a new agent capable of getting into Saudi Arabia without any questions being asked,' Jahandar added. He walked back into the suite and headed for the bedroom.

'I would prefer it, gentlemen, if you would now go straight to your own suite and keep a very low profile. Stay out of sight and only use room service for your needs. When the dust has settled on this unfortunate accident I'll let you know.' Shayhar and Javid laughed and with a last glance at the dying point of light on the horizon they left the suite.

Jahandar picked up the cellphone he had just used to detonate the bomb and dialled a number. 'I trust you are doing as I instructed,' he said when Stuart answered and then nodded slowly. 'You have two, possibly three, days after the water has been exhausted. As a doctor your wife will know what to do and should be able to survive that long, but not for much longer,' he said cruelly and broke the connection. Jahandar reached into a bowl and scooped up a handful of nuts before sinking back into the fine cotton sheets to begin cracking them in his clenched fist.

Later, when the drug baron had closed the windows, turned out the lights and was beginning to give himself up to sleep a light breeze blew across the room, cooling his half-naked body. A window had been opened and Jahandar was instantly alert to danger. He inched one hand under the pillow and curled his pudgy fingers around the moulded grip of the pistol he habitually placed there every night.

'Don't show me your hand with anything other than lifelines in it and you'll keep it,' a voice hissed in the dark. A glitter of reflected moonlight revealed the long blade hovering above his face. Jahandar released his grip and removed his hand.

'Now that's a whole lot healthier, sir,' the whisperer dripped sarcasm with every word. 'If I had caught the merest glimpse of a gun I would have removed your head in seconds and without any regrets.'

The blade danced in front of Jahandar's sweat-streaked face as an invisible hand groped beneath the pillow to remove the 9-mm magnum automatic. 'Now, do please tell me why you thought it a wise move to blow Changeez and myself into tiny pieces for the little fish to dine on?'

'Your faces are now being shown on television and in every newspaper in the country so it wouldn't have been long before the hotel staff had recognized you and called the police. If you're captured and questioned I have no guarantee that you would remain quiet about my identity and my multimillion-dollar business would be destroyed in a matter of hours.'

'Better that Changeez and I should disappear instead, yes?'

'With regret, I can assure you,' Jahandar said. 'You have been good employees.' He used a corner of the sheet to wipe away the sweat that was trickling into his eyes.

'I cannot make you disappear so easily, Jahandar, but I can make you dead,' Behrouz said as he aimed the barrel at the round face beneath him and pulled the automatic slide back to chamber the first round.

'Why act in such a foolish way when I could still make you a very rich man, Behrouz,' Jahandar whispered in a softly beguiling voice. The curling finger decreased in pressure on the trigger and Behrouz waited patiently for the man to continue.

'If you do one more simple job for me I'll guarantee you ten thousand dollars in hard cash.'

Behrouz swallowed noisily and sat down at the end of the bed, the automatic still levelled at the big man's head. 'What would I have to do?'

'I'll tell you when the time comes,' Jahandar hissed back. 'Now, go and dry yourself before you saturate the end of my bed with seawater and then get some sleep in the sitting room.'

'How can I trust you after what you've done to Changeez?'

'You can't but I can guarantee that you'll remain poor if you don't do as I say,' the big man sneered and he rolled over and closed his little eyes, nervously thinking about the automatic that still pointed at his head.

Behrouz stared at the motionless hulk for a few more seconds with hate battling greed until finally the muzzle drooped and he slipped the gun into his sodden trouser pocket. He then rose to his feet and leaving a trail of wet footprints across the parquet flooring he left the room and quietly closed the door behind him.

The following day Jahandar rose early and after showering and dressing went through to the sitting room to find the crumpled figure of Behrouz still sleeping off his exhaustion from his long swim back to shore the previous evening. With slippers whispering on the varnished wood he returned to the bedroom and summoned the two bodyguards to his suite. Jahandar then returned to the sitting room and quietly waited by the door until the bell chimed. He swiftly admitted the big men who advanced on the sleeping man with automatics drawn.

The doorchime had disturbed Behrouz and he was just opening his eyes when he became aware of the two men standing over him and the gun barrels that were only centimetres from his face.

'Would you kindly return my weapon, Mr Behrouz,' Jahandar said as he walked towards the frozen tableau. 'Very carefully,' he swiftly added, his palm outstretched.

Behrouz half sat up and reached into his trouser pocket to touch the cold metal. With finger and thumb gripping the butt he slowly withdrew the weapon and held it up. Jahandar snatched it away by the barrel and nodded at the two bodyguards who backed away a few steps as their employer pointed his weapon at the terrified Behrouz.

'So, I was a fool to trust you,' Behrouz whimpered as he cringed away from the threat of the gun aimed at his left eye. 'You'll kill me anyway.'

'Kill you? Not at all, Behrouz. I still expect you to fulfil a little task for me for which you will be paid very handsomely indeed.' Jahandar lowered the weapon until it hung by his side. 'You will return to the mainland with us in a day or two and then you will receive your instructions. Please remember, Shayhar and Javid are expert at killing and if you should be tempted to leave or try to do me any harm they will have no qualms about ending your existence.' There was a long, silent pause. 'Do I make myself clear?'

Behrouz nodded and Jahandar beamed as he turned and took a bowl of pistachios from the glass coffee table before waddling back into the bedroom. The two bodyguards crossed the large room to where the flat-screen television stood. Javid threw himself into one of the armchairs as Shayhar used the remote to switch the set on. Behrouz wearily lay back on the settee as a large image of Changeez sprang into view. He sat up with a start as the news presenter gave Changeez's full name and then invited viewers to report any sighting of the fugitive to the nearest police station. Then his own face replaced that of his dead boss and the request was repeated. Behrouz knew he could no longer simply walk away from Jahandar and his men for he desperately needed the drug baron's help to escape back to Iran.

Helen sat perfectly still as she listened to the silence broken only by the light hissing of the mild tinnitus she had suffered since leaving college. From the time when the two men had left her alone she had tried hard to suppress the rising panic that threatened to destroy any rational thinking and she wrapped her arms around her knees and pulled herself into a tight ball. Helen tried to imagine what Stuart might be doing but then realized, knowing him as well as she did, that he would obey the kidnappers demands if they had been threatening her life. However, she was also confident that being a resourceful man he would be able to find a way of turning the tables and finding her.

Helen smiled as she recalled the time when they had first met three years ago. The same Saudi Arabian oil company that employed Stuart had also offered her the lucrative position as company doctor. At that time Stuart had been very interested in a type of illegally distilled and distributed alcohol called siddiqui. To reduce the boredom of living in the country Stuart took up distilling as a hobby and set about perfecting a highly potent spirit in his spare time. This had led them both into a number of life-threatening situations and as they overcame each problem to survive her love for the ruggedly handsome geologist had blossomed and grown.

Helen's shoulders relaxed a little and she felt around in the dark until her fingers brushed across the side of the litre bottle. Without thinking Helen picked it up and started unscrewing the cap. As she raised the bottle to her lips she instinctively checked herself for any symptoms of dehydration and on discovering that she could still produce a sufficient quantity of saliva in her mouth she replaced the cap. This may have to last a very long time, she thought and only then did Helen realize that she had no way of measuring time. She couldn't even estimate how long she had been held captive and the feeling of panic returned. She pushed all thoughts of her imprisonment away and thought of Stuart and his hazel eyes; eyes that made her heart skip when they opened every morning. She then recalled in minute detail the happiest day of her life when they had travelled to the Western Highlands and were married in the sixteenth-century Barcaldine Castle. The local people commonly knew it as The Black Castle as it was built in 1600 by Sir Duncan Campbell, the Black Duncan. She recalled the beautiful view that stretched up Loch Creran to the brooding majesty of Glencoe and a deep longing filled her soul.

Her mind then shifted to linger on the fine lacework of her wedding dress and then with a wry smile remembered seeing Stuart in his traditional kilt for the first time.

A rustling sound interrupted her thoughts and she sat bolt upright, straining her ears to detect any movement. Helen sat immobile for a minute before the rapid rustling happened again. The sound seemed to travel across the chamber and she surmised that it was a small animal running.

'Rats,' she shouted in disgust and drew her legs up, gripping them even tighter with her arms.

To overcome the upsurge of horror Helen began to list all the moments in their short married life that Stuart had made extraspecial with either a whispered word, a gesture or one of his broad infectious smiles. Helen smiled and began to sing 'Wild Mountain Thyme' which was Stuart's favourite and one of the traditional folk songs that they had danced to at the reception.

> O the summer time has come
> And the trees are sweetly blooming
> And wild mountain thyme
> Grows around the purple heather.
> Will you go, lassie, go?

The sound of her voice filled the silence before echoing slightly to remind Helen that she may be in her burial chamber—her voice faltered and then stopped on the second line of the chorus.

> And we'll all go together,
> To pull wild mountain thyme . . .

Stuart braced himself against the rise and fall of the small fishing craft as it rode the waves that rolled in to break on the beach at Askar. The buildings on the shore were dwindling in size as the fishing boat ploughed its way towards the wreck of the *Fifi*.

The bewhiskered captain was expertly using the wheel with only the thumb and forefinger of his right hand. The other fingers were lost when he put his hand into a dark hole in a reef that proved to be the home of a particularly vicious moray eel.

'We should be over the reef by *dhuhr* prayer time, *insh'allah*,' the captain shouted to Stuart and Alan who were tending their dive equipment on the aft deck.

'Twelve noon,' Stuart repeated for Alan's benefit as he checked his regulator. 'We can anchor over the site once we've located the buoy and start diving immediately.'

Alan nodded and returned to his task of thoroughly checking the air cylinders that they had collected from the apartment. They had stopped off at the Aquatique dive shop on the way to Askar and filled all six, anticipating that they would be doing more than one dive despite being warned about multiple diving on the same day by the PADI dive instructor who owned the shop.

After about ten minutes the captain noticed a small boat with a white sail racing towards them. It was a single-handed Laser-class competition dinghy and the occupant was too preoccupied with extracting every ounce of sailpower from the light sea breeze to notice the larger craft bearing down.

The captain spun the wheel and the fishing boat swung violently to starboard throwing Alan off his feet. 'What the heck are you up to?' he shouted as he rose to his knees and then flung himself onto a rapidly rolling oxygen cylinder that was threatening to smash into Stuart's legs.

'It's the captain's special evasive technique,' Stuart shouted as he watched the Laser swing to port to fill the sail. The person in the dinghy was still oblivious to any danger and continued to counter balance the craft by leaning back over the port side with feet rigidly placed against the centre board as the Laser heeled at a forty degree angle.

The captain spun the wheel again and the boat tried to change course yet again but the prow only swung at a snail's pace to starboard and the correction was too late. With a harsh, drawn-out sound of calico being torn in half the heavy oak prow ripped through the fragile sail and fibreglass hull and both men ducked as the radial mast with its sail whipped towards the fishing boat, narrowly missing Stuart; and then the small craft was rolled over and was driven beneath the heavy hull.

'The stern, quick,' Stuart shouted as he ran to the rear of the fishing vessel. Alan quickly followed as the captain pulled the throttle back and left the wheelhouse to join the two men. The fishing boat lurched to a wallowing halt, rising and falling in the residue of its own wake.

Alan was the first to spot the lone sailor and dived over the side before Stuart could react. With powerful strokes learnt and perfected in the heavy surf of Bondi Beach, Alan cleaved the calm sea until he was amidst the wreckage of the Laser. He kicked to rise a little in the water and twisted his body to catch a glimpse of long trailing hair slowly fading beneath the surface. Taking a deep breath he jack-knifed his muscular body and kicked hard to drive himself down into the crystal waters. Salt began to sting his unprotected eyes as he searched frantically amongst the sinking flotsam until he spotted the figure slowly descending with half of the Laser hull. With lungs bursting he rose to the surface and after taking a brief gulp of air he powered himself down again. The figure was now much deeper and Alan had a hard muscle-twisting task to overcome his own buoyancy before he was within reach to grasp the white shirt the sailor was wearing. He turned and began kicking hard, pulling the figure behind him as he looked up at the shimmering surface that seemed impossibly far away.

His lungs were about to give up when he felt the pull on his shoulder stop. Looking down he saw that Stuart had swum down and taken up the task of bringing the unconscious person to the surface so that Alan could save himself.

With no encumbrance to inhibit his arms Alan struck out and with a loud inhalation of air he surfaced to flop down onto his back, his chest heaving with the effort to draw as much oxygen as possible into his body.

Stuart broke the surface and pulled the person up until he was able to support the dead weight. 'Help me get her to the boat,' he panted as he tried to swim with one arm around the motionless person while the other worked to move them towards the boat that lay dead in the water. Having recovered his breath Alan swam to Stuart's side and only then did he notice that the unconscious person was a young woman.

'My God, it's a sheila,' he panted as he grabbed a firm upperarm and helped tow the woman towards the boat hook being held over the side by the captain. Stuart ignored the spike and shouted up to the captain that he should unfold the steps that were stowed amidship. The stainless-steel ladder was soon unhinged and swung over the bulwark giving both men something substantial to climb with the dead weight of the young woman between them.

It was only a matter of minutes before they had the unconscious woman lying on the deck and covered with one of the captain's goat hair blankets. Alan went below to the galley and began preparing some hot chocolate for them all, adding a good shot of whisky to each mug. 'For medicinal purposes,' he said when Stuart raised an eyebrow on sipping his.

Stuart had briefly examined the woman and on seeing the bruise that was colouring her right temple he said, 'I guess she was knocked out when she was flung overboard.' He ran a finger over the purple bump.

'She's beautiful,' Alan observed as he studied the smooth complexion and full lips. Her long eyelashes curled above high cheekbones and her raven hair was tied back in a severe, practical ponytail.

'When you've finished ogling the poor girl, Alan, perhaps you could contact the Manama yacht club and see if she is known to them,' Stuart said with a slight grin. 'As far as I can remember from the brief few seconds before we ran her down the registration on the sail was an O and a G or, possibly C and the number was forty-three.'

Alan nodded with eyes still lingering on the recumbent figure then he quickly rose to his feet and hurried into the wheelhouse. After being passed from one member of staff to another he eventually managed to get through to the secretary of the club who immediately referred to his membership ledger.

'Yes, we have a Laser OC43 registered in the name of Reem Sfeir. She was logged out at nine-thirty this morning and is expected back at midday.'

Alan reported what had happened and that she appeared to have been rendered unconscious. While he was talking Stuart appeared at the wheelhouse door. 'She's awake and seems to be perfectly okay,' he said giving a deep sigh of relief.

Alan passed this on and then suggested that they could bring the young woman to the yacht club on their return. The secretary agreed and said that one of the members of the club, who happened to be a doctor, would be able to make himself available to check Ms Sfeir when they returned to port.

After thanking the secretary for his help Alan hung up and turned to look out of the window at the beautiful apparition that sat upon the stern rail watching the gulls diving into their wake. The bleached jeans and the white cotton shirt tied at the waist had dried sufficiently in the hot sun for Alan to be able to see the curvaceous figure being backlit by the brilliance of the midday sun reflecting off the sea.

'Jeez,' he whispered and Stuart turned his head.

'What was that Alan?'

'Nothing, mate, let's get going to the dive site, shall we? However, shouldn't we have her looked at by a doctor first?' he said with a concerned look on his face while still staring at the young woman.

Stuart smiled to himself. 'I've already asked her if she feels up to joining us on a teasure hunt and she agreed.' He tapped the captain on the shoulder as he pointed to the open sea. 'Okay, Captain, can you get us out there as quickly as possible?' The captain nodded and pushed the throttle forward.

Alan wandered to the stern of the boat and stood beside the woman who turned her head and sized him up with friendly eyes that glowed with bright flecks of hazel. 'You are Mrs Reem Sfeir?' he asked, and felt his throat constricting with nervousness.

'It's Miss Sfeir, but I'm called Reem by all those who rescue me from the monsters of the deep,' she murmured and Alan was struck by the warm sensuality of her voice. 'I understand from Mr Taylor that you risked your life to swim down to me and to get me back to the surface.'

'I had help from Stuart, I didn't do it all by myself,' Alan stuttered.

'Well, I believe that if you hadn't done what you did I would be dead now and for that I am truly indebted to you,' Reem said quietly as she placed her hand over Alan's that was nervously gripping the stern rail.

Totally embarrassed by her words Alan changed the subject. 'What does Reem mean?'

'It means white antelope and like my namesake I should have been fast enough to get out of your way,' she said as she looked back to where the boiling arrow-shaped wake pointed to the final resting place of her beloved Laser. 'I just didn't see you until it was too late,' she added sadly.

'I'm truly sorry about that, Reem,' Alan said as he studied the beautiful profile. 'Our captain tried everything to avoid you but it was the last swing to starboard that proved insufficient to prevent the collision. Luckily you do not seem to be badly hurt. However, I have a doctor on standby to give you a check-up on your arrival back at the yacht club.'

'That won't be necessary, Alan, I know that I'm perfectly okay.'

'You never can tell,' Alan insisted.

'I can because I'm a nurse with a proficient level of medical knowledge on concussion and similar ailments.'

'That's interesting,' Alan said. 'Stuart's wife is a doctor at the Bahrain Specialist Hospital.'

'What a strange coincidence.' Reem tilted her head with one elegantly arched eyebrow. 'I know most if not all of the doctors in the hospital so I must have met or even worked with her at one time or another.'

'Dr Helen Taylor, that's her name.'

'I know her well. A very attractive doctor whom I have had the pleasure of teaming with on occasions,' Reem exclaimed, her voice tinged with surprise.

As the fishing boat continued chugging its way to the dive site Alan made every excuse to remain sitting by Reem to ask and answer scores of questions about their respective jobs and lives. Alan remained ambiguous about the reason for their expedition to *Fifi* and explained their jaunt with a little white lie, saying that it was their first opportunity to explore the old shipwreck and search for treasure.

The scene of the two as they sat talking on the stern rail reminded Stuart of his own courtship days. He covertly watched from the wheelhouse with a benign expression that occasionally hinted at becoming a smile as he observed his friend's efforts to charm the attractive woman.

Fifty minutes later the fishing boat throttled back and drifted to a standstill. Without a word Alan stripped off his shirt revealing his impressive musculature and slipped over the side. He used his face mask to search for the buoy that was luckily still tethered at a depth of thirteen metres. Without lifting his head from the water he waved his hand to indicate the direction and the captain gently moved the vessel forward while Alan held on to a rusting ringbolt on the side of the hull. Finally he lifted his head out of the water and ran his hand across his throat to indicate that the captain should cut the engines. 'We're right overhead,' Alan shouted up to Stuart as he pointed downwards.

Stuart smiled and reaching behind his back grasped the dangling zip-cord and pulled it up over his shoulder to seal his wetsuit. 'Let's go treasure hunting, then,' he said and reached down to pull Alan aboard.

Reem was a little puzzled for the visibility in the water exceeded fifteen metres and she could see no sign of a shipwreck beneath their hull. Stuart's remark had creased her brow further while she wondered about the kind of 'treasure' he was referring to. She looked at the Australian as he tugged on his wetsuit, puzzled that he hadn't mentioned anything concrete and on the contrary had been very evasive about any treasure.

The old captain muttered to himself as he went to the bow and dropped the heavily corroded twin-fluke anchor over the side. The short chain rattled noisily until only rope was running through the chock. When only half of the neat coil on the deck was gone the anchor hit the seabed and one of the flukes bit deep into the sandy bottom, swinging the boat round to align with the current. Without even looking at the two men who had finished putting on their equipment the captain returned to his wheelhouse to begin washing himself for the *dhuhr* prayer.

The friends went through their pre-dive check before sitting side by side on the bulwark. Alan gave Reem a broad smile before biting down on the mouthpiece and on a signal from Stuart they both rolled backwards and into the calm, tepid water. Accompanied by a mass of silvery bubbles they momentarily sank and then rose to the surface where they spent a few moments neutralizing their buoyancy. Alan waved to Reem who was leaning over the rail and with Stuart leading the way they sank beneath the surface.

10

Both men swam down to the tethered buoy and then onward until they were able to stand on the seabed. Alan's face mask briefly fogged up and in the effort to clear it he tasted sweet water, which told him that they were in the fresh-water upwelling; it wasn't long before Stuart began pointing at a depression in the seabed that had been the site of the original chest. He tapped his dive buddy on the shoulder and then waved his hand in a wide circle and Alan immediately understood that they should begin to search the seabed in an ever-widening spiral, using the depression as their starting point.

Positioning themselves about two metres apart they began swimming alongside each other while skimming through the top few centimetres of sand with spread fingers. The visibility behind them was reduced by the clouds of fine silt but this fortunately settled by the time they completed one circle to begin the next.

After circling three more times Stuart paused and raked in the sand until he had uncovered what seemed to be a large, deeply pitted iron tube. Alan helped to scoop the sand away from the heavily corroded object until they realized that they had found a medieval ship's smooth-bore cannon. Stuart gave the thumbs-up sign and the two men continued searching. They swam another seven metres and found two more cannons before Alan's hand hit a different shape and he stopped to investigate more closely. Stuart joined him and they soon cleared enough sand away to reveal a similar chest to the one they had recovered earlier. Stuart pointed upward and as Alan swam to the surface Stuart stayed down to inflate another buoy and tether it to the chest before joining him.

'Fantastic,' he gasped on breaking the surface beside his friend. 'It is exactly the same as the other one.'

Still gripping his mouthpiece Alan nodded and struck out for the anchored fishing boat. Stuart kept pace and both were soon on board with Alan excitedly telling Reem of their find. 'An old sea-chest,' she responded with a look of disbelief on her face.

'We found a similar one the other day in almost the same spot,' Alan exclaimed and Stuart touched him lightly on the arm before he could mention what it had contained.

Reem didn't miss the slight movement. 'And what did you find inside? I heard Stuart mention treasure earlier.'

Stuart turned to face the young woman and spread his hands in a gesture of defeat. 'You've obviously guessed that we found something of value and it was . . .'

Alan interrupted him with an enthusiastic description of the necklace and the other pieces of jewellery, his face glowing with excitement, until Stuart said the one word 'Helen' and Alan stopped mid-sentence with an apologetic expression. 'Go on, Alan,' Reem said eagerly as she looked from one man to the other.

'Reem, you should know that some rather vicious people learnt about the treasure we found and are now holding Stuart's wife ransom for what we may have found today,' Alan said wretchedly.

'Oh, my God,' Reem exclaimed, startling the captain on the foredeck who was just finishing his prayers. 'They're holding Doctor Taylor? Do the police know?'

'Yes, and they are currently looking for her but we don't hold out much hope of them finding the kidnappers or Helen. The only way is to do as they ask until we get the opportunity to either follow, or catch them,' Stuart muttered as he finished attaching one end of a long rope to an old deck cleat and throwing the rest over the side. He changed his air cylinder for a full one and then with a short wave to the couple he toppled back into the sea. Alan watched his friend's blurred image recede with the tied rope paying out behind him and then began removing his dive gear.

The captain returned from the foredeck and reverently placed the rolled prayer mat inside the wheelhouse before moving to Alan's side. 'We have something to pull from the sea?' he asked and Alan nodded.

Reem sat on the bulwark and waited, her eyes fixed on Alan as he tested the rope tension.

Nineteen metres below Stuart had located the new buoy and the half-buried chest and was swiftly running the rope end through the iron rings at both ends. He tested the knots and when satisfied tugged on the rope until he received an answering pull from above. With powerful beats of his long legs he began returning to the boat.

Alan felt the tug and began pulling in the free length of rope before it resisted his efforts and he wound the rope once more around the cleat before taking the strain. The muscles of his back and upper arms became visible cords of power and the young woman openly admired Alan's physique.

'A little help wouldn't go amiss,' Alan grunted and Reem, red-cheeked, hurried to help pull on the rope. As the two struggled to free the chest from the suction of the sand Stuart surfaced and climbed aboard where he quickly stripped off his diving gear and joined the couple at the rope.

Suddenly they were able to take a step back and Stuart knew that the chest had been released from its watery vault. 'Gently, we only have the weight of the chest to contend with now,' he warned. Within minutes the chest had broken the surface and had been hauled onto the deck.

'Shall we open it now?' Reem asked as she tried to disguise her excitement.

In answer to her question Stuart placed a crowbar under the oxidized lock hasp and levered until the last remaining fragments of iron gave way. Alan grasped one side of the lid and pulled while Stuart pushed up on the other until their tanned faces were a darker shade of red.

Reem jumped down from the rail where she had been sitting. 'Let me help,' she said enthusiastically as she knelt beside Stuart and pushed up on the rough rim of the lid. The seal was broken with a sudden 'crack' and the lid squealed as three pairs of hands raised it to an upright position.

'It only needed a woman's touch,' Reem said smugly as she gazed upon a dark piece of rotten canvas that covered the contents and the two men laughed. Alan moved round to the front of the chest as Stuart took a corner of the canvas between thumb and forefinger and gently pulled it to one side, folding it carefully as he went until he had fully uncovered rows of beeswax bars not dissimilar to the one they had already found.

'This must be the rest of the plunder from the seventeenth-century raids on Bahrain,' Alan whispered as he removed one of the heavy packages and held it up to show Reem. 'We found one of these in another chest that we raised from the same shipwreck and it contained a beautiful pearl necklace.'

'They were in perfect condition, too,' Stuart added as he took another package and placed it on the deck. Using the dive knife that was strapped to his calf he teased away at the wax. The others watched eagerly as he slowly uncovered a linen bundle and after sweeping away the pieces of wax he slowly tugged at the ends of the fragile linen until he was able to unroll it completely. There were sudden intakes of breath as the sun fell upon a perfectly preserved opera necklace for the first time in four hundred years.

'They are positively beautiful,' Reem gasped. 'It's the most beautiful pearl necklace that I've ever seen,' she added as she tentatively touched one of the large lustrous pearls with her fingertip before exclaiming, 'They're Jumana pearls!'

'What's a Jumana?' Alan asked.

'It's an extremely rare pearl with a light silvery sheen in the lustre. Can't you see it?'

'I can see that they must be something special. I'd also say that they are perfectly graduated from ten to fourteen millimetres in size and strung on gold wire,' Alan murmured. 'What do you reckon, Stuart?'

'Mmm, my guesstimate would be from two to three million dollars.'

Alan began lifting out the beeswax packages until he had ten lined up on the sun-bleached decking planks. 'That means we've got a minimum of twenty-two million dollars in front of us,' Alan shouted as he jumped to his feet. 'Jeez, that's a bloody fortune.'

Stuart remained on his knees and looking up at his prancing friend he said, '*We* haven't got a fortune, Alan, the kidnappers have,' and instantly dampened Alan's high spirits. He sank back onto his haunches with a grim expression.

'We have to come up with a plan that will trick them into releasing Helen.'

'Or track them to where they're holding her,' Stuart added.

'I think you should leave it to the police,' Reem said as she tore her eyes away from the pearls and went to sit on the bulwark.

'Let's discuss it with Walid,' Alan asserted.

'I agree, three heads are better than two.' Stuart rose and signalled to the captain that they needed to up-anchor and return to shore. The fisherman left his wheelhouse and grumbled his way to the bow; passing the open chest and exposed pearls without looking at them he began hauling in the anchor.

'Four heads,' Reem said with a little irritation in her tone.

'Pardon,' Stuart asked raising one eyebrow.

'I'd like to help you find your wife, Stuart, and as a fairly intelligent person I believe I can contribute towards that task.'

A flicker of a smile crossed Alan's face and Stuart briefly nodded. 'Thank you, Reem, but I think we should get you checked by the doctor who is waiting for you at the marina.

'I can reassure you as a fully qualified nurse that I know that I am perfectly healthy and that there is only one doctor I wish to consult with.'

'Who's that?' Alan asked.

'Doctor Helen Taylor.'

Helen took a very tentative sip of the tepid water from the plastic bottle and wrinkled her nose at the taste. Her painfully dry throat and cracked lips had prompted her to draw upon the precious fluid and after two small swallows she recapped the bottle and stood it on the stone floor where it reassuringly leant against her hip.

Helen let her mind wander back to the romantic wedding and honeymoon in Barcaldine Castle during that first snowfall in Argyll. She could almost feel the heat of the blazing fire that hissed and crackled in the huge fireplace of the Grand Hall where they had exchanged vows. The smell of the wood smoke mingling with the ancient panelling and musty trophies on the walls teased her imagination for a few seconds before she returned to the reality of the dank stone chamber.

After a few minutes she began to conjure in her mind the gentle wonder of her wedding night in the old castle, while outside they could hear the 'clock-clocking' sounds of the wild capercaillie.

Helen sat up with a jerk, realizing that the sounds were real. The imaginary game birds had become the reality of echoing footsteps coming down the long passageway that led to the heavy door of her prison.

'Help!' she screamed and then continued shouting for help until the approaching sounds stopped outside the door. Stuart had arrived at last and she breathed a deep sigh when a key turned in the lock and bolts noisily slid back in their rusty restraints. The door squealed as it swung open and flashing lights forced Helen to shut eyes that had only known inky blackness for so long.

'Is that you, Stuart?' she asked, her voice hoarse as she slowly opened her eyes to see a vague silhouette before her. There was a momentary silence that Helen was about to break when a flashlight shone directly into her face, blinding her as a man with an Iranian accent spoke.

'No, it's not your husband, Mrs Taylor. I believe he has failed to retrieve the items that I wanted and therefore I have no choice but to carry out my original threat,' Jahandar said in a cold businesslike tone of voice.

Helen recognized the voice and her heart sank. She slumped back against the cold wall and shielded her eyes from the glare of the flashlight with her hands. 'You plan to kill me?'

Jahandar didn't answer immediately and waited, impatiently tapping his foot until Javid had unlocked the padlock and removed the chain from Helen's wrists. As the bodyguard stepped back behind his boss Jahandar spoke.

'Nobody is going to kill you, Mrs Taylor. We will leave that to nature. If one day in the distant future your body is discovered it will be considered an unfortunate accident—a foolish tourist who was accidentally trapped in the old dungeon.' He shuffled back through the door and just before it was fully closed Helen could hear him dialling on a cellphone. Jahandar began speaking in a low threatening voice but Helen couldn't make out what he was saying.

After what seemed like an age to the doctor Jahandar re-entered the chamber and shuffled across to where she sat. Half expecting to be killed on the spot Helen cringed away as he leant over her huddled form and placed a cellphone to her ear. 'Say something to your darling husband,' Jahandar snarled and Helen eagerly tried to grab the instrument but her hand was batted away by the drug lord.

'Stuart is that you?' she cried and hearing his familiar voice she burst into tears. 'Yes, yes, I am well and chained to a wall in a . . .'

'Enough,' Jahandar shouted and snatched the cellphone away and covered the microphone. He stalked back through the doorway to continue his conversation with Stuart. 'I believe you have found more packages, Mr Taylor. You found many inside an old wooden chest and I will tell you how I know. Your stupid old captain had phoned a friend to tell him about the wonderful discovery by his customers. This friend just happened to be a first cousin of one of my men.' There was a long pause that almost stretched Stuart's nerves to breaking point before Jahandar continued.

'You will now place everything you found, and I mean everything, in a canvas holdall and leave it at the reception of the Ramada Palace Hotel for collection by a man called Issa ben Ali. Do you understand, Mr Taylor? If you involve the police and don't do this by five o'clock today your wife will die of thirst in a dark place that is never visited.'

Jahandar switched off his cellphone. 'Your husband tried to trick me, Mrs Taylor, and for this he must pay a forfeit—you.' He began walking up the passageway to the surface, laughing as he went. The door thudded shut and the iron key rasped as it was turned in the lock.

Helen reached out to touch her bottle of water and felt nothing. Crouching down with outstretched arms she slowly searched until she had crossed the chamber. It was after recrossing for the third time and when the muscles of her legs had begun to suffer painful cramp that she came to the terrifying conclusion that the bottle had gone. It had been taken by Jahandar to ensure Helen's death happened a little sooner than originally planned.

The old captain slowly guided his fishing boat into the exclusive marina with some trepidation. The salt-stained vessel, streaked with rust and smelling of fish was in marked contrast to all the beautifully groomed boats moored in neat, serried ranks. With years of skill in evidence he eased his boat up against the jetty where a number of men were waiting to assist them.

Stuart and Alan had packed the contents of the chest into their dive bags on the final approach to the marina and instructed the captain to take good care of the old chest as the Bahrain National Museum would be coming to collect it later. As the last items were lifted from the chest they uncovered a folded piece of vellum that had been folded twice and sealed with wax. Stuart placed it with the beeswax packages intending to study it when out of sight of any inquisitive eyes. Alan paid the charter fee and added a handsome tip that the captain clearly appreciated and Reem gave him a smile that had him wishing he were thirty years younger.

A rather short man wearing fawn linen slacks and an expensive Ralph Lauren polo shirt walked towards the fishing vessel as the last mooring line was tied and swept an imperious gaze over everyone on board before fixing Reem with a look of irritation.

'Are you Miss Reem Sfeir?' he abruptly asked in Arabic and the young woman who was leaning against the rail nodded and waited for the man to continue.

'I've been waiting for three hours to attend to you,' he said by way of introduction and stepped aboard. 'I was told that you had been badly injured in a yachting accident and needed the urgent services of a doctor.'

'Thank you, Doctor, but you were sadly misinformed about my condition. It's correct that my yacht was run down by this fishing boat but I was fortunately rescued by these two gentlemen and I am perfectly okay.'

'I am Doctor Farouk and a specialist at Salmaniya Medical Complex so I'll be the one who decides whether you are okay, not one of these lowly educated fishermen.' He waved a hand dismissively at the others.

The captain rushed from the wheelhouse, his face suffused with colour and Stuart gently arrested him with a hand on his the barrel-like chest. He then turned round from the heap of dive gear that he had been sorting to face the doctor and spoke harshly in Arabic. 'There are no poorly educated fishermen on this boat,' he said. 'If you wish to make a habit of insulting people make sure you get your facts right.'

Doctor Farouk was taken aback at seeing a Western expatriate on such a battered vessel but recovered quickly. 'I would like to point out to you that my time is extremely valuable,' he snapped. 'You should have used the radio to say my services were no longer required.'

Reem stood upright and moved away from the rail. 'It was made perfectly clear to the club secretary by this gentleman that I was unhurt and as a trained nurse I would know whether I needed to be examined by an overpaid, self-centred practitioner or not,' she retorted as she slipped her arm through Alan's.

Dumbstruck, the doctor turned on his heel, walked to the side of the boat and jumped onto the quayside where he strode off in a huff towards the clubhouse.

The sudden outburst of applause from those on the boat was joined by that of a stocky man with an uncontrollable bushy moustache. He separated himself from the small group of men he was with and advanced on the fishing boat with a broad infectious smile as he pounded large, beefy hands together.

'Bravo,' Major Safa cried as he boarded the boat and slapped a hand between Reem's shoulder blades making her stagger against Alan. 'You've found yourself quite a spirited mermaid, Alan,' he teased as he shook everybody's hand. Even the captain had his hand engulfed and pumped warmly until he couldn't help but smile too.

'She's not my mermaid, Walid,' Alan said with embarrassment colouring his face.

'But he would like her to be,' Reem said with a mischievous grin as she gripped his arm tightly. Alan's normal ruddy complexion reddened even further and he turned to Stuart for moral support but his friend only had one thought in his mind.

Stuart grabbed Walid by the arm. 'Any news of Helen?' he said as he studied the major's face for positive signs. 'Has the search produced anything that would lead to her whereabouts?'

'Sorry, Stuart, but so far we haven't been able to develop any leads,' Walid answered sadly. 'Major Kazemi has now widened the search pattern and is pulling in the usual suspects.'

'Like Claude Rains in *Casablanca*, I suppose,' Alan said morosely.

'There is no need to be so cynical; the dragnet approach does throw up some good leads.'

'I suggest we drop Reem at the hospital and then discuss our options at my apartment,' Stuart said and apart from Reem they all agreed.

'If you don't mind I would like to join you. I feel committed to helping you find Dr Taylor and going back to work now would be a betrayal of my own sense of duty,' Reem said heatedly.

Alan boldly squeezed her arm and Stuart smiled his appreciation. 'Any help now, Reem, would be invaluable so we'll all go together. Is that okay with you, Walid?'

Walid nodded and they all went ashore to join the sergeant and walk to the police cruiser that was parked nearby. Stuart and Alan waved goodbye to the captain who returned their friendly gesture with enthusiastic arm flapping and cries of *be-ashoofak badayn*, see you later, that continued long after they had climbed into the car and driven off.

On arrival at the apartment Stuart unpacked the sports bags and they all helped to chip away at the beeswax with various implements until only the wound linen separated them from the contents. Walid was amazed by what his friend had found and as the pearl jewellery was revealed and laid out on the glass coffee table the level of conversation died to an awed silence.

'Magnificent,' Walid finally gasped as he raised a multi-strand choker to study the deep lustre of the pearls. 'I've never seen anything so perfect in my life.'

Reem unrolled a larger package and her sudden intake of breath caused all to look at what was being uncovered. She slowly lifted the necklace by a golden clasp that was studded with small diamonds. Their eyes followed her as she was forced to stand up to keep unravelling the graduated pearls until a very long rope dangled from her fingers.

'My God, that's magnificent,' Alan whispered. 'Put it on and make it more beautiful,' he added and then blushed at his own boldness.

Reem ducked her head through the loop to let the necklace settle around her bare neck and fall to just below her narrow waist. Alan held his breath as he studied the glowing pearls nestling against her smooth, golden skin.

'Unfortunately, Reem, as beautiful as you now look you will have to remove the necklace for it is part of the ransom for Helen's life,' Stuart said.

Alan sighed and stepping behind Reem helped her remove the rope and place it beside the growing collection of collars and chokers. Precious rings and bracelets had also been unwrapped and they were put with the pearls until there was nothing left to unwrap.

'There must be the best part of forty million dollars on that glass top,' Walid murmured. 'A reasonable motive for kidnapping and killing.'

Stuart winced at the words and Walid quickly placed a reassuring hand on his shoulder. 'But we shall definitely find Helen and she will be alive my friend,' he avowed.

'Walid's right, Stuart,' Alan said. 'And I'm also going to give the bastards a bloody good lesson in how to treat a sheila.'

'Sheila?' Reem queried.

'Streuth, girl, excuse my French,' Alan apologized. 'Sheila is Australian slang for girl, or lady. My other language was unforgivable.'

Reem laughed and gave the embarrassed geologist a quick hug. 'That's okay, Alan, I understand what you must be feeling for your friend and it does you credit.'

'What's this,' Walid said, interrupting Alan's moment of pleasure as the warm, shapely form briefly pressed against him. Walid was holding up the sealed piece of vellum that had been tucked in one of the sports bags. Stuart took the fragile material from him and after prying the wax seal open he began unfolding it on the parquet floor.

As the last fold was opened and pressed flat columns of fine, spidery calligraphy and numerals could be seen. The ink that had been used was badly faded in places and on some of the creases it was non-existent.

'Looks like a ship's manifesto to me,' Alan muttered as he ran a forefinger down one of the columns. 'But it's all Greek to me.'

'Not Greek but Latin,' Reem said as she peered over his shoulder, her breath against his cheek. 'That looks like *frumentum* which means grain.' Her finger rested on one of the spidery words before moving to the next word *bos*. 'And that's ox or animal.'

Hey, there's your favourite word, Alan,' Stuart said as he pointed to *vinum*.

'I must admit I wouldn't say no to a nice glass of lightly chilled Chardonnay,' Alan chuckled. 'Are you permitted to drink, Reem?' he asked.

'I'm not Moslem, Alan, I'm Catholic and I never limit myself to communion wine only.'

Their laughter was cut dead by a cellphone ringtone. Walid immediately reached into his pocket but stopped when Stuart took his own cellphone from the table. Everyone waited with bated breath as Stuart looked at the caller display. 'It's them,' he said grimly and pressed 'receive'.

'*Es salaam alykhum*, Mr Taylor. I have given you plenty of time; what have you to report?'

Stuart recognized the cold voice. 'What have you done with my wife? I wish to speak to her.'

'In time, in time,' Jahandar snapped back. 'Now what have you got for me?'

'We found six more beeswax packages,' Stuart answered. 'But I'll not give them to you until I have proof of life. You must put my wife on the phone now.'

There was a long period of static hissing before a panic-stricken voice called out his name. Stuart pressed the receiver hard to his ear as though it would bring her closer. 'Helen, are you all right?' he asked. 'Where are you?' Stuart listened to Jahandar's instructions with blood draining from his face until the phone finally cut to the faint crackling of a disconnected line.

'What did he say—did you speak to Helen—is she okay,' Alan rattled his questions like machine-gun fire as Stuart slowly replaced his cellphone on the coffee table. Walid raised a hand to silence Alan and walked over to grip Stuart's shoulder.

'I heard her. She is alive but we have to leave everything at the Ramada Hotel,' he murmured disconsolately. 'And no police are to be involved otherwise Helen will be history.'

Walid nodded slowly. 'That's the normal request of a kidnapper but I can assure you, Stuart, every member of my team is exceedingly discreet when it comes to shadowing people. They have to because quite often their own lives depend on being invisible. As usual I will organize some of my men and participate in the tracking, with Shehhi as my runner. We do not have to involve the local Bahraini police.'

'What can Stuart and I do while your ninja are at work, Walid?' Alan asked.

'Be patient and wait,' Walid replied as he speed-dialled a number. Sergeant Shehhi was already using his cellphone in the far corner of the room and putting the armed response unit on standby.

Walid hung up. 'I have notified Major Kazemi that we will be instigating an operation that involves tracking a drug runner and I have been given the green light to use whatever means to apprehend the suspects.'

'As it is now four-fifteen we had better start packing these beauties into a bag,' Alan said and Reem went to the kitchen to fetch rolls of kitchen paper and to retrieve one of the sports bags.

'This is to protect the pearls,' she said on her return and she started unrolling some paper in preparation for wrapping one of the necklaces. While Stuart, Alan and Reem were winding the soft paper around the precious items Walid quietly spoke to Shehhi who immediately left the room. They heard the front door open and close and Stuart gave Walid a questioning look.

'There is one vital piece of equipment I need before we can take the bag to the hotel,' he said with an enigmatic smile.

Shehhi soon returned and handed something to Walid who nodded with a satisfied look on his face. He crossed to where the bag stood and placed something on the side. As Walid leant back from his handiwork the others could see that he had put a red sports club decal on the canvas.

'What on earth is that for, Walid,' Stuart asked as he ran a finger over the smooth vinyl patch.

'That, my friend, can talk to satellites three hundred kilometres above our heads which then talk to me to let us know where the sports bag is to within ten metres precisely.'

'A very cunning GPS transmitter,' Alan said admiringly.

'And only two millimetres thick,' Walid added. 'It was easily disguised in the sandwich of vinyl plastic. We use them a lot to track bags and cases that pass through airports carrying drugs into the kingdom.'

'Wow, I'm with a bunch of spies,' Reem thoughtlessly exclaimed.

'This is no James Bond movie, Reem, a woman's life is at stake and this is an actual police investigation,' Walid said as he turned to stare into Reem's green eyes with the same concern her own father showed when she first left home for medical college.

Reem bowed her head slightly in acknowledgement of Walid's gentle rebuke and then turned to face the others. 'I'm so sorry, Stuart. I didn't want to sound flippant about the situation. I know it must be extremely worrying for you and your friends.'

Stuart dismissed her apology with a light wave of his hand. 'Please stay in the apartment with Alan until I return,' he said and then picked up the sports bag. 'If all your men are in position I think we should get this show on the road.'

Walid looked at Shehhi who gave an affirmative nod. 'Let's go kill the *ibn el-kalb*,' he growled.

'Son of a dog,' Walid translated.

11

Major Walid Safa had scattered his undercover team throughout the hotel. They had been thoroughly briefed and each man knew precisely what was at stake so they were careful not to draw any attention to themselves. Shehhi had instructed each squad to exchange places in fifteen-minute shifts, thereby avoiding the same face being seen in any one place for too long.

Stuart left the bag at the reception desk with the strict instruction that it was to be collected by no one but Mr Issa ben Ali. He had then left the hotel to return to his apartment with some reluctance. Walid had explained earlier that Issa ben Ali had been the name of a Bahraini ruler who had been deposed by the British in 1923 and had obviously been chosen by the kidnappers as a joke.

As Walid perused the tourist souvenirs in the gift shop he was able to watch the hotel front desk reflected in the window. Three more of his team in smart business suits were drinking coffee, reading and studying racked travel pamphlets at strategic points in the spacious lobby.

The squad had just been replaced by the next shift when a man approached the reception desk and after a minimum exchange of words was given the sports bag. Walid immediately recognized Behrouz, the wanted gunman. The major strolled out of the hotel and into the heat of the afternoon sun rubbing his nose; it was the signal to the pursuit squads to prepare for action. He made his way across the busy road and climbed into an unmarked car to join Shehhi and await the emergence of Behrouz. As he looked through the tinted one-way glass a dark-green Mercury saloon pulled into the hotel's service road and stopped at the entrance just as Behrouz, carrying the sports bag, came out looking nervously both left and right. The car door slammed shut behind him and it drove off to integrate smoothly with the heavy traffic.

Shehhi slipped into drive while giving instructions on his throat microphone. Walid observed one of their chase cars pull away from the kerb fifty metres in front of the Mercury and accelerate to maintain a safe distance. He turned to look through the rear window as the second chase car turned into the main road and took up position behind their control car. Shehhi kept at a steady distance behind the target and began giving a full description and plate number to all team members, including those in two more vehicles that were positioned well ahead and waiting for instructions on when and where to replace the existing chase cars.

The convoy slowly threaded through the eastern part of Manama until they passed the Yum Yum Tree food court and approached the port area. Walid instructed the car behind to overtake him and for the car in front of the target to increase its distance to avoid being noticed on the low traffic roads.

Without warning the Mercury suddenly turned right and headed towards the quayside. The chase car in front of Shehhi slowed and then followed, stopping one hundred metres from a junction where it met a quay lined with moored fishing boats and recreational powerboats.

Walid indicated to Shehhi to pull up behind the stationary chase car. They both walked past the chase car and Walid indicated to the four officers to stay put before walking on to peer round the corner in the direction that their target had taken. He jerked back on seeing the Mercury parked only thirty metres from the junction. Behrouz had slung the sports bag over his shoulder and was climbing into a St Martin mini-speedboat.

'Very clever,' Walid said as he looked over the sergeant's shoulder. 'Wherever he's going he'll have a car waiting for him so it's useless commandeering a boat to follow. We'd also stand out like a spare hump on a camel if we try to follow by water.'

'The GPS will give us our next clue as to where he is going,' Shehhi said briskly and he quickly trotted back to the car to alert the IT team at police headquarters. In the few seconds it took for Walid to rebrief the men in the chase car and to return to his own vehicle Shehhi had an answer.

'The speedboat is heading towards the Ras Sanad mangrove forest which obviously means he'll be going past it and on to Al Eker. There's no way he can navigate a boat to dry land in that mangrove swamp.'

'Al Eker would be an excellent place to rendezvous with a car,' Walid said as he vigorously tugged at his moustache. 'We'll wait until we see in what direction the bag travels before we position all our chase cars.'

Shehhi reversed to the main road and then, followed by the chase car that had been in front of them, they slowly drove to the Verandah 2 coffee shop in Adliya to await further news from the IT team.

Walid was hyperactive and impatient to get moving by the time he had finished his second espresso when Shehhi received the call: Their target had come to a halt in the district of Al Daih and had then remained stationary for more than five minutes.

'That must be where they are holding Helen,' Walid muttered as he stood up. Without the need for any instructions Shehhi hurried from the café talking rapidly into his throat mike, hotly pursued by the men from the two accompanying chase cars.

Walid threw a few notes down onto the table to cover the bill and was soon climbing into the car. The rear tyres spun before getting a grip and launching the car out of the car park followed by the other two cars.

Shehhi switched on the blue police lights and put his foot down. As the traffic magically parted they sped northward on Alsalah Highway until they entered Al Daih. The sergeant followed the transmitted instructions from the IT team until the three cars had arrived at the visitors car park of the Bahrain International Hospital. The team spread out and after searching each parking bay that was protected from the searing sun by stretched canvas covers they were able to pinpoint the target as a brown Ford Taurus.

Shehhi and Walid removed their weapons from their holsters and holding them in the regulation two-handed grip advanced on the car. It was unoccupied and the doors had been left unlocked; two bomb specialists hurried past the armed officers to inspect the vehicle for booby traps. Mirrors on long telescopic rods were passed underneath and the bonnet was tripped open and searched for any abnormal additions.

On being given the all-clear signal Walid advanced and looking inside the rear he instantly saw what he had feared most. The sports bag was on the back seat and it was clear that it had been emptied. The GPS decal had been removed from the bag and was now cheekily stuck on the rear window. They had been rumbled.

'Oh, my God,' Shehhi groaned. 'This doesn't look good.'

Walid looked over his sergeant's head into the front of the car and was immediately shocked by the cloying stench of blood that covered the dashboard and pooled on the floor and in the passenger seat.

'It's like a slaughterhouse, sir,' Shehhi whispered in horror as he held his nostrils and backed away from the scene.

There was a shout from behind both men and Walid spun round to see one of the bomb specialists staring into the trunk that he had just levered open. His eyes were wide open with horror and Walid hurried to the rear of the car to see a severed head resting on a corpse.

'Is it Mrs Taylor, sir?' Shehhi whispered as he stood beside Walid and tried to make out the features beneath the mask of blood.

'I don't think so, Sergeant. It's definitely a man but we cannot be sure who it is until the head has been cleaned up. The body is also male so we will need to do a full post-mortem to see if the head matches the body and also check the DNA to ascertain the identity of the person. Let's hope that the head does belong to the torso otherwise we will have the job of identifying two people,' he added wearily. 'However, this will not happen unless you get this crime-scene investigation underway and make a request for a coroner to attend.'

Shehhi glanced once more into the trunk before taking a deep breath and turning away in disgust. 'I take it that we shouldn't make any mention of this to Stuart . . . Mr Taylor, sir?' He jerked a thumb over his shoulder at the open trunk.

'That's right, Shehhi. He's right on the edge as it is and learning that the kidnappers will resort to this kind of violence could push him over.'

'Perfectly understood, sir.' Shehhi began issuing instructions into his mike to close and quarantine the immediate area. Walid quietly ordered the team nearest to him to keep the growing number of curious bystanders at a distance.

Earlier that day Jahandar had been waiting at Al Eker in the back of the Taurus that Javid had stolen only thirty minutes earlier. He impatiently rotated his thumbs over his voluminous stomach as Behrouz climbed into the passenger seat beside Shayhar. He passed the sports bag to Javid and as the bodyguard put the bag next to Jahandar his drawn features showed a fine sheen of sweat that betrayed his need to have immediate access to his cache of 'pistachio nuts' back at the villa.

Jahandar unzipped the bag and removed one of the wrapped parcels. A four-strand choker and a number of emerald rings cascaded onto his lap, their large oval-cut stones reflecting green fire in the evening sunlight. He sighed with pleasure and gave an orgasmic groan before quickly rewrapping the jewellery.

'I have what I wanted and you have completed the task I set you,' Jahandar said softly, eyeing Behrouz through half-closed eyes as he fondled the sports bag that now lay upon his lap with suppressed rapture. He briefly tapped Javid on the knee and the bodyguard gave an imperceptible nod of his head. As Behrouz was seated directly in front of Javid he was unaware that Javid had noiselessly slid a length of thin wire from his belt loops and was grasping the miniature toggles at each end in his fists.

'Wait,' Jahandar hissed as his hand stopped caressing the side of the bag. 'I think we have been betrayed.'

With a puzzled expression Javid let the garrotte drop between his knees and he looked askance at his boss for new instructions.

'This sticker, decal, call it what you may, is too thick,' Jahandar snarled as his fat fingers scrabbled at the edges of the vinyl patch. He managed to lift a corner and the decal was peeled from the bag and held up to the light to reveal the dark shadow of the GPS transmitter and the fine coil of wire that acted as its aerial.

'You were bugged, Behrouz, you bloody imbecile. You've led them to us and we're now being tracked,' Jahandar screamed. 'Javid!'

The bodyguard whipped the wire up and over the head of the startled Behrouz who didn't have time to raise his hands in defence. The firmly gripped wire efficiently sliced through his throat to be stopped only by bone.

Shayhar avoided looking at the slaughter that was taking place beside him and only glanced down at the blood splattering his trouser leg before quickly pulling off the dangerously crowded highway. The car slowed down on a service road that ran parallel to the highway before Shahyar decided to turn into the main drive of a large hospital. As Behrouz continued to pump blood onto the dashboard and into his own lap Shayhar drove into the sparsely used car park and stopped in one of the covered bays.

With the embedded wire crossed at the nape of the neck Javid gave one last jerk on the toggles and burst into maniacal laughter as the wire noose was completely closed between two vertebrae, slicing through the spinal chord and completely severing the head that tumbled down the blood-soaked chest and into the footwell.

'They will come and investigate now that we have stopped so we must leave immediately,' Jahandar said as he pasted the decal onto the glass of the rear window and then began removing the parcels from the sports bag. 'You have plastic shopping bags in the trunk, Shayhar?' he snapped and without waiting for confirmation instructed Shayhar to pack the jewellery in the bags and put the remains of Behrouz in the trunk.

The three men checked the car park for onlookers and when all was clear the two bodyguards swiftly lifted the body out of the front seat and unceremoniously dumped it into the trunk. Javid returned to the front passenger seat and grabbing the head by its hair pretended to kick the head like a rugby ball to his partner before nonchalantly tossing it into the groin of the corpse. Shayhar grimaced at his partner's grisly sense of humour and slammed the trunk shut.

Jahandar ignored the behaviour of the drug addict and with a distinctive rolling gait moved away from the car as fast as possible. He made his way out of the car park and headed for the line of taxis outside the main entrance to the hospital. As he climbed into the first taxi at the head of the queue he powered the window down and instructed Javid and Shayhar to return to the villa. They took the next ranking taxi while Jahandar told his driver to take him to the international airport. As the taxi drove down the hospital drive he leant back and checked the inside pocket of his jacket for his passport. He discovered that he still had his bodyguards' passports as well as his own and he smiled.

The Mozart ringtone sounded harsher than normal to the nervous man waiting in the kitchen. He dropped the half-finished glass into the sink and dashed into the living room to reach the cellphone lying on the coffee table.

'Stuart, bad news I'm afraid,' Walid said. 'The car was dumped and so was the sports bag, minus all the trinkets.'

'We don't know where they've gone or where they're holding Helen!' Stuart shouted angrily. 'Damn it man, they could be killing her right now.'

'Steady, my friend. The forensic team has only just arrived to start work on the car and as soon as I have any news I'll let you know straight away.'

Stuart took a deep breath and sat down. 'I'm sorry, Walid. It's just the thought of what might be happening to her that's got me so wound up.'

'I fully understand, no apology needed,' Walid said softly. 'Just try to relax for a short time, stay where you are and I'll call you.' The line went dead and Stuart placed the cellphone on the table.

'Bad news, Stuart?' Alan asked as he watched his partner sink back into the cushions, his face white and drawn.

'We don't know yet, just keep your fingers crossed that the forensic team can find something useful. Walid said that we must be patient and just wait a little longer.'

'I'll make us all a cup of tea,' Reem said trying to lighten the atmosphere. She jumped up and strode long-legged into the kitchen followed by Alan's admiring gaze.

'You can't go far wrong with that girl, mate,' Stuart murmured when he saw Alan's besotted expression. 'Intelligent, good sense of humour, supportive and a reasonable figure.'

'What!' Alan exclaimed. 'Reasonable figure, reasonable? She's bloody marvellous, mate. Open your eyes Stuart, Reem is an absolute doll.'

'Glad you think so, Alan,' a distant voice in the kitchen called out before bursting into laughter. 'You have a pretty powerful voice, too,' Reem added as she walked into the room carrying a tray. 'It can certainly travel a fair distance.'

Alan sank back into his chair, the colour in his face matching the crimson cushion supporting his head. Stuart chuckled and the deep lines of worry briefly faded to restore his handsome looks.

Stuart turned to Reem with a mock-serious expression. 'For a sheila, you're bloody marvellous, Reem,' he joked in a broad Australian accent.

The strains of Mozart's Eine Kleine Nachtmusik destroyed the brief moment of forgetfulness. Stuart snatched up the cellphone and hit the receive button with a pounding heart.

'Stuart, I think I have some promising news,' Walid said and before Stuart could interrupt he went on. 'We have found a couple of tourist leaflets in the glove compartment, one for the Ramada Hotel which was used as the kidnapper's pick-up location and another one for a popular tourist site.'

'What is it, what is the other leaflet about?' Stuart demanded.

'It's the Qal'at al-Bahrain Fort,' Walid declared with undisguised excitement. 'They may be holding her there because I know that some parts of the ruin are very run-down and rarely visited by tourists or guides.'

'I'm on my way now,' Stuart exclaimed. 'I'll meet you there.'

'Wait,' Walid said. 'There's something else. The team found a scrap of paper beneath the front seat with some strange figures on it.' Walid then began reading them out while Stuart jotted them down on the back of an envelope. He folded the envelope and thrust it into his hip pocket while gesturing to Alan to stay in the apartment.

'I'll meet you at the fort, Walid,' he said. Without waiting for an answer Stuart dropped the phone into his jacket pocket and began hurrying to the door.

'We're coming too,' Alan cried out, grabbing his jacket and Reem's arm. 'If there's a chance we can help find Helen you can count us in, mate.'

Stuart smiled, nodded and then hurried from the apartment. It took the trio fifteen minutes to weave through the traffic and make one detour to avoid another particularly violent street demonstration before they arrived at the main entrance to the impressive sandstone fort. Armed men in full body armour and helmets studied the friends through tinted visors until a familiar stocky figure pushed his way through the cordon and waved to them to follow him.

Walid greeted the three with a stony, expressionless face. 'This may be the place; I cannot be absolutely sure and we must hope that Helen is being held in a part of the fort that is rarely visited.'

'What part of the fort would that be?' Stuart asked impatiently.

'I have already dispatched a team to the far side of the ruins to cut off any escape that way while the rest of the SWAT team are covering every exit,' Walid explained. He looked down at his Rolex Oyster. 'They'll complete the trap in precisely fifty seconds.'

As Walid finished talking everyone glanced at their own wristwatches and at the designated time a whistle sounded and the SWAT team rapidly began to close the net round the medieval fort.

'We'll join these guys and go round the other side of the fort if that's okay with you, Walid,' Alan said and he gave the thumbs-up sign to the team leader who looked at the major for confirmation. Walid nodded and instructed the SWAT lieutenant to keep the couple at the rear before he hurried to his car.

Stuart followed Walid as he got back into his car and Shehhi quickly drove along the road circling the ruins until he reached a point where another SWAT team was waiting. 'This is my team,' Shehhi said in a proud voice. 'We plan to search this part of the perimeter for any likely hiding places, sir.'

'I trust Shehhi's instinct in these matters,' Walid murmured for Stuart's benefit and Shehhi's chest swelled with pride when he heard his superior officer's comment. He climbed from the car and acknowledged the men's whispered greetings as Stuart followed the major. Walid thrust an automatic pistol into his hand. 'I know that it's illegal for you to have a firearm but I will waive that regulation in the light of the circumstances,' Walid said grimly. 'Use it wisely.'

Stuart nodded and checked the magazine.

As the SWAT team spread out and began to filter through the stone walls that were badly deteriorating and had collapsed through neglect Walid and Stuart kept pace, their senses becoming ever more acute as they progressed into the fort.

Walid and half of the team reached the opening to a dark, downward-sloping passageway. Walid advanced to the front, his helmet light switched on and his weapon at the ready. After ten paces they were confronted by an iron gate that was padlocked. An engineer produced a small pair of bolt cutters from one of his many trouser pockets and cut through the high-tensile steel as though it were butter.

Walid turned to the team and whispered into his throat mike to address those outside. 'This gate was locked from the outside so we can expect that there are no kidnappers down here. That means they could be somewhere else in the ruins.'

With no further words necessary Sergeant Shehhi lead the team back to guard the entrance to the shaft and to continue the search elsewhere. Stuart stayed close behind the major as he strode quickly along the tunnel until once again a formidable barricade stopped them. The engineer bent to study the rusting lock plate in a heavy oak door. He reached into another of his numerous pockets and produced what appeared to be a small piece of plasticine and a tiny black tube with a ring at one end.

Seeing Stuart's puzzled expression Walid explained, 'Time-delay pencil detonator and C4.'

The plasticine was expertly shaped and pushed into the large keyhole. As the detonator was inserted into the putty-like consistency and the hooked finger of the engineer slipped through the safety ring there was a faint sound from beyond the oak door.

'Wait,' Stuart shouted, his voice reverberating along the passageway behind them. 'I think I heard someone on the other side.'

The engineer removed his finger from the safety ring and pressed an ear against the door. 'I can hear something, sir,' he confirmed in a low voice. 'It sounds like somebody singing. Something about "and we'll all go together, to pull wild something or other"—I can't quite hear the rest.'

'Wild mountain thyme; it's Helen, she's singing Wild Mountain Thyme!' Stuart shouted exuberantly as he joined the other two to put his ear to the rough oak. A soft contralto voice could now clearly be heard and Stuart felt an overwhelming sense of relief that caused his eyes to prickle with tears.

'She must be warned to keep away from the door,' Walid said and Stuart began pounding on the door with his fist until the engineer handed him a small hammer that had magically appeared from yet another of his innumerable pockets. There was an answering thump and a small voice shouted words rendered unintelligible by the thickness of the wood.

'She can't hear us,' Stuart cried out in frustration.

'Somehow we need to make our warning as loud as possible.'

'Will this do it, sir,' the engineer said. He was holding a bullhorn in his hand.

'Don't tell me you had that in one of your pockets as well,' Stuart said.

'No sir, I was carrying it just in case we had to clear tourists away should the kidnappers start shooting.'

'Well done, lad. That's perfect,' Walid said as he switched the bullhorn on and placed the bell end against the oak panel. He then told Helen to keep as far away from the door as possible and to knock twice on the door if she understood.

The men waited anxiously for a reply and after a few tense seconds they heard two faint thumps on the timber. Walid nodded to the engineer who waited until the three men had trotted back up the passage and Walid's headlamp was no more than a faint firefly in the blackness. Then he held the detonator in place, pulled the ring free and began running towards the distant flicker of lights.

Stuart counted to ten beneath his breath and was blinded by the sharp flash of light that was instantly followed by a thunderous 'crack' that hurt his ears; as he clapped his hands to the side of his head Walid was already running to the door closely followed by the engineer.

As his ears ceased to ring Stuart heard running feet and looking round saw Shehhi rushing down the passageway to investigate. Stuart raised his hands to show that all was okay and they both went to investigate the results of the C4 explosion.

Walid was inspecting the large splintered hole where the cast-iron lock had been and Shehhi helped the engineer free the bolts at the top and the bottom of the door.

'Now,' the sergeant said and they all pushed against the door to feel it give before swinging open on its massive rusty hinges.

'Is that you Stuart?' a timid voice said in the blackness before a pale oval face became visible in the light of the three headlamps.

'Yes, sweetheart,' Stuart cried as he pushed past Walid and enfolded his wife in his arms. 'Yes, you're safe now.' His voice stumbled over the words as tears unashamedly ran down his cheeks.

'I knew you would find me,' Helen croaked as she wrapped her arms around his neck and held him tightly. 'Did you bring any water with you?'

Walid immediately turned to Shehhi who magically produced a canteen. Stuart removed the cap with shaking hands and watched as Helen drank long and deep.

Walid went into the chamber and using his headlamp he studied Helen's prison, noting the chains and ring bolts set into the walls. 'This looks like blood, sir,' Shehhi whispered as he took one of the chains and inspected it closely. Walid directed his light onto the chain and then turned to illuminate Helen's wrists that were held high as she tilted the canteen back to drink.

'They had chained her in total darkness and complete silence. It must have been mental torture for the lady, sir,' Shehhi growled and Walid could feel the hate radiating from his sergeant.

'Don't worry, Shehhi, we'll get the bastards and they'll wish that they hadn't been born.'

'I'd also like to be there when you do, sir,' the SWAT engineer said with uncharacteristic menace. The three men crossed the chamber to where Stuart was still holding his wife as though afraid that he might lose her again if he let her go.

'Time to leave this place and let the forensic guys check it out. We also need to get Helen to a hospital for a thorough check-up and treatment for those wrists.'

Stuart glanced down and was horrified to see the badly chafed and bloodied skin where Helen had futilely tried to rid herself of the manacles. While he fretted over Helen's wounds Shehhi used his throat mike to instruct the whole team to do a quick sweep throughout the ruins and to notify them of Helen's rescue. His earpiece rattled to the resounding cheers broadcast by two dozen throat mikes. Even Walid had to remove the offending piece of technology with a broad grin on his face.

'You've got some great chaps, Walid,' Stuart said as he grabbed his friend by the hand. Helen reached up to pull Walid's blushing face down for a resounding kiss on the cheek and Shehhi erupted with laughter at his superior officer's embarrassment.

The squad of officers guarding the entrance applauded as they watched the four emerge into the sunlight. Unused to the bright light Helen shielded her eyes until a thoughtful police officer rushed forward and offered her his military plutonite sunglasses. Walid acknowledged the officer's kind gesture as he led Stuart and Helen to the waiting paramedics.

'I'm perfectly alright, I don't need these guys,' Helen protested but Walid held his hand up.

'You must be professionally checked in the hospital and I won't take no for an answer,' he said firmly and Helen knew that she had little choice but to allow the paramedics to take her to the ambulance.

She was just about to get in when Alan and Reem ran to her laughing with relief. 'Thank God, you are alright, Helen,' Alan said fervently as he grabbed her wrists and held tight as though to reassure himself that she really was alive.

Helen winced as his grip put pressure on her wounds but marvelled at seeing his face again. Without saying a word Reem put an arm round her before looking heavenward with a thankful expression.

'We'll follow the ambulance,' Alan said as he led Reem away to where the car was parked.

'I'll ride with you to the hospital,' Stuart whispered. He helped her up into the ambulance and kissed her on the forehead before easing her down onto the stretcher. The ambulance was about to pull away when Walid leapt into the vehicle followed by Shehhi.

'Helen is now a material witness and able to identify the kidnappers so she must have maximum protection. My sergeant has orders to stay by her side until such time as we catch them,' Walid said.

'And it will be my pleasure to ensure no harm comes to you, Mrs Helen,' Shehhi added with determination.

'As I said, my friend, you've got men to be proud of,' Stuart said to Walid as he raised his hand in a friendly gesture to the sergeant who grinned broadly in response.

While they drove to the hospital Helen told them that despite her inability to understand much Farsi she had overheard one of the men repeating the word 'jahandar' and another word that she recalled having heard before being kidnapped.

'Which word was that,' Stuart asked as he held her hand.

'*Foroodgaah*,' but I cannot quite put my finger on it or remember what it means or even what language it's in.

'*Foroodgaah* is Farsi for airport,' Walid said. 'Modernization of the Persian language was begun in 1924 by a military organization that coined new words, *foroodgaah* being one of them,' he explained before realizing the reason the kidnapper's had mentioned the word. 'Damn! I think they're planning to leave the country.' He snatched the microphone from the dashboard. 'And Jahandar may be the name of one of your kidnappers,' Walid added before garbling a priority alert to airport security in Arabic. He then sent the same message to Police Headquarters for the attention of Major Mohammad Kazemi adding a request for a squad of top officers to circulate in the departure halls with photofit descriptions of the wanted men.

Later, as the police spread throughout the airport, a taxi pulled into the dropping-off zone outside the main entrance. Jahandar opened the door and without alighting slammed it shut again when he spotted the alarming number of uniformed security guards and police. One officer began striding purposefully towards the stationary taxi and Jahandar leant forward and tapped the driver on his shoulder.

'Drive, go, leave now,' he nervously snapped and the driver turned with a suspicious look to be confronted by an automatic pistol aimed at his forehead. He quickly faced to the front and gunned the taxi into the traffic causing a coach packed with tourists to screech to a halt. The police officer held his hand up to stop the taxi and was forced to jump out of the way as the terrified driver pressed his foot down hard on the accelerator.

Jahandar looked through the rear window at the officer blowing frantically on his whistle whilst trying to activate the radio on his shoulder at the same time.

'Keep going or I will kill you,' Jahandar snarled and he tapped the driver on the cheek with his automatic to emphasize his point. The driver said nothing and with hands gripping the wheel fed the car along the airport service road and into the traffic flowing along the main highway back to the city.

The taxi had crossed the Hamad Causeway and was passing through the diplomatic area when Jahandar, screwing a silencer onto the barrel of his gun, commanded the driver to turn right; as they approached the Standard Chartered Bank he told the petrified man to pull into the car park and stop the car. The driver did as he was told and as soon as he had parked the car and applied the handbrake Jahandar put the muzzle of the gun to the back of his head and squeezed the trigger. He then calmly removed the silencer and slipped the gun back into his pocket.

Leaving the vehicle, with only a cursory glance around the car park to check that he hadn't been observed, Jahandar wearily walked to the highway in the debilitating heat. His beige linen suit had begun to stain from excessive perspiration as he hailed the next cruising taxi and gave a location two blocks from the building where Stuart and Helen had their apartment. When the bright orange cab passed Farooq Mosque on Khalaf Al Asfoor Avenue he speed-dialled an unlisted number and, on being connected, asked uneasily, 'Is that the Magician?'

12

Walid had left the hospital with Helen's security in the hands of Shehhi and hurried back to headquarters to report to Major Mohammad Kazemi. As he drew closer the streets were thronged with demonstrators and he was forced to a crawl when he reached the police cordon that ringed the building. He waved his police pass at the officers manning the barricades and turned into the underground car park. Instead of taking the lift he hurried up the three flights of stairs and was breathing heavily when he finally entered Major Kazemi's office.

'Where have you been?' Kazemi asked peevishly. 'You were supposed to be on the street observing the latest tactics we have been using against the riotous scum who believe they have the same rights as the members of our government.'

'We have successfully saved the doctor, Helen Taylor, from the kidnappers and she is currently being attended to in hospital,' Walid said as he sat down, completely unperturbed by Kazemi's attitude.

'That's not why your government was given our extremely kind permission to let you and your anti-terrorist team enter Bahrain.'

'I appreciate that, Major, but you must understand that the kidnappers may have been acting under orders from the leaders of the insurrection,' Walid lied. 'Therefore it was of extreme importance to apprehend these men and question them to gain a lead as to who the front-runners may be.' He casually stroked his untidy moustache as he held Kazemi's look with a steady gaze that soon unsettled the major, making him turn away to fiddle with some papers on his desk.

'Are those men in custody?' Kazemi muttered.

'No, we were too late to catch them at the place where the woman was being held captive but I will soon have some information that I feel will lead to an early arrest.'

The major's head jerked up and he fixed Walid with glittering eyes. 'Are you saying that you released the woman but didn't catch the kidnappers?' he sneered. 'The great Major Walid Safa who smashed a powerful terrorist ring in his own country but is unable to catch a couple of cheap crooks in mine?'

'We are very near to closing the case . . .'

Walid was interrupted by a ringtone and Kazemi grabbed a cellphone from off the desk. 'Yes, it is,' he declared ambiguously and spun his high-backed chair to face away from Walid while he listened to the caller for a couple of minutes before speaking tersely as though to a servant. 'You will guarantee safe delivery and ensure that you are not interrupted in this task by anything or anybody.' Kazemi spun around to face Walid as he closed the phone and tossed it onto the blotting pad before him.

'Major Safa,' he barked. 'You will make sure that you are not distracted from your designated duties in my country and that you will not get involved in this kidnapping case again. Is that clear?'

'If it is proved that the kidnappers are involved in the current civil unrest that has so far caused five civilians to be shot to death in the street by your men then they will still be within my remit,' Walid growled and as he stood up he added: 'My team are naturally under my orders and I will make sure that they understand that they obey no instructions other than my own. Is that clear, Major Mohammad?'

Kazemi fought hard to control his rising rage and Walid watched the man's face redden and his hands clutch a pencil until the knuckles showed white. 'You can be sure that I will be contacting your superiors concerning your hostile attitude and total lack of cooperation,' he snarled as the pencil snapped. 'I'll have you thrown out of Bahrain in the blink of an eye.'

'We are of equal rank, Kazemi, therefore I suggest you lodge any complaint you have with your own superior officers before you go over their heads and contact mine otherwise you could end up being a political embarrassment to your government,' Walid said quietly as he strolled out of the office and through an astounded department of eavesdropping officers.

The streets were still resounding with the chants of protesters as Walid made his way back to the hospital. Stuart and Alan had left the hospital since Helen had been given sedatives and would be sleeping until the next day. Using his cellphone he called and arranged to rendezvous with them at the apartment within the hour.

The sun was three finger-widths above the sea when Walid arrived and the three men settled down at the kitchen table as he listed the next steps that he and his team hoped to take in order to apprehend the kidnappers. When he reached the point about his discussion with Major Kazemi he took the scrap of paper that had been found in the abandoned car from his pocket and smoothed it out on the table's surface.

'Isn't that vital evidence?' Alan asked, raising one eyebrow.

'In our hands it may prove to be vital; in Major Kazemi's it'll only be toilet paper and that's why I took it,' Walid said with a glint in his eye while scanning the hastily scrawled figures.

Alan tried to suppress his laughter unsuccessfully as he too studied the figures over and over while Stuart retrieved the folded envelope from his pocket to study the same figures he had copied.

After a few minutes of silence Alan gave a despondent sigh. 'I can't make any sense of them,' he said. 'They seem to be telephone numbers but why would anyone put full points between some of the figures and add what seems to be accents after others, unless they were Europeans?'

There was a sudden exclamation from Stuart. 'That's because they're not telephone numbers but longitudinal and latitudinal figures with minutes and seconds.'

Stuart jumped up and went to a small bookcase where he removed an old survey map of Bahrain. He returned to the table and stabbed his finger along the scale above the island and then down the vertical scale until he had the two groupings of numbers that corresponded to those on the scrap of paper. He then followed the lines with his fingers to the point where they intersected on the island of Bahrain.

'Whatever it means, it's there,' he said as he tried to read the legend printed in a tiny indistinct typeface with broken serifs.

'That's the site of the A'ali burial mounds,' Walid said aloud. 'Of what interest can that possibly be to the kidnappers? Helen was hidden in the Qal'at Al-Bahrain fort which is a long way from there.'

'What would the mounds be used for, what's buried there?' Alan asked as he too tried to read the map.

'They are four thousand years old and it's where the ancient Dilmun people buried their dead. There are over 85,000 mounds covering thirty square kilometres of the island. Many hundreds are at A'ali with some as high as twenty metres,' Walid explained before stopping abruptly when he realized that he was lecturing two geologists who most probably knew all the geographical features on the island.

'I had read about them, Walid, but I didn't know that there were so many,' Stuart said out of politeness.

'Do you think we could get to this graveyard before it gets too dark to reconnoitre?' Alan asked as he rose to his feet, anxious for action of any kind.

'Let's do it now,' Walid said and the trio quickly departed for A'ali.

From the relative safety of the stolen Chevrolet Jahandar observed Walid arriving at the apartment building and he settled himself down to await the next development. After he had lit his fourth cigarette he recalled the Magician's threatening words with a light shudder. 'You will guarantee safe delivery and ensure that you are not interrupted in this task by anything or anybody.' The Magician's tone implied 'or else' and Jahandar knew that he couldn't afford to fail. He also remembered the second call from the mystery man, warning him not to return to the villa and Jahandar made a mental note to tell his bodyguards.

He jerked upright and reached for the ignition key when he spotted three men leaving the building's underground car park in a battered Jeep and turning right to head for central Manama. Jahandar pulled out into the late-afternoon traffic and keeping five cars between him and the Jeep he began following. They had just passed the United States Embassy when Jahandar's cellphone rang. He fumbled in his jacket pocket and depressed the receive button.

'Sir, the woman has been found by the police and we are at the villa. What do you want us to do now?' Javid whined despite feeling the exhilarating euphoria that accompanied every heroin hit.

'You must immediately leave the villa and make your way to the A'ali burial mounds on Sheikh Khalifa bin Salman Highway. Look out for a cream-coloured Chevrolet in Avenue 38. I will be nearby and expecting you to arrive within ten minutes. Is that understood?'

'Yes, sir,' Javid said but he was speaking into a dead phone. He relayed the instructions to Shayhar and they quickly left the villa only minutes ahead of a police raid that was being orchestrated by Major Kazemi. He had been advised by Walid to pay the property a visit and when he asked in his normal brusque manner for a reason Walid had told him that it was an anonymous telephone call.

As Stuart and his friends drove along A'ali Highway an amazing scene confronted them. Hundreds of prehistoric mounds rising high into the sky seemed to stretch to the horizon.

'Some of those are unbelievably high,' Alan said in a hushed voiced.

'And one of them is hiding a secret that is of great interest to the men who took Helen,' Stuart added and Walid grunted his agreement.

As they turned into Avenue 38 and headed south Alan gazed in awe at the ranks of burial mounds flashing by. 'How can we tell which one to investigate?' Walid grunted his inability to give any answer and continued studying the figures on the scrap of paper. Suddenly his cellphone rang and he listened for a brief moment before turning to Stuart.

'Headquarters have informed me that a man in a light-coloured suit was seen leaving a hotel car park where a taxi driver had been murdered. The man walked to the highway where he hailed a taxi. A description of the taxi was given and we traced the drop-off to a point close to where a cream Chevrolet was stolen. It was only a few blocks from your apartment, Stuart.'

'It could be a coincidence.'

'Or, it could be that one of the kidnappers has been following us,' Alan muttered as he turned to look out of the rear window.

Stuart glanced in the wing mirror at the small line of cars and trucks that blocked his view and he was unable to spot the cream-coloured sedan pulling into the kerb and the black car that parked behind it.

Stuart turned right into Wali Al Ahed Highway and then right again to circle the burial mounds that had slowly been losing the pink colour of the setting sun and were now casting long, dark shadows against each other.

'We need more information,' Walid said, staring out of the car window at the hopeless task before them. 'Something that will pinpoint which of these mounds is the most important.'

'Then we might just as well call it a day,' Stuart murmured as he put his foot down to filter the Jeep into the fast lane. He was unaware that a black Toyota rental car had joined Sheikh Khalifa bin Salman Highway shortly after them and was now keeping pace as they hurried back to the apartment.

'I wish to pray, Stuart, so please drop me at the hospital and I'll first check with Shehhi that all is okay with Helen,' Walid said. 'Then I'll visit the mosque for prayers before returning to headquarters to see if the major had been successful with his raid on the villa, that's if he bothered to act on my advice at all.'

Stuart gave a sympathetic nod and set course for the hospital. As he drove past the Al Fateh Grand Mosque Walid's cellphone sounded its familiar ringtone and the major smiled an apology at his friends before answering.

'That was central. They found the cream Chevrolet on Avenue 38,' Walid said.

'Heck, mate, we were there only a few minutes ago,' Alan said with surprise. 'So he had been following us.'

'And then changed cars. That can only mean that whoever he is has partners and they're all after us for some reason that I just cannot fathom,' Stuart added grimly.

'The scrap of paper, Stuart,' Walid said quietly. 'Interpol ran a check on the fingerprints found on the murder vehicle and they identified one of the men as a fellow who calls himself Jahandar. It appears that he is an Iranian drug lord who has the law in his own country in his pocket and always remains one step ahead of every international law agency. He's the low-life I've been trying to catch for over a year.'

'But what about the paper, why does he have an interest in those figures,' Alan asked. 'I mean, we don't even know where they're leading us.'

'I would hazard a guess, Alan, that they point to where his local mules have hidden drugs that he imports into Bahrain for transporting into the Saudi market,' Walid said as Stuart pulled up outside the hospital. Before leaving he said, 'That little piece of paper could be worth millions of dollars, Stuart. Keep it safe and watch your backs. Both of you.'

'Give Reem my regards,' Alan shouted after the major who was briskly striding towards the main entrance. Walid turned to acknowledge his words with a brief wave and a knowing smile.

Walid entered the reception area and went to the desk to ask for Doctor Taylor. The young woman politely informed him that the doctor had discharged herself and had returned to medical duties.

'She is currently attending to a patient in Gynaecology,' she said. Walid thanked her and strode off, following the directional arrow on the board listing the various departments. 'You cannot go there without an appointment, sir,' she called after him but Walid simply kept on walking.

When he reached the right corridor he instantly spotted Sergeant Shehhi standing guard outside a door. The officer's hand had automatically moved to his holstered gun before recognizing his superior and he smiled sheepishly.

'I like your reflexes, Shehhi,' Walid said, clapping the man on the back. 'She's in there with a patient, a lady patient?'

Shehhi nodded. 'Doctor Taylor is attending to an elderly woman and her daughter, sir. I checked before I allowed them admittance and they are perfectly bona fide patients. They've been coming to the hospital for more than three years.'

'Good man, I guess we'll both have to wait until she has finished with them,' Walid said, slumping wearily into one of the many chairs that lined the corridor. 'I'll wait until *isha'a* prayer time so I suggest that you go to *maghrib* prayer now, Shehhi.'

Shehhi grinned his thanks before checking a signboard on the wall for directions to the hospital mosque and then hurrying away down the corridor. Walid watched him go until he turned the corner and then sank back into the leather cushions and allowed his eyelids to droop as fatigue took control of his body.

A hand on his shoulder gently shook him awake and he sat upright with surprise and embarrassment when he realized that he had fallen asleep.

'Major Safa,' a warm voice said. 'It's so nice to see you here.'

Walid looked up at Helen's smiling face. 'My apology, Helen, I should not have been sleeping when I'm supposed to be guarding your safety.'

'My dear Major, it's perfectly understandable,' Helen said before turning to the white-haired woman waiting patiently beside her.

'Madame Kanoo, you may leave now and I will notify you about the test results as soon as they are known.' The black-robed woman nodded and limped away.

'I've now finished for the day and will be returning to the apartment,' Helen said. 'Will you be escorting me, Walid?'

The major beamed his reply and with a vigilant Shehhi leading the way they left the hospital, stopping briefly at reception for Helen to sign out. They had walked halfway to the car in the humid air before Walid remembered Alan's message.

'Is the young nurse here today?' he asked Helen.

'Do you mean Reem? She left the hospital only a few minutes ago.' Walid looked around and immediately spotted the young nurse climbing into a bright yellow Fiat 500.

'And there she goes. Excuse me, Helen, but I must give her a message or Alan will never forgive me,' he called over his shoulder while running to intercept the little car that was slowly leaving its parking bay. 'My apology, Reem, but Alan sends his regards and asks if you would like to join him for dinner,' he puffed to the startled woman.

'Ah, Major Safa,' she said as the friendly features and the very unruly moustache triggered her memory. 'Tell him I would be delighted and would he please call me to make arrangements.' She handed Walid a hospital business card; he gave her a smart salute and a smile. She laughed, powered the window up and drove off slowly with all thoughts on the rugged, sun-bronzed Australian.

Walid returned to the waiting car and they headed back to the apartment. The major sighed wistfully on missing his regular prayer time as they passed the magnificent mosque. The two minarets and the massive golden dome were now floodlit, creating a wondrous sight for Moslems and Christians alike. Walid sighed again and Shehhi gave his superior a sympathetic glance as he accelerated into the fast lane and drove north on Al Fatih Highway.

They delivered Helen safely home and Walid gave Alan the small card and Reem's message. Before the major could turn to be greeted by Stuart the stocky Australian was squinting at the small print and rapidly dialling the number.

'He's in love,' Stuart joked as he shook Walid's hand before hugging his wife. Shehhi stalked across the room to the picture window and studied the windows of the apartment building opposite, paying special attention to the darkened ones for any signs of movement before closing the drapes completely.

Walid sat on the divan at Stuart's invitation and stretched his legs. 'We have a few hundred burial mounds to search,' he said. 'Any ideas on how we can make this task easier?'

Stuart watched his wife busy herself with the coffee percolator as he took the envelope from his pocket and looked at the coordinates again. 'Could these be so precise that it highlights just one of the mounds?' he asked nobody in particular.

'I checked, Stuart,' Alan said. 'The mounds are so tightly packed across those acres and the figures so imprecise that it is impossible to isolate twenty let alone one.'

Walid looked over Stuart's shoulder before removing the original scrap of paper from his pocket and rotating it slowly. 'There is something extra on this that you didn't copy, Stuart,' he said slowly as he held the paper up to the light.'

'I don't know how I missed that,' Stuart said as he looked through the backlit paper. 'It appears to be the letter W, what could that stand for?'

Walid rotated the paper once again and then paused. 'Not a W but an M,' he exclaimed. 'I believe that it isn't a letter at all but a quick sketch of a double burial mound. It could be one of the royal mounds where they interred a queen alongside her husband.'

Alan took the paper from Walid's hand. 'I think I spotted a double mound on the south side of the site,' Alan said as he handed the paper back to the major. 'In fact, I'm pretty sure I did. That must be the one the traffickers have been using.'

'I suggest that we take a look at it tomorrow morning, Walid,' Stuart suggested. 'Will we need any special permission from the government to go into the burial site?'

'My status in the country should be sufficient so I don't think we'll worry the authorities.'

There was a knock at the door and the friends all fell silent.

'I suggest we set fire to the paper before it falls into the wrong hands again,' Stuart whispered as Shehhi and Walid took up position on either side of the front door, their automatic pistols held at the ready. Walid nodded and Stuart set fire to the small piece of paper with a match and watched as the paper was speedily reduced to ash in an empty coffee cup. There was another, more insistent knock at the door.

'It's Reem, Helen,' a muffled voice called out and everyone visibly relaxed. Helen unlatched the door and welcomed the young nurse with a kiss on both cheeks.

'You were quick,' Helen said. 'Did you have any urgent reason for hurrying?' she teased with a straight face and then grinned when Reem's face coloured with embarrassment.

'Leave her alone, Helen,' Stuart said with a chuckle as he led Reem into the living room where Alan was waiting nervously.

'So good of you to come, Reem,' Alan stuttered as he took her extended hand in his. 'We've err . . . decided on Trader Vic's for dinner,' he added as he reluctantly let go and immediately tried to think of a viable excuse to hold that delicate hand once again.

The following morning Walid went into police headquarters to check-up on any progress in the hunt for the kidnappers who had somehow eluded the raid on the villa. Before he went he ordered Shehhi to accompany Helen to work and act as her bodyguard for the rest of the day. Stuart and Alan decided to visit A'ali to seek the double burial mound.

Alan was still smiling to himself as they drove through Manama, recalling the pleasant meal and conversation he had enjoyed with Reem. Although there had been four other chattering people at the same table it was as if they were alone in their own world of discovery.

'You're quite keen on the girl, aren't you, Alan,' Stuart said when he became aware of his friend's prolonged silence.

'She's beaut, mate,' Alan said as he gazed out of the car window at the Adhari Theme Park passing by. 'I don't know how to explain it but every time I see her something happens in my head and I get a strange giddy feeling.'

'You've got it bad, my friend,' Stuart said with a smile before braking suddenly with a curse on his lips as a large truck careered across the double lanes to block their way. As they waited for the huge vehicle to move Stuart noticed a black Toyota with an open window stop on the opposite side of the highway. He thought it a peculiar thing to do in such humidity until the barrel of a silenced pistol emerged and pointed towards him. Pulling the stick shift into reverse he floored the accelerator and roared back, turning the wheel while briefly applying the handbrake to spin the car until it faced the way they had come. Two of the lanes were backed up with traffic and the third was clear for a hundred metres back to the service road access. With smoking tyres they suicidally shot past the stationary lines of traffic and pulled into the side road. There they were confronted by oncoming traffic and Stuart had to brake to a halt.

He opened his door and jumped out. 'Come on, Alan,' he shouted. 'Our friends have caught up with us and they don't want to play nicely.'

Alan shot a quick glance around and was galvanized into action by the sharp double crack of a 45-calibre bullet puncturing the rear window and the windscreen, barely missing Stuart. The two friends zigzagged along the sidewalk and then turned down an alleyway between two factories. They emerged to be greeted by a fusillade of bullets coming from the same Toyota and they quickly backtracked down the narrow alley. They had covered half the distance when they heard the roar of a car engine echoing between the walls of the factories.

Alan glanced back and then shook his head. 'Back to the car, Stuart?' he asked.

'We go straight across the double highway. That way they can't follow us in a car and we may stand a better chance.' They pelted out of the alley and across the service road without stopping. Stuart paused at the first three lanes coming from his left and timed the flow of the approaching traffic.

'Now,' he shouted and ran out behind a passing Ford Caprice and cleared the first lane with the following Porsche a whisker away. Without any hesitation he ran between four more speeding cars to reach the central reservation.

Stuart looked sideways to find Alan right beside him, red-faced and panting like a horse. 'Well done, mate,' he panted himself and looked back across the lanes of fast-moving traffic. The black Toyota was standing at the entrance to the alley and three men were looking across at them.

'We'd better keep going, Stuart,' Alan shouted above the constant pandemonium of the traffic. 'We can't spend the rest of our lives here.'

Stuart nodded and looking right he began to count beneath his breath until he suddenly shouted, 'Now, Alan!' and sprinted across the next three lanes. Alan matched him stride for stride, putting all his faith in Stuart's judgement until after what seemed an eternity of near-death moments they stumbled onto the safety of the pavement.

'Wow,' Alan shouted, clapping Stuart on the back. 'That was some high. We must do that more often.'

Stuart grinned and then looked across all six lanes to see that the mystery car had disappeared from the alley. 'We'd better find a taxi,' he said and trotted towards the distant theme park. 'The interchange is only a kilometre away which means they could be on this side of the highway in double-quick time.'

As the two heavily perspiring men trotted towards the nearest taxi rank at Adhari Park they could hear the faint screams of children riding the big dipper and the log flume. Stuart glanced back but was unable to see any pursuing cars.

As they approached the gates a large crowd of people spilled out of the park and across the service road. They began to chant anti-government slogans and banners were unfurled and raised aloft.

'Just what we need, mate,' Alan declared as they were caught up in the whirling mêlée of angry Bahrainis and swept into the main highway. Cars screeched to a halt to avoid hitting pedestrians and were in turn struck from behind by cars caught completely unawares. The throng of men and women continued to move across the lanes until all six lanes were blocked and traffic was at a standstill in both directions.

Stuart jumped up to see over the heads of the protesters and spotted the black Toyota parked in the service road. 'They're not far away, Alan,' he shouted above the chanting. 'Keep your eyes open.'

Alan nodded and they continued pushing their way through the crush, trying to reach the other side where they had originally abandoned the Jeep. As the throng thinned and they staggered into the open they found themselves confronted by a line of angry riot police with shields and vicious-looking batons held at the ready.

'Whoops,' Stuart muttered and turned, preparing to dive back into the thick of the protesting crowd. 'Whoops, again, Alan,' he repeated when he spotted the three men.

They were poised on the edge of the throng and staring thoughtfully at their quarry. Two of the men held pistols by their sides and the third, an obese shape in a dark business suit beckoned Stuart to come closer.

'Mr Taylor, I have assumed that you have a piece of paper with numbers on it so just give me what you've found at the A'ali burial site and we'll leave you and your friends alone,' the fat man said.

Stuart turned to Alan. 'We'll have to run for it and hope for the best,' he whispered. 'On three, run like hell,' he added before giving the count. Both men began running parallel to the front of the crowd and the line of riot police.

As they ran towards a nearby warehouse Shayhar and Javid instinctively raised their guns and fired. Their rounds passed between Stuart and Alan and found targets in the police line.

Three officers crumpled, one screaming in agony and many of their colleagues rapidly drew their weapons and fired into the crowd. Jahandar had begun shuffling back into the crowd the moment his two bodyguards had raised their weapons. They soon joined him as he struggled through the pandemonium that had ensued when the shooting began.

As protesters were felled by a fusillade of baton rounds and bullets Stuart and Alan raced to reach the open door of the warehouse. When barely forty-five metres from safety Alan was punched in the middle of his back by rubber bullets and knocked face down onto the hard concrete. Stuart stopped and as he bent to help his friend he was spun around and down by another round that dislocated his left shoulder. Within seconds the riot police had pinned them to the ground, their wrists cruelly fastened with plasticuffs. The pain that erupted in Stuart's shoulder caused him to sink into unconsciousness but before he passed out completely he heard a voice screaming close to his ear.

'You killed two of my men. You'll pay for that, Taylor.'

Everything went black.

13

Stuart woke and then almost passed out again from the excruciating pain as he tried to move his arm. He was lying on a concrete floor that was splattered with dried vomit, urine and excrement and his wrists were still plasticuffed behind his back. He painfully moved centimetre by centimetre until he was sitting upright against the crudely plastered wall.

'Are you all right, mate,' Alan croaked as he staggered to his feet and crossed the cell to where his white-faced friend sat. 'You look bloody crook to me.'

'It's my shoulder. It's either broken or dislocated. Do you know where we are?'

'I think they call it Jaw prison and it's been said on the street that it's bloody notorious. Human rights observers were permitted to visit pre-selected parts of the prison but they either overlooked or weren't permitted to inspect the detention centre, which is where we are now being held.'

'I've heard that human rights mean nothing in here,' Stuart murmured as he moved slightly to ease the throbbing in his shoulder. 'Have you been able to ask for Major Safa while I was out of this world?'

'I'm afraid not, cobber. The only social chit-chat I've had so far is a stick across my head, three punches in the face and a boot up my rear for talking.'

'Friendly lot aren't they?'

There was the sound of heavy boots approaching and stopping outside the steel door, causing both men to stop talking. A faint murmuring of voices could be heard followed by bolts being drawn and the screech of rarely oiled hinges. The door swung inward and two burly prison guards in stained uniforms entered the cell. They hurriedly pulled the prisoners upright by the arms, eliciting a cry of agony from Stuart. One gave a tobacco-stained smile at his prisoner's discomfort and made a crude comment in Arabic that caused his partner to laugh.

'I think that guy would laugh while garrotting his own mother,' Alan said on seeing Stuart's painful expression and doubled up as he was viciously punched in the stomach. An officer smoking a Cuban double corona suddenly entered the cell. He was exceptionally tall and had to duck to avoid striking his head on the lintel.

'You are Mr Stuart Taylor and Mr Alan Short,' he said in a nonchalant tone of voice. Seeing both men nod he introduced himself: 'I am Major Mohammad Kazemi of the Bahraini police.'

'Then you must know Major Walid Safa,' Stuart replied and was struck across the face with a short bamboo cane wielded by the guard gripping his arm.

'I do not think I have come across that name, Mr Taylor,' Kazemi lied as he drew deeply on the cigar. 'However I do happen to know that you shot two of my police officers who were dutifully trying to control an unruly mob of criminals and terrorists.'

Stuart remained silent for he had realized that the officer had exactly the same voice as the riot policeman who had screamed at him in English; the same officer who had known and shouted his name while he was losing consciousness.

Kazemi blew a large smoke ring in the direction of the two men. 'You will be brought before a preliminary hearing to be held in the prison later today when it will be decided whether you are to be tried in a criminal court of law or face trial in a shariah court,' he snarled. 'Naturally I would prefer the latter and I will attend whichever court is chosen for I was a prime witness to your murderous actions. You can be assured, Mr Taylor, that the outcome is a foregone conclusion.' His malevolent laugh hung in the air like the pungent smoke polluting the cell and he turned abruptly and left the two men to the mercy of their jailers.

For the next ten minutes the two friends were subjected to beatings with canes, fists and heavy boots. Stuart's shoulder became the obvious target for his tormentor and he felt the agonizing pain begin to diminish as once more he sank into unconsciousness. Seeing that his victim could no longer feel anything the guard stopped swinging his cane and turned to help his colleague thrash Alan into a senseless state.

The jailers stood back, their arms weary from all the effort and looked down at the two unconscious foreigners. 'That's for killing our brothers,' one shouted and they both hawked loudly and spat onto the faces of the still figures before stomping out of the cell and slamming the steel door shut.

Walid had requested news of the kidnappers from Major Kazemi who had responded by reminding the Saudi of his orders, the only reason for his presence in Bahrain.

'Major Safa, you are here to study our crowd-control techniques, not to chase kidnappers,' Kazemi shouted as he left the office. Walid had to content himself by studying the incoming reports of disturbances in various parts of the city and analysing how counter-measures were being deployed. Real-time CCTV constantly fed the large flat-screen monitors in the main communications centre. Each revealed peaceful demonstrations being brutally suppressed by the riot police, many of whom were mercenaries who had been recruited from different countries in the region to assist the security force in restoring civil order. Walid winced as every baton struck a defenseless head or body and had to leave the room in disgust when live rounds were indiscriminately discharged into the crowd.

Answering the insistent ringing of the telephone in his temporary office he was immediately overwhelmed by Helen's distressed voice.

'I've been watching the television news and the street riots are worrying me, Walid. The hospital is becoming over-crowded with civilians who have been wounded with batons and bullets,' she cried. 'It's now mid-afternoon and I still haven't heard anything from Stuart and although his cellphone rings he doesn't answer; this is not like him at all. What can I do?'

'Calm down, Helen. I'm sure Stuart and Alan are perfectly all right,' the major said, trying to reassure his distraught friend. 'They most probably left their phones in the Jeep while doing a bit of reconnoitring amongst the burial mounds.'

'Is that where they said they were going? Is there any way that you can check on that?' Helen asked.

'I'll instigate an investigation into any recent road accidents and also a check with all the major hospitals,' he said in the calmest voice he could manage. 'I'll get back to you as soon as I have any news and please, don't worry. You know how resourceful Stuart is at getting out of trouble.'

With a steadier voice Helen thanked Walid and rang off, enabling him to turn to his computer and begin hunting through the road-accident reports and hospital intake listings. Two fruitless hours later he was preparing himself mentally for the latest list of names to come from the new wave of demonstrations when the door opened and one of his team members entered.

'Sorry to disturb you, sir,' the young lieutenant said after smartly saluting his superior. 'But two expatriate men were arrested at the Adhari Park demonstration this afternoon after supposedly shooting two police officers dead.'

'That's terrible news, lieutenant, but why should it be of specific interest to me?'

'The arrest report doesn't show any names and when I asked the duty officer who they were he told me that Major Kazemi had taken charge of the arrest himself and that the identities were a security matter and to be considered strictly confidential. On checking the CCTV discs and probing the Bahraini officer a little further I learnt that both men had been taken directly to Jaw prison which I found to be very unusual. He also told me that one of the men had an Australian accent.'

'And the other one?'

'He had been rendered unconscious by a baton round and had been stretchered from the scene of the demonstration. That I saw myself as I was able to find the CCTV recording that monitored the incident.'

'Well done, lieutenant, do you have the disc?'

The young officer gave a mischievous grin. 'I thought you would ask, sir, so I appropriated it without anyone knowing.' He reached into a side pocket and proudly flourished the DVD. Walid took it and inserted it into his drive and waited nervously for the images to run, hoping that they wouldn't show what he had secretly begun to fear.

The coarse picture showing the bottled-up traffic on the main highway suddenly expanded as the camera zoomed in to a medium close-up of the angry crowd being confronted by a double line of riot police. Two civilians in Western dress stood in the no-man's land separating the protesters from the grim-faced men wielding riot shields and weapons.

'Can we get a close-up of those two men?' The lieutenant nodded and operated the zoom control with his mouse and the coarse image became even more pixelated but Walid was still able to identify the faces of his friends.

'Okay, pull back a little so I can get a broader picture of what happened,' he instructed and was mystified to see that his friends weren't facing the police but apparently talking to someone in the dense crowd. Suddenly both men began running and almost immediately after they had started to sprint Walid saw policemen fall to the ground.

'Those were the officers shot dead, sir.'

'Well, it's very clear from this disc that the running men didn't do the shooting,' Walid said grimly. 'They were clearly unarmed.' He continued to watch as his friends were brought down by rubber bullets. 'Right, I've seen enough. Do we know where Major Kazemi is right now?'

'The duty officer said that the major was going to question the terrorist suspects at Jaw prison, sir, and that he wouldn't be returning to the office today.' The lieutenant watched as uncontrollable anger flickered across his superior's face. This was a sight that he and his comrades had never, ever seen and the young man felt a momentary pang of pity for the person this rage would be directed at. Thank God it's not me, he thought.

'Lieutenant, I want you to return to our quarters and prepare both teams for an operation that may possibly end the drug-running from this damned country into ours,' and Walid clenched his fists.

The young man snapped to attention and smartly saluted with eyes shining eagerly. 'Yes, sir. I'll have everyone ready for the GO the moment you give the signal. Will Sergeant Shehhi be returning with me?'

'No, I need him for another task,' Walid said as he returned the salute. He then snatched up his briefcase and hurried from the office.

Jahandar had melted into the crowd of demonstrators as fast as his fat legs would carry him, expecting his bodyguards to be close behind to shield him from any of the stray rounds being fired by the police.

'I saw the police shoot both of them,' Javid said in an excited voice.

'Rubber bullets,' Shayhar clarified. 'I don't think they were hit with live ammunition.'

Jahandar nodded and kept moving until they had cleared the crowd and could see Stuart's abandoned Jeep. 'Search it for anything that may be a clue to the whereabouts of the consignment,' he ordered, wiping his brow with a large silk handkerchief. He hurried on, ignoring the Jeep and threaded his way through six lanes of horn-blowing stationary traffic and crossed the double highway to where their car was parked in the service road.

The two bodyguards caught up with Jahandar as he was ponderously levering himself into the back of the Toyota and Shayhar handed him a scrap of paper.

'It's all we could find,' Javid said apologetically and watched over the seat back as Jahandar unfolded the scrunched up page and scrutinized the figures.

'It's enough,' he muttered. 'This was written by that fool Behrouz and the numbers are most probably directions to where Changeez stored my last consignment in Bahrain.' He fell silent and sank back into the upholstery as he repeatedly read the figures to himself. 'They don't make any sense,' he muttered. 'I'm going to need Taylor to tell me what these mean.' He crumpled the paper in his frustration and stuffed it into his trouser pocket. 'He and his friend were circling the A'ali burial mounds for a very specific reason and these figures undoubtedly play a vital role: Changeez has hidden the cargo somewhere within the A'ali burial site and it may be inside one of the hundreds of mounds. Taylor must now know which one it is.'

'But the police have taken him into custody,' Shayhar complained as he started the engine. 'There's not much we can do about that.'

'Patience, fool. We simply wait and we watch,' Jahandar murmured. 'I have an idea where they may have taken Taylor and his colleague. They are both expatriates and the police will want to keep their arrest as quiet as possible until they have decided on a specific crime with which they wish to charge them. That means they will detain them where they are least expected to be held.'

'In a police station?' Javid asked.

'Don't be such an incompetent. That's the first place any embassy official would go to make inquiries if a missing-persons report is filed. No, I believe that prison is more likely,' Jahandar said and rubbed his sweating palms on a silk cloth. 'Until convicted by a court it isn't normal for detainees to be sent to a prison. That makes it the perfect place for the security police to do any initial questioning of suspected terrorists or even foreign undesirables.'

Shayhar U-turned the car and then stopped. 'Which prison should I drive to?'

'Jaw prison on King Hamad Highway. It's an all-male penitentiary for hardened criminals and it's very remote. We'll begin our wait there.' Jahandar speed-dialled a number and then began to talk in a low tone of voice that had both bodyguards wondering how important the person at the other end could be.

'What do you want, now?' an authoritarian voice demanded.

'I need a little more time,' Jahandar whispered so that his men couldn't hear. 'The one person who has the vital information that leads to the consignment has foolishly got himself arrested in one of those stupid street demonstrations and I am now waiting for him to be released on bail. As soon as he makes an appearance I'll persuade him to help me locate your special delivery.'

'You have twenty-four hours, Jahandar,' the voice purred in his ear. 'If by then you haven't recovered my property you will pay back every dollar I wired to you in Iran plus 50 per cent interest. Do you understand?'

Jahandar swallowed hard. 'I understand perfectly,' he said. The line went dead and he closed the cellphone with a shaking hand.

'Is everything okay, boss?' Shayhar inquired as he studied Jahandar's abnormally ashen face in the rear-view mirror.

'Mind your own business,' the fat man snapped. He loosened his tie and undid the top shirt button before slumping back into the soft leather seat seething with rage. Shayhar shrugged and silently estimated how long it would take to reach the notorious prison where two innocent men were incarcerated with hundreds of guilty men.

Walid collected Sergeant Shehhi and Helen from the hospital and leaving a very apprehensive Reem on ward rounds he broke all speed limits to eventually filter onto the Hawar Highway and travel south into the more desolate region of the island. He explained his worst suspicions to his passengers as they raced through the flat, arid landscape that was broken only by the distinctive outline of the Ras Hayyan transmitting station. Four and a half minutes later they drove through Jaw, a small village that was only a few hundred metres from the large prison complex that bore the same name. Walid tugged on the wheel and the car veered across the traffic lanes, startling a number of horn-blowing motorists as he swiftly left the highway and filtered into the small service road leading to the main prison gates.

Shehhi and Helen gripped the safety straps to prevent themselves from being thrown about as the car raced through the complex of buildings until finally it skidded to a halt outside the reception block.

Without waiting for the others Walid leapt from the car and raced up the steps and into the air-conditioned building. A sleepy-eyed prison officer looked up from the *Alwasat News* he had been half-reading. He panicked when he saw a stranger running towards him and his hand went to the alarm button. The man stopped short of pressing it when he saw the police warrant being held in front of his face.

'Major Safa to see Major Kazemi immediately,' Walid demanded breathlessly as he jabbed a finger at the telephone that stood before the bewildered officer. 'Do it now or suffer a reprimand from your superiors. I know the major is here and that he arrived earlier today escorting two prisoners.'

The prison officer tugged at his collar and read the warrant card again and then quickly pushed his chair back as Walid leant over the counter top and poked him in the chest with a stiff forefinger. 'If you don't want to lose those two stripes on your sleeve you'd better pick up the phone immediately.' It was at that point that Sergeant Shehhi also arrived at the counter and the prison officer decided to do as he was told.

After briefly gabbling into the phone behind his cupped hand he paused, listened and then hung up. 'Take the first door on your right and proceed to the detention centre where you will be met,' he stuttered nervously. 'The way is clearly marked!' he shouted after the two running men and then his eyes popped when a bare-headed woman entered the reception hall.

'No women allowed,' he shouted at her, pointing to the doorway.

'I'm with them,' Helen snapped, pointing towards her friends as they disappeared through a swing-door. The prison officer sat down with compressed lips and simply nodded towards the chairs in the waiting area.

'Thank you,' Helen said sweetly as she tossed her long auburn hair and strode to the most comfortable-looking chair with her long *abaya* swishing provocatively around her ankles. The officer retrieved his newspaper but was unable to concentrate on any words for he was frequently compelled to lift his head and glance at the long hair that caught the golden light of the setting sun.

The guards threw pails of water over the two senseless men until they regained consciousness, coughing and spluttering. Stuart instantly regretted waking; the pain that shot through his shoulder and down his arm was unbearable.

'The pigs are ready for another lesson in street protests,' one said as he aimed a kick at Alan's stomach. The pain caused by the steel-capped boot caused the Australian to double up and retch.

'My little piglet seems to be having some trouble with his arm,' the other laughed as he swung his baton down on the damaged shoulder. Stuart cried out involuntarily as the blow sent waves of agony down his arm and chest.

Lighting cigarettes the two men leant against the open door while studying their victims with predatory expressions on their faces. As one turned to make a remark he found himself looking into the blazing eyes of an enraged Walid. He had time to draw a breath of surprise before a clenched fist struck the bridge of his nose, smashing both bone and cartilage into a bloody pulp.

The other guard raised a baton to strike the unknown assailant but his wrist was held from behind in a paralysing grip, forcing him to release the weapon. Sergeant Shehhi then spun the man around and rammed his knee up into his groin. The guard doubled up and collapsed with a long-drawn-out scream.

'I believe the English have a strange expression for this crude act of justice,' Walid said as he stared pitilessly at the two groaning guards.

'And what would that be, sir,' Shehhi asked as he hurried to help Alan sit up.

'Tit-for-tat!' Stuart staggered to his feet and leant on Walid's arm.

'That's the one. Now let's get you both to a doctor.'

'I happen to know where I can find one in a hurry, sir.' Shehhi winked at the major and ran from the cell. Walid helped Stuart across the cell to where Alan was sitting with his back against the wall and lowered him carefully.

While Stuart was telling Walid what had occurred at the theme park, with a number of interruptions from Alan who had some embellishments of his own, two more prison guards entered the cell and taking one look at their comrades they quickly drew their pistols. Fearing a jail breakout they cocked their weapons. Walid rose to his feet and showing his empty hands he reached slowly into his top pocket to extract his police identity card. Only when the pistols were lowered did he attempt to speak. 'I am Major Safa of the Saudi Security Force and I have irrefutable proof that these two men are innocent of any crime and that proof was taken from monitored CCTV at police headquarters.'

A senior prison officer arrived on the scene and Walid explained once more who he was and why he had defended the prisoners who were blatantly being tortured. With due deference to Walid's high rank the officer ordered the two guards to place their injured colleagues under arrest and to take them to the infirmary.

'I have a doctor coming for these prisoners and we'll wait until they have been treated before taking them with us,' Walid said with determination.

Helen rushed into the cell closely followed by Sergeant Shehhi. The prison officer was scandalized to discover that a foreign woman had entered his prison. He was about to protest at such an extreme violation of prison regulations but stopped when he saw the expression on Walid's face.

With tears in her eyes Helen checked her husband's condition and immediately tended his heavily bruised, dislocated shoulder. 'What kind of men beat a prisoner when he's injured,' she shouted over her shoulder while professionally tearing her *abaya* into long strips to bind his bent arm against his chest. The officer was unable to give a reasonable reply and resorted to keeping silent while rapidly thinking of a way to put all blame onto the two guards.

Walid helped Alan remove his shirt to enable Helen to examine his hideously bruised abdomen. After painful prodding that was accompanied by a constant stream of apologies for the pain caused Helen pronounced Alan undamaged internally.

'You have wheelchairs?' Helen asked the officer in a peremptory manner that deeply offended him.

'Yes, madam,' he replied coldly.

'Then order them now,' Walid demanded loudly and waited, tapping his toe on the concrete floor as the frightened officer used his cellphone to instruct the infirmary. While they waited Helen opened the small medical bag that never seemed to leave her side and administered a shot of morphine to both men, thereby easing the worst of their pain.

'That'll hold you until we get to the hospital and I can do a proper check on you both,' she murmured as she ran her hand down Stuart's cheek.

Within ten minutes they had been transferred from the fetid cell to Walid's cruiser and were heading back to the city with Shehhi at the wheel.

'You've got a pretty good knee action, Sergeant,' Walid murmured and his old comrade grinned. Both officers were unaware that Jahandar and his men were waiting for them.

14

While he was standing by the vending machine drinking coffee from a plastic cup Major Kazemi saw the rapidly approaching police car through the window. As it braked violently to a halt outside the reception block he crushed the empty cup and rushed to the car park at the rear of the building. The major had no wish to answer Walid's awkward questions and he instructed his driver to return to police headquarters at Manama.

Major Kazemi saw the black sedan parked on the shale shoulder of the highway with some satisfaction but gave no sign of recognizing the three men in the car as he swept past. The Magician had given him strict instructions that there would be no face-to-face contact with the Iranian suppliers and he remained poker-faced and looked straight ahead until they had left the parked car far behind.

Jahandar, in turn, had noticed the police car as it filtered off the service road and joined the Hawar Highway but had shaken his head when he saw that it only contained a driver and one passenger, a Bahraini police major he was unfamiliar with.

Another thirty minutes later a second police car appeared on the service road and turned onto the highway. It headed for Manama and Jahandar could see that the car was filled to capacity and the brief glint of auburn hair against a rear window convinced him that it was the wife of his prime target.

Jahandar tapped Shayhar on the shoulder and as the Toyota's engine had been idling to keep the air-conditioning going he could quickly move away. 'Wait!' Jahandar snapped. 'Let them have a kilometre headstart before we pull out otherwise they'll become suspicious.'

The three men watched the car dwindle into the distorting haze rising from the tarmac and as it faded from sight round the first gentle curve Jahandar tapped Shayhar once again: 'Now you can go.'

The Toyota spat stones into the air as they pulled off the rough shoulder and onto the relatively smooth road surface. Within minutes Shayhar had closed the gap and with eyes heavily shielded against the sun they soon had their quarry in sight. He eased his foot off the accelerator to maintain a steady distance between the two vehicles.

'At the first opportunity you will snatch Taylor from the hospital and bring him to me,' Jahandar commanded as he cracked his knuckles and stared fixedly at the police car they were following.

I only have until lunchtime tomorrow, he thought and a shiver ran through his obese stomach as he considered the possibility of failure and the consequent penalty.

They had passed the rows of mega-sized petroleum storage tanks when the police car began to slow and the gap was closed. 'Slow down, keep your distance,' Jahandar shouted and Shayhar began lifting his foot before noticing that the police car was accelerating to regain its original speed, opening the gap between the two vehicles.

'Do you think they know we are following them?' Javid said, his first words since leaving Jaw.

'No, he slowed for another reason,' Shayhar said confidently.

'He may have but I am certain they now know we are tailing them because of the way you have matched their speed,' Jahandar snarled. 'Idiot.'

'You told me to slow down,' Shayhar protested.

'But I didn't tell you to speed up again, did I?' Jahandar slapped the driver on the back of his head. 'Slow down and let them get a little further ahead.' The traffic was becoming heavier as they drove through the suburbs and the police car often vanished from sight as a mixture of cars and trucks came between them.

'If only we knew where they were going so that we could stop following them and take our time getting there,' Javid muttered.

Jahandar grunted, marvelling at the man's glimmer of intelligence. 'There are two places they are likely to go. After a spell in Jaw Prison it will either be to get some rest at the apartment or to be repaired at a hospital.'

'Her hospital?' Shayhar interjected.

'Yes. And knowing the reputation of Jaw Prison I would place my bet on Major Walid taking the two men to hospital for a check up,' Jahandar conjectured. 'Turn off this road now and take me to the office of the Two Seas Marine Supplies that Changeez had on the docks. After that you will go to the Bahrain Specialist Hospital and collect Mr Taylor for interrogation.' Javid turned to look at his employer and grinned inanely. 'Alive, do you understand?' Jahandar snapped.

The assassin touched the concealed sheath that hid his long, razor-sharp knife. 'I understand perfectly,' he purred.

Shayhar turned off the highway and used the minor roads that shadowed the highway through the district of Tubli towards the dockyards. Within ten minutes they had pulled up outside a small warehouse on an abandoned lot that was covered with fly-tipped rubbish.

'Changeez had quite a fancy business,' Javid observed sarcastically.

'It'll do for our purposes,' Jahandar snapped as he struggled to ease his way out of the car. 'When you've got Taylor bring him here but don't be seen doing it.' Both men nodded and the car accelerated away leaving the large man standing by a small access door. He was slightly out of breath by the time he had taken a duplicate Yale key from his pocket. The key turned easily and the door swung open on well-oiled hinges.

Jahandar stepped into the blackness and brushed wildly as something touched his face: it was a thin pull cord and on giving it a tug a pale orange light illuminated the cavernous interior. The warehouse was completely empty apart from a small half-glazed office that had been erected in one corner behind stacks of crates.

The office contained one battered chair and a very rickety desk. Every surface was covered in a thick layer of dust and marked with faint wood beetle and cockroach spoors that meandered mindlessly in circles.

Jahandar gingerly picked up an old exercise book leaving a clean rectangle of polished mahogany and flicked through the pages. Dust motes rose into the air and he quickly took a handkerchief from his pocket and held it over his mouth and nose. The columns of Arabic figures had been written in cheap ink that had faded to a pale, almost illegible lilac colour and Jahandar knew that they had nothing to do with Changeez or the shipments that he had made to Manama. He threw it across the small room making more dust rise and he stepped out into the warehouse to avoid breathing it in while he waited for his men to return with Stuart.

Shayhar pulled into the hospital car park and stopped as far from the parked police car as he could. Both men made their way to Accident & Emergency and found the reception area in chaos. The escalation of street protests had increased the number of casualties requiring treatment for brick, baton, boot and bullet wounds and the two Iranians had to push their way through the bloodied crowd to get to the reception desk.

One of the three harassed receptionists who wore a black headscarf and *abaya* was eventually convinced that Shayhar was a relative and coerced into giving him the information they sought. The perspiring Bahraini informed them that due to the shortage of beds Mr Alan Short had been discharged in the care of a nurse but Mr Stuart Taylor had been admitted for treatment in a first-floor private room because of his injury. The Iranians melted back into the crowd and made their way through the pandemonium to the stairs.

When they reached the landing Javid turned into the corridor and immediately spotted a police corporal keeping guard outside one of the rooms. He had a small book in his hand and the chair he was sitting in was tilted back against the wall.

He looked up at the two approaching men. 'State your names and reason for being on this level,' he demanded as he tilted the chair forward and began to stand. Without saying a word both men took silenced pistols from behind their backs and executed the officer with deadly precision.

Shayhar ejected the empty clip and pushed in a fresh one before rushing into the room the officer had been guarding. He had only taken two steps, closely followed by Javid, when both men were thrown backwards by the impact of two .45-magnum rounds pounding into Shayhar's chest. Javid rolled from beneath his fallen partner and taking his gun fired randomly into the room before running down the corridor to the stairs. As he turned the corner and took the first step downward a bullet passed through the wall and wood splinters pierced his cheek.

Javid leapt three steps at a time until he reached reception. The solid mass of people jostling for attention was an impenetrable obstacle and he fired bullets into the ceiling to clear a path to the main door.

The crowd went silent and all heads turned to stare at the wild-looking man waving two guns in the air. 'Out of my way,' Javid screamed and men and women, frozen with fear, began to push back against the press of bodies to make way. The sudden impact of a bullet penetrating the bottom step made Javid look up the stairway to see Walid aiming his pistol. Javid leapt into the crowd knowing that the policeman dared not shoot again with so many people around.

A middle-aged man with a bloody bandage about his head reached out to grab Javid and the panicking gunman jammed his gun into the man's stomach and pulled the trigger. The sudden explosion and the man's collapse sparked more panic and the crowd surged away from the gunman, clearing a path to the main exit.

Brandishing his weapons Javid rammed the glass door open and ran from the hospital. As he went down the marble steps he spotted the line of waiting taxis. He went to the first car and pulled the man from behind the wheel by his shirt collar. The protesting driver attempted to fight back as he tumbled from the vehicle but Javid callously shot him in the mouth before jumping into the seat and starting the engine.

Walid appeared at the top of the marble steps as the taxi pulled away and aimed his heavy automatic but he couldn't be sure who the occupant was and he held his fire. When Javid sped away Walid noticed the crumpled figure surrounded by four of his fellow taxi drivers and realized what had happened.

'You swine,' he muttered through clenched teeth as he took aim. His first shot passed through the rear window, narrowly missing Javid's head and exited through the windscreen. Walid's second shot ripped through the rear tyre but the vehicle was able to keep moving and merge with the traffic beyond.

Walid holstered his weapon and used his cellphone to issue an all-points bulletin giving a description of the hijacked taxi. He then hurried back into the hospital to ensure the security personnel cordon off the scenes of the fatal shootings before going up to Stuart's room. The young policeman's body had been respectfully covered with a crisp linen sheet but the gunman's body still lay uncovered in the doorway and Shehhi was going through the man's clothing seeking some form of identification.

'Stuart is perfectly okay, sir,' he said when he saw his superior coming along the corridor. 'The stray bullets didn't go anywhere near him.'

'Excellent. Any luck with this man?'

'I couldn't find a thing, sir. It's as though all his personal details, including clothing tags, had deliberately been removed.'

'That makes him a professional,' Walid mused as he looked into the unseeing eyes and studied the features for any national characteristics. 'He looks Iranian.'

'I believe you're right, sir. I smelled his breath and I know for a fact that he ate *ghormeh sabzi* recently. It's a mixture of Persian limes, seasonings and strong spices that most Iranians adore.' Shehhi sniffed again. 'He's unmistakably from that region.'

'Well spotted, Shehhi,' Walid said. 'It seems your nose is as useful as your right knee.' The major laughed as he stepped over the body to enter the room and check on his friend. Helen was bent over Stuart with a deeply concerned expression on her face.

'What have you done to upset the Iranian people lately?' Walid asked as he placed a hand on his friend's good shoulder. 'They seem to have developed a violent dislike to you. Enough to kill to get you and then to kill to get away.'

Stuart winced as he sat up with Helen's arm supporting his shoulders. 'Who's been killed, Walid?'

'The police corporal guarding your door, a patient downstairs and a taxi-cab driver,' Walid replied sadly.

'My God, all these terrible things can't be happening because of a few trinkets from an ancient shipwreck,' Helen said as she searched Walid's eyes for some explanation.

'You're right, Helen,' Walid said softly. 'It's not just the pearls but vast quantities of drugs flooding through this country and into Saudi that's motivating these sons of Satan to do anything and everything.'

'I had a feeling that the man who kidnapped Helen had interests in other things and now I know it for sure,' Stuart said bitterly. 'I wish Alan and I had never found those pearls. They've proved to be nothing but bloody trouble, bringing us into contact with killers and drug runners and exposing everyone around us to mortal danger.'

'Talking of which, I will assign some officers to guard Alan and Reem,' Walid said and he speed-dialled headquarters. Once connected he asked to be transferred to Major Kazemi's extension and it rang unanswered for a full two minutes before an excited junior officer picked up the receiver. Apparently nobody knew where the major was. The colonel had requested the major's presence in his office early that morning and was now making everyone's life hell, demanding that Kazemi be found immediately. Walid sympathized with the junior officer and after organizing protection for Alan and Reem he hung up and told Stuart of his suspicions regarding the Bahraini major.

It was at that moment that Shehhi backed into the room. 'Trouble, sir,' he said raising his hands above his head. 'The SWAT team is here and they're coming on heavy.' Three men in full body armour and brandishing Heckler & Koch machine-guns eyed the occupants as they followed the sergeant and entered the room. The young nurse who had been helping Helen gave a choked-off cry of surprise and moved closer to the doctor. One of the SWAT team batted her on the side of the head with his gloved hand and she fell to the floor. Helen immediately knelt beside the young girl and cradled her head in her lap.

'Do that again and you'll end up in a police cell,' Walid said as he held up his police identification. The man backed away with doubt in his eyes as a senior officer entered the room and tugged off his balaclava.

'Major Safa,' he cried out. 'What are you doing in the middle of this mess?'

'I believe I'm part of the trouble that brought you here, Captain Dabal,' Walid said with a grim smile as he recognized the officer. Helen ignored the two men, turning away to help the young nurse to her feet.

'Some assassins tried to kill this patient and my sergeant and I managed to rout them but not before they had killed three people,' Walid explained quickly.

'Why would assassins want to kill this particular man, Major?' the captain asked with a raised eyebrow. 'And how were you so sure that an attack would happen that you would put one of your own officers on guard outside this door?' the captain added before recognizing Stuart despite his heavily bruised face. 'Wait a moment, aren't you Mr Taylor, the man whose wife was kidnapped?'

'That's right, Captain,' Stuart answered. 'And this is Doctor Taylor, my wife, whom you and your men helped Major Safa to release and for which I will forever be in your debt.'

'It was the same men who tried to exact their revenge today,' Walid added, holding the captain's gaze until he saw all suspicion fade.

'Revenge is a powerful motive for killing, Major, but as one assassin is dead and the description of the other has been circulated I have very little left to do here except to organize my men and check the people in reception for any militant agitators.' Dabal flicked a casual salute to Walid before walking to the door. As he stepped over Shayhar he turned his head. 'Take care, Major, after *maghrib* prayer a curfew is in force throughout the country and anyone on the streets after eight o'clock will be treated as a troublemaker, a militant, and shot.'

Walid nodded, his smile rapidly evaporating as the harsh reality of what was happening to the Land of Two Seas hit home. 'It's a disastrous law to impose in any country, on any people. I wouldn't like to be the one who decides when to shoot to kill,' he murmured.

The captain paused and looked down at the corpse. 'I think you've already made that decision,' he said and then turned to disappear down the corridor and attend to the chaos that had ensued in reception. The three heavily armed men who held their guns tucked tightly into their shoulders, ready to fire, followed him.

'The only difference was that this murderous bastard wasn't some harmless civilian demanding his civil rights,' Stuart said loudly enough to carry out of the room and down the corridor to the departing men.

'One of these days you'll get yourself into trouble,' Walid laughed humourlessly as he thumped his friend on the arm and then threw his hands up in horror when he saw the pain race across Stuart's face. 'Oh, so sorry, my friend. I forgot you're in a great deal of trouble already.'

'It's not with this particular government, Walid. It seems our big problem lies more with murderous drug importers,' Helen said as she helped to ease Stuart into a more comfortable position.

'Whom I will gladly terminate given the chance to do so,' Walid said with feeling before apologetically smiling at the young nurse. 'I'm not normally this bloodthirsty, young lady, but those who drag people into the hell of drug addiction deserve to be put down like the mad dogs they are.'

The young woman smiled her agreement and Sergeant Shehhi grunted his approval as he listened to his major while applying a small amount of ointment to where the officer had badly scratched the nurse's cheek.

'It is close to eight o'clock, Walid,' Stuart observed looking at his watch lying on the bedside table. 'If we want to avoid sleeping in one of these bloody awful hospital beds tonight we should all make a move.'

'I'll stay, sir, they may try again,' Shehhi said as he sat down in the vacant chair by the bed and placed a heavy automatic in his lap.

'Good man, Shehhi.' I'll get a man to relieve you at eight in the morning.'

'As much as I appreciate the kind thought I think we all need to get a good night's sleep in our own beds,' Stuart said. 'I don't think they will try again now they know I'm guarded by the police.' While talking, Stuart had struggled out of the bed and walked to the wardrobe where his clothes had been hung. Helen watched in amazement.

'You're not going anywhere tonight, darling.'

'Well, I'm not staying here.' He turned his back on everyone and removed the medical gown. 'Thanks to all the street protesters this bed will be needed tonight by someone who is more badly hurt than I am.'

Helen had to agree and hurried over to Stuart to help him put his shirt and trousers on. The young nurse stood up to give Helen a helping hand but was waved back with a thankful smile. 'I can manage Noor. I suggest you go to reception and help where you can with the many incoming patients there.' Noor nodded eagerly and with a brief wave she stepped over the corpse that was being photographed and hurried down the corridor.

'Nice girl,' Shehhi said quietly and then quickly looked away from the others as he felt his cheeks glow.

'And she's very attractive, Shehhi,' Walid said, trying hard to keep a straight face. 'Look, I won't be needing you any more tonight so why don't you go down and give the captain and the medical staff a hand,' then Walid added thoughtfully, 'but don't forget the curfew, your Saudi uniform may not save you from trigger-happy mercenaries.'

Shehhi nodded and then confirmed the meeting time for the next day before hurrying out of the room. Walid looked round and saw that Helen had rigged a sling to ease the strain on Stuart's shoulder and that he was now fully dressed and ready to leave.

'I'll drop you and Helen at your apartment,' Walid said as he watched the arrival of more crime-scene investigators at the entrance to the room.

'I can't possibly join you, darling,' Helen suddenly said above the noise arising from reception. 'There are too many injuries that will need serious attention.' Stuart made as though to protest but then fell silent knowing his wife's dedication and he squeezed her hand in silent agreement.

'You realize that the curfew will not permit you to get home at all tonight?' Walid said quietly, knowing the answer before she spoke.

'I'll get a little sleep later in the staff room and take a taxi home in the morning.' Turning to Stuart she said, 'Just make sure you rest that shoulder, darling.'

'You can't take a taxi with the streets as they are,' Stuart argued strongly.

'He's absolutely right, Helen. I will send a car to pick you up at eight o'clock which will get you home in perfect safety,' Walid said while descending the final steps and discovering that Captain Dabal had organized the crowd into orderly lines which had to pass the scrutiny of SWAT officers before they were permitted medical treatment. Even the badly wounded on the gurneys were being searched for weapons and their identity documents checked.

'This is awful,' Helen exclaimed. She gave Stuart a farewell peck on the cheek and rushed into the mêlée, joining the other doctors attending to the more seriously wounded people who were being forced to queue.

Walid shook his head at the scene and shielded Stuart's shoulder from the press of people as they crossed the reception lobby to the main door. He briefly nodded at Captain Dabal who was questioning a bewildered student with blood trickling into his left eye from a very serious head trauma.

Reaching the door they both looked back and caught sight of Shehhi and Noor leading an elderly man to the examination rooms. They exited the hospital and as the door closed behind them the sudden silence was overwhelming. Stuart glanced up into the crystal-clear night before gingerly climbing into the police cruiser.

Walid's cellphone warbled when they reached the car and he mouthed the word 'Alan' to Stuart as he listened with growing anger before telling the Australian that he would have a warrant issued instantly for Major Kazemi's arrest. He switched the phone off and started the car.

'It seems Alan was in a spot of trouble with Major Kazemi but it has been resolved. I'll tell you all about it later.'

'You are sure he is all right?'

'Perfectly. And in Reem's good hands.'

'He'll like that. Now please take me home, Walid,' Stuart said wearily.

'No sooner said than done, my friend.'

15

Alan shifted in the passenger seat to ease the muscular pain and regretted his decision as another stab of pain ran across his abdomen. He wasn't aware that he'd betrayed his discomfort until Reem noticeably reduced the speed of the car.

'It's okay, Reem,' he said. 'Just a little twinge.'

'Don't get macho with me, Alan. I'll be the judge of whether the little twinge you felt requires me to take it easy on this rough road or not,' she said briskly, her eyes studying the road ahead for more potholes.

They had passed easily through the first roadblock where polite Bahraini police waved them through when they saw Reem's nurse's uniform. Eyebrows had been raised at Alan's badly bruised face but the officers correctly assumed that he was the patient.

At the second roadblock as Reem was weaving through the concrete chicane a more senior officer stepped out of the guard hut and glimpsed Alan's battered face. Greatly alarmed at seeing one of the prisoners he wanted dead Major Kazemi shouted and raised his hand to point at the old Datsun Cherry as it was cleared by the guards and started accelerating along Al Fatih Highway.

Alan heard shouts fading away and turned in time to see an officer urging his men to fire their raised weapons. The Bahraini police officers seemed reluctant to shoot at an innocent-looking nurse until a mercenary pulled his trigger first and the bullet shattered the wing mirror on Reem's side. Then more rifles began to fire ineffectually. The men shooting were either poor marksmen or didn't have their hearts in the task and the bullets harmlessly passed over the vehicle. Kazemi and the mercenary had no scruples about killing women and their bullets peppered the boot with metallic bangs that made Reem and Alan hunch their shoulders defensively with each new strike.

Reem kept her nerve and floored the accelerator sending the tachometer into the red zone. Alan squeezed her shoulder in encouragement, feeling an overwhelming sense of admiration for the plucky young woman as she screeched round the first turning, taking them out of the line of fire.

As they entered the side road and the roadblock flicked out of sight Alan caught sight of a black car emerging from behind the concrete blocks and accelerating in their direction. 'We have company, Reem.'

The young woman nodded, her eyes fixed on the junction coming up and with perfect judgement she twisted the wheel to enter a service road that acted as a filter for Mina Salman Avenue. When they reached the main road they were immediately confronted by another roadblock. This was a simple affair comprising scores of rubber traffic cones that closed the road down to one lane that was guarded by four policemen. Two guards waved Reem down and on identifying her outfit they smiled and let her through to the next guards who waited thirty metres further on. As she came to a halt and wound her window down Alan looked back and saw one of the first two officers pointing at the back of the Datsun. He's spotted the damn bullet holes in the car, he thought. Alan then swore beneath his breath when he saw a black car racing towards the roadblock, its headlights flashing.

'You'd better go,' Alan whispered urgently behind one hand as the other slipped the shift into drive. 'Go fast,' he said out loud and Reem slipped the brake and jammed her foot down on the accelerator. The surprised officer who was settling himself down to ask the pretty young woman the formulaic questions jumped back as the Datsun shot away from the roadblock, narrowly missing the toecaps of his boots.

Alan kept looking back and saw one of the confused police officers leap in front of the black car with his hand raised, only to be swept into the air like a rag doll as the car powered through the roadblock without slowing. The remaining guards drew their weapons and began pouring bullets into the back of the large car as it left the roadblock. One of the officers stopped shooting and quickly wrote down the car registration before dialling for an ambulance.

'He ran him down. He ran that poor man down,' Reem screamed as she stared into the rear-view mirror. 'Who is that driver?'

'It's the same man who tried to get Stuart and myself officially executed for murder,' Alan said as he put an arm around the sobbing woman whilst ignoring the shooting pains in his side. 'We have to lose him or we'll both die like that policeman.'

'But why does he want you dead?'

'I don't know, Reem,' Alan said with a puzzled look. From what I can gather he is the Bahraini officer who was appointed to liaise with Major Safa on the drug-running investigation but that's all I know.'

'Maybe you know something he wants but without knowing it yourself.'

'Now you've really got me confused,' Alan said and then ducked his head as something heavy hit the car. He turned to see the black car fast approaching and the driver pointing a large automatic at them. Reem had also seen it in the mirror and she swerved across all lanes, narrowly missing an oncoming truck to speed down an on-ramp against the thin line of traffic. A large 4x4 hastily slewed to one side as the Datsun raced towards it and Reem managed to squeeze the compact car through the narrow gap. She then slowed, unlike Alan's pounding heart, to weave through the few oncoming cars driven by men sounding their horns in dismay at the way all women drive.

Alan averted his gaze from the disconcerting sight of the oncoming traffic and checked behind; the black car had suffered a head-on collision with the 4x4 that had thought it safe enough to accelerate and merge with the traffic on the main road above.

He faced forward again and gave the attractive nurse an admiring glance. 'You can take it easy, Reem,' he sighed as they emerged onto the road that would take them to his apartment. 'The man chasing us was silly enough to think he could drive down a one-way street the wrong way.'

'Who did he think he was, a woman?' Reem declared and she laughed out loud, feeling the tension drain as she slowly guided the car to the correct side of the road. As she slowed to drive more sedately they spontaneously broke into laughter again and Alan fondly patted the slender hand that still gripped the gear stick.

'That was beautifully done, Reem,' Alan said. 'I couldn't have done better if I'd tried.'

'I know, now sit back and try to relax those damaged stomach muscles, before I have to return you to hospital for more treatment,'

Reem said in a mock-bossy tone. Alan grinned and sank back into a well-worn calfskin seat and closed his eyes.

'Shouldn't you let Major Safa know what's happened before you drop off to sleep?'

Alan grunted his agreement, annoyed with himself at being so remiss, and he quickly speed-dialled Walid. After listening to a summary of the events that took place since the couple had left the hospital a horrified Walid promised Alan that he would have any hunt for the Datsun called off immediately and an all-points bulletin would be issued for the arrest of Major Kazemi for the deliberate killing of a police officer—the crime he had accused Alan and Stuart of committing.

Reem dropped Alan off at his apartment and after promising to take extreme care and to double lock her doors she left for her own apartment that she shared with two other nurses from the same hospital. Alan waited until her Datsun turned the corner before climbing the few steps in the lingering heat of the day and entering the cool atrium. He opened his apartment door and walked down the short corridor carefully checking every room for intruders before getting a cold beer from the kitchen and sinking back into his favourite armchair.

His cellphone began emitting a cheeky ringtone and Alan saw that it was a call from Stuart. 'Yes, Stuart, what's new with you and Helen?'

'I've heard from Walid that you were almost killed by Major Kazemi. Are you and Reem okay?' Alan was warmed by his friend's concern and he quickly reassured him that they were both okay.

'I have a strong feeling that this cat-and-mouse business isn't going to end until we find whatever it is that everyone is looking for,' Stuart said.

'And where are we going to find whatever it is we're expected to know about?' Alan said, confusing his own thoughts even more.

'We'll continue where we left off.'

'A'ali burial site?'

'Right. We know the answer lies in one of those royal double mounds. Remember how the fat man in the crowd demanded what we'd found in A'ali. I suggest we start searching the moment the curfew lifts in the morning,' Stuart said, his natural enthusiasm for solving a mystery overcoming all his concerns. 'Remember how we spotted a double mound on the south side of the site? It looked very much like the mysterious M on the scrap of paper so I believe we should check that one first.'

Alan was swept along by the excitement in Stuart's voice and he readily agreed to join his friend in the morning. Stuart then called Walid and outlined his plan before asking if some form of protection could be extended to Helen and Reem.

'Easily done,' Walid replied. 'Men will be appointed to the task after the *fajr* dawn prayer and I'll be accompanying you to the burial site.' Stuart welcomed his friend's moral support and a meeting time was set.

The sun had yet to reveal its brilliant tip above the horizon when the muezzin finished calling the devout to prayer. At the same time a modified black Hummer rolled quietly up to the main hospital entrance and two men in full body armour leapt out with automatic Heckler & Koch sub-machine guns at the ready. Shehhi and a young corporal rushed up the steps and into the reception that appeared to be an oasis of peace compared to the previous evening. Shehhi went to the desk and asked a petrified receptionist to inform Doctor Taylor that her escort had arrived.

The woman dialled the staff room with shaking hands. After a few nervously mumbled words she hung up and turned to face the ruggedly handsome man with the sub-machine gun hanging across his chest.

'She will be here in five minutes,' she stuttered as she nervously flicked through the paperwork on her desk. One of the doors to the examination rooms opened and a nurse with a small plaster on her cheek skipped into reception.

'Shehhi,' she squealed. 'Is that you under all that camouflage?' He smiled broadly and then blushed as he watched Noor gaily approaching.

'You look so . . . so gallant,' she added as she touched him on the sleeve in a modest greeting. 'Have you come to take me to breakfast?'

'I'm here as protection for Doctor Taylor although it would have been nice to spend some time with you. But I have to tell you that I am a little bit older than you.'

'I would say quite a bit older but that is of no consequence, Shehhi,' she teased. 'So, we will have to meet again at a more opportune time. Agreed?' she said, extending her hand.

Shehhi took the delicate hand smelling of antiseptic wash in his own and squeezed gently. 'I would really like that, Noor,' he said and then quickly withdrew his hand when he heard muffled laughter. He spun around to catch the corporal with a hand over his mouth and a mischievous twinkle in his eyes.

'If I hear a word of this back at barracks you'll be doing KP duties for the next six months. Do you understand, Corporal?' he demanded through clenched teeth and the young policeman paled.

'Yes sir, not a word, sir.'

More laughter made Shehhi turn again and he couldn't help grinning when he saw Noor laughing as well, her even white teeth and free-flowing raven hair shining in the light streaming through the plate-glass windows. Helen was now standing beside the nurse, smiling kindly at the veteran's discomfiture but Shehhi only had eyes for Noor.

A completely mystified receptionist kept looking from one person to the other. 'Will you be returning later, Doctor Taylor?' she finally asked and Helen shook her head. 'After last night I need some more sleep.' She smiled at the woman and turning on her heel she lead the way to the entrance. Shehhi gave Noor a farewell smile and strode after the doctor. Using hand signals he ordered the corporal to leave the hospital first and check security. The young man raced ahead and with gun at the ready he opened the doors and went out onto the steps.

Walid was waiting by the car, his head swivelling constantly as he visually checked every vehicle or pedestrian approaching the hospital entrance. He gave the signal to advance and the three descended the steps and climbed into the car.

'*As salaam alykhum*, Walid,' Helen greeted the major cheerfully.

'*Alykhum es salaam*, Helen. Corporal Ahmed will be your bodyguard for the day and I trust he will not make a nuisance of himself. However, I would stress that you should act on his orders if a situation arises. He is a professional bodyguard and has secret-service experience in my own country.'

'Wow, you are a very accomplished young man,' Helen said to the back of the driver's close-cropped head.

'Thank you, madam,' he replied sheepishly.

It was Shehhi's turn to laugh and the young man visibly blushed. 'No words in the barracks, sir?' the corporal said meaningfully to the still chuckling Shehhi sitting beside him.

'No words, Corporal,' Shehhi agreed and laughed again.

Arriving at the building fifteen minutes later the corporal went ahead to check the lobby and the stairs before signalling the all-clear.

When they reached Helen's apartment Walid raised a finger to his lips and opened the door before waving the corporal in. The young officer crept in on silent, rubber-soled boots and was immediately hit over the head with a large flower pot. Fortunately the riot helmet prevented his skull from being fractured.

Stuart was raising the pot for a second strike when his wrist was clamped in an iron-like grip. 'It's me, my friend,' Walid cried and Stuart looked around in astonishment. Helen immediately dropped to her knees beside the fallen officer and checked his pulse.

'Fortunately, you just stunned him, silly,' she reprimanded her crestfallen husband as she helped the young officer to stagger to his feet. Walid slipped the corporal's arm over his shoulders and helped him into the living room where he eased him down onto the settee.

'He's had worse happen to him in the barracks,' Walid assured Stuart who was standing with an apologetic expression on his face. 'A brandy wouldn't go amiss, though,' he added brightly and Stuart hurriedly poured a stiff measure from a Montrose pottery decanter.

'Is he permitted alcohol, Walid?' Stuart asked, noticing how the young man had perked up at the sight of the golden drink in his hand.

'Not normally, but under these circumstances a little stimulation will make him more efficient at carrying out his orders for the day.'

Stuart handed the glass to the corporal with a muttered apology for hitting him. 'When there was no ring or knock at the door I thought that the kidnappers had returned. That's why I struck you.'

'That's okay, sir. *Lisan at-tajriba asdaq*,' the corporal said with a smile after sipping the twenty-year-old spirit.

'Experience is the best teacher,' Walid translated with a slight frown as he watched the young policeman take another sip of brandy. 'I'll lay a bet that he won't enter a house the same way again without doing the proper checks.'

'I won't. Another mistake like that could kill me, sir,' the corporal said and handed the unfinished glass back to Stuart. 'And that could, too, if I drank too much,' he added, nodding at the remainder of the liquid that Stuart was absently swirling in the glass.

Walid grunted his approval. 'Moslems must avoid alcohol to have unpolluted minds in prayer, Stuart. We also need clear minds when preparing for any dangerous missions that require firearms.'

'Time for us to leave,' Walid said.

Stuart briefly hugged his wife and murmured in her ear. 'I want you to lock the door after we have left and not to answer it to anyone but Walid or myself—is that understood?' Helen nodded slowly and the corporal gave the universal thumbs-up sign.

The two friends were met by Shehhi in the lobby with his wicked-looking weapon still slung across his chest and ready for any eventuality. In a matter of minutes the Hummer arrived at Alan's building where he was waiting outside in the soaring temperature of the new day.

'That was rather foolish, Alan,' Stuart commented from the back as the Australian climbed into the front passenger seat beside Shehhi. 'You could easily have been picked off by a drive-by thug.'

'And a very good morning to you to,' Alan answered cheerfully.

'I don't think they'd attack now,' Walid said quietly. 'They'll wait for us to find something before they make any move so we'd better keep our eyes open at the burial site.' He continued to scrutinize the other vehicles on the road and realizing the wisdom of his words the others fell silent and also made a point of studying every car they overtook and especially those that passed them.

Eventually, Stuart broke the unnerving silence. 'We're heading for the double mound on the south side of the burial site first. Do you know it, Shehhi?'

'I can't say I've seen the one you refer to but if you can point it out I'll get us to it.'

'Sergeant Shehhi drove captured Iraqi tanks in the Kuwait war and loves destroying cars in demolition derbies for a hobby—he'll get us anywhere, especially in this big bastard,' Walid mused aloud, making Alan glance at Shehhi with increased respect.

'To the south the Bin Salman Highway cuts through the burial site but as there are no roadside fences I will be able to leave the road at any point and drive into the site, sir,' Shehhi said as he swerved round a slow-moving pick-up carrying two hobbled camels.

Stuart looked round the interior of the Hummer and became aware of the weapon racks on the roof and between the rear seats. Most held heavy-gauge shotguns for close-quarter fighting but the two between Walid and himself held strangely shaped weapons that were unfamiliar. He ran a hand over the blued steel barrel of one and prodded Walid in the arm to get his attention.

'Ahh, these are my silent beauties, Stuart,' Walid said proudly as he unclipped the gun and lifted it from the rack. 'This is a Heckler & Koch MP5-SD with a non-detachable integral silencer. The vented barrel reduces the bullet muzzle velocity to below the speed of sound.'

'So that makes it quiet?'

'This is more than quiet, it's almost silent even on fully automatic.'

'Ammunition?' Alan asked, peering over the seat with covetous eyes locked onto the weapon.

'Standard 9mm.' Walid put the gun back into the rack and patted the stock lovingly.

The spell of mutual admiration was suddenly broken by Shehhi's warning cough. 'Is that the double mound you saw the other day, sir,' he said, jerking a thumb in the direction of the burial site that they were now passing.

Stuart gazed out at the fabulous scene that had survived for seven millennia before land values rocketed and property developers began to level most of the burial sites. It was only a mere sixty years ago that the sites had been given their true place in history by Danish archaeologists. The remaining few thousand mounds were then saved and preserved for future generations to marvel at. The dusty landscape was littered with dried mud mounds as far as the eye could see. They rose as high as two storeys and were nine to twelve metres in diameter. One in particular drew his eye for it adjoined another to form a shape not dissimilar to a woman's breasts rising above all others.

'Let's see if it is the one,' Stuart said and Shehhi pulled the Hummer off the road to side-slip down the steep bank to where the vast burial site began. A double strand of camel-proof barbed wire blocked their entry and Shehhi took a pair of wire cutters from the well-stocked toolbox. It was a neat job that only took fifty seconds and then they were through the fence and powering between the giant molehills towards the double mound.

Shehhi brought the Hummer to an abrupt halt at the foot of a steep mud slope and everybody jumped out to gaze in wonder at one of man's earliest architectural wonders. Shehhi, meanwhile, had unclipped one of the MP5-SDs and was observing everything but the royal mound. His eyes flicked from side to side in order to catch any form of fleeting movement amongst the tightly packed mounds. To prevent any misunderstanding by patrolling highway security forces Walid had attached a Bahrain Police pennant to the Hummer's whip aerial.

'So this is a Dilmun royal burial mound,' Alan said, gazing up at the eighteen-metre tomb. 'So where is the entrance?'

'This way,' Stuart shouted from where he had wandered round the mound. 'It looks like the crude entrance to a tunnel and we are definitely going to need flashlights if we want to explore the interior.'

While Shehhi stayed on guard Walid opened the large toolbox and took out three Surefire military flashlights. He trotted round the mound and gave one to each of the waiting men. The tunnel was on the opposite side to the rising sun and they stumbled into a murky darkness, forcing them to switch the flashlights on before they could progress any further. The low headroom made all three men stoop as they walked along until they suddenly found the way blocked by fallen rubble. Stuart placed his flashlight on the floor and went to shift one of the stones but a stabbing pain raced across his chest, forcing a low grunt to pass his lips.

'Leave it, Stuart, you're not well enough yet,' and Walid placed his flashlight in his friend's hand. 'Alan and I will clear the way.' He bent and quickly began to pass pieces of rock to Alan who stacked them neatly along the passage. Sweat dripped from their noses and down their necks and pain shot across Alan's abdomen as they worked. Soon there was a hole large enough for them to squeeze through and they found themselves in a spacious cavern with a high domed ceiling. Their powerful beams lit up a rough dirt floor littered with stones and rotting wooden crates that had been discarded by archaeologists long ago.

'Not exactly a cosy place to live,' Alan said as he swept his light up the rough, curving wall to where it began to descend again, eighteen metres above their heads. 'Doesn't even have a chimney.'

'It's a crypt, you chump,' Stuart laughed. 'The inhabitants didn't have to be cosy.'

'I think you guys need to see this,' Walid called out. He was standing beside the old wooden crates and Alan and Stuart soon realized that what they had taken for a crate was in fact a coffin.

'The ancient Dilmun didn't use coffins, they just curled the remains within a circle of stones on the ground,' Stuart exclaimed. 'And if anyone had been put in a wooden box it would have disintegrated hundreds of years ago.'

'And that would include the bodies, too.' Walid aimed his flashlight through the splintered lid of a second coffin and as Stuart peered through the cracks the glint of metal caught his eye. He very carefully tried to lift the lid and it cracked in half with an explosion of fine wood dust that seemed to hang motionless in the beams of the flashlight.

Alan pulled back when he glimpsed the stark whiteness of a grinning skull. 'Cripes, the place is inhabited,' he said as Stuart lifted the other half of the lid to reveal a desiccated skeleton dressed in the remnants of a very old uniform.

'If I'm not mistaken he's not a Dilmun and is more probably the mortal remains of a sixteenth-century Portuguese seaman.' He pointed to the rusting blade showing through holes in the decaying scabbard. 'That's definitely a naval officer's sword.'

'How can you tell he's sixteenth century?' Alan asked, picking up a beautifully engraved dagger encrusted with emeralds to study it more closely.

'The coins, my Antipodean mate,' Stuart said, flipping coins to Alan and Walid. 'Note the obverse field which shows a castle over water and the reverse which is clearly the shield of Portugal. I would hazard a guess that these were minted during the reign of Manuel the First who was sometimes referred to as The Fortunate.'

'Why fortunate,' Walid asked as he slowly turned the coin over.

'He brought about the golden era of Portugal through exploration and a great deal of global discoveries. He even sponsored Vasco Da Gama who opened up the trade routes to India and when Pedro Cabral crossed the Atlantic, King Manuel was able to claim Brazil for Portugal.'

'Quite a character,' Alan commented, tossing the coin back into the coffin to join the small pile that had spilt out of a rotting sack that had been placed between the officer's dried, powdery boots.

'That still doesn't explain why one of Manuel's naval officers was buried in a six-thousand-year-old Dilmun mound,' Walid said.

'And why his wife was buried alongside him,' Alan added as he looked into the second coffin that he had just wrenched opened. Stuart and Walid gasped when they saw the faded beauty of the emerald-green silk gown and the mother-of-pearl designs on the fragile slippers that still encased the slender bones of her feet.

'That looks like a jewel casket,' Stuart muttered, aiming his light at the dark oak box that lay at the woman's feet. 'I guess the grave robbers thought the same thing,' Alan said as he pointed at the lid that had been forced open to remove the contents. As the flashlights lit the interior a flicker of bright red revealed that the thieves had missed a small gold ring set with a single ruby.

'Pretty,' Walid said as he bent to pick it up. 'Although it's not worth much in today's market.'

'With true provenance a sixteenth-century ring could be very valuable to a collector of such objets d'art,' Stuart said as he swept the chamber with his flashlight for more items of interest. 'I would estimate a value of eight thousand pounds sterling.'

Walid raised his eyebrows in surprise and dropped the ring into his pocket. 'Then I'll make sure the proceeds of its auction go to a good charity such as the Islamic Relief Fund.'

'Great idea, Walid,' Alan murmured. 'I also think that this couple would have approved for I reckon they were murdered and their bodies hidden here by people who believed that they would never be discovered.'

'He may have been the owner of the chests you found in the Gulf,' Walid surmised. 'The first necklace may have belonged to the woman, and her husband was probably shipping the other chest of pearls to Lisbon for profit.'

'Judging by the uniform he is wearing he may have been the captain of the ship we found, which would explain how he came to have such wealth,' Stuart said, fingering the gold frogging on the uniform jacket. 'The crew killed the couple when they were ashore and hid their bodies in this mound before setting sail for Portugal with a prepared story about the couple being murdered by Bahrainis.'

'The ship could then have been attacked by ships of the Emir of Hormuz and sunk off the coast where we found it,' Alan said excitedly.

'Where the grisly secret wouldn't be known for another five hundred years,' Walid finished and Stuart nodded his head solemnly.

Alan broke the brief moment of silence that followed Walid's words. 'There has to be more to this than two skeletons and a single ruby ring.'

'You're right, mate,' Stuart said, sweeping the walls of the chamber with his light. He paused and swept the beam back to stop on a dark shape in the opposite wall at ground level. He walked across and saw that it was a small tunnel.

'This must be the connecting passage with this mound's twin,' he cried out and Alan and Walid hurried across. Stuart dropped on all fours and shuffled forward into the darkness. The powerful beam lit up the rough-hewn walls of the narrow tunnel that was painfully scraping his back through the thin cotton shirt. He had progressed about three metres when he emerged into the second chamber that was as cavernous as the first.

As he stood up and swept his beam across the black space Alan and Walid crawled in to join him and their flashlights helped to reveal the whole interior of the chamber.

'What's that over there?' Alan cried as he shone his light against the far wall to reveal a small stack of wooden boxes. The pale colour of the wood clearly indicated that the boxes were brand-new and not of sixteenth-century origin and the three men hurried across to investigate.

Alan took a Leatherman multi-tool from his pocket and unfolded a miniature chisel with which to prise open one of the lids. The small nails, releasing their hold on the softwood lid, creaked eerily in the vacant chamber and the lid slowly lifted. Alan applied even more pressure and the lid leapt up and off to reveal hundreds of tiny glassine bags solidly packed inside the box.

'My God,' Stuart whispered. 'It looks like drugs to me.'

'We've found the drug runners' distribution centre,' Walid said with triumph in his voice. 'This is what I've been working towards for the last twelve months.'

'My heartiest congratulations, Walid. Now what shall we do with these? We can't leave them here,' Stuart asked as he tentatively lifted one of the boxes. 'Wow, it feels like ten kilograms to me.'

'And there's twelve boxes. That's a pretty tidy profit for someone,' Alan said as he picked up two boxes.

Walid beamed from ear to ear. 'We'll put them in the Hummer and take them back to headquarters,' then he too took two boxes and headed for the tunnel. It took the three men ten minutes to transfer the boxes to the first chamber and then, with backs painfully bent they carried them out of the mound and into the broiling heat.

Stuart's cellphone gave its familiar ringtone and on answering it he heard the familiar voice of Jahandar.

'Listen to me carefully, Mr Taylor. I am currently entertaining a young lady by the name of Reem who I believe is known to you, yes?'

'You bastard.'

'That kind of language will only make me angry and pretty little Reem wouldn't like to have an angry host, would she?'

'What do you want?'

'What you will find or, what you have already found in the A'ali burial site. That's all I want, Mr Taylor. She will then be of no further use to me and she can return to carry on her invaluable work at the hospital.'

'Wait!' Stuart said and covering the phone with his hand he related what had happened to the others. The expressions of the three men revealed their shock and anger and after an ominous silence Walid spoke first.

'No matter what we do they will kill Reem,' Walid said quietly. 'So, we will have to hand over the drugs or he'll kill her now and hide her body in the desert.'

'You mean the bastard wins and Reem disappears. Is that how it goes?' Alan shouted, his face as pale as sun-bleached bones.

'Reem needn't die, my friend,' Walid whispered. 'It all comes down to how we arrange the handover.'

Stuart nodded grimly as he took his hand off the microphone. 'Okay, you win. As soon as we've found what you want I'll give you a call.'

'You have until noon tomorrow or you will try my patience and you know what will happen then.' Jahandar broke the connection and Stuart switched off his phone.

'Now what?' he asked Walid.

16

Sheikh Abdullah Al-Tahlawi climbed out of his opalescent salmon-pink Lamborghini Gallardo with the usual difficulty brought about by his passion for Italian food. The pale-faced obsequious man who had arrived earlier by taxi stood rigidly by the open door with his arm outstretched to assist the puffing man.

Smoothing his *thawb* over a well-rounded paunch with nicotine-stained fingers he ignored the outstretched hand of Tony Whitmore, the UK Trade and Investment officer, and instead waited with signs of impatience as his servant tended to the creasing and draping of his *smaagh* head cloth, making sure it reflected the latest style adopted in Jeddah.

Tony was used to the manner of this particular sheikh and he let his hand fall to his side. He turned and followed the man who had the power to veto a $20-million contract. This was for the supply and construction of a new metal foundry, a project he had spent the last six months arranging. It was intended to introduce the finest British technology into Bahrain and involved installing induction furnaces and four giant crucibles capable of producing the highest-grade stainless steel for the many oil companies in the region.

As they walked into the coolness of the embassy he recalled the three contracts he'd already lost to the Chinese and knew he couldn't afford to let this one slip through his fingers. Failure meant a recall to London and a less luxurious life for him, Dorothy and his two troublesome teenagers who had been thoroughly spoilt by the good life offered on the island.

They entered Tony's office and after introducing the sheikh to the three principal members of his support team he invited his visitor to sit. The thin servant stood behind his master with his back against the wall as Sheikh Abdullah lowered himself into the leather club chair and coffee and dates were placed on the table. After thirty minutes the meeting was adjourned at the sheikh's request while he had a few words in private with Tony Whitmore. As soon as the door had closed on the three trade officers the sheikh gestured at his servant to pour him more coffee.

'Mr Whitmore,' he said, his soft, feminine tones contradicting his vicious character. 'This contract will be allowed to proceed further but only under a specific condition.'

'I am quite sure our British tenders will be able to meet any additional conditions you put in the contract and will look forward to working with you and your government,' Whitmore said politely in a calm voice that belied the nervous tension involuntarily making him clench his fists under the conference table.

'It is a condition, or rather a favour, that I wish from you, that has not been written into the contract but one that I personally wish you to be bound by.'

'Oh?' Whitmore exclaimed in puzzlement as his nails bit into the palms of his hands.

'As an officer of this embassy you can claim diplomatic immunity, yes?'

'Naturally.' Whitmore unclenched his hands and tried to relax as he waited for a clue as to where the conversation was leading.

'Therefore you can travel to and from Saudi Arabia without having your vehicle searched. Yes?'

Tony pushed his chair away from the table and stood up. 'Sheikh Abdullah Al-Tahlawi, I regularly visit our contact office in Dammam with embassy papers and that's all I carry. I am not sure what you are about to suggest but I should warn you that I cannot jeopardize Britain's good relations with this country or with the Saudis.'

'That relationship also depends on mutual trading agreements that profit both parties.' Abdullah raised his eyebrows and Whitmore nodded his accord. 'The loss of the contract currently on the table would affect that relationship?' Whitmore was forced to nod again and the thought of seeing such a big feather for his cap being blown away made him physically shiver.

'Mrs Dorothy and your two pretty daughters would not be too happy either?' Sheikh Abdullah whispered spitefully. The servant leaning against the wall had watched the scene being played out in silence and now he felt a stab of sympathy for the trade officer as conflicting emotions flickered across his face.

'What is it that you want me to do that is so important that it would terminate a twenty-million-dollar contract if I don't comply?'

'It's very simple. On the first day of each month I wish you to put four small wooden boxes in the trunk of your car, cross the King Fahd Causeway and deliver them to an address in Al Aziziyah.'

'What's in the boxes?' Whitmore asked but the sheikh remained silent, his eyes fixed upon Tony.

'Okay, if you refuse to tell me at least let me know what's in it for me and my family.'

'After the first trip you will receive the signed contract you so desperately want and for each subsequent journey thereafter you will receive two thousand dollars in cash for your extravagant family needs.'

Whitmore sat down opposite the sheikh, his eyes flicking from the sheikh's sardonic smile to the immobile servant standing behind him and he perceived a slight movement on the sergeant's face, one that hinted at an expression of pity.

'Don't worry about Ahmed,' the sheikh hissed. 'He is the soul of discretion because he knows his life depends on being so.' Whitmore nodded slightly.

'Does that mean yes?'

'Yes, damn it!' Tony snapped and then immediately regretted his discourtesy.

A brief frown clouded Sheikh Abdullah's face before he beamed innocently and stood up to reach across the table. 'Now we can shake hands, Mr Whitmore, yes?'

Whitmore took the clammy hand in a light grip before quickly withdrawing and sitting down with a heavy heart to wipe his damp hand on his linen-clad thighs beneath the table.

'This is the number I wish you to call as soon as I have left.' Abdullah flicked a small piece of pasteboard across the polished table to hit Whitmore's hand. It had a single telephone number on it.

'Your call is expected and no matter what the man says you are to refer to me only as the sheikh and not to give my real name. If you do, something unfortunate might happen to members of your family. Do you understand what I am saying?'

Whitmore thumped his fists on the mahogany. 'I understand that I am no longer negotiating with a gentleman but a common blackmailer.' His sudden outburst took Sheikh Abdullah by surprise and he jumped back with a shocked expression on his face before the mocking look slowly returned and he gave a falsetto giggle. 'My dear Mr Whitmore, there is no need to be so emotional. No harm will come to your family if you do as you are told.'

'I assure you Sheikh Abdullah, if anyone touches my children your name will be headline news around the world. Of that you can be sure.'

The sheikh smiled. 'I think it's time to ask the rest of your colleagues to return to the meeting. You can give them the good news and then we can adjourn until the signing of the contract. That will be on the second day of the month for we both know where you will be going on the first, don't we Mr Whitmore?'

Tony glowered at the sheikh as he stomped to the double doors leading to the anteroom.

Major Kazemi left the police compound and instructed his driver to go to the Two Seas Marine Supplies warehouse. The corporal sitting beside the driver turned to look at his superior with raised eyebrows.

'It's time I met Jahandar face to face,' Kazemi muttered to himself, ignoring the corporal who simply shrugged and went back to staring out at the drab surroundings while his mind drifted back to the third-rate belly dancer he had slept with the previous night.

'Will we need the Uzis, sir?' the corporal asked.

'Only side-arms.' The major removed his Glock 18 from the well-waxed holster and checked the magazine load. 'This is just a friendly meeting and I do not anticipate any trouble. However, I want you both to be on your guard with holsters unfastened. Is that clear?'

'Yes, sir,' the police officers chorused loudly and Kazemi sank back in his seat to speed-dial a number; he recognized Jahandar's voice straightaway.

'Ah, you are still at the warehouse, yes?' Jahandar said that he was and Kazemi snapped back. 'You have acquired what I want and it's ready for collection?'

'It's not with me yet, sir. I have just told Mr Taylor that he has to deliver the crates by this time tomorrow or lose a friend.'

'Explain!' Kazemi growled.

'I have taken a friend hostage and have her here with me now.'

'You stupid fool! You dared to kidnap another person and run the risk of stirring up yet another hornets' nest. Have you forgotten what happened last time you tried such a childish plan? You failed miserably and achieved nothing.'

'I gained a very valuable chest of precious jewels and pearls that were worth about three million dollars. I wouldn't call that nothing!'

'It is only loose change compared to the value of what is being transferred to the Saudi Arabian market every month,' Kazemi shouted. 'Get it into your thick head now, Jahandar, that what we have been dealing with over the last two years is worth a lot more than just mere baubles.'

There was a long silence on the line and the major's anger slowly subsided. 'I will shortly be arriving at the warehouse and I expect a sensible plan from you when I get there.' Kazemi broke the connection.

The two corporals shifted uneasily in their seats and said nothing. The powerful limousine glided along Kuwait Avenue with hardly a sound, apart from the sporadic 'popping' sound of distant gunfire.

'Sounds like our guys are putting down another demonstration,' the driver ventured to say and his hollow laugh cut to silence when there was no response from the rear of the car.

The major's ringtone sounded and he flipped the cellphone open. After a brief moment of listening he snapped, 'Mr Whitmore, if that is your real name, how did you get my number?'

Whitmore simply said 'the sheikh' and Kazemi went rigid. 'And what were your instructions?' He listened in silence for a few seconds before interrupting the trade officer. 'You must be ready shortly after midday tomorrow to make a run to an Al Aziziyah address that I will give you with the boxes.' After a brief check to ensure Whitmore's number had been stored he snapped the phone shut.

The car turned off the main road and wound through a few side streets before slowly coming to a stop outside the office of the Two Seas Marine Supplies. The corporals checked their weapons and returned them loosely to the holsters and the three officers left the unmarked car to enter the thick humid atmosphere of the office. The rusted bell over the door warned that customers were on the premises. The door behind the reception counter opened and Jahandar waddled into the sticky heat.

He did a double-take on seeing three uniformed officers and quickly adopted his most obsequious expression.

'How can I help you, officers,' he asked as he leant his heavy weight upon the counter.

'I spoke to you on the phone,' Kazemi said as he lifted the flap in the counter top and walked through to stand beside Jahandar. 'You are Jahandar?'

'And you are the Magician?' Jahandar countered.

'No, I am his personal assistant and you should be careful when using that title in public,' Kazemi snapped back.

'Then who are you?'

'That is of no consequence and you will simply address me as Major,' Kazemi said brusquely as he stepped through the warehouse door which had been opened from the inside by Javid, Jahandar's bodyguard. The major ignored the automatic held loosely in the bodyguard's hand and brushed past him followed by his two corporals who, with hands resting lightly on holsters, kept their eyes fixed on both men. The interior of the warehouse was considerably colder than the office and Kazemi loosened his collar to allow the perspiration that had gathered around his neckband to evaporate.

'You are holding the hostage here?' he asked.

Jahandar nodded and pointed to a remote corner where a stack of cardboard containers stood. 'The woman is behind that stack. She cannot identify you as she has been blindfolded,' he added while his short stumpy legs tried to keep up with the long strides of the major.

The two corporals separated and walked midway across the warehouse to tactically cover the two men should anything untoward happen. Javid ignored them and sat down on one of the rickety cane chairs near the door and began cleaning his nails with the point of a long knife.

Major Kazemi approached the cartons and on rounding the high stack of illegally imported malt whisky he saw Reem. It was immediately clear that she had been assaulted for someone had ripped her nurse's uniform and unfastened the delicate silk bra to expose her breasts. Only the skimpy panties maintained any modicum of modesty for the young woman. Reem was handcuffed to one of the roof support columns and a black bag covered her head.

An Indian wearing a food-stained cream *kurta* and cradling an ancient AK47 in his lap sat on a small oil drum beside her, his lascivious eyes constantly travelling up and down her indelicately exposed body.

'Who is she,' Kazemi inquired angrily as he studied the woman's condition.

'She's a nurse from the same hospital as Helen Taylor. It appears she has become a close friend of Alan Short.'

'I vaguely recognize the name.'

'He is Stuart Taylor's colleague, Major,' Jahandar said with a smug expression. 'They are also great friends which makes Mr Short my leverage on Taylor to find and retrieve our drugs.'

'And who did that?' the major shouted suddenly, pointing at the tattered state of Reem's clothing that did nothing to protect her dignity.

Jahandar cringed mentally as he realized that his unbridled moment of lust could be exposed. 'One of the hired men who picked her up became a little over-excited and wanted to see and touch the merchandise for himself. At great risk to myself I managed to stop him before he could consider raping the woman.'

'Who was this animal,' Kazemi snarled.

'The man guarding her,' Jahandar swiftly lied, pointing at the Indian. 'His name is Kumar and he cannot understand us as he speaks no Arabic, only Urdu.'

Kazemi strode towards the man who believed he was the subject of praise and looked up at the major with a broad smile on his unwashed face. In one single action the Glock slid from its holster and flipping the safety switch off with his thumb Major Kazemi fired a 9mm round into the grinning face. Only the briefest flicker of surprise showed on the Indian's face before he died and fell to the warehouse floor.

Fifteen metres away Javid leapt to his feet and the two corporals automatically levelled their weapons at him. With his eyes fixed on Javid one of the men checked what had happened and then lowered his gun.

'I will not tolerate that kind of depravity in my organization, Jahandar, do you understand?' Kazemi shouted as he returned the weapon to its holster without bothering to look at the man he had just killed.

Jahandar looked away from the cold, penetrating gaze and nodded towards the young woman. 'I have given Taylor until tomorrow noon to deliver all the boxes or I will kill his friend's girlfriend.'

'You will do precisely what I say and nothing else,' Kazemi ordered, drawing himself up to tower over Jahandar. 'I want no witnesses to this operation and therefore tomorrow as the sun rises at *fajr* prayer time, you will cut this woman's throat. You will then place the knife that was used in the dead Indian's hand and pin a note to his chest with five precise words written in her blood.'

'What words?'

'*Rapist and defiler of women!* Now do you understand me?' Kazemi said, quietly watching Jahandar's face for any sign of disagreement. 'This way her death will not be linked to my import and export activities.'

'Brilliant, Major,' Jahandar said deferentially as he stared at the half-naked woman whilst thinking that it was a waste.

Stuart slammed the rear door on the Hummer and turned to face Walid. 'We have what they want, now how do we guarantee that we can safely exchange the boxes for Reem?'

'I don't know how many they are but we are four which means two marksmen can be hidden with the silenced MP5-SDs while the other two handle the face-to-face confrontation with whoever turns up.'

'Why not get the whole Special Forces team involved?' Stuart asked.

'The more men the less chance of secrecy and we could run the risk of scaring them into running off and killing Reem,' Walid answered in a quiet voice.

'Where and when do we make the exchange?' Alan demanded impatiently.

'I won't know that until I call,' Stuart said as he recalled the number from his address book and hit the dial button. There were a few tense seconds as the phone rang before it was answered.

'You have what I want, Mr Taylor?'

'I do and we will make the exchange at the A'ali burial site.'

'No, Mr Taylor, we will make the exchange where and when I say or the woman dies. Is that clear?'

'Where do you want us to meet?'

'The Tree of Life at sunrise,' the voice demanded and the connection was cut.

'The Tree of Life?' Alan said, mystified.

'It's a giant mesquite tree that is reputed to be four hundred years old. It stands alone in the middle of a small desert on an eight-metre-high sandy hill. The locals believe that the tree's long life is due to Enki, the mythical god of water,' Walid explained.

'And it is reputed to be the original location of the Garden of Eden,' Shehhi reverently added in Arabic.

'That's all very interesting but where exactly is it?' Alan asked.

Stuart gave a small smile. 'It's just over five kilometres south of Jebel Dukhan which at 135 metres above sea level is the highest point in Bahrain,' he said. 'You should know that, Alan,' Stuart added. 'After all, you've been working here as a geologist for the last two years.'

'Ah!' Alan exclaimed. 'You mean the Mountain of Smoke, don't you?'

Stuart nodded. 'That's the rough translation.'

Alan gave a smile. 'Well, I know all about that place because I was doing a survey in that area only last month. When it's humid it is often surrounded by a dense mist which gives the appearance of swirling smoke, hence the name.'

'We can make good use of the Hummer's cross-country strengths by leaving the Hamad Highway near the Jaw Prison and head into the desert using the compass,' Shehhi said confidently.

'I suggest that we don't wait for morning but go later tonight to find the best positions for our weapons. They have to be at a fair distance and out of sight of anyone waiting by the Tree of Life. Walid and Shehhi are best qualified for that. Stuart and I will arrive at the appointed time as though we are by ourselves.'

'I know that the effective range of the suppressed MP5-SD is 180 metres and therefore we'll find cover that gives us a clear view of the Tree without risking being seen when the sun rises,' Shehhi murmured.

Walid patted him on the shoulder and said, 'We'll use two ghillie suits from the Hummer locker,' referring to the desert camouflage they had packed before leaving Saudi Arabia.

The four men got into the 4x4 and Shehhi gunned it into life to drive Stuart and Alan back to the apartment. The two policemen quickly shook hands before leaving and Stuart lingered outside to watch the Hummer pull away into the setting sun until it had completely disappeared in the haze. 'God protect them,' he thought.

Walid stripped and oiled the two MP5-SDs while Shehhi concentrated on his driving. 'We have sufficient ammunition?' he asked and Walid gave the thumbs-up sign. They both fell silent as the road unrolled, their eyes studying every vehicle for any indication that they may be carrying their adversaries.

As the sun sank below the horizon and the muezzin called the faithful to the *maghrib* prayer the traffic dwindled. Within a few minutes they had passed through the village of Askar and were rapidly approaching the infamous Jaw Prison. With a brief glance at the compass on the dashboard Shehhi instinctively slowed and left the highway to venture into the formidable desert.

After a kilometre of jouncing across the sand that was dotted with scrub they found the start of a primitive dusty trail that was clearly used on a regular basis by wild camels. They followed this relatively smooth path until they came upon a more frequently used tarmac road, wind-blown with a thin covering of sand.

'Go left, Sergeant, and then continue for another kilometre before turning right,' Walid instructed as he finished reassembling the second weapon and checking the compass as well as a small folded map for directions.

The Hummer purred along on the comparatively smooth surface, whipping up small whirlpools of golden sand. Shehhi saw tyre tracks leaving the road and turned to follow them into an even more desolate environment.

Walid pointed to the right after they had travelled another kilometre and Shehhi headed towards a dark smudge on the blood-red horizon. 'That's the Tree of Life, Shehhi.'

'It's over four hundred years old and yet it is only ten metres high,' Walid added. 'Nobody knows what source of water keeps it alive in these hot and dry conditions which adds further to the belief that the tree is symbolic of life itself.'

Shehhi grunted in admiration as his keen eyes searched the sandy waste around the Tree. Every undulation was analysed and logged in his brain until he had a topographical picture covering every fold, rise and dip in the sand lying within two hundred metres of the tree. As they drew near to the spreading boughs of the mesquite a small shack caught their eyes and Shehhi slowed to a stop and used his binoculars to study every detail of the dried mud building.

'Looks like an information centre for tourists,' Walid said. 'There's no vehicles so we can assume that any staff who work there have left for the day.'

'The other side of the Tree could provide a good hiding place for the Hummer,' Shehhi said as he swept the slightly undulating landscape with his glasses. 'There appears to be a few small dunes to the north behind which we can hide the vehicle from the approach road. The dunes are under two hundred metres from the Tree and therefore would provide perfect cover for one of the weapons.'

'Drive north-west, Sergeant,' Walid instructed as he peered into the approaching darkness. 'I think we have a very shallow wadi over there which would be ideal for the second weapon.'

The Hummer powered over the rough surface and then slid to a halt on the lip of the little gully in the sand. Walid clipped a walkie-talkie onto his belt and leapt out of the 4x4 with one of the MP5-SDs in one hand and a ghillie suit in the other. The vehicle backed up and then roared away to the distant dunes that were slowly being lost to sight as day was rapidly transformed into a moonless night.

Walid spread the ghillie on the bed of the wadi to lie down. With the weapon by his side he slipped into an uneasy sleep. Shehhi circled the Tree and drove on to the dunes he had spotted earlier. On reaching them he crested the first rise and descended into the slack beyond where he stopped and parked the vehicle. Taking the ghillie suit Shehhi returned to the crest and swept the surface with the camouflaged material until all signs of his tracks had been eliminated. He knew the light breeze would disguise any that remained. With sand filtering into his boots he returned to the Hummer and got in. He switched off the interior courtesy light and set the alarm on his watch as he settled down to wait. Very soon his eyelids became heavy and he slipped into the light sleep of a trained hunter.

Javid mentally praised Jahandar for his foresight in bringing him to the Tree of Life information centre hours before the planned meeting. The caretaker was still on duty but when they told him that they wished to sit quietly and contemplate the possible meaning of the Tree and would be leaving soon anyway the old man had locked up and driven off home in his battered pick-up.

Picking the lock had been a simple task for someone as skilled as Javid and soon he was hiding inside and watching through one of the sand-scoured windows as Jahandar drove off to return to the warehouse in Manama. Another hour elapsed before he saw and then heard the distinctive low rumbling of a Hummer as it approached the rough road that circled the Tree of Life. He watched as it roared off to stop at the wadi he had reconnoitred earlier; a hiss of air escaped his lips as he saw a heavy-set man jump from the vehicle and disappear into the wadi carrying a weapon in one hand and what seemed to be a large bundle of rags in the other.

As the Hummer roared off into the darkness Javid grinned, 'So, they're setting up a crossfire, are they,' he muttered to himself and settled down into the caretaker's chair to make a telephone call.

'They have arrived early, as you predicted,' he said after being connected.

'Then you know what you have to do.' There was a click and the call ended.

Javid waited until he was sure that the men who had arrived were either asleep or preoccupied with their preparations for sunrise before making his move. He opened the door of the shack a mere fraction and studied the starlit terrain for five minutes. With no moon to cast any shadows and no movement or light in the vicinity of the two policemen he decided to make his move and edged the door open to sneak out into the night.

Slipping his sandals off and crouching low he began running across the sand and into the extreme black shadows beneath the Tree of Life. The widespread boughs hissed slightly in the gentle wind that constantly beat grains of sand against his bare ankles. Javid paused and looked towards the wadi and then at the crest of the dune before leaving his temporary sanctuary and sprinting towards the steep slope behind which he knew the Hummer was hidden. Glittering particles of sand captured by the glimmer of starlight flicked up from his heels as he ran and his shoulder muscles tensed, anticipating a bullet that could speed from the distant wadi in less than a second.

Javid reached the first dune and slowly crawled up the slope to look over the crest and down into the slack. The dark shape of the Hummer was directly beneath him and taking all precautions he sidled away until the Hummer was a good fifty metres to his right before attempting to slither down the slope and into the slack. Javid removed a large steel tube from his hip pocket and proceeded to screw it onto the barrel of his automatic before sinking down to begin his slow crawl towards the vehicle. When he was within touching distance of the tailpipe he slipped his favourite thin-bladed knife from its sheath and resting on his elbows he inched his way along the side of the Hummer.

Shehhi had almost drifted into sleep when the door he was leaning against gave way and he felt himself falling backwards. The first thing he glimpsed as his eyes opened was the deadly glitter of a knife blade raised high. Hitting the sand he rolled to his left and kicked upwards with his feet. A fiery pain seared through his leg as the blade descended and sliced deep into his thigh muscle. His hand snatched at the automatic in his side holster as he attempted to twist away from the immediate danger of a second knife strike when a loud cough sounded by his ear. The bullet from the silenced automatic creased his shoulder and he rolled the other way to kick up at his assailant with the undamaged leg. Shehhi missed but managed to slide his weapon free from its holster and was raising it in a two-handed grip, searching for the assassin, when the weapon above coughed once more.

The bullet entered his forehead and jerked his head back into the unyielding sand before the sound made by Javid's gun could travel the same distance.

To make sure of his kill Javid slid his knife free from the muscular thigh and cut the Saudi officer's throat. He then ran to the crest of the dune and stared into the darkness concealing the distant wadi. He waited with a pounding heart until he was sure he could detect no sign of movement coming his way. Only then did his heart begin to slow and his shoulders slump as the familiar post-kill relaxation kicked in; the excessive release of adrenalin fading with each passing second.

Javid slid back down the dune and went to the back of the Hummer where he found the small wooden boxes. He quickly lifted them out and stacked them on the sand. He had been given strict instructions on what to do and he began the task of transferring the boxes, two at a time, to the base of the Tree. Within the encircling steel rail intended to keep tourists at a safe distance from the ancient trunk he began digging with the foldable spade he had taken from the Hummer. When the hole was big enough he buried the boxes and smoothed the sand until all signs of any disturbance had been eradicated.

The sweating killer gave one last lingering look in the direction of the wadi and sensing no signs of life he grunted in satisfaction and began loping away from the Tree of Life. Stealing the Hummer for his getaway would have alerted the man in the wadi and given him a perfect target in his night-vision scope the moment he left the cover of the dunes. He preferred the silence of barefoot jogging and he followed the trail that led back to the metalled road where he had arranged for Jahandar to pick him up within the hour. With the drugs safely hidden they could return to the city to deal with the young woman in the factory as ordered by the Magician.

17

The insistent vibration of the cellphone in his breast pocket instantly woke Walid. He opened his eyes and judged by the lack of light in the east that it was still far from the appointed time for the exchange.

'They're on to us, Walid,' Alan said when he answered. 'They're planning some form of trap for you and Shehhi during the night.'

'How do you know this?' Walid whispered.

'Reem has managed to escape. She hasn't told me how yet but I now have her safe in my car. Her Farsi isn't that good but she understood that the men who were holding her were planning some kind of trap at the Tree of Life.'

'I'll tell Shehhi, Alan. Thanks for the warning. Glad to hear Reem is okay,' he added before ending the call and picking up the walkie-talkie. He knew something was wrong when Shehhi failed to respond and he swiftly donned the ghillie, checked his weapon and tentatively raised his head above the edge of the wadi.

The silhouette of the Tree of Life could be faintly discerned and all was serenely still. Walid swept the area with his night glasses and was satisfied until on his third pass he noticed that something had changed: the door to the tourist centre was open.

Walid dropped the glasses and raising the weapon used its more powerful scope to study the door. Although he was unable to detect any movement in the darkness he still cocked the MP5-SD and slipped the safety off. He edged himself over the rim of the wadi and began crawling on his elbows towards the building. Despite the early morning chill the all-encompassing ghillie suit soon had him sweating heavily and when he finally reached the small building moisture was trickling into every crevice of his body. At the open door Walid raised himself to a crouch with the weapon held tight into his shoulder and ready to fire. He kicked the door wide open and jumped inside, tracking the barrel left and right to cover the dark interior. It was completely deserted and Walid straightened up and lowered the gun. Unclipping the flashlight from his belt he studied the room in minute detail and spotted the cigarette butts that had been stubbed out on the desktop.

'No tourist guide would do that to his desk,' he murmured. With growing anxiety Walid left the shack and immediately noticed a solitary set of bare footprints going towards the Tree of Life and back again. The marks were obviously made by someone who wished to travel soundlessly.

An icy moment of fear gripped him and he quickly switched off his flashlight and bending double he began trotting towards the distant dunes where he calculated Sergeant Shehhi had parked the Hummer. Puffing heavily he topped the crest of the first dune and instantly spotted the Hummer one hundred metres to his right. Walid slithered down into the slack and ran towards the vehicle, his vision blurred by the flow of sweat that ran from his hairline.

He saw a dark shadow sprawled on the sand beneath the driver's open door. 'Shehhi,' he croaked, half hoping that it was somebody else's body but on slamming the door shut he was able to see his friend's face. Blood had trickled from the neat round hole in his forehead and the sand was stained with blood from the slash beneath his chin.

Walid threw himself down to kneel beside his sergeant and grief distorted his face as tears flowed unashamedly down his cheeks. His friend and dependable back-up in many life-threatening situations had been heartlessly slaughtered. Walid opened the door and reached for the sergeant's ghillie on the driver's seat and spread it gently over his body. He then took the phone from his pocket and was about to dial when it started warbling his favourite ringtone.

A voice hissed malevolently, 'You tried to trick me, Major, and for that you will now pay the ultimate price.'

'And you'll dearly wish you hadn't killed my sergeant,' Walid shouted uncontrollably. 'You'll be begging me for a merciful death by the time I've finished with you.'

'Control yourself, Major Safa. The two of you were heavily armed and waiting for me at the Tree of Life. What did you expect me to do?'

'If you had simply made the exchange in the morning nothing would have happened.'

'You expect me to believe that?'

'You are holding the young nurse which meant we dared not fire in case you took revenge on her. However, I have to explain that we were also there in case you reneged on the deal,' Walid explained.

'Well, that's all rather academic now and I should add that neither of us will have the nurse for I shall return to the city and cut her throat.' There was a soft click and Walid was left holding a dead phone.

'Thank God, Alan's got her in a safe place,' he murmured aloud. The major slowly sank down on tired legs to squat on the sand beside his old comrade as he speed-dialled police headquarters and requested to speak to Captain Dabal.

Reem's captors disappeared behind the packing cases and she listened to their receding footsteps and the clatter of the steel door opening and closing. Silence fell upon the warehouse and she tried once more to slip her hands through the handcuffs. Even with the bag over her head and despite her limited Arabic after six years in the Middle East she understood that they were leaving her to prepare a lethal trap for Stuart and Alan.

The young nurse moved her jaw until the crude gag slipped down. Then shaking her head violently Reem leant forward and was rewarded by the bag sliding off her head. The sunlight streaming through one of the dusty windows briefly blinded her and she squinted until her pupils were dilated. Reem gasped on seeing the crumpled figure of her executed guard in the shadows.

She could now hear the faint buzzing of flies and her eyes wandered up the body to the shattered head lying in its own pool of blood. Although she was used to the sight of extreme trauma in the hospital she was still forced to look away and take deep breaths in an effort not to gag.

The sound of a muezzin gave Reem a reasonable indication of the time and knowing that her kidnappers could return at any time she quickly looked around for any means of escape. The stacked packing cases obscured her view of the whole warehouse and she was limited to the area at the rear that had a small glazed office in one corner and light machinery in the other. Although the light was fading Reem could see that the floor was littered with swarf from a small metal lathe.

Reem bent her knees and with her back against the hard steel column she slowly slid down until her hands could touch the concrete floor. She felt arounds but was unable to detect any of the small coils of metal shavings; as her thigh muscles tightened in painful protest she sidled around the column until she finally touched something.

She blindly selected a small coil of the razor-sharp metal and after slicing her fingertips a few times managed to straighten it out. Pushing herself upright again she began to twist and turn the metal strip in the lock of the handcuffs. It took her precisely one hour to find the right angle until she heard a satisfying click and the cruel bracelet dropped open releasing her hand. With a sigh of relief Reem slowly brought her arms forward. Having had them forcibly held behind her for so long had stiffened both shoulders and she bit her lip to prevent herself from crying out in pain.

Without a backward glance at the body Reem hurried into the inner office and was astonished to see that the floor was ankle deep in pistachio shells. There were dozens of empty cellophane bags scattered everywhere and she could see by the printed legends that they were the retail bags for the nuts.

Reem swept sheets of dust-covered paper off the steel desk and uncovered a very old Bakelite landline phone. She raised the handset to her ear but there was no dialling tone: running her fingers along the old cord she also found that it wasn't connected. With feet crunching noisily on the discarded shells Reem gingerly left the office and avoiding the scattering of metal shavings she cautiously went round the packing cases. Discovering that she really was alone in the building she began walking towards the distant door but fear increased her pace until she was running hard whilst clumsily trying to refasten her bra and the remaining buttons on her uniform.

Just as she reached out to grasp the handle she heard voices in the reception office on the other side of the door. In panic she looked around for somewhere to hide and in the dark shadows on the opposite side of the warehouse she spotted a large white removals van. Reem slipped her shoes off and ran silently across the concrete. When she stopped to lean against the vehicle the door behind her opened and the familiar voices of her two kidnappers could clearly be heard arguing in Farsi.

Fumbling in the shadows she found that the rear door had been left unlocked and as she tentatively pulled the lever down angry exclamations from the other side of the packing cases broadcast her escape. Reem quickly hid herself just as the whole warehouse was suddenly illuminated by the brilliance of white arc lights. She held her breath as running feet crossed the warehouse towards where she was hiding.

'The main doors were left unlocked,' a high-pitched voice said angrily. 'She could be talking to the cops right now.'

'Then we should get out now and stop wasting time,' Javid said. 'We've got the drugs and they can be recovered at any time I choose.'

'Check the van first. The silly bitch may have hidden in the back instead of running for it,' Jahandar shouted as he returned to the outer reception office.

The sound of sandals flip-flopped closer, matching the beat of Reem's heart until the van's rear doors were suddenly thrown open and a bright flashlight probed the interior like the finger of death. The whole vehicle creaked on its suspension as the killer jumped up to stalk around inside. The brilliance of the beam of light left no corner untouched and with a grunt of disappointment Javid leapt down again.

'Nothing here,' he shouted and Reem heard Jahandar's faint reply exhorting him to hurry. Javid's sandals beat out a faster rhythm as he ran to the warehouse door to join his boss outside.

Silence fell once more throughout the cavernous warehouse and Reem, shaking like a leaf, rolled out from under the van and stood up. She crept to the door and pressed her ear against the warm metal to listen for any movement on the other side. All was as still as a morgue and when she opened the door there was no sign of the two kidnappers. Reem cautiously peered round the doorframe to see a steady flow of cars and trucks passing both ways. Headlights briefly flashed across the entrance to illuminate her white uniform with its blood-stained cuffs.

Realizing that she was in no danger Reem backed into the outer reception office and picked up the phone on the desk. Hearing a dialling tone she tapped in Alan's number and waited anxiously for him to answer.

'Alan Short, how can I help you?' the familiar baritone voice asked and Reem heaved a sigh of relief.

'Alan, it's Reem!'

'My God, Reem, where are you?' Alan said and she felt his concern conveying a welcome protective feeling.

'I don't know where but it's an old warehouse and judging by the smell it is near to fishing boats,' she said as she turned to flick through the small stack of invoices in an out-tray. 'I think the company is called Two Seas Marine Supplies but the address on the invoices is only given as a post-box number.'

'I'll find you, Reem, don't worry,' Alan said confidently as he waved the piece of paper he had written on. Stuart took it from him and began dialling directory enquiries.

'Don't stay in the warehouse, stay nearby but only show yourself when you see me arrive. Is that understood?' Alan said, sensing Reem's fear.

'Please, don't be long, Alan, I'm afraid they might return.'

Alan quickly reassured her that it was most unlikely while he watched Stuart use the other phone. Seeing his friend scribble something down he gave one last reassurance and said goodbye to the distraught woman.

After a few brief words the two men agreed that now that the curfew had been temporarily lifted Alan would go straight to Reem while Stuart went to the Tree of Life to give extra support to Walid and Shehhi at the time of their appointment with Jahandar.

It had taken the operator only seconds to give Stuart the address of the company and three minutes for Alan to make it to his car and race towards the Umm Al Hassam district.

Stuart called Helen but it was the corporal who answered the phone. He explained to the young officer that he was going to the Tree of Life to meet Walid and to tell his wife that he would see her later in the morning.

Reem crossed the narrow street using a gap in the traffic and was standing in an alley between two decrepit businesses when she recognized the car moving slowly towards her and coming to a standstill outside the warehouse. She waited until she saw Alan's familiar figure get out of the vehicle. He looked around frantically as he searched for her and she stepped out of the black shadows and into the poorly lit street. Alan waved and ran across the street, dangerously weaving his way between the moving cars and took her in his arms.

'I managed to escape from them, Alan,' she sobbed into his shoulder. 'They murdered one of their own men and his body is still in there.' She waved a hand in the rough direction of the warehouse.

'You're safe now,' Alan said as he tightened his arms round the openly crying woman in an effort to comfort her. 'This place will soon be crawling with police so I don't think they'll be returning here in a hurry.'

Reem looked up and then with a start recalled Javid's words. 'They said they had laid a trap for you and Stuart,' she said hurriedly. 'You must warn Stuart now.'

'They are obviously planning to bushwhack us in the morning. We'll take extra care when we go to the Tree of Life.'

'The trap wasn't about tomorrow morning but tonight, Alan,' Reem said wide-eyed.

'My God, the trap won't be for us but for Walid and Shehhi,' Alan said in alarm. 'And now Stuart will also be caught in the same trap.' He quickly shepherded Reem across the road and into his car where he dialled Walid's number. After a few seconds he heard his friend's sleep-blurred voice. He rapidly warned Walid of the kidnappers' plan and Stuart's forthcoming arrival before hanging up and driving back to his apartment. Reem slowly slumped sideways to rest her dishevelled head against Alan's shoulder. Exhaustion took its toll and she sank into a shallow yet troubled sleep.

With an irritated swat at a mosquito that had settled on his wrist Major Kazemi picked up the phone and dialled. It rang for a couple of minutes before it was finally answered.

'You have my property?' Kazemi demanded as he hit the dashboard with the flat of his hand. There was a brief silence during which the major turned his hand over to find the squashed remains of the insect.

'I have your precious boxes and they are in a perfectly safe place,' Jahandar replied.

'And the woman is dead?'

There was an even longer pause before the drug baron timidly replied. 'Unfortunately, while I was recovering your property the woman managed to escape.'

Kazemi drew in a deep breath and let it out with an angry roar. 'You had your orders, Jahandar,' he shouted. 'Carry them out, now.'

'But she has gone.'

'Then find her and finish the job.'

'I will put my best man onto it, right away,' Jahandar whined and he gave Javid a piercing look that left the killer unmoved.

'You will then give my property to the Englishman who will call your number very soon. The name he will give you is Tony Whitmore and you are to make arrangements to hand over four of the cases plus the Al Aziziyah address in Saudi Arabia for him to make a delivery. You will then store the eight remaining cases in a safe place and I do mean safe, this time,' Kazemi said in a low menacing tone. 'Make any mistakes this time and you'll greatly regret you ever heard of me or the Magician.' With that threat the connection was abruptly cut.

Jahandar closed his phone and tapped Javid on the shoulder. 'Take me to the marina at Zalluk and make it quick,' he muttered. 'I then want you to return to Manama and find that woman. When you do just make sure you kill her and anyone else who is with her.'

Javid accelerated away from the Umm Al Hassam district and using the highway sped towards the north-west coast of Bahrain to connect with the road that led directly to the coastal spa town of Zalluk.

The dazzling white Boston Whaler Conquest was moored fifteen metres offshore and was just visible in the gloomy evening light. It was one of the many large pleasure craft anchored in the exclusive marina used by wealthy boat owners. Javid drove towards the harbour until he was forced to slow to a stop at the guarded entrance to the yacht club. The uniformed man on duty yawned and stepped out of his small office but waved the car on when he saw the membership badge in the windscreen. Javid drove directly to the spot on the sea wall where the whaler's dinghy was tied up; Jahandar left the car and waited until Javid had driven back the way they had come before waddling in the taxing humidity to the small rowboat.

Three dinars induced a fisherman who was lounging between tides to row Jahandar out to the ten-metre sports boat that was gently rising and falling on the light sea swell that had slipped past the harbour wall.

After agreeing to return on Jahandar's signal he very quickly rowed back to shore to enjoy a long shisha pipe at the café.

Jahandar quickly went below deck to start the engine and switch on the air-conditioning and it wasn't long before the cabin was awash with super-cooled air. Feeling more at ease in the pliant comfort of calf-leather seating and surrounded by mahogany panelling Jahandar poured gin and tonic into cut-crystal and waited for Mr Whitmore to call.

Javid drove directly to the hospital where he knew the young nurse worked in the hope that she would return. Not wishing to draw attention to himself he drove within the national speed limit with dipped headlights and scrupulously slowed to drive below the lower limit in the urban areas.

The nondescript Ford crawled into the car park and parked as far away from the main entrance to the Bahrain Specialist Hospital as possible. Javid sank back in the seat and fixed his heavy-lidded predatory look on everybody leaving or climbing the steps up to the brightly illuminated entrance. He was concealed by the heavily tinted windows and Javid was confident that the car wouldn't cause any undue interest if checked by security staff with Traffic Registration in Manama.

Switching on the interior light Javid started checking his armoury. First on the list was to wipe Shehhi's blood from the finely honed carbon blade and slip the knife back into its hidden sheath. He then took the automatic from his pocket, disassembled it and oiled every moving part. He ran the cleaning rod through the barrel a number of times and with great care he reassembled the weapon and checked the firing mechanism. When he was perfectly satisfied with the action he replaced the magazine and screwed the suppressor back onto the barrel before putting the gun down on the seat beside him. All the time he had been working he had used his peripheral vision to keep watch on the comings and goings at the hospital entrance but of Reem there was no sign.

The muezzin at the nearby mosque had begun his call for the nightfall *isha'a* prayer when the cellphone began playing the first few bars of Mama ya Mama, a popular Arabic hit. Javid picked it up and was immediately assailed by the voice of a very angry Jahandar. 'Where the hell are you. What are you doing?'

'I'm obeying your orders and waiting at the hospital for the woman to return to work so that I can do mine,' Javid replied morosely.

'You're totally wasting your time. She is bound to be at her home, surrounded by bodyguards, and recovering from her experience,' Jahandar thundered. 'Where does she live, Javid?'

'I don't know,' Javid said sheepishly.

'Idiot. Now listen carefully, I have just had a call from Mr Whitmore and you are to give him four of the cases at nine o'clock tomorrow.'

Javid suddenly sat upright. 'I have to return to the Tree of Life tonight?' he said in a suspicious manner. 'The police could still be there.'

'No questions, do as you're told and just dig them all up and deliver them to the marina in the morning. A tall Englishman dressed in a cream linen suit will meet with you and arrange the transfer of the cases to his vehicle. Then you will leave and return to the task of finding that damned woman.'

Javid drew in a deep breath to repeat his concern about the police presence but realizing the futility of such an argument decided against it and hung up before Jahandar had a chance to insult him any more. He drove slowly from the hospital car park and headed out of the city and back to the Tree of Life. Tension knotted the muscles in his scrawny neck for he knew that there was a very good chance that the police would still be there. If he waited until they had left he would have the problem of regular morning staff opening the site early which would drastically reduce his window of opportunity. Javid shrugged resignedly as he turned onto the Hawar Highway and headed south. It was not long after switching to the King Hamad Highway and bypassing Jaw Prison and the Royal Academy of Police that he turned right onto a sand-blown road that would take him to the camel track that led to the Tree of Life.

Javid was tempted to leave the road and cut across the desert as the crow flies but he didn't trust the old Ford sedan to survive the rough, undulating surface. He dipped the headlights when he saw stationary lights in the distance and slowed to a crawl. When he estimated that he was only a kilometre from the lights Javid pulled off the road to stop and cut his lights completely. He got out and scrambled onto the roof to gain a better view and calculated that there were at least four vehicles. However, the lack of any moon made seeing anything detailed absolutely impossible.

Picking up the automatic and patting his sheathed knife beneath his shirt he began to lope across the sand in the direction of the car lights. His open sandals left his toes vulnerable to the occasional sharp stones but he instinctively suppressed any cries of pain that might alert those studying the terrain around the Tree.

After ten minutes Javid was close enough to creep past the tourist reception building and be able to identify the Hummer parked at the foot of the first dune. There was also a white police cruiser with its distinctive dark blue stripes and a white van that Javid assumed belonged to the coroner. A Jeep, the fourth vehicle parked alongside the big 4x4 was unfamiliar and Javid crouched down and searched the area to locate each of the policemen present.

Two men were in deep discussion by the Jeep. One was clearly a Western expatriate and the other, wearing a Saudi police uniform, was stocky with a bushy moustache. Four more policemen whom Javid identified as Bahrainis by their uniforms were in conference over the shrouded figure on a stretcher at the back of the white van. Javid stayed where he was and waited, searching for more officers. His patience was rewarded when he spotted two men in white coveralls coming over the dune and slithering down the soft, sandy slope towards the vehicles.

'Crime scene investigators,' Javid muttered to himself as he watched the two men join the four officers. 'Well, they won't find anything I didn't want them to find,' he chuckled quietly as he flattened himself into the sand.

Once more his assassin's patience was tested for it was another hour before the body of Shehhi was loaded into the van and driven off, followed by the officers in the cruiser. The vehicles passed within fifty metres of Javid's unseen prone figure and it was not long before the Hummer and the Jeep also left the symbolic Tree of Life, the sole witness to the callous butchery. Javid watched them fade into the night without sensing the wave of hatred for the killer that radiated from the Hummer.

As the sound of the engines faded and only the light hiss of blown sand could be heard Javid rose to his feet and jogged towards the Tree. He had equipped himself with a small spade and after identifying the exact spot he began digging.

The dull thud of metal striking wood told Javid he was in the right spot and he proceeded to unearth the cases until he had all twelve stacked neatly under the Tree. He pulled his sleeve up to check the time before throwing down the spade and trotting back to his car. He approached the Ford with extreme caution born of habit and seeing nothing untoward he ran the last few metres to climb in and drive without lights towards the Tree.

Forty minutes later, with the cases neatly stacked in the boot and on the back seat, he left the Hawar Highway and headed towards Zallaq to keep his rendezvous with Mr Whitmore. His mind briefly wandered and a wicked smirk spread across his face as he thought about the subsequent hunt for the young nurse and her agonizing demise at his hand after he has had his pleasure.

18

Stuart felt a sense of foreboding when he spotted the police cruiser and the coroner's van as he stopped by the famous Tree of Life. The burly figure of Walid detached itself from the small group of police officers and went to meet the geologist.

'What happened?' Stuart called out as Walid drew near to his car.

'Terrible news. Sergeant Shehhi has been murdered,' Walid replied, his voice breaking.

'Good God, Walid! I am so sorry,' Stuart said and then reluctantly asked his friend. 'How did it happen?'

The desolate Walid slumped down on the sand and leant against the Jeep. 'They have already established that the killer had arrived before Shehhi and myself had taken up our positions. Forensic evidence showed he had been hiding in the building and it's my guess he had been spying on us both and pinpointed our respective positions for the morning meeting between you and the kidnappers.'

'But how did he manage to kill someone as experienced as Shehhi?'

'Some scuffs on the inside of the Hummer door suggest that Shehhi had been leaning against it when it was yanked open, causing him to fall backwards. He was then stabbed in the thigh and shot in the head after falling out onto the sand. The medical examiner said that the killer cut Shehhi's throat after the shooting as there was a lot less blood from that severe trauma than is normal.'

'Strange thing to do after you've killed someone.'

'Not if you're uncertain of the head shot being fatal or if you are simply a psychopath,' Walid growled. 'One thing they couldn't clear up was why Shehhi had been stabbed in the leg before being shot dead. The large amount of blood that had flowed from that wound meant his heart had still been pumping healthily.'

'I guess we'll never know how it happened,' Stuart said, his voice heavy with sympathy for his friend's loss as he pulled on his arm to help him to his feet. 'I just know that we have the task of finding the bastard and bringing him to justice.'

'Or killing him like a rabid dog,' Walid declared harshly.

Stuart nodded slowly. 'But first we have to visit the hospital and break the news to Noor.'

'Shehhi was always secretive about his private life but I do know that the two of them had formed a strong bond in the short time they'd known each other. I was ever hopeful that he would meet a nice girl one day, marry and raise a family of his own,' Walid said sadly.

'I guess she'll take his death badly?'

'It'll break her heart.'

'I did overhear that the forensic study revealed something else,' Stuart said with a thoughtful expression. 'It would seem that the cases taken from the Hummer had been dragged a short distance before all tracks in the sand were brushed away, possibly by the single palm frond that was discovered lying near the Tree of Life.'

The two watched as the police cruiser and the coroner's van carrying Shehhi's remains drove away. 'Then I suggest that it's our turn to set a trap,' Walid said and they solemnly shook hands under the stars in an unspoken vow to avenge the slaughter of their comrade.

The friends climbed into their respective vehicles and drove to the main road that led back to city. There they hid the Hummer that Walid had been driving behind a row of palms that lined the highway and using a small hand compass drove the Jeep back into the desert, taking a wide circuitous route that would bring them back to the Tree of Life. It wasn't long before they encountered the familiar dunes and with lights switched off they approached to within a kilometre of the Tree before stopping in a slack and killing the engine. Both men struggled ankle-deep across dune after dune with fine sand filling their shoes and rubbing their heels painfully until they reached the last crest that overlooked the Tree of Life.

Walid removed his Yukon Tracker infra-red binoculars from the case and scanned the area surrounding the Tree. For the next two hours the two took turns in performing this ritual before Stuart suddenly jerked upright. The glasses were no longer scanning but fixed on headlights approaching the spot and he reached to touch Walid on the shoulder without removing his eyes from the binoculars.

Walid squeezed Stuart's arm for he had also seen the lights. The headlights were painful to look at through the light-intensifying glasses and Stuart lowered them and wiped tears from his eyes. The car stopped a few metres short of the protective barrier around the tree and the lights were extinguished. They both watched as a shadowy figure left the car and strode to a spot close to the tree. They waited patiently until they heard the faint *chink* of metal on rock that told them that the man was digging. They continued to wait and Stuart briefly used the glasses again to see a small stack of boxes growing beside a hole as Javid lifted each one out.

'Do we take him?' Stuart whispered as he handed the glasses to Walid.

'As much as I'd like to tear the head off the bastard with my bare hands, I think we should be patient as this could be the big opportunity to find out who his contacts are and who's heading this drug-smuggling operation. With a bit of luck we could end up taking them all down, Stuart.'

Stuart nodded and smiled grimly. 'So we follow this one and kill him later when we've been introduced to his boss?'

'In memory of Shehhi, I'll kill them all,' Walid murmured as he continued to watch the toiling man beneath the concealment of night.

As he lay awake suffering the rasping snores of his mistress, Major Kazemi was still fuming about Reem's escape and Jahandar's words were still ringing in his ears when the loud warbling of his phone abruptly interrupted his ugly thoughts.

He nudged the buxom form beside him and was rewarded with an annoyed grunt and a naked shoulder turning away from him. Esraa was a married woman who at first had thought that a tall, handsome police major might be the ideal daring knight who would rescue her from the arranged, loveless marriage to an obese man twice her age. Esraa soon realized her mistake—the handsome major was far from romantically inclined and only used her to relieve the sexual frustration caused by the breakdown of his own marriage. Her 'gallant' major had even fallen into the insulting habit of putting one hundred dinars into her purse before she left the shabby apartment he rented for their sweaty encounters. Esraa constantly felt abused but continued to tolerate Kazemi's sexual depravity as the only means of injecting a little excitement into what was a dull, pointless existence.

The drowsy woman ignored the persistent nudging in the small of her back and kept her eyes tightly closed. With his patience pushed to the limit the major finally leant across the woman who was reeking of stale whisky and grabbed the phone. The caller was one of the police corporals who was on night duty in the communications centre.

'Sorry to trouble you at this hour, sir, but I've just received news that Sergeant Shehhi of the Saudi Arabian special police force has been murdered, by a person or persons unknown, in the vicinity of the Tree of Life,' he said in a brisk, almost cheerful tone of voice. The corporal then winced as the major's phone was thrown to hit a bedroom wall with a splintering crash before it cut to silence.

The tousled head beside him rose off the pillow and then dropped again as Kazemi roared out in anger, 'That bloody stupid Iranian!'

The enraged major grabbed Esraa's mobile phone and began dialling a number while repeatedly kicking the recumbent figure on her plump rear. 'Coffee, make me coffee now,' he shouted at the sleep-befuddled woman. Esraa rolled out from under the covers and staggered to her feet as an ill-tempered voice pierced Kazemi's eardrum.

'Who the hell is this,' Jahandar shrilled.

'You stupid man, you let your man kill a police officer,' Kazemi shrieked back.

There was a moment of static silence and Jahandar spoke in much more subdued tones. 'So what? You wanted your property and we got it for you the hard way and the four boxes will be given to Mr Whitmore in the morning.'

'So what? You ask me "so what" after that imbecile you employ killed an officer of the Saudi Arabian police who, incidentally, is on special duties involving illegal drug trafficking? This stupid act could result in massive political repercussions and questions will undoubtedly be asked that may prove embarrassing for me.'

'Nothing will link this death to me or to you and the whole thing will blow over in a couple of days,' Jahandar insisted. 'By that time the delivery will have been made and the goods distributed right across the peninsular. All evidence gone.' The high voice grated on Kazemi's nerves but he found he had to accept the logic of the man's words.

'And what about the woman called Reem?'

'Javid will be taking care of her after he has met with Mr Whitmore.'

'Make sure it looks like an accident. I don't want it to be vaguely linked to the death of the Saudi or to the kidnapping. Is that clear?'

'Perfectly, Major.'

'How do you know my rank?' Kazemi demanded, astonished by Jahandar's use of his rank.

'Remember, I met with you at the warehouse when you were in uniform. I'm very familiar with badges of rank, Major.' Jahandar underlined his point with a sardonic slur.

The calm manner in which Jahandar answered the question had further annoyed the major and he abruptly ended the call by tossing the phone back onto the table. He lay back against the pillow and thought about his next steps. He couldn't return to his own apartment or the office for fear of being arrested and he needed the proceeds from all twelve boxes before attempting to leave the country. As his forehead wrinkled in concentration his voluptuous mistress wandered back into the bedroom carrying two espressos. He watched as Esraa approached the bed, her full breasts swaying with each step taken and the old familiar sensation in his groin presaged his growing passion. All strategic thoughts were swept from his mind to be replaced by lust as he took the proffered cup and placed it beside hers on the table. He then reached up and grasped warm flesh before tumbling a surprised Esraa down onto the bed. Breathing heavily he rolled over on top of her and began forcing his legs between her reluctant thighs while burying his face in her neck. Esraa sighed and turned her head to look through the bedroom window at the flashing neon lights across the street. As the colour reflected on her face alternated between blue and yellow she finally gave up the struggle and resigned herself to yet another bout of violent coupling that would further brutalize her youthful fantasies of romance and love.

Jahandar put the phone down and went up the short stairway to the open deck at the stern of the Boston Whaler that was now moored at the quay. After the heated conversation with Kazemi he knew he wouldn't be able to sleep. He lowered his cumbersome figure into the moulded seating and had just raised the glass of brandy to his lips when he spotted headlights. They had paused at the security office and were now slowly entering the marina. As the vehicle drove along the quayside he recognized the old Ford that Javid had been driving earlier that day. The car stopped forty metres from the cruiser and the interior courtesy light briefly revealed the shadowy figure of Javid.

Jahandar downed the remaining drops of brandy and raised his hand to summon the man who immediately scuttled across the cobbles and jumped aboard. 'Why have you come into the marina?' Jahandar hissed as Javid sat beside him.

'It would seem more suspicious if I slept in the car. If you recall, both the villa and the warehouse have been exposed and are most probably being watched by the police as we talk. The spare bunks on your fishing boat seemed more preferable to being spotted on the street,' Javid said, his surly manner not going unnoticed by his employer.

'You have the boxes in the car,' Jahandar asked, jerking a thumb in the direction of the parked Ford, and Javid nodded.

'Good. I've made arrangements for you to meet Whitmore in the morning at the Bahrain International Circuit which is only a short distance from here.'

'The Formula One race track? Isn't that a little too exposed for a daylight transfer?'

'Firstly, Javid, there will be no racing and as there are no events imminent the place will be deserted and secondly, you'll drive past the main spectators' entrance as well as the car parks and turn down the approach road that leads to the pit area. Whitmore will be parked two hundred metres from the main road. That's where you will transfer only four of the boxes to his car,' Jahandar explained as though talking to a child and Javid grunted in reply. 'I would now recommend that you get some sleep for you have an early meeting with Mr Whitmore at seven o'clock.'

As Javid followed Jahandar down into the cabin two figures flitted from shadow to shadow until they had reached the Ford. Walid tested the door handle and found that Javid, in his haste to report to his boss, had neglected to lock the car. With ears keenly attuned for any sounds coming from the Boston Whaler the two men began the arduous task of transferring the boxes to the Jeep that was parked close to the marina entrance gates.

Walid's police identity card had enabled them to enter the marina and now, carrying box after box, they ran on bare feet suffering the sharp flints in the rough shale that made up the road. It was four in the morning when Stuart slid behind the wheel and started the engine with his fingers crossed. After a three-point turn they slowly purred away into the night while the drug smugglers snored and wheezed in deep sleep.

The call of the muezzin woke Jahandar and throwing on a silk robe he left the main cabin and kicked the snoring figure lying on the bunk bed in the lounge before stumbling sleepily to the coffee percolator. 'Wake up and get a move on, Javid, you've got an important meeting in precisely one hour.'

Javid's animal instincts brought him to full consciousness and he threw the thin sheet off his naked body and leapt to his feet.

'And get some clothes on, you look disgusting,' Jahandar added while ladling ground coffee into the filter.

Javid threw the big man an irritable look as he began gathering up his clothes that had been carelessly scattered the night before. 'There's plenty of time,' he muttered. 'It'll only take fifteen minutes to get there.'

'And you'd better not be late,' Jahandar snarled.

Javid rinsed his hands and mouth at the tiny basin before noisily using the toilet. The full, rich aroma of filtering coffee greeted him when he emerged and he greedily snatched one of the filled cups to drink outside as he studied the quayside. Although the sun had yet to rise a few powerboat owners were already preparing their vessels for a day's cruising. Javid ignored the occasional friendly wave in his direction.

Jahandar struggled up the few steps and sat down, looking up at the killer as though expecting immediate action. 'Stop daydreaming, Javid and get going,' he commanded. 'It's now quarter to the hour and Whitmore will be waiting.' His falsetto voice cut through Javid's thoughts and he tossed the coffee grounds that remained in his cup over the side.

'I'm going,' Javid grunted and he leapt ashore and hurried over to the parked Ford. The door opened to his touch and it wasn't until he sat behind the wheel that he fully grasped the fact that he hadn't locked the vehicle the night before.

'Shit,' he muttered, giving a guilty glance over his shoulder towards the moored Whaler where Jahandar was coldly staring back at him. It was then that he noticed that the covered boxes stacked on the back seat were no longer there. Javid quickly started the car and accelerated along the quayside to leave the marina. After a while he pulled over and stopped the car. He leapt from the car and a quick check showed that the boxes he had hidden in the boot had also vanished. The colour in his face drained to become a sickly yellow and Javid slowly climbed back into the Ford and gripped the wheel tightly.

'Jahandar is not going to like this,' he thought and a shiver went through him. The loss, for the second time, of heroin with an estimated street value of $13 million left him feeling paralysed and Javid sat transfixed for a good five minutes before a viable plan began to form.

He started the engine and drove quickly to the Bahrain International Circuit. As instructed, he ignored the turn-off to the main entrance and only turned left when he reached the road leading to the competitors' pits and general service areas.

He immediately spotted Whitmore's Mercury which was parked facing him and Javid drove on past to execute a U-turn at the junction. As he slowly returned to the waiting car Javid checked behind and in front for any other vehicles before slowing to a stop alongside the large sedan. He powered his window down and waited until Whitmore had done the same before attempting to speak.

'You are here to collect something?' Javid asked in a conspiratorial manner.

'Four boxes! You have four boxes and the address I have to take them to?' Whitmore snapped, eager to be away from such an unsavoury-looking character.

'No,' Javid said, raising the automatic and reaching across the intervening gap to press the large suppression cyclinder against the official's temple. 'They were stolen from you, Mr Whitmore, by an interfering person who will shortly pay for his action,' he added and before the trade officer could react he pulled the trigger twice.

Javid quickly dropped the automatic onto his passenger seat and accelerated away. As he approached the main road he checked behind for any movement and was satisfied to see that the early-morning desert silence remained undisturbed by any human activity. It took him fourteen minutes to return to the Boston Whaler and he parked in exactly the same spot as he had earlier that day. Jahandar was sitting in the stern indulging in an early shisha and puffing clouds of blue smoke that wafted across the harbour in the light breeze. The sun had yet to make sitting outside impossible and Javid leapt aboard to sit beside the smoking man.

'It went well?' Jahandar asked. 'Four boxes transferred and the rest hidden safely?'

Javid nodded confidently. 'Whitmore was there and I gave him the boxes as instructed. The other eight have been returned to the same place by the Tree of Life as I thought that it would be the safest place for them. The police would never think of returning to the scene of a crime to look for something buried there.'

Jahandar gave a nod of satisfaction and took a deep draw before expelling a cloud of apple-scented smoke above his head.

'Now go and find the nurse and kill her,' he murmured as he leant back and closed his eyes as he savoured the sweetly scented smoke.

Major Kazemi received the news from Jahandar just before the midday *dhuhr* prayer and he immediately dialled the unlisted number he had been given by the sheikh.

'Yes, Major Kazemi?' a voice answered.

'The first four boxes are on their way,' Kazemi reported and Jahandar's man is now searching for the woman.'

'I expect all loose ends to be dealt with within twenty-four hours, Major,' the sheikh said quickly. 'And that includes Jahandar and his filthy assassin. You will start looking for their replacements the moment you have everything neatly tidied up, is this understood?'

Kazemi assured his master of his success and politely waited until the man had rung off before calling two of his men who were still on duty at police headquarters and giving them the same instructions.

'I also want you to monitor all information regarding Major Safa and his movements and those of his friends,' he said and both men heard the urgency in their superior's voice. They immediately put all other work aside and began rifling through the latest paperwork that filled their in-trays.

It was as Corporal Shaheen reviewed the witness statements on the hospital shootings that Alan Short's name arose in an unofficial note attached to the case file. Further investigation of all paperwork associated with the same incident linked Alan's name with Stuart Taylor's. By cross-checking the name of the interviewer Shaheen discovered that both men had communicated with Major Walid Safa. He quickly noted down Alan Short's address and picked up the phone.

'As the woman wasn't in her own apartment I have guessed that she may be under the protection of the man she was very well acquainted with,' Shaheen said confidently.

'That was quick work, Corporal,' Kazemi praised lightly as he wrote down the address. 'I now want you to find Corporal Mamood and meet a man called Javid who I have ordered to wait for you at the address. He will be in an unmarked car and I trust that you will be using one yourself. Make sure that you take two untraceable pistols. After you have shot Alan Short and the woman you are to kill Javid with the other pistol. That gun is to be put in the hand of Alan Short and the other in the hand of Javid. When you call headquarters to report the shootings you tell them that you investigated an anonymous phone call to find all three dead in what seems to be a fatal shooting involving two insanely jealous men fighting over a woman.' Without another word he hung up.

The two corporals paid a brief visit to the evidence storeroom. While Mamood distracted the duty officer with pictures of his family Shaheen took two tagged automatics from a closed-case evidence box. The men then gave their excuses and hurriedly left headquarters to drive to the Al Manzil building in the district of Al Mahooz.

After speaking to Shaheen the major quickly dialled again. 'Jahandar, you must instruct Javid to meet two police corporals outside the Al Manzil suites immediately. He must then follow them to a specific apartment and wait outside until the officers have killed a man and a woman called Reem. Javid must then enter and check that the couple is dead before taking the guns the officers have placed in the dead couple's hands and shooting both officers with them. Javid is then to replace the guns where he found them and disappear before anyone sees him. Is this understood?'

Jahandar nodded as he rapidly repeated the plan. He phoned Javid to pass on the major's very precise instructions, not realizing the double-cross being played on him.

The Al Manzil residential suites were much favoured by Western expatriate workers for the high standard of comfort they provided. Alan's one-bedroom suite had every luxury that a single expatriate geologist could wish for. A fully equipped kitchenette adjoined the expansive and comfortably furnished lounge and the large double bedroom and bathroom. Alan's quadrophonic sound system and giant flat-screen satellite television were his pride and joy and Reem closed her eyes and relaxed into the soft cushions of the settee as the whole room resonated with the soothing sounds of a piano concerto. Alan smiled as he watched her unwinding while he mixed two martinis. Dropping two olives into each glass he walked across the room to sit beside her and she stirred and opened her eyes.

'Ah, the perfect drink to accompany Mozart's No. 21,' she murmured as she reached up to take the condensation-streaked glass. Their hands touched briefly and they felt a light electrostatic tingle caused by the nylon-rich carpet.

'Mozart and I always have that effect on beautiful women,' he murmured.

'Thank you, kind sir, the maiden said,' Reem said with a low chuckle. She turned her head away to hide the rising colour of her cheeks but Alan reached up and took her chin between thumb and forefinger to encourage her to face him. He studied her dark eyes that were half veiled by dark long lashes and leant forward to kiss her on the tip of her nose.

'Why did you do that?' Reem asked in a voice so soft that he hardly heard her. 'For the simple reason that I think I'm falling in love with you, Reem.'

Her eyes opened wide and she looked intently into the ruggedly handsome face, searching for something that would reveal some insincerity but all she could see was an open, frank belief in what he had said.

'We are from totally different cultures and backgrounds, Alan,' she whispered, permitting her hand to be taken and held in his. 'I'm a Maronite Catholic from Broumana in Lebanon and you're a Protestant from Port Jackson in Sydney. We're from peoples who are literally poles apart.'

'Reem,' Alan said, holding his forefinger against her full lips. 'We are not different people but simply a man and a woman. Religion and culture could never influence how I feel about you for I am greatly attracted to you. You're an intelligent, beautiful, thoughtful and very sensitive young woman. Perhaps you will think that I am being too forward and possibly offensive for I know that I'm a lot older than you.'

It was Reem's turn to place a hand against Alan's mouth. 'If you can put our social backgrounds to one side then I can do the same about age,' she said and then hurriedly went on as she brushed an unruly lock of hair from his forehead. 'And even though there are social and age differences I'm simply happy that fate threw us together even though we've also been thrown into great danger.'

Alan placed his glass on the coffee table and shifted closer so that he might place an arm around Reem's slender waist. 'Do you really mean that, Reem?'

'Yes, with all my heart,' Reem said and then hesitantly leant towards him and coyly tilted her head back to let Alan brush her lips with his own. With fading inhibitions Reem placed a hand on the back of his head and pulled him to her, crushing their lips in a passionate kiss.

Alan felt his heart racing as their tongues tentatively touched and then wound around each other. He pulled her tight against him and as her arms went around to hold him even tighter he felt a sudden iciness run down his back.

'Oh God! What's that?' Alan gasped as he jerked away in shock and Reem apologetically showed him her half-empty glass.

'I'm so sorry, Alan, I must have forgotton that I was still holding my drink.'

'Well, that dry martini has certainly dampened my ardour,' Alan laughed, pulling the cold, saturated shirt away from his back.

'*Wet* martini, actually,' Reem said and she couldn't stop herself from laughing. 'You'd better take that off before the air-conditioning gives you a chill,' she said with some concern.

Alan went into the bedroom to strip off the damp shirt. He tossed the garment into the open laundry basket standing in the corner of the room before opening the wardrobe to select a crisp cotton replacement. He was suddenly confronted by Reem standing a scant few centimetres from him and for a moment neither moved.

Her eyes flicked over his broad shoulders and down to the flat, work-hardened stomach before swiftly returning to his face with undisguised passion. Alan let the shirt drop and pulled her into a tight embrace before searching out her lips with his own. Reem responded eagerly and they kissed long and hard. Their arms wound around each other to bind their bodies together tightly. Alan felt the heat growing between them as her full breasts pressed hard against him.

When their tongues eventually untwined and they drew apart gasping for breath Alan slowly began to unfasten the buttons of her blouse. The soft silk slid from her olive shoulders and fell to the floor to be quickly followed by the plain white skirt. Within seconds they were both naked and they fell upon the bed in each other's embrace and began a sensuous exploration of each other as they lay pressed tightly together.

'I love you, Alan,' Reem gasped as she moved her legs apart to allow Alan to discover how ready she was. 'I love you so very much,' she whispered hoarsely as the intense passion of their lovemaking made her whole body quiver. All too soon they were both overcome by an intensely pleasurable sensation and a release that neither had experienced before. Bathed in perspiration Alan collapsed upon Reem who continued to caress his body.

'Earlier, when I said I was falling in love with you, Reem, I really meant to admit that I had already fallen in love with you but I was frightened to say so in case of rejection,' Alan panted as their bodies remained ecstatically fused together.

The young woman sighed from deep contentment and kissed Alan's neck while wrapping her arms and legs around his strong body to hold him even tighter.

The strident ringing of the landline phone sliced through the apartment, bringing the two satiated lovers back to earth.

19

As he sat in his office Captain Dabal could observe the rest of the department through the glass dividing wall and it was with great interest that he noticed Corporal Shaheen rapidly thumbing through a small stack of case notes. He knew the man wasn't on any particular case and the urgency with which Shaheen flicked through the paperwork was intriguing. Dabal was aware that the man's loyalty lay with Major Kazemi so he waited for the officer to give him a clue as to the major's current location.

It was mid-afternoon and the muezzin was calling the *asr* prayer when Shaheen, after making a quick telephone call, pushed his chair back and hurried to where Corporal Mamood sat and spoke hurriedly in his ear. Both officers left the squad room and the captain discreetly followed after giving specific instructions to the duty sergeant. He hurried down the corridor just in time to see the men going into the storeroom where court evidence was kept. Dabal lit a cigarette and leant against the wall to wait patiently while looking at a magnificent view of the city through a tall grimy window. The cigarette was only half-burned when the two preoccupied corporals emerged and without noticing his presence hurried down the corridor. He soon saw the men cross the street and climb into a dusty blue Chevrolet that instantly pulled away to disappear in the stream of heavy traffic.

When he re-entered the squad room he was immediately handed a case file by the sergeant who had a knowing look on his face. Dabal hurriedly flipped the pages until he saw that some of the names listed had been highlighted with a yellow felt-tip pen and a chill ran down his spine.

'Go and check in the evidence room for any missing items,' he instructed and the sergeant hurried from the squad room.

Captain Dabal went back to his desk to contact the major. 'Major Safa, I believe that Alan Short's home address is known to Major Kazemi and to some others who plan to do him and Miss Reem harm,' Dabal explained and then listened for a few moments before terminating the call with a brief *ana afham*, I understand.

Dabal opened the case file again and after checking dialled a number that took a while to be answered. 'Who is this?' a weary voice enquired. 'Don't you realize that you've interrupted the most memorable moment of my life?'

There was a muffled giggle in the background and Dabal grinned before apologizing for his poor timing. The captain then quickly told Alan about the suspicious behaviour of the two corporals. Alan assured him that he and Miss Reem would take precautions and immediately leave the apartment.

Captain Dabal closed the case file in front of him and put it back on Corporal Shaheen's desk where the sergeant had found it. Dabal then added the two corporals' names to the list of men wanted for questioning about the hospital shooting and beckoned to the sergeant to come into his office.

Stuart listened with growing dread as Walid relayed Captain Dabal's latest intelligence. 'So what's our plan, Walid?' he asked when the major had finished.

'Not our plan, Stuart, mine. I've already assembled a team of my men who knew and loved Shehhi and we're staking out the apartment building. If and when the two corporals turn up I've been given the power by Captain Dabal to arrest them on the spot and if they resist I have given myself the judicial right to execute them. It's as simple as that.'

'Wow! But what if they manage to get inside the building and try to enter Alan's apartment?'

'Our friends won't be there. Alan and Reem have already been warned by Captain Dabal about the danger and are most probably already driving to you and Helen. Dabal has also promised to clear the area around the Al Manzil suites of all Bahraini police patrols for the next two hours and is leaving this one entirely up to my special unit.'

'I feel so useless,' Stuart mumbled in frustration and he looked up as Helen's arms reassuringly tightened around his waist as she leant her warm body against his.

'Don't feel useless, my friend, because as soon as Alan turns up at your place I want you to put Reem into Helen's care and then go with him to meet Captain Dabal at police headquarters. You have millions of dollars' worth of heroin in your Jeep and you must turn it over to the Bahraini Drug Squad before it's too late.'

Stuart smiled grimly and reluctantly stood up as he bid Walid farewell. The front door bell rang and he hurried to the door. Alan and Reem were waiting outside.

'Thank God you're both alright,' Stuart said as he hurriedly pulled them inside and quickly closed the door. 'I've just spoken with Walid and he's told me that a trap has been prepared for the men who are expected to appear at your apartment.'

'It was a Captain Dabal who called us,' Alan said. 'We haven't had a chance to talk to Walid yet. Shouldn't we go and help him?'

'No, it's official police business and we shouldn't get involved.'

Helen sat down on the settee. 'I agree with Stuart,' she said wearily. 'Haven't we had enough danger?'

Reem nodded in agreement. 'Okay, we'll stay put and ride out the storm,' Alan said as he sat beside her.

'There's no sitting around comfortably for you my friend,' said Stuart. 'We've been asked by Walid to go downtown and deliver the heroin to the Bahrain Drugs Squad. I'm sorry, Helen, but you have to stay here and care for Reem.'

'I can care for myself!' Reem said indignantly. 'I'm not a child. I don't need a babysitter.'

'I can vouch for the fact that she's no child, Stuart,' Alan murmured as his eyes dreamily dwelt on Reem's face while he warmly recalled their moments of intense passion.

Reem blushed and moved closer to him and Stuart clearly recognized the silent signals passing between the couple. 'Okay lovebirds, Alan will also stay here with Helen while I drive to police headquarters in the Jeep.'

He grabbed his jacket from off the armchair and went to the door where Helen kissed him lightly. 'Take care, darling. Don't take any foolish chances.'

'I never do, Helen. Just double lock this door after I've gone and don't open it for anyone other than Walid or myself.'

As he made his way down to the car park in the basement Stuart smiled to himself as he recalled the look of bliss on Alan's face. 'It's about time the stupid galah settled down with a good woman,' he thought.

He was soon speeding along Palace Avenue towards Police Headquarters and was unaware that his departure had been observed and that a Ford was close behind. Javid had ignored his orders and played a hunch that Stuart Taylor's apartment may deliver more fruit than that of Alan Short. Stuart's familiar face seen through the windscreen of the Jeep proved him right.

It was after they had passed the Hoora School for girls and stopped at the next set of traffic lights that Javid decided to make his move. He took the automatic from his pocket and while nudging the steering wheel with his knees to maintain a straight course he swiftly screwed on the silencer. He watched the lights change to red as they both approached the intersection and he slowed down to stop alongside the Jeep. Still staring ahead Javid powered the window down and slowly began to raise his weapon from where it had been lying in his lap. His phone rang and with his concentration shattered he dropped the automatic back into his lap and snatched the phone from the seat beside him. 'Yes!' he barked.

'Javid, you have been a very naughty boy, haven't you,' Jahandar said softly and a chill passed through the assassin's body, making him clutch the instrument even more tightly. 'Mr Whitmore has just been found by the police. He had some rather nasty holes in his head.' There was a long ominous pause and the only sound that could be heard was Javid's heavy breathing. 'Where are the four boxes?' Jahandar went on, his voice assuming a deadly edge.

'I can explain.'

'Do so, now!'

Javid watched the lights turn green and his quarry slip away as his mind raced in an effort to find an excuse. 'Whitmore didn't come to the rendezvous alone. He had a bodyguard who told me that he knew what the boxes contained and that we should split them between us. When I said that we had to stick to the original plan he drew a gun on me and forced me to transfer all the boxes to Whitmore's car. He then told me to disappear or he would make my disappearance more permanent.' Javid paused to draw breath but there was still no response from his employer.

Horns blared behind the Ford and Javid pulled away to follow the red Jeep that was now two blocks distant. It was not long before the density of the traffic increased and he lost all sight of his quarry.

There was a brief intake of air, a sound of impatience in his ear, before Jahandar spoke. 'You're lying to me, Javid,' he whispered. 'I can hear it in your voice. You clearly didn't have the boxes when you met with Whitmore and you killed him to hide the truth.'

'No—no—Whitmore's bodyguard must have killed him to get all four boxes for himself. We have to find the bodyguard.'

Jahandar ignored the man's protestations. 'I do not know how or when you blundered and why you killed Whitmore but your life now depends on rectifying your mistake. So, I would suggest that you do not harm Taylor or his friends, just in case they happen to know the whereabouts of the missing boxes and you must get busy recovering all four of the boxes. Have I made myself clear?'

'Perfectly clear,' Javid stuttered. 'However, I do know that the boxes were definitely in my car when I arrived at the marina which means someone took them while I was sleeping on your boat.'

There was another long ominous silence. 'Are you saying that all twelve boxes have vanished and that you didn't bury eight of them by the Tree of Life?'

'I'm sure I can recover all of them, Jahandar, just give me a little time,' Javid said in a panic-stricken voice.

'You left the car unlocked and let someone steal heroin worth thirteen-million-dollars belonging to the sheikh, the Magician? By God, Javid, find that delivery or we'll both be cut and fed to the sharks.'

'I'll return to the marina and question the nightwatchman. He must have seen someone drive onto the dockside road late last night.'

There was no response and the line remained silent a full minute before it went dead. Javid snapped the phone shut with shaking hands and wrenched the wheel to take a left turn and head back towards the marina.

Walid had hunched up in his seat and was waiting patiently outside the Al Manzil suites when a dark saloon pulled into the kerb and two uniformed policemen got out.

'They're our targets,' Walid murmured to the three grim-faced men in the car. He slid the automatic from his shoulder holster and checked the magazine. 'We'll follow them into the building to make sure that no passers-by are hurt and then trap them inside the apartment.'

As the corporals used the revolving door and disappeared into the main lobby Walid, followed by the three heavily armed men, crossed the road and entered the building in time to see the lift doors close behind the two policemen. They stepped into the second lift that was waiting and after ten seconds Walid gave the signal to push the button.

When they stepped into an empty corridor the team quickly spread out with weapons cocked and silently padded after Walid. With a double-handed grip on his automatic Walid neared the open door to Alan's apartment just as Corporal Mamood emerged with a look of disappointment on his face at finding nobody at home. This immediately changed to one of complete surprise when confronted by the major and his men and he instinctively reached for his holstered weapon.

'Stop or I will fire,' Walid shouted. His automatic remained centred on the man's chest. Mamood paused and as his eyes narrowed, calculating his chances, Shaheen leapt out into the corridor and fired his standard-issue Glock automatic. The nine-millimetre bullet narrowly missed Walid to strike one of his Special Force men in the chest. The officer was knocked back a few paces by the force of the heavy-calibre bullet but was saved from serious injury by the Kevlar vest. Walid crouched and fired his weapon, instantly killing Shaheen with a bullet through the head. Mamood tried to pull his weapon from the holster, prompting the two officers behind Walid to open fire. The Heckler & Koch machine-guns rammed Mamood back against the wall and he slid down to sit upon the parquet floor before toppling lifelessly to one side.

With his ears still ringing from the deafening thunder of the discharged weapons Walid checked both corporals before nodding with satisfaction. He then picked up Shaheen's pistol and removed Mamood's weapon from the holster before firing once into the corridor floor and dropping both guns into polythene evidence bags. Walid then turned to check on his downed team member but the man had already removed his protective vest and shirt and was proudly displaying the nastily developing bruises on his chest to his team-mates.

'Good job, guys,' Walid said as he indicated that they should leave the scene of the shooting. 'Back to base and remember, don't speak to anyone about this mission. I shall answer any questions that arise.'

With broad grins on their faces the three men nodded and trotted back to the lift leaving Walid talking to police headquarters and waving curious and shocked residents back into their apartments.

Walid only had to wait ten minutes before Captain Dabal arrived with his own clean-up team of forensic investigators and the coroner. 'They didn't want to come quietly then?' he asked with a wry smile of greeting as he studied the shredded chest of Mamood and the neatly drilled hole in Shaheen's forehead.

'I didn't have a chance to read them their rights. That one came with all guns blazing,' Walid said indicating Shaheen. 'And the other one tried to join the party.' Walid handed the polythene bag containing the weapons to one of the forensic officers. 'We now need to find Major Kazemi before he tries to silence Reem and Alan.'

Dabal nodded as he prodded Mamood with the toe of his boot. 'He might be a little harder to find than these two fools.'

'He didn't kill Shehhi with his own hand but I'm sure he is connected to the person or persons who did murder my friend. This drug ring is a lot bigger than we think and I have a feeling it goes right to the top.' Walid shook the captain's hand and strode down the corridor. 'I'll let you know if I hear of anything, *insh'allah*,' he called over his shoulder as he raised a hand in brief farewell before stepping into the lift.

Walid arrived at Stuart's apartment a few minutes after his friend's return from police headquarters. As the front door swung open he greeted Stuart with a warm bear-hug. 'I praise Allah that you are unharmed,' he blurted out before turning to Alan and pummelling him on the chest. 'Good to see you haven't encountered our rotten apple in the barrel, my friend.' A look of puzzlement crossed the Australian's weathered face. 'Major Kazemi,' Walid explained. 'He'll be seeking the whereabouts of the heroin and that means you and Stuart will be the first people he'll want to have a 'friendly' talk to. That's why I need to get to him first. I have a lot of questions that need answers and he is the only man who might be able to provide them.'

'Stuart has a confession, Walid,' Alan said as Reem joined the men in the hallway.

'I haven't given the heroin to the Bahrain Drug Squad yet. I only got halfway across town before I realized that Alan and Reem were in mortal danger even in my apartment—more so, as the drug runners have already been here.'

'The boxes are still in the Jeep?' Walid asked incredulously.

'The car is well-locked in the basement car park.'

'And I don't need to tell you that cars can easily be unlocked by determined killers. How long has the Jeep been down there?' Walid asked as he slipped the automatic out of his shoulder holster and checked the load in the magazine.

'Roughly two hours,' Stuart said as he watched Walid hurry out through the front door. 'Nobody can get into the car park without alerting the security guard.'

'One or two unarmed guards wouldn't cause these bastards any trouble,' Walid called out as Stuart and Alan hurried after him. The three men stepped into the lift and Stuart punched the button three or four times as though it would make the electronic circuitry work faster.

They cautiously emerged into the grim gloom of the car park where dingy concrete walls were barely illuminated by the insufficient fluorescent tubes. There was only a scattering of cars belonging to the wives of residents who had driven to work in the second car and the bright red Jeep stood out like a ripe cherry on a cupcake. Clutching the fire extinguisher he had taken from a wall bracket Stuart walked closely behind Walid who held the automatic close to his side. Alan fingered the broad-bladed hunting knife that was always sheathed at his waist.

The three friends spread out and approached the Jeep with extreme caution. As they drew nearer it became clear to them that someone had broken into the car and taken all the boxes. The front and rear windows had been smashed and the rear door had been left wide open.

'Surely someone must have heard this,' Alan muttered as he looked around the silent car park after studying the mess a jemmy had made of the rear lock.

'The security guards are only just round that corner at the foot of the ramp,' Stuart said as he put the extinguisher down and began walking towards the exit. Walid strode after him and the two men walked to the small glazed clapboarded security box beside red-striped barriers. One of the arms had been wrenched from the vertical post and tossed to one side and the safety-glass windows and wood panels of the security box were indiscriminately perforated with neat round holes.

With a sick feeling of foreboding Walid pulled the small door open to reveal the crumpled forms of the two security guards. 'They've been and gone,' Walid groaned. He retrieved his mobile from his *thawb* pocket and dialled Captain Dabal.

'You have some news for me Major Walid?' he asked almost immediately.

'Not the news you were expecting, Captain. The drug runners tracked Stuart back to his apartment and stole the heroin from his car in the underground car park, killing two security guards in the process.'

'I thought Mr Taylor had taken the drugs to the Bahrain Drug Squad?'

'He was going to but had to return urgently to his apartment.'

'So, we're back to where we started and the drugs could be crossing the border to vanish into the vastness of your country this very minute.'

'Not necessarily, Captain. I've sent out an alert to my own border control before calling you. I've also ensured all ports on the Saudi coast are now monitoring any foreign-registered boats seeking berths.'

'I'll have a clean-up team sent to the car park and I'll meet you in Stuart's apartment for a council of war. We have to recover the heroin before the top brass begin their investigation. Our jobs could be on the line, Walid, unless we can bring in this rogue major as soon as possible.'

'I agree, Captain.' Walid said goodbye and asked his friends to return to Stuart's apartment.

Major Kazemi drove swiftly along Highway 71, glancing briefly at the A'ali Burial Mounds as he sped past, and headed back to the Hamala Beach Resort where he had rented a small waterside villa. The twelve boxes of heroin were stacked in the back of the Toyota Land Cruiser. They were covered with a lightweight tarpaulin and his recently used Glock automatic lay on the passenger seat within easy reach. The big 4x4 belonged to a distant cousin who was unaware of the trouble that Kazemi was in and who believed it was only going to be used as substitute transport for a few days.

Kazemi felt no remorse over killing the two guards. When he had smashed the windows of the Jeep his whole focus had been on the boxes and the uniformed men had simply been a distraction, an obstacle in his way that needed to be cleared. After transferring the drugs he had called the sheikh and had been instructed to dispatch the whole shipment to Al Aziziyah on the Saudi peninsular.

He drove through the gates and headed for the villa as he rang another number. 'Jahandar, I have done your work for you and recovered the shipment. The sheikh is not at all happy that your thug assassinated the only courier with impeccable credentials so, I now expect you to find a replacement or failing that to get all twelve boxes to the mainland yourself.'

'That is very good news, Major,' Jahandar said, his high voice revealing his nervousness. 'I will immediately arrange transport. In the meantime can you deliver the boxes to me at the Zallaq Marina?'

'No, Javid must collect them from me at the Tree of Life where you lost them in the first place.'

'That could be dangerous.'

'The police would never expect anyone to return to the Tree so soon. The site has been closed to the public and it is remote enough to prevent questions being asked about boxes being transferred from one vehicle to another. I have a 4x4 that can cross the desert and approach the Tree from the west. I suggest that you do the same and meet me at midnight tomorrow.' The phone line went dead.

Jahandar cursed quietly to himself as he contacted Javid. 'Stop whatever you are doing and get down to the marina right away,' he shouted the moment he heard Javid's voice.

20

Switching to high beam Major Kazemi powered the Land Cruiser off the highway to challenge the black wasteland that ran either side. Soon the last trace of civilization was left behind and he was subjected to the clattering of shale beneath the vehicle and the ever-hissing sand in the wheel arches. He was now solely dependent on the dashboard-mounted compass and his pigeon-like instinct to travel in the right direction. The occasional wadi appeared as a dark river in the car's halogen beams and he was forced to seek crossing places where the walls had been eroded by the weather.

After eight kilometres of torturous driving he spotted a dark irregularity on the otherwise perfectly level horizon. The unimposing height of the Tree of Life could now be clearly identified against the lighter star-bright sky and Kazemi slowed down, switched off his lights and approached the rendezvous site with extreme caution. When he was two hundred metres from the Tree he stopped, switched off the engine and powered his window down to listen. The slight hissing of sand grains moving across the stony surface and the irregular ticking of the engine cooling were the only sounds and he confidently restarted the engine to drive within metres of the steel ring fence.

The major climbed the short ladder attached to the back of the Land Cruiser and went onto the roof to study the surrounding landscape for any sign of lights before climbing down again. He performed this routine every fifteen minutes until he caught a brief flash to the north-west. Using his binoculars he could see that it was in fact two headlights and the vehicle was heading directly towards the Tree of Life. He checked his watch before climbing down, drumming his fingers on the hood while watching the vehicle draw closer.

The dark shape resolved into a Nissan X-Trail that stopped suddenly scattering a small shower of small stones towards the brightly illuminated major. With a hand resting on his leather holster Kazemi stepped quickly out of the twin spotlights and into the protective darkness as the door opened and Javid lithely leapt from the vehicle.

'*As salaam alykhum*, Major Kazemi,' he said as he quickly scanned the immediate area before fixing the major with narrowed eyes. 'You have brought the heroin?'

'It's here and you have your instructions,' Kazemi replied as he tried to see through the tinted windows of the X-Trail. 'Where's Jahandar?'

'He was unable to come and sends his apologies,' Javid muttered as he went to the back of the Land Cruiser and tried the door catch. The door was locked and he looked at the major with one raised eyebrow.

Kazemi showed his keys to the gunman before triggering the door release button. 'This shipment must be in Saudi Arabia by tomorrow or you and Jahandar will learn how the sheikh got his reputation for making people disappear.'

Javid grunted in response and began unloading the Land Cruiser as quickly as possible. Soon all twelve boxes had been transferred to the X-Trail and he climbed behind the wheel. The door was suddenly wrenched open and he found himself looking into the business end of a nine-millimetre Glock automatic.

'If you should mislay those boxes again I will assume you have double-crossed the sheikh and I will tell him of my conclusion,' Major Kazemi snarled. 'You know what his orders to me will be?'

Javid nodded and leant away as the major slammed the door shut. He quickly started the engine and pulled away, going the way he had come. Kazemi returned to the Land Cruiser and drove in the opposite direction towards the infamous Jaw Prison. He soon reached the relaxingly smooth King Hamad Highway and turned south to drive twenty kilometres to the artificial fish-shaped islands where his friend had invested in a luxury villa. When he arrived he garaged the Land Cruiser and went into the kitchen where a body was lying. Kazemi believed he was perfectly justified in shooting his friend of ten years simply because firstly, he had refused to loan him his car and secondly, was about to report his whereabouts to the police after recognizing his face on a television news channel.

After dragging the corpse into the utility room the major prepared the percolator and began scrambling eggs and toasting bread for a very late supper before retiring to the bedroom. After the killing in the car park he was still feeling high and craved the compliant sensuality of Esraa beneath his naked body.

Without encountering any signs of life whatsoever Javid crossed the wilderness beneath the awe-inspiring canopy of stars and when he reached the skimmed surface of the highway he sped towards Zallaq Marina. The boxes that had jounced around while he had been driving over the rough terrain were now lying motionless beneath the light tarpaulin that the major had tossed to Javid, as a man might toss a bone to a dog.

As he walked through the marina checkpoint the Boston Whaler was brightly lit in the stern and Javid could clearly recognize the obese shape of his employer lounging in one of the moulded plastic seats.

Javid had parked the X-Trail a kilometre from the marina and walked the rest of the way after carefully locking the vehicle. He walked purposefully towards the boat with his long fingers lightly resting on the hilt of his sheathed dagger.

'You are very foolish to arrange for us to meet here,' Javid said in a low voice as he stepped over the gunwale and lowered himself into the seat opposite his employer. The boat moved slightly in the still water with each of his movements and Jahandar frowned on being interrupted in his quiet meditation. 'They stole the heroin from my Ford when it was parked here. If they knew we had returned they would do it again and what's more hand us over to the police.'

'I didn't see you arrive in the car,' Jahandar said softly between deep draws on the shisha pipe. Smoke dribbled between his lips while he studied his employee, becoming aware of a new kind of tense atmosphere that had grown to separate them. 'What have you done with the heroin?' he asked as his eyes casually roamed to where Javid's hand lay against his waist. A thumb was hooked into the thin leather belt while the palm rested against the hidden weapon that Jahandar knew was always kept sheathed there.

Javid saw the direction of his employer's gaze. 'I have been thinking very carefully, Jahandar, and come to the conclusion that I no longer wish to be ordered around like a personal slave. With the amount of heroin in those boxes I would be rich for the rest of my life. I could return to Iran and live like a king in my old neighbourhood.'

Jahandar sighed deeply. '*Kull bayt wa fihi balu'a,*' he murmured.

'I know that every house has its sewers but I plan to climb out of yours.'

'That kind of thinking can be bad for your health,' Jahandar said as he slid a hand under the cushion that lay beside him. 'You have forgotten that the sheikh threatened to feed us to the sharks bit by bit if anything happened to the shipment.'

Javid laughed abruptly and his nicotine-yellowed teeth gleamed in the boat's lights. 'You think a threat like that will stand between me and my dream?' A swift movement of his hand produced the long, slender-bladed dagger and he pointed it at Jahandar. 'Remove your hand from under that cushion and make sure it is empty. You've seen how fast I can work with this and I wouldn't hesitate to use it if you try to kill me.'

Jahandar placed the fingertips of both hands together under his chin and thoughtfully studied Javid for a few seconds before speaking again. 'Very well, Javid, from now on we are partners and I will ensure that you get a bigger cut of the fee tomorrow.'

'As they say, tomorrow never comes. Fifty-fifty is what I would call bigger and I want it now,' Javid muttered as he picked up the silk cushion beside Jahandar to reveal the silenced Smith & Wesson automatic. As he picked it up he slid the blade back into its sheath. Javid began rebuttoning the shirt that had been open down to the waist since leaving the uncomfortable humidity of the underground car park. 'I believe we now have a favourable working relationship that can only be improved if you agree to help me sell the shipment and return to Iran.'

'You still want to double-cross a Bahraini sheikh?'

'And who the hell does he think he is?'

'I believe he's a powerful man who will want to feed us to the sharks or at the least bury us up to our necks in an ant nest.'

'That can't happen if I kill him first, and that's exactly what I'll do. I need to know how to get to the man so that I can make sure nobody interferes with my plan.'

'My only contact with the sheikh is through Major Kazemi. He passes on all instructions and acts as the enforcer if they're not carried out,' Jahandar said as he detached the shisha mouthpiece from the pipe and slipped it into his vest pocket.

'You have the major's telephone number?' Javid asked as he removed the magazine from the automatic and tossed the weapon onto the silk cushion.

Jahandar pointed to his pocket to warn Javid before slipping a hand in to retrieve his mobile phone. He stabbed at a few keys and showed the number to Javid who made sure he had memorized it perfectly before nodding his head.

'I'll call and make him the offer—our heroin for four million dollars. Do you think he'll accept that?' Javid asked, knowing full well what the answer would be. When Jahandar shook his head Javid grinned. 'Then I shall arrange a meeting to discuss the offer further and that's when I'll get the information on the sheikh from him.'

'You think it will be that easy?' Jahandar asked in a sour voice. 'You'll be lucky if you leave any meeting with the major with your head still on your shoulders.'

'If anyone is going to lose his head I can assure you it won't be me.' Javid stood up and leapt over the gunwale. Jahandar watched with envious eyes as the lean figure strode away and along the waterfront until he had disappeared into the gloom beyond the marina gates. He looked round for his phone before remembering that Javid had taken it with him. He couldn't call the major to tell him of Javid's plan which meant he wouldn't be able to distance himself of the double-cross.

Arriving at the only decision left to him Jahandar heaved himself to his feet and wheezing heavily he made his way into the fore cabin where he began packing what few items of clothing he would need after leaving the boat. Then hooking a finger in the inset brass ring he lifted a floor panel and with extreme care extracted the large canvas bag that he had secreted in the engine compartment. He knew that the value of the contents was far greater than a paltry share of the heroin that Javid was gambling their lives on. The plain-looking bag in his hand contained $40-million worth of historic pearl necklaces and assorted jewellery. Jahandar planned to be as far away as possible when the sheikh learned of Javid's double-cross.

Major Kazemi had just finished his meal and was planning to retire to the bedroom with a book and a mellow single-malt whisky when his cellphone rang. He picked it up and listened in silence for two minutes before speaking.

'You want four million dollars for the boxes?' His face hardened as the caller confirmed his words. 'Then you have a deal but you'll need to give me twenty-four hours to raise the cash. Call me tomorrow at the same time.' He hung up without waiting for an answer and immediately dialled an unlisted number.

'Yes, Major?' a shrill voice answered. 'I trust you are calling to give me good news about the shipment.'

'*Es salaam alykhum*, Sheikh Abdullah. I have good news and a little bad news. Jahandar has the cases in his possession but the problem is that we have been double-crossed by him and his servant. They are now demanding five million dollars cash for delivery to the mainland.'

There was a moment of silence during which Kazemi could only hear the static on the line as sweat trickled from his hairline. The sheikh finally responded in a low silky voice. 'Major, I would have preferred it if you had got all your facts right before calling me on this number. Firstly, from what I understand, you are the one with the problem for they have demanded the money from you and not me.' There was a slight pause before the sheikh continued in a more threatening tone of voice. 'Secondly, and I wish to emphasize this point, if you do not have the cases delivered to the mainland by *dhuhr* prayer tomorrow I will send some people to remove your feet, hands and head.'

The major's knuckles whitened as his grip on the phone tightened and his pulse quickened. 'I will make sure that the cases are in Saudi by midday, sir.'

Without any warning the line was cut and it was only on glancing down at his watch that Kazemi realized he had been given a mere eighteen hours to live. He selected a speed-dial number and impatiently rapped his empty glass on the table as he waited for it to be answered.

'That was quick, Major,' Javid said. 'You have the money already?'

Major Kazemi could hear the suspicion in the man's voice and he replied smoothly, 'Yes, the sheikh gave me precisely four million in used one-hundred-dollar bills and I wish to complete the exchange today. Is Jahandar aboard his boat at the marina?'

Javid hesitated before speaking while he revised his original plan of meeting the major at the Formula One track. 'Yes, he is still in the Zallaq Marina and he has the boxes with him. I will tell him that you wish to see him in one hour and that you will be bringing the money as we agreed.' As he cut the connection Javid smirked at his new idea of having both the heroin and the money. After killing the major and Jahandar he would use about two hundred dollars from the four million to secretly arrange for the drugs to be shipped to Hawar Island and then on to Dukhan on the Qatari coast where he knew of a distributor he could deal with.

Thirty minutes before the agreed time Javid drove through the marina checkpoint to be greeted with a casual wave from the Filipino watchman. Driving past the moored luxury cruisers he started comparing the different styles, trying to decide which model he would select once he had his money. As Javid reached the point where the Boston Whaler had been moored he slammed on the brakes. A large empty space between the moored vessels plainly showed that Jahandar had taken the vessel and left the marina. Javid left the car and walked in shock to where the boat had been tied up and gazed towards the marina entrance and the emerald sea beyond. Treacherous son of a sow, he thought. He quickly returned to his car and went into the small town where he parked the Ford with its precious cargo before walking back to the entrance of the marina to wait for the major to arrive.

Javid had smoked his second cigarette when a Land Cruiser slowly approached the marina gates. The driver's window powered down and a hand briefly appeared waving a police warrant. The watchman nodded and indicated that the driver could proceed. Javid watched the large vehicle cruise along the wharf as he dialled a number. 'He's gone,' he said the moment the connection was made and he saw the brake lights flare crimson. 'No, he doesn't have the boxes, I do, and I'm prepared to continue with the exchange provided you do it my way.' Javid listened for a few seconds and then continued. 'In precisely five minutes I want you to throw the money out of your window and then drive on to the end of the dock. There you will switch off your engine and wait until I have collected the bag and driven out of the marina. After checking the money I will call you and tell you where I have parked the car and you can collect the drugs. Do you understand?'

The major fumed but managed to keep the anger out of his voice when he agreed to follow the instructions. Javid immediately walked to the watchman's hut, much to the surprise of the Filipino who was reading a dog-eared copy of the Qur'an. The look of surprise remained on his face as the thin blade slid through his thin uniform to penetrate his heart in one swift killing stroke. Javid wiped the blade on the man's jacket and after locking the door he strode quickly back to the road leading to the town centre. Javid walked along the main street studying the few pedestrians braving the oppressive humidity until he saw the ideal scapegoat. He tapped the shoulder of a heavily bearded man in traditional dress who was getting into a dilapidated and heavily corroded Toyota.

'I'll give you fifty US dollars if you'll collect something I forgot on the marina quayside,' Javid said, eyeing the frayed collar and cuffs of the man's *thawb*. The Bahraini nodded, his eyes betraying his need as he held his hand out for the money.

'There's no watchman on duty so you can drive straight into the marina. After one hundred metres you'll see a bag by the side of the road. Pick it up and bring it back to me here,' and he placed twenty-five dollars on the open calloused palm. 'The other twenty-five dollars will be for when you return,' he said in answer to the questioning look in the man's eyes. The villager nodded eagerly at the thought of a month's money for such a simple task and he got into his vehicle and drove towards the marina.

Javid waited until the vehicle had turned the corner before hurrying back the shorter way that led to the gates of the marina. When he was within fifty metres of the watchman's hut he stopped in the dark shadow of a palm tree and watched as the Land Cruiser began driving towards the end of the dock leaving a black bag standing on the cobblestones. Suddenly the old Toyota rumbled into view and with squealing tyres turned off the street to pass through the entrance gates. There was a teeth-setting crash of gears as it accelerated along the dock road, emitting a dark noxious cloud, until it suddenly braked and stopped beside the bag.

The Bahraini climbed out and Javid watched him place the bag inside the car before climbing in himself. The Toyota coughed up more smoke and was halfway through a three-point turn when the Land Cruiser suddenly roared into life and hurtled along the road. Suspecting a change of plan Javid drew back further into the shadows and watched as the bigger vehicle blocked the Toyota's way. The startled Bahraini opened his door and was innocently climbing out to remonstrate with the other driver when two nine-millimetre bullets entered his skull.

Major Kazemi ran to the vehicle and quickly searched the filthy interior before springing the boot and discovering that it contained nothing but a freshly slaughtered lamb. Javid watched the major storm back to the Land Cruiser while his own anger at being betrayed began to stimulate his need to kill something, anyone. Javid now knew that the promise of exchanging the four million dollars had simply been to draw him out into the open and kill him, enabling the major to walk away with the shipment and the sheikh's money. The 4x4 roared through the gates and swept past the palm Javid was leaning against; he impulsively reached for his gun but instead took out his mobile and dialled.

'That was foolish, Major,' Javid snarled. 'As a punishment for that childish trap I will keep the shipment and sell it to another buyer.'

'You are finished, Jahandar. I'm talking to a dead man,' the major shouted. Javid realized that in using his employer's phone he had misled Kazemi into believing he had been speaking to Jahandar.

'I'm long gone on my boat, Major. You cannot harm me or get your shipment back,' Javid whispered and switched the phone off.

Major Kazemi held the dead phone to his ear for a long time before throwing it down on the seat beside him. He was aware that he now had to find the Boston Whaler and recover the sheikh's heroin before morning or his life wouldn't be worth a single *fils*.

The friends were gathered in Stuart's apartment and while Helen and Reem prepared a light supper the men sat around the coffee table to plan their next move. Corporal Ahmed leant on the balcony rail and kept watch for any suspicious activity in the street below.

'I propose that we try and end this by striking the head off the serpent,' Walid said. 'We have the name and description of the sea-going cruiser which I have reason to believe is owned by the man whom Reem heard being called Jahandar.'

'You think Jahandar is the boss of this drug ring, mate?' Alan asked.

'It may be Major Kazemi,' Stuart added thoughtfully.

'That's also a possibility,' Walid said. 'The hunt for him is still continuing but like the snake he is he seems to have slipped through our net and found a hole in which to hide.'

'So our best chance is to capture this Jahandar fellow and beat the crap out of him until he tells us where the drugs are and the whereabouts of Major Kazemi.'

'No, Alan,' Walid said in a firm voice. 'That's not the way I would do things in this country or anywhere else, either. As much as I'd like to avenge the murder of Sergeant Shehhi, I will still stick to the rules for interviewing suspects. If I can possibly take Jahandar alive, along with any associates who may also be aboard; they will all be questioned according to Bahraini police procedure.'

'That's a bloody pity, Walid. I was really looking forward to finding the bastard who did for Shehhi and sending him to Paradise.'

'As was I,' Stuart added. 'However, what's the plan. How do we find this cruiser?'

'As you know a watch was put on all Saudi ports so he cannot go that way without being apprehended,' Walid said while unrolling a map of the area and using glasses and an onyx ashtray to weigh down the corners.

'And I have a twenty-four-hour watch on the channels between here and here,' Captain Dabal added, running his forefinger along the Hawar and Qatari coastlines. 'The moment the boat is identified an Apache helicopter gunship will be scrambled and the boat ordered to return to Bahrain or be sunk.'

'So, we just sit and wait?' Stuart said as he leant back in the settee.

'No, you must eat,' Helen said as she and Reem entered the living room with trays heavily laden with extra-hot curry and pitta bread. 'And that includes you, Ahmed,' she called out to the corporal leaning over the balcony. Soon all conversation ceased as the friends helped themselves to the dishes arrayed before them and began eating with a noisy gusto that only hungry men can achieve. The muezzin in a nearby minaret began calling the faithful to *maghrib* prayer; glancing out of the window at the rapidly setting sun Walid rose to his feet. After smiling apologetically to Helen he left the apartment, followed by Captain Dabal and hurried to the building's dedicated mosque on the top floor. As the two officers departed Corporal Ahmed remained on guard. He strolled out into the bright orange light cast by the sinking sun to finish his meal on the balcony. Two hours later, long after prayer time, the landline phone rang. It was Dabal and Stuart nodded as he listened to the captain.

'It seems they have detected the Boston Whaler off the coast of Hawar and a helicopter gunship has been despatched to intercept it,' he said on hanging up.

'Excellent,' Walid said thumping the table with his fist. 'Now we should be able to get some answers to what's been going on.'

'Dabal said that although it's still high tide the boat is following a rather dangerous course, one that goes over some of the more prominent coral reefs. He also added that it seems to be running at full throttle with the main current that sweeps past Hawar.'

'The man obviously doesn't know local conditions,' Stuart surmised. 'So, what will happen?'

'Unless action is taken by the captain within the next thirty minutes the boat will be swept past Hawar towards the Qatari coast and then be carried over a long sandbar that is well-known for wrecking the craft of careless navigators.'

'We'll wait for the gunship report and then meet Captain Dabal at the docks to give Jahandar a big welcome home,' Walid muttered.

'Right by your side, mate,' Alan growled and Reem put an arm around his shoulders to help smooth the rage on his face. Stuart nodded his head sympathetically and rose to help Helen with the coffee.

Ahmed came into the living room from the balcony and swung his Heckler & Koch sub-machine gun around and across his chest before sitting down in a chair that he had placed beside the front door. Stuart switched on the television and the group watched the latest news on the street riots. The commentator announced that pro-democracy students had barricaded themselves in the university building and were throwing roof pantiles down onto the police who were attempting to storm the front door. The commentator coolly described the actions of the SWAT team who were firing live rounds through windows.

'When will all this killing end?' Alan said.

'When the elitist minority who have all the wealth in this country start to listen to the poor majority,' Walid answered morosely.

21

As soon as Javid had left the marina and disappeared from sight Jahandar released the boat from its wharfside cleats and climbed the short companionway to the wheelhouse to start the engine. Within minutes he had reached the old mooring buoy in the middle of the small harbour. A clinker-built dinghy was tied to the buoy and leaning out over the side while swearing beneath his breath Jahandar wasted precious minutes and broke three fingernails untying the barnacle-encrusted rope. He then retied the rope to the cruiser's transom and returned to the bridge to push the throttles forward and continue on out to sea with the dinghy bouncing in its wake.

When all sight of land had sunk below the horizon Jahandar throttled back and began to transfer bottles of water and a little of the cheese from the refrigerator to the dinghy. With extreme care he lowered the canvas bag into the tiny boat before returning to the wheelhouse. He tied off the steering and advanced the throttle levers halfway. As soon as he was satisfied with the Boston Whaler's heading he cautiously lowered himself over the side into the dinghy. As soon as he gained a secure footing he let go of the cruiser's gunwale and crawled to the prow of the dinghy to untie the painter, freeing himself from the cruiser. The boat rapidly dropped back and rocked violently in the wake of the Boston Whaler that was steadily moving away towards the distant island of Hawar.

Perspiration saturated the expensively tailored linen suit as Jahandar strained to raise the stubby mast and set about hoisting the single sail. A light breeze soon bellied the thin canvas and with his hand resting on the tiller the dinghy began to make way against the current and head back towards Bahrain. After an hour of steady sailing when Jahandar was beginning to identify landmarks on the thin coastal smudge on the horizon a sudden roar filled the air above his head and a military helicopter rushed by. It was about fifteen metres above the small waves and the downdraught from the rotors caused the sail to flatten and the dinghy to heel dangerously before it was able to right itself and the sail could belly out once more. Jahandar craned his neck to watch the aircraft fly in the direction of Hawar and a satisfied smirk creased the corners of his tight little mouth.

The sun was at its highest, broiling down on the small dinghy as it approached the six-kilometre stretch of Jazair Beach. Jahandar could clearly see the sea walls of the Bahrain Yacht Club harbour and as he crouched beneath the protection of the spare sail he had found in the footlocker he finished the last bottle of water and a few crumbs of cheese.

He pulled hard on the tiller and the dinghy heeled over and headed towards the shore. He deliberately bypassed the harbour entrance for he was aware that it was restricted to yacht club members only and his appearance would undoubtedly raise eyebrows and some awkward questions.

The dinghy neared the shingle beach and Jahandar swung the tiller to run parallel until he was a safe distance from the built-up area that surrounded the harbour. He ran the boat ashore and pulled the sail down at the last moment before the keel grated harshly on the pebbles. In case he was being watched Jahandar lowered the mast and folded the sails neatly as though it was his normal practice. In an ungainly fashion he used the last of his strength to pull the boat out of the water and well above the high-tide mark. Taking the canvas bag from the dinghy and clutching it tightly to his side he strolled up the beach until he had reached the Jazair Beach road where he waited in the hot sun to hail a taxi that was returning to the city.

The driver suspiciously eyed the large man who demanded to be taken to the city centre as he settled his gross weight across the worn back seats. He continued to study Jahandar in his rear-view mirror until a ten-dollar bill was passed to him with the curt instruction to take him to the Ritz-Carlton Hotel.

The receptionist at the front desk also gave Jahandar a strange look when he saw the filthy condition of his clothing but was mollified by the explanation that Jahandar had been in a minor boating accident.

Twenty US dollars surreptitiously slid across the desk beneath the completed registration form and the receptionist immediately produced the mandatory smile.

'Thank you very much, Mr Hosseini, I do hope you enjoy your stay,' the clerk murmured as he deftly pocketed the money while reading the false name and address given by Jahandar. He rang the bell to summon a bellhop. Once in his room Jahandar gave the Indian boy one hundred dollars and told him to buy the cheapest mobile phone with a twenty-dollar pay-as-you-go card and bring it back within the hour. The calls he wished to make couldn't be trusted to go through the hotel switchboard or an easily tapped landline.

The young Indian was as good as his word and returned within twenty minutes with a cheap Nokia that was registered in the name of Aishwarya and ready to use, plus thirty-one dollars in change. Jahandar smiled, knowing that the name meant prosperity, and he told the overwhelmed lad to keep the change as he ushered him out of the room and locked the door.

'Major Kazemi?' Jahandar asked as soon as the phone was answered.

'Who is this?'

'This is Jahandar, Major, and I have something extremely important to tell you.'

'And I have little to say to thieves except that they die very painfully.'

'Just listen to me very carefully. Javid is the one who has betrayed us both. He has the twelve boxes and wants four million dollars for them.'

'So it wasn't you who arranged the exchange at the marina?' Kazemi asked in a puzzled tone.

'Exchange? No. Javid stole my phone and undoubtedly pretended to be me.'

'And which sewer is the rat in now?'

'That I do not know. I was hoping that you would be able to tell me as you have all the resources of the police department.'

'I have no resources because I am now wanted by the police myself.'

For a few seconds Jahandar fell into an amazed silence. 'Where are you now?' he finally worked up the courage to ask.

'That is of no importance to you. However I require you to find your servant and recover the heroin.' The imperative tone in his voice made this an order and not a request and Jahandar bit his tongue before replying.

'I will do my best to find Javid,' he muttered between clenched teeth and he flinched inwardly as the line went dead.

After leaving the marina Javid went directly to where he had parked the Ford and was soon driving through the city on the Bin Salman Highway to the docks at Guraifa. He was fully aware that he had to leave Bahrain before Major Kazemi and the sheikh caught up with him and he had decided to steal a small seaworthy boat and head for the Iranian coast.

As he passed the Asian School two patrol cars with light bars flashing overtook him and sped towards the area that was crowded with shipping warehouses. Javid slowed to cruise below the speed limit and at the next right turn he lost himself in the labyrinth of corrugated iron sheds and warehouses that lined the water's edge.

The old car rumbled past a disused shipyard with rows of rust-streaked hulks, flaking anchors and massive chains whose links had been rendered immobile by years of corrosion. Javid cruised on until he saw the quayside where a motley collection of leisure cruisers and fishing boats were moored. He turned into a small alley, stopped the car and after a few moments of making sure that he hadn't been seen he got out and walked slowly back to the main road to scan the various vessels. As he walked along the wharf he could hear the water gently lapping against the rotting timbers and the hulls but his mind was far from being lulled into a sense of false security. Javid's hunter instincts were finely tuned and he spotted the two police patrol cars a long way ahead. They appeared to be parked at the quayside for a specific reason and Javid sat on a large steel bollard to give the appearance of being a casual labourer. He picked at a bit of beef lodged between two front teeth with a well-used toothpick as he looked askance at the police officers who were idly talking and smoking.

It wasn't long before the object of their interest appeared at the breakwater and motored slowly towards the quay. It was the Boston Whaler and Javid instantly recognized the profile and livery as it passed him. He could clearly see that the man at the helm was a police officer who was expertly juggling the throttle levers to bring the boat to a halt on the quayside. One of the waiting men caught the thrown rope and tied it to a bollard before catching a second rope and mooring the bow.

Javid waited but there was no sign of Jahandar and the two officers jumped ashore to make their report to the waiting men. As one of the senior officers turned Javid stood up and walked back to the car. He had recognized the man as being the same heavy-set major he had briefly seen by moonlight at the Tree of Life. He started the Ford and crept further down the alley to where large rubbish skips had been left against the walls. He pulled in behind a high skip that suddenly disgorged a dozen screeching cats. The high-sided container effectively hid the vehicle from any curious looks by anyone walking by on the main road. Javid watched the feral cats skitter away and vanish into the gloomy interiors of the warehouses looming on either side. He admired the animals for like him they were true survivors that had been abandoned and shunned by the community at large and had created their own closed society and lived by taking that which was no longer given. As he waited his mobile warbled and saw that the caller ID was anonymous. He listened and heard a very familiar voice at the other end.

'*Es salaam alykhum*, Javid,' Jahandar said. 'So you still have my phone, then?'

'It has been very useful,' Javid answered warily.

'Have you got your own Saudi distributor for the drugs yet,' Jahandar said, aware that he had never disclosed the name given to him by Major Kazemi.

Javid thought quickly and recalled that Jahandar still had the jewels in his possession and said, 'I'll give you twenty-five per cent for the distributor's name.'

'Give me fifty per cent and I must accompany you to the address I give.'

Javid could afford to be generous when he knew that he would never be honouring any agreement. 'Very well, it's a deal, so listen carefully. Come to the Guraifa docks at eleven thirty and bring everything you need for the journey.'

Javid avoided telling Jahandar that he had two surprises for his ex-employer. One, they would be sailing on Jahandar's boat and two, it would be the last trip of his life.

Major Dabal, Walid and Corporal Ahmed searched the fishing cruiser from stem to stern but found nothing to connect the boat with the man they sought. The helicopter team had reported that on absailing down onto the runaway vessel they had found it deserted and the helm lashed with a short length of rope. They managed to untie the wheel and alter course seconds before the boat would have struck the fateful sandbar that had claimed so many lives. After further questioning by Dabal the pilot recalled that he had briefly passed over a tiny sailing dinghy that was heading for the Bahrain Yacht Club.

'He doubled back and fooled us,' Walid surmised when Captain Dabal phoned him with the news. 'They led us astray by making it look as though they had fled to Qatar and then, like cunning jackals, they simply returned to their lair.'

'I'll have somebody check at the yacht club,' Dabal said.

'Don't bother yourself, Captain,' Walid sighed. 'If I know these people they wouldn't do the obvious and moor there. I believe they have bypassed the harbour and probably beached the boat on a more deserted part of the coast before hitching a ride.'

'I'll also have all the beaches and taxi companies checked.'

'That'll be our best course of action right now and while that's happening I'll meet you at the docks with Corporal Ahmed and we'll take a closer look at the cruiser to see if there are any clues as to their current whereabouts.'

Walid gave strict instructions to his friends that they should stay in the locked apartment until he and Ahmed returned and Stuart reluctantly gave way and agreed. Alan was more than happy to be able to stay and keep Reem company and Helen was unable to disguise her pleasure that Stuart couldn't be tempted to do anything foolhardy, as he so often was. Walid gave Stuart a sympathetic look as he left the apartment, knowing that his friend always wanted to be where the real action was taking place.

The muezzin was calling the faithful to the *maghrib* prayer and the sun had been halved by a perfectly flat and burnished horizon when the two officers and Ahmed clambered aboard the Boston Whaler to begin their investigation. Every square centimetre of the vessel was searched, including the large engine compartment and bilges before Walid decided to call it a day.

'They've left nothing here that can be of any help to us,' he concluded and gave a deep sigh as he sank into one of the saloon seats. Captain Dabal nodded his agreement but continued to flip and unzip mattresses and cushions while the corporal optimistically went on opening locker after locker.

'Major Kazemi seems to have completely vanished off the face of the earth as well,' Dabal added in a morose voice.

'Why don't you give him a call and ask him where he is?' Walid said sardonically.

The captain was about to laugh at the major's outlandish remark when his breath caught in his throat and he shoved a hand into his pocket. 'Major, I do believe you may have given me a good idea.' He took out his phone and stabbed at the buttons. 'We were so concerned with physically apprehending Kazemi that we didn't consider calling him.' He pressed the phone to his ear and listened with an intense expression.

'Ah! Good afternoon, Major Kazemi. This is Captain Dabal. I was hoping that you would be kind enough to meet with me so that we can discuss your next course of action.' He listened briefly before hurriedly continuing, 'Don't hang up, Major. Please listen to me. Our meeting can be held on neutral ground of your choosing and I will come alone and unarmed at any time you specify, naturally. It's important that you understand that this meeting will be to your great advantage. If you don't agree to this then the only alternative left to me is to continue the manhunt which, as you well know, can only have one outcome.'

Walid could see Dabal holding his breath as he listened to the major's reply and then he exhaled and winked at Walid. 'I am in complete agreement with that, Major Kazemi,' he said and closed the phone.

'You managed to convince him to meet with you?' Walid asked with one sceptical eyebrow raised.

'I have and it'll be in the Manama Souk at eleven tonight,' Dabal said jubilantly.

Walid was familiar with the old market in the heart of Manama and he knew that the maze of crowded streets would be the perfect meeting place for the major to suddenly appear and disappear if he thought there was any hint of a trap.

'Where in the souk are you to go?' Walid asked.

'There's a couple of streets where gold traders operate and I am to wander along them until I am approached by an old coffee vendor who will take me to the major.

'What is your plan to apprehend the man?'

'I have no plan yet. I am simply going to suggest to him that telling me the whereabouts of the heroin will guarantee him safe passage out of the country.'

'You do not have the power to promise a drug smuggler and possible murderer his freedom, Captain. That decision has to be taken at a higher level than our petty ranks permit.'

'Going through the right channels will tie us up in red tape and waste a lot of valuable time. I'm seeing him in three hours and you and I will have to take responsibility for the meeting,' the captain said earnestly, lightly touching Walid who was deep in thought.

'We are the only ones who know you have made contact with the major and as long as we keep it like that our jobs will be safe,' Walid finally murmured as he turned his head and fixed his eyes on the young corporal standing nearby.

'You can trust me, sir.'

'Good lad.' Walid clapped the corporal on the back with a meaty hand and turned to the captain. 'As much as I disagree with your plan I have to admit that it is our only chance of getting a lead on the heroin. We must stop that shipment leaving Bahrain and crossing over to the mainland at all costs. What kind of back-up can we arrange for you?'

'None. I want Corporal Ahmed to stay and guard this boat and for you to stay clear of the souk until I tell you to come in. If there is any trouble I'll use my favourite back-up,' Dabal said, raising his trouser leg to reveal the Smith & Wesson revolver. 'That will make up for this loss,' he added as he opened his jacket, removed his trusty Glock from the shoulder holster and gave it to Walid. 'I have to show Kazemi that I am unarmed so please take care of that until we meet in the lobby of the Oriental Palace Hotel at midnight.'

Knowing that the hotel was close to the gold souk and therefore near to the meeting place, should any trouble arise, reassured Walid a little and he nodded and slipped the heavy gun out of sight beneath his jacket.

'I shall be there and should anything go wrong before midnight make sure that you call me,' Walid insisted as he watched the captain stand up to leave the boat and head back to the city. Walid quickly extended his hand. 'Take care, Captain Dabal,' he said softly. 'You're an excellent police officer who will rise in the ranks very quickly but only if you stay alive.'

'If I do, Major, it will be because of officers like yourself. I wish I could work on your team permanently,' the captain said hurriedly as he turned away to hide the rising colour in his cheeks. Dabal jumped ashore and strode away to where he had parked his patrol car.

Javid watched as Dabal left the vessel and he ducked back into the alley until the officer had driven away. He checked his watch and then continued watching the vessel until he saw the cockpit light go out and the two remaining men clamber ashore. One was a corporal and the other was the same bulky man he had seen carrying a rifle by the Tree of Life. His hand automatically went to the knife and he fondled the sheath while keeping watch on the two men. They paused to shake hands and then the corporal returned to the vessel, turning briefly to salute the older man as he drove past and took the road leading back to the city centre.

Javid waited patiently until it was eleven o'clock before slipping quietly across the road and onto the dockside where he paused beside a stack of salt-bleached pallets to stare into the dimly lit main saloon. He could vaguely make out the figure of the police officer. After a long day he had succumbed to tiredness and was slumped on the divan clutching a mug of cold coffee with both hands. Javid studied the dock both ways before moving closer to the stern of the vessel for a better view of the interior. The young officer had begun to snore lightly and Javid noticed that the night tide had fortunately raised the gunwale of the boat to be level with the dockside. Javid slowly stepped over the side and down onto the rear bench seat with one foot. The boat dipped beneath his added weight but the movement was slight and the policeman remained in a deep sleep. With arms outstretched Javid balanced on his right leg as he cautiously brought the other leg over the stern. With indiscernible movements he made his way towards the open saloon.

Corporal Ahmed was experiencing a nightmare: he was eating his favourite ice cream in a strange girl's bedroom when the chocolate flake suddenly transformed into a black, writhing snake. In horror he threw the cone and imaginary reptile through an open window and his coffee cup flew from his hands to smash into pieces on the deck.

The police officer awoke with a start and was confronted by a shadowy figure leaning towards him. Realizing that he was no longer dreaming the officer snatched at the pistol on his hip and screamed as his hair was grabbed and pulled, forcing his head back.

A flicker of reflected light in the dim saloon silenced his scream as his trachea and carotid artery were both expertly severed by the assassin's knife. Javid leant to one side to avoid the spurting blood and kept the dying man's head pulled well back. The corporal's legs thrashed wildly for a few seconds before being stilled by the onset of unconsciousness and then death.

Javid silently waited in the darkness for a few minutes to make sure that nobody had been alerted by the policeman's brief scream before leaving the saloon and going ashore where he flitted from shadow to shadow until he had made it back to the alley unobserved.

It took Javid only a matter of minutes to park the Ford by the Boston Whaler and unload the twelve boxes. These were rapidly stacked in the saloon beside the corpse and after retrieving the spare ignition key he had stolen from Jahandar and taped inside the port navigation light he waited by the mooring ropes for Jahandar to appear.

It was precisely eleven-thirty when a taxi drove slowly along the dockside road and Javid waved at the driver as he drew near. Jahandar eased his bulk out of the door, his mouth open in astonishment. He reached back inside and withdrew a large canvas bag before paying the driver. As the taxi drove away he hauled himself and his luggage aboard.

'It's my boat!' he exclaimed to the smirking Javid.

'And now it's mine,' Javid said, unlooping the mooring and lithely climbing up to the controls. 'Where are we headed for?'

'Al Aziziyah, Saudi Arabia. There is a private villa on the coast near the desalination plant. That's where we need to go,' Jahandar said, his voice muffled by the decking.

The engine started on the first turn of the key and while Jahandar made himself comfortable in the saloon Javid eased the throttle forward and the craft slowly made headway and motored towards the harbour entrance.

At eleven o'clock the Boston Whaler had cleared the docks and with navigation lights switched on was safely heading out to sea on a course that would take them round the north coast of Bahrain. Javid hoped to pass beneath the King Fahd Causeway that linked the island to the mainland before turning towards the Saudi coast under cover of darkness.

When he was approximately four kilometres offshore Javid went below and removed the body of the police corporal from the saloon. Jahandar's nose wrinkled with distaste as he added more deep cuts to the arms and legs before rolling Ahmed over the side for the night predators to feast on.

At precisely eleven o'clock Captain Dabal began to walk up and down the gold souk. The labyrinth of narrow streets were still thronged with traders, buyers and late-night tourists, and the few coffee sellers Dabal saw were busy meeting a constant demand for their tiny cups of a strong and bitter Turkish brew. The aroma of roast lamb and spices assailed him at every corner and his stomach began to rumble from neglect. His feet were hurting in his new shoes and he was beginning to think that Major Kazemi wouldn't keep the appointment when an elderly man with the traditional stack of cups and a large brass coffee pot emerged from an alleyway and caught Dabal's eye. With a slight nod of his head the captain followed the shuffling man along a circuitous route that left Dabal dazed by its intricacy until the old man stopped at a green door. The coffee seller rapped once on the thick panels and then quickly walked away, leaving the captain standing alone in the shadows.

Heavy bolts slid in corroded locks and the door creaked open, releasing a flood of bright light that illuminated the squinting captain.

'Come in, Dabal,' a voice commanded and the captain recognized it as Major Kazemi's. 'I trust you were not followed and that you are unarmed?'

'No, I was not followed and yes, I am unarmed.' Dabal opened his jacket to reveal the empty holster as he stepped into the small room that was decorated and furnished as a traditional *majlis*. The major had seated himself cross-legged on one of the large silk cushions that lined the walls.

'Sit there,' Kazemi ordered pointing to a spot opposite him. 'Then remove your back-up very carefully and give it to this man.' As he spoke a burly man entered the room carrying a small coffee tray in one hand and an Uzi machine-gun in the other. 'I have always known about your liking for American guns and to say that you would come unarmed is totally out of character.'

Holding the weapon between thumb and forefinger Dabal placed it on the tray that was being held by the towering servant. He then took one of the small, steaming cups and one of the medjool dates that were presented in a delicate porcelain bowl.

'It would appear that although you are a member of a drug-smuggling operation you haven't forgotten your manners when it comes to extending hospitality.'

'Let's forget about being polite and get straight down to what you want,' Kazemi snarled before slurping his coffee down and tossing the empty cup to one side.

'Very well, Major. All you have to do is give me the current location of the heroin and I will ensure that you will receive a reasonable sum of money and the freedom to purchase an air ticket to anywhere in the world you wish.'

'You don't have the authority to offer me that,' Kazemi snapped.

'I don't need the authority. I will simply give you the money and escort you to the airport and gladly see you onto the first available plane. I'll face the consequences of my actions after the event,' Dabal replied in an equally brittle tone.

'My life is on the line if I tell you about the drugs.'

'I will guarantee an armed escort for your protection until you leave the country.'

Major Kazemi fell silent as he thought carefully about Dabal's offer. He knew that with the money he had been paid for handling previous shipments he had enough to start a new business in South America. However, would it be far enough away from any retribution by Sheikh Abdullah? Dabal watched the major's face as he weighed the pros and cons of the offer until he suddenly looked up and straightened his shoulders.

'I accept, Captain. Give me your hand and let's seal this deal like gentlemen.' Kazemi spat on his palm and extended it towards the captain. Dabal rose and reluctantly grasped the hand of the treacherous officer.

'It's a deal. Now, where are the drugs?'

'They are being held by a man called Javid whom I will now call.' He took a mobile from his pocket.

Javid had just finished washing the blood off the decking and the gunwale when the familiar ringtone of Jahandar's phone was heard in the saloon. He checked the caller ID and was shocked to see Major Kazemi's name. Javid walked to the stern and was about to throw the phone into the boiling wake when curiosity overcame caution.

'What do you want, Major?'

'Javid, it's not what I want but what would be beneficial to us both. I have a proposition that you cannot afford to ignore.'

'You forget, Major. I have the drugs which represent a great deal of money.'

'And that's all they do represent because they cannot buy you real protection from the retribution that will soon follow. Remember, Javid, no matter where you go the sheikh has all the money and power in the world to catch up with you.'

'And what can you do to prevent that? You're only a mere major in the police and a wanted man yourself.'

'I can assure you that I have the sheikh's full confidence and I will be able to convince him to leave you alone and to even give you twenty-five per cent of the street value in US dollars if you hand over the full shipment for me to dispose of as I wish.'

'You'll give me four million dollars in cash for lifetime protection from the sheikh?' Javid whispered as he mentally added that sum to what he could get for the ancient jewels in the canvas bag.

'The value is still thirteen million. You'll get three and a quarter million and not a dollar more and we'll make the exchange at a place of your own choosing.'

'I won't argue about the odd few thousand, Major.' There was a brief pause. 'I accept but insist that the exchange takes place at Budaiya Marina at *fajr* prayer time,' he said adamantly.

'I won't be able to get the money during the night. How about midday?'

'Get the money from the sheikh by dawn or the deal is off and I sail.'

'You're on a boat?' Kazemi said in surprise.

'You'll recognize it. It used to belong to Jahandar.'

The line went dead and Kazemi closed his phone and looked across at Dabal. 'He wants to meet at Budaiya Marina on a boat that used to belong to his boss, Jahandar,' he said and then added in a more eager tone. 'When do I get money and protection?'

A cold chill had run through the captain on hearing Kazemi's reference to the Boston Whaler and he was unable to think about anything but Corporal Ahmed for a few moments before speaking again.

'I want all the drugs in my possession before our deal is completed. I think it would be best if you kept your appointment with Javid because he knows that you're a wanted man and he won't think he is being led into a police trap if you could be ensnared at the same time.'

Dabal rose to his feet and held his hand out to the tall servant. Kazemi nodded and the man reluctantly returned the Smith & Wesson and the captain went to the door. 'You must make your own way to the marina but I assure you that you will be watched every step of the way.' He bent down and slipped the pistol back into its holster.

Kazemi remained seated and once more nodded to the big man holding the Uzi. With two long strides he reached the door and unlocked it with a large key he had taken from his belt. 'I will see you at dawn, Captain,' Kazemi said curtly and Dabal tapped his wristwatch in token agreement before stepping through the open door and into the dark alley beyond.

The shabby green door slammed shut and the high humidity couldn't remove the chill that Dabal was feeling as he quickly dialled Walid's number. It was answered almost immediately.

'It's only eleven-thirty. What's wrong?'

'I hope nothing is wrong, Walid, but we had better make a check to see if the Boston Whaler is still where we left it because Major Kazemi has just informed me that Javid is now in possession of the vessel.'

'What! But Corporal Ahmed is on board guarding it. You must phone him immediately and call me back.'

Walid strode across the lobby of the Oriental Palace Hotel and out to the forecourt where he had parked his car. As he opened the door and sat in the driver's seat his phone rang.

'There is no answer,' Dabal said breathlessly. 'Corporal Ahmed isn't answering his phone.'

'I'll call Stuart and Alan and we'll meet them at the dock,' Walid said decisively. 'We may need extra help.'

'No need for that, Major. I can get a SWAT team at the mooring in thirty minutes.'

'And I can be there in fifteen, Captain. Please bring a couple of extra weapons,' Walid snapped and ended the call. He then dialled again to give instructions to his friends; soon after he had reached the dockside road and as arranged met up with the two geologists outside the Port

Authority building. As he briefed Stuart on what had happened since they had last been together Dabal screeched to a halt beside them.

Stuart took the back-up Smith & Wesson offered by the captain and Alan took the Mossberg shotgun that was kept inside the patrol car for riots.

The three men then climbed into Dabal's car that swiftly accelerated down to the docks and round the corner into the wharfside road. Walid and Dabal immediately saw that the Boston Whaler was gone and the patrol car stopped dead where the boat was last moored.

'I'll put out an all-points on the vessel; it couldn't have gone very far,' Dabal said as he reached for the microphone clipped to the dashboard.

'No, leave it, Dabal. We know where he is planning to be at dawn and now we know that he is arriving by water and not by road.' Walid laid a restraining hand on the captain's that was gripping the microphone.

'But what about Ahmed?'

'I'm sorry, Captain, but I believe you won't be seeing the corporal again. The man we are dealing with is totally ruthless and I believe he is the man who murdered Shehhi at the Tree of Life.'

The four men sat in silence for a moment thinking of what they would do to the killer before Dabal restarted the engine and slowly pulled away from the empty mooring.

'We must prepare a trap to catch this man,' Stuart said.

'And when we've got him we must forget the word justice,' Alan added. 'And that's why we cannot get a SWAT team involved for they would be compelled to witness against us.'

The two police officers stiffened for they had been sworn to uphold the law and reneging on their oath to become avenging vigilantes went against everything they had been taught. Walid was about to protest when a clear image of Shehhi lying in the sand with his throat cut appeared before his eyes. The pain he felt when he first grieved for his friend returned in an emotional tidal wave and words caught in his throat as he silently agreed with Alan's sentiment.

'If we just shoot the man it would be an act of murder. It is our duty to try to bring him in for a proper trial,' Dabal said half-heartedly.

'The man has no compunction about killing those who get in his way and I'm sorry to say it but he has undoubtedly murdered your corporal. He will also kill Major Kazemi to get both the money and the drugs in the morning,' Alan argued. 'So, we will try to bring him in as you suggest, Captain. However, there is a very good chance that we will fail.'

Dabal fell into a troubled silence and he turned to look at the senior officer with eyes that pleaded for help.

'You need not be present, Dabal,' Walid murmured. 'We will claim that he tried to escape.'

Dabal looked deep into Walid's eyes and recognized the cold determination to avenge Shehhi and all legal and moral objections to what had been suggested suddenly evaporated. They seemed so irrelevant in the light of the terrible crimes that Javid had already committed.

'He will be mine,' Walid whispered as he stared unseeing out of the car window. 'He must pay for Sergeant Shehhi and Corporal Ahmed.'

'Then let it be so!' Captain Dabal reluctantly concurred.

22

Major Kazemi locked the villa and left Durrat al Bahrain as the first faint streaks of light appeared on the horizon and arrived at Budaiya Marina just as the sun began to show through the morning sea mist. Muezzin after muezzin seemed to follow him the length of the island as they called the *fajr* prayer time.

He passed the Mohammed bin Khalifa mosque, turned right into Road 5553 and slowed his pace until he saw the turning on the left that would take him to the moorings. His eyes scoured the area for any suspicious vehicles as he entered the narrow access road to the moorings on the huge breakwater.

Boats of all descriptions that looked like abandoned toys in a sandpit were beached on a large empty lot beside the road and after passing seven chandleries he came upon scores of pleasure craft. They were moored on both sides of four jetties that jutted thirty-five metres into the harbour. There were plenty of parking places alongside the road and Kazemi pulled into one of the empty bays and opened his window before switching off the ignition.

The gentle lapping of water against hulls, shroud lines clattering against masts and the screech of the odd seagull were the only sounds disturbing the slumbering harbour. Kazemi stepped out of the car and into the morning humidty with all his senses fully alert as he looked round slowly for any sign of life. A distant metallic clang quickly drew his attention to a lone figure on a yacht that was moored to the last jetty on the breakwater. He was sluicing down the decks with buckets of seawater.

A car door slammed and Kazemi turned round to see that a Jeep had parked at the far end of the road. There were four men inside who sat staring straight ahead at the rising sun. The major thought he could recognize Captain Dabal but the car was too far away for him to be sure. He ignored the policemen and began studying each of the jetties in turn but was unable to identify anything that resembled a Boston Whaler.

The major crossed the road and reaching the parapet of the breakwater he looked down on scores of launches and pleasure cruisers anchored and moored to brightly coloured buoys. One of the boats was the Boston Whaler and although it was moored fifty metres from the sea wall he could clearly recognize the slender man reclining on the long seat in the stern.

Kazemi picked up a small pebble and threw it to splash behind the vessel. Javid instantly sat bolt upright and looked round with a hand inside his jacket.

Kazemi waited until Javid was facing his way before raising a hand to attract his attention. The bodyguard nodded and pointed at the slime-covered sea wall and then at the small dinghy tied to a rusting ringbolt.

The major swung himself over the parapet and climbed down the rusting rungs to where the little rowboat bobbed in the gentle swell. He put the short oars into the rowlocks and was soon propelling the light craft towards the cruiser.

'You're not carrying anything,' Javid snarled as the rowboat bumped against the stern of the anchored boat. 'You're not coming aboard unless you have six and a half million dollars on you.' He slipped a large automatic from beneath his coat and pointed it at the major who had shipped oars and was patiently looking up at the assassin.

'I came to warn you. Not to give you any money,' Kazemi said calmly. 'There are four men on the breakwater—'

'You've betrayed me?' Javid interrupted with a menacing growl as he pulled the slide back to cock the weapon.

'—four men who want to recover the shipment you took and to hand you over to the police but I can safely get us both to the Saudi mainland if you do as I tell you to.'

'And if I don't?'

'Then you will no doubt have a gun battle on your hands that you cannot win.'

'What's your brilliant plan then?' Javid said sarcastically as he lowered the weapon.

'We must leave immediately before the men on the sea wall get suspicious and then, once we have rounded the headland and are in the next bay, we can switch to a faster boat and open the seacocks on this one.'

'You have such a boat waiting there?'

'No. We have to take one that is moored offshore,' Kazemi said confidently as he began to climb over the side. 'I suggest you raise the anchor and get this boat moving before the men above stop looking at us and start shooting.'

'Have you cleared the deal with the sheikh yet?' Javid muttered.

'Look, we have no time for that now.'

'Well, have you?' Javid screeched raising the gun again.

'No. I can only do that when we have the drugs well out of his reach. Only then can I negotiate from a posititon of strength.'

Javid's eyes narrowed and his pressure on the trigger increased to take up the fraction of slack in the mechanism.

'Let's discuss this later otherwise neither of us will be in a position to negotiate.'

Javid shot a glance upward and saw two heads peering over the sea wall parapet. 'I see only two men,' he shouted as he hurried to the flying bridge. He soon had the engine started and he thrust the throttle forward as the first bullet whistled past his ear to punch a hole in the windshield. He swung the wheel and the next volley harmlessly raked the sea. As the boat raced away from the sea wall he kept spinning the wheel to make them a more difficult target. Soon the shots were sending up small plumes of water in their wake and he knew they were out of range of the pistols. The Boston Whaler disappeared from the shooters' sight as it rounded the bluff.

As the vessel violently avoided the gunshots in its race away from the huge breakwater Kazemi staggered into the saloon. A small intake of breath was his only reaction when he saw the massive figure of Jahandar facing him. He advanced on the motionless man until he was able to see the ragged round hole in the drug lord's forehead. A thin trickle of blood had run from the wound past the unseeing eyes and down the side of the pudgy nose to the corner of the open mouth, giving the impression that the dead man was drinking his own blood.

The major didn't have to look to know that the heavy-calibre bullet had removed a large piece of skull from the back of the head.

'I see you have terminated your employment with Jahandar,' he shouted above the noise of the engine and the sea slapping the sides of the hull.

'He was under the impression that he could take the shipment back without giving me any recompense for my trouble,' Javid shouted back. 'Come up and help me select a suitable boat.'

Kazemi quickly climbed to the flying bridge and began surveying the various moored craft. His gaze soon settled on a twelve-metre powerboat. The outstanding pedigree of the Sunseeker Portofino made it the obvious choice as the major knew that the sleek sports cruiser was capable of achieving thirty-four knots—more than sufficient for their needs. He pointed to the craft and Javid spun the wheel and pulled alongside, causing the Sunseeker to rise and fall in the surge of water created between the two vessels.

A large Jamaican emerged from the cabin wearing Bermuda shorts and a plain white T-shirt. He stood with arms folded across an impressive chest as he studied the policeman on the Boston Whaler with an air of curiosity.

'Can I help you officer?' he asked in a lilting accent. 'Is there a problem?'

'No problem, sir,' Kazemi called back. 'Just a routine enquiry. Are you the owner of this vessel?'

'No sir. I wish I was but I'm just the security guard employed by the company that owns it,' the man replied with a broad smile.

'Enough of this polite crap,' Javid muttered and taking the gun from his pocket he aimed it at the man's face.

'Javid! No!' Kazemi shouted but he was too late. The trigger was squeezed and the man's head was thrust back by the impact of the nine-millimetre bullet. The security guard fell backwards onto the leather seating as the deafening gunshot reverberated across the water.

Javid ignored the protestations of the major and began hastily throwing the boxes over the side into the Sunseeker's seating area. Kazemi kept the two craft together while they rose and fell until the last of the drugs had been transferred and then he jumped the narrow gap to board the luxury sports boat.

Javid, still aboard the Boston Whaler, went below and opened the seacock valves that were normally used to drain bilge water when the vessel was dry-docked. Fountains of seawater began to gush into the boat and Javid grabbed the old canvas bag from beside Jahandar's body and quickly joined the major.

A quick search of the dead Jamaican's pockets unearthed the ignition key and Javid hurried to the cockpit and started the engines. Kazemi went forward and untied the mooring rope and then a muffled shout from Javid reminded him of the stern line. The major hurried back and climbed down onto the diving platform to release the tether. As he dropped it over the side and stood up the engines of the Sunseeker suddenly roared and the sea boiled behind him. Before the major could steady himself the Sunseeker leapt forward and he lost his balance and toppled into the foaming water.

The Sunseeker raced seawards and Kazemi surfaced, spluttering and coughing up sea water. With salt-infused eyes he made out the stern of the boat powering away as he was lifted by the powerful wake it left behind. He also caught a brief glimpse of another boat that was moving across the small bay in the same direction and on the next uplift of water he identified it as an official customs boat. It was a slow stubby-hulled boat that he knew could never catch the Sunseeker when it was at full-throttle. He quickly shed his uniform jacket and he began swimming with an energy-conserving stroke towards the distant shore where he planned to retrieve his car and return to the villa at Durrat Bahrain.

Before Javid made his escape the four friends had watched as Major Kazemi left his car and walked across the road to look over the parapet.

'It looks like he's going his own way now,' Alan said as they observed the major climbing over the wall and disappearing from sight. They waited a few seconds and then left the Jeep and raced across the road to see where the major had gone.

As they cautiously raised their heads to look over the rough stone blocks they saw him rowing a small skiff towards a Boston Whaler.

'That looks like our missing boat and I would like to place a bet that Javid is aboard her with all the drugs,' Stuart said, clenching his fists.

'Looks like you're right, Stuart. So, it's on with plan two,' Walid muttered and he hurried back to the Jeep with Captain Dabal in hot pursuit.

Stuart and Alan remained at the parapet as the Jeep raced back along the breakwater. They watched as Kazemi was permitted to tie his dinghy to the larger boat. A lean, swarthy man appeared and seemed to be pointing some kind of weapon at the major. That same man then spotted the two friends at the parapet and he spun on his heel and nimbly ascended the ladder to sit at the helm on the flying bridge.

'That must have been Javid,' Stuart said as he tried to make out the man starting the engine. 'And it looks like they have both decided to do a runner.'

The sudden roar of an engine seemed to add a full point to Stuart's words and Alan pulled the Smith & Wesson from his belt.

'They're getting away,' he exclaimed and instinctively fired. He was unable to see whether he had hit anything or not and just kept firing until the magazine was empty. They both watched with dismay as the Boston Whaler grew smaller and then disappeared round the bluff.

The two friends stepped down from the parapet and turned to see Walid's Jeep turning at the beginning of the breakwater and racing away towards Manama.

'I reckon we should get back to the ladies and leave the outcome of this to the law enforcers,' Stuart said, tucking the warm weapon back into his belt. They strode along the breakwater towards the wharfside road with eyes on the lookout for a cruising taxi.

Walid drove to the corniche where he accelerated with the sea on his right. The morning traffic was light and he was able to maintain a good speed until the Budaiya Fort came into view.

'Everyone thinks this is just an old tourist attraction but if you turn right just past the fort you will come to the Rapid Response centre I told you about,' Dabal said with a quiet smile. 'We keep a nice toy hidden there that has cut my drug enforcement budget by nearly two million dollars. I think you'll appreciate what it can do, Walid.'

Walid looked askance at the grinning captain and then concentrated on slewing the car round the next corner and heading directly towards the sea. The fort loomed ominously on their right and soon they were passing a long row of anonymous sheds. As they approached a gate topped with razor wire an officer in full riot gear and a machine-gun slung across his chest held his hand up and Walid braked to a stop. Dabal nodded to the man who instantly recognized the captain. He broke into a smile and ran to open the gate and as Walid drove past he performed a crisp salute for the senior officer.

'Nice guys you have here,' Walid observed.

'And they're tough, too. They're as loyal to me as your own team are to you, Walid,' Dabal said proudly. 'And they'll back us all the way in this little venture because they have all suffered at the hands of drug smugglers.'

'How do you mean.'

'Well, for example take Bassam. He had a little sister called Esraa whom he dearly loved. Pushers at the school gates got her hooked on marijuana, cocaine and then heroin. She stole money, was forced to sell her body for a fix and finally died from an overdose at an unknown drug dealer's party for rich paedophiles when she was only 14 years old. Her body was found discarded on a rubbish tip.'

'A pattern that is so familiar right across the region,' Walid murmured as he followed Dabal's directional hand gestures until they arrived at a large corrugated shed on the water's edge.

'All the men in this team have similar stories and that's why every one of them is prepared to flay any drug dealer alive if they can catch him,' Dabal said with a catch in his throat as they left the Jeep and entered the small door at the side of the building.

Walid stepped back, astounded by the sight before him, for within the oversized boathouse was moored a Pegasus Class military hydrofoil. On the foredeck was a deadly OTO Melara sixty-two-calibre gun capable of firing eighty-four rounds a minute over a distance of twenty-two thousand metres. This he had learned during a cultural exchange with the US naval base in Norfolk, Virginia.

Captain Dabal's crew had been alerted and the engines were already burbling away as they went up the gangplank and received salutes from four officers.

'Do you like my little surprise?' Dabal asked and then laughed as he noticed the expression on Walid's face. 'You obviously do. Let's go to the bridge and meet Lieutenant Ashique.'

'I don't know what to say, Dabal, except let's go and get the bloody bastards.'

'Now that we've flushed them into the open it will be easy to apprehend them.' Dabal held a door open and Walid stepped onto the bridge to be confronted by an array of high-tech instrument consoles manned by grim-faced sailors.

'They know whom we're going after and they're eager to get into the chase,' Dabal murmured in Walid's ear. The major was introduced to Lieutenant Ashique, a young baby-faced officer and an older officer with a heavily weathered face who was simply referred to as Yazzan.

'Yazzan is in charge of the automatic fire control system and as a reformed addict takes great pleasure in sinking drug dealers,' Dabal said by way of listing the officer's professional credentials.

Dabal took the young lieutenant to one side and after a brief murmured discussion returned to where Walid was studying the flight deck of the hydrofoil. The main doors of the boathouse were opening and the lieutenant gave orders to the coxswain who eased the twin throttles forward and immediately the sound of the powerful Mercedes-Benz marine engines were echoing in the building and the vessel slowly moved out to the open sea.

Walid clutched at an overhead rail as the boat leapt forward to speed through the water creating a boiling white wake that was as straight as an arrow. A sailor entered the bridge to join Yazzan and they both sat before a bank of glowing screens.

'That's the fully-automatic firing control. Once the target has been found by radar and locked on lasers paint the target and the gun will then constantly adjust for every pitch and roll. This gives the weapon pinpoint accuracy up to twenty-two thousand metres,' Dabal explained as he pointed at each of the different screens over the sailors' shoulders.

'Standby gentlemen,' the lieutenant warned as the sound of the engines changed. 'We're switching to gas turbine.' A sudden whine overlaid the normal rumbling and Walid felt a dramatic increase in the speed. Then without warning the deck tilted, forcing him to grab the back of Yazzan's chair to maintain his balance.

'We're rising on the planes,' Dabal said with a broad grin when seeing the surprised look on Walid's face. 'Now we're really going to move.'

As the hull rose above the sea the lack of friction allowed the hydrofoil to reach maximum speed and by the time Walid had steadied himself the four aquaplanes had fully raised the boat and it was cutting through the waves at forty-eight knots. Dabal tapped a large dial in front of the helmsman. 'We're now doing the equivalent of eighty-eight kilometres per hour. We'd be exceeding the speed limit if we were in downtown Manama.' He smiled broadly but his eyes remained icy cold. 'We'll soon run the bastards down.'

His words were sharply punctuated by a loud chorus of '*Na'am, Naqib,*' by every seaman on the bridge. That single shout of 'Yes, Captain,' demonstrated the unity and dedication of the whole crew. Walid was about to compliment Dabal on his team when alarm bells sounded.

'I have a fast-moving target, Captain. Bearing two-four-zero,' Yazzan shouted as he rapidly tapped keys before him.

'I don't like the sound of fast-moving,' Walid muttered.

'Anything above thirty knots is fast moving at sea which makes targeting it that much more difficult,' Dabal said.

'But not difficult for us, right Yazzan,' the lieutenant added with eyes glittering now that the hunt was on.

The man in control of the deadly unmanned gun on the foredeck simply grunted as his eyes flicked from one screen to another, occasionally murmuring instructions to the man seated beside him. His fingers danced over the keys as though they had a life of their own and lights flickered on and off on the screens until a loud pinging noise came from the loudspeakers.

'Target painted and locked on, sir,' Yazzan called out and the lieutenant raised his binoculars to study the small, hazy shape that was passing under a span of the King Fahd Causeway. 'Exactly six thousand metres and closing,' Yazzan called out and began to chant new range figures as they sped towards the distant boat.

Dabal gratefully took the spare pair of binoculars handed to him by the helmsman and as he spun the focusing ring the unfamiliar lines of a Sunseeker cruiser sprang into view.

'It's not the Boston Whaler, Walid,' he said. 'But the man at the controls looks familiar. Take a look.'

Walid took the binoculars and after bracing himself against deck movement he studied the fast-moving powerboat.

'That's him but where's our second man? Kazemi was wearing a uniform and I can't see him.'

'I don't know but I have a feeling that this is our killer. He is running too fast to be innocent. They must have switched boats at the off-shore mooring,' Dabal said. 'Let's catch them just after the causeway, Captain.'

Lieutenant Ashique nodded and the hydrofoil raced towards the spectacular, twenty-five-kilometre highway over the sea that provided a trade umbilical cord between Saudi Arabia and Bahrain. It was also Major Kazemi's foremost link with drug distributors in the kingdom.

As Javid looked up at the vast network of steel girders that supported the main span he was passing under he happened to glance back and see a distant boat following the same course. He raised the binoculars and holding them with one hand he focused the lenses until he saw the mid-grey hull flying above the sea on foaming legs.

A cold chill went through his body and he spun the wheel to send the boat on a new course directly towards the coast of Saudi Arabia. As he ran parallel to the causeway the boat was now close enough for him to catch brief glimpses of his pursuers between the concrete pylons that supported the eight-lane highway high above. He instinctively knew that it was a military craft and that his best chance was to stay as close to the causeway as possible to prevent the use of what seemed to be a no-nonsense gun on the foredeck.

As the hydrofoil passed under the causeway the lieutenant ordered the gas turbine to be cut and the hull slowly sank down into the sea while the craft reverted to diesel power. The hydrofoil turned to chase the Sunseeker which was still running parallel to the causeway and Javid instantly wrenched the wheel to double back beneath the highway.

The computer calculated the change of course and the proximity shell exploded by the stern with enough percussive strength to throw Javid forward against the wheel. He gasped as the metal rim was rammed against his ribs and he immediately spun the wheel to move behind another concrete pillar.

The hydrofoil stayed on the left of the causeway to shadow Javid's course and he heard an amplified buzz and then an authoritative voice echoed beneath the causeway.

'You have no chance of escape. Give yourself up now and it will be a lot easier for you.'

Javid looked between each of the concrete towers at the ominous grey shape that followed his progress like a predatory shark. He knew that the disembodied voice was right but he also knew that if he did give himself up he would be surrendering to the hangman's noose in Bahrain or the headsman's sword in Saudi Arabia.

the boat was turned to head away from the causeway. Their object was to lead us away from where they had left the vessel.' Both men swung their glasses to focus on the pillar behind which the Sunseeker had sheltered before it suddenly veered seawards.

'And there's one of them, sir,' Yazzan cried, pointing to the base of the column. 'There seems to be an unusually dark lump just above the waterline.'

'Well spotted, Yazzan,' Lieutenant Ashique said. 'Shall we heave to, sir,' he asked eagerly.

'They won't be going anywhere for quite a while so I think we should take care of that first,' Walid said as he pointed at the slowly sinking boat. 'We don't want a dozen wooden boxes filled with heroin floating to the surface later.'

'Yazzan, use both incendiary and high-explosive rounds and destroy the interior of that boat before it sinks completely,' the lieutenant ordered and Yazzan grinned as he began changing the type of shells to be loaded. Within seconds he had completed the programming and he looked at the sailor beside him.

'The honour is yours, lad,' he said softly and the young man beamed with delight. He reached across to Yazzan's keyboard and pressed one key with a flourish. The bridge was instantly subjected to sixty seconds of rolling thunder as eighty-four large-calibre shells reduced the sleek pleasure craft to a flaming inferno. The dead Jamaican had rolled from the sinking Sunseeker and disappeared long before the craft was vaporized. They all watched as the subsequent fireball rose hundreds of feet into the air.

'Now let's go catch us some fish,' Walid said as he checked the load of his automatic pistol.

When they approached the pillar the helmsman listened carefully to the lieutenant's instructions. The strong currents flowing between the massive columns constantly created new whirlpools that could easily ram the hydrofoil against the concrete structure.

Walid and Dabal waited on the heaving foredeck they could clearly see that the fugitive was clutching a large bag against his body as he kept his balance on a narrow ledge less than a metre above the waves.

'Drop any weapons you have and jump into the water; we will lower a ladder for you. If you refuse you'll be shot where you stand,' Walid said, his voice amplified by a megaphone.

Javid glared across at the major and then took his beloved Glock automatic and with an exaggerated action for all to see, threw it into the sea. He then leapt into the water still clutching the bag; using that as a float he kicked and thrashed his way to the hydrofoil. Yazzan hinged back a section of rail, unrolled a Jacob's ladder and then waited to give the man a hand in climbing aboard.

Placing the bag strap over his head Javid grabbed at the swaying ladder with both hands and as the boat rolled towards him he reached for the highest rung and let the vessel pull him up as it rolled the other way. A powerful hand gripped him by the arm and pulled him the rest of the way to lie gasping on the steel deck.

'Where's Kazemi?' a gruff voice demanded and Javid instantly recognized Major Walid.

The killer staggered to his feet and with a sneer on his face told both officers that Kazemi had jumped into the sea back at Budaiya Marina.

'We'll soon get him and he can join you on the scaffold,' Captain Dabal said in an emotionless tone as he indicated to the lieutenant on the bridge to back away from the causeway.

It wasn't the wet clothes that sent a sudden chill through Javid as he looked at Walid and saw the same pitiless eyes watching him. Hatred for the man who had ruined every one of his plans released a massive amount of adrenalin and before anyone could stop him Javid had slipped the long blade from its scabbard and lunged at Walid. The razor-sharp weapon sliced through the uniform jacket and shirt and penetrated the major's side before anyone could make a move. Javid pulled the blade out releasing a stream of blood and drew his arm back for a second strike when his head seemed to explode with pain and darkness fell. Yazzan watched the man fall and lowered the Uzi that he had used to hit the back of Javid's skull.

Walid slowly lowered himself to the deck clutching at his side as Dabal shouted for a medic. He knelt by the wounded officer and taking the sharp weapon that had fallen from Javid's nerveless hand he quickly cut away the clothing to reveal the wound that was streaming bright red.

Dabal pressed a wad of shirting against the incision to stem the flow of blood and shouted again for a medic just as two corpsmen rushed onto the foredeck to take control. Walid was still conscious when he was carried below. The wound wasn't fatal but they needed to get their patient to a hospital as soon as possible to avoid infection spreading from the minute pieces of material that had been driven deep into the wound.

Dabal gave orders for the fastest possible return to base and soon the hydrofoil gas turbine was screaming in protest as throttles were held wide open. With its hull held high above the waves by the four aquaplanes the military craft virtually flew across the ocean.

As Yazzan stood beside the drug runner who was slowly regaining consciousness the Special Response officer called Bassam walked across the foredeck to stand beside his comrade. He looked down at the waking man with pure hatred in his eyes.

'Are we really taking him back for a trial in court?' he asked beneath his breath.

'Chances are that a good lawyer will save him from the rope,' Yazzan replied.

Javid had struggled into a sitting position and was looking up at the two men with an uncomprehending, dazed expression on his face. Salt spray occasionally dampened all the men including the impassive Captain Dabal.

'Guard him well, Yazzan. If he tries to make a run for it you know what you have to do.' Dabal turned his back on Javid and paced across the deck to the bridge.

'Now where can I run to?' Javid sniggered, waving an arm around to encompass the ocean surrounding them.

'Good question, pig,' Jazzan said. 'Where could he run to, Bassam?'

'He could try to run on water. The Christians believe Jesus did that.'

'Do you think he has the same powers as Jesus?'

'Yes, I do. Look! He's trying to run for it now,' Bassam called out as Javid rose to his feet with a sneer.

'You're stupid fools if you believe a man can walk on water,' Javid said as he pushed wet hair from his eyes and rubbed the painful lump on the back of his head.

Yazzan raised his Uzi. 'But if I did believe you could walk on water that might pose a bit of a problem.'

Javid looked down the muzzle of the weapon and then up into the eyes of the man holding it and he knew what was going to happen.

'That's murder!' he shouted as he was gripped by panic. 'You can't just shoot a man down in cold blood.'

'You have, many times,' Bassam roared in disgust and he took his automatic from its holster.

'I think he's trying to run, Bassam, so to honour Corporal Ahmed and your sister you had better stop him,' Yazzan said in a quiet voice that could hardly be heard above the roar of the engine and the sea breaking against the aquaplane legs.

'Thank you, Yazzan.' Bassam raised his pistol as Javid backed away with his hands held before his face until his back was pressed against the wet rail.

'For Ahmed and my dear Esraa,' Bassam said as he fired. The two gunshots were lost in the wind and the sounds of the sea and the impact of the nine-millimetre bullets in the head punched the drug runner over the rail.

Both men went to the rail and looked back at the white wake that stretched as straight as an arrow but there were no signs of the killer.

Bassam went below and Yazzan returned to his post on the bridge.

'Where's the prisoner,' Captain Dabal asked politely as Yazzan placed the soggy canvas bag at Dabal's feet.

'He tried to escape, Captain.' Yazzan calmly sat before his screens.

'How?'

'By walking on water.'

'Did he get away?'

'No, sir.'

A small smile flickered across Dabal's face.

23

Major Kazemi waited for an hour in the shadow of a fisherman's hut before walking briskly towards the breakwater. The hot sun and light breeze blowing in from the sea had dried his shirt and slacks by the time he reached the parapet wall and he cautiously looked round it to study the road running the length of the breakwater.

His car was still parked where he had left it and he made sure that it wasn't a trap before hurrying to the vehicle and getting in. He was surprised that there wasn't a police watch on the car although he was sure that someone had noted the registration number back at police headquarters.

The key was still in his trouser pocket and he thanked Allah that he hadn't put it in his uniform jacket that was now lying on the sea floor. The car started immediately and soon he was heading south on the Janabiyah Highway. The journey back to the villa in Durrat Al Bahrain was completed without incident just as the afternoon *asr* prayer was being called at the nearby mosque. The high, pitch-perfect voice calmed his nerves as he poured himself a stiff whisky and switched on the television news. Apart from coverage of more violence on the city streets there was no mention of any occurence at Budaiya Marina.

As the major ran over the events of the last three days he came to the conclusion that his lost wealth and glorious future were the fault of one man only. Stuart Taylor had personally interfered and motivated the police forces of two countries to destroy his successful business. As his mind seethed over each downturn in his good fortune Kazemi began to formulate a plan to get his revenge and leave the country before either the police or the sheikh's men caught up with him.

The sun was touching the horizon and turning the sea the colour of the whisky in his tumbler. By the time he had finished the bottle of 18-year-old Glenlivet he had decided on his plan of action. Kazemi picked up the phone and dialled. His head was beginning to spin and when a voice answered he subserviently explained what had happened without taking a breath and before the man he had called could comment he snapped the phone shut.

Kazemi sipped the last drops in his glass as he nervously waited for a ring-back but nothing happened. The sheikh had washed his hands of him and was expecting Kazemi to sort out the problem alone, or else. With a low groan he lay back on the settee, his mind a chaotic tangle of thoughts on witness elimination, revenge and escaping the sheikh's wrath until he sank into fitful sleep.

The following evening, Friday, Dr Helen Taylor left the hospital and drove back to the apartment unaware that she was being followed. As it was a holy day all street protests had been postponed until after the *dhuhr* midday prayers. This followed an appeal on television the day before by the country's leading imams. The dark blue Land Cruiser had discreetly lingered five cars behind Helen for the whole journey and then parked at the kerb as she descended into the underground car park beneath the apartment building.

The driver waited ten minutes and then crept down the dark ramp to check for any police presence. All signs of the shooting had been eliminated and every bloodstain meticulously removed. Most of the bays contained vehicles and Helen's car was still ticking intermittently as the engine cooled. The bay assigned to Stuart's car was vacant for he and Alan had been recalled to the office to tend to urgent seismic reports from a recent oil survey.

Major Kazemi put his hand in the *thawb* pocket and fingered the cold metal of the Taurus .357 Magnum that had been a gift from his father when he had entered the police academy twenty-two years ago. The lift pinged and he quickly removed his hand and strode to the bank of four lifts in the centre of the car park. An elderly Bahraini emerged as the door hissed open but ignored the anonymous-looking man in the long *thawb* and *smaagh* head covering. Heavily framed dark glasses completed Kazemi's disguise and he brushed past the Bahraini without a word and entered the lift.

The carpet in the passageway muffled his footfalls as he strode to No. 203. Kazemi pressed the button and the muffled chime delicately sounded within the apartment.

Five seconds elapsed before the light in the peephole was dimmed and he knew he was being scrutinized by the person inside. There was the sound of a chain being applied and the door opened and Helen's face peered through the narrow gap.

'Can I help you?' she asked guardedly.

'I'm sorry to trouble you but I live one floor down and my wife has suddenly collapsed. I don't know what it is but someone told me that you are a doctor and you were the first person I could think of.'

'Is she conscious?'

'No. She simply clutched at her chest and fell down. Do hurry, please,' Kazemi pleaded.

Helen closed the door to unbolt the chain and then opened it wide to find herself staring into the barrel of a large revolver.

'Step back inside and do not scream,' he snarled as he pushed Helen back and closed the door behind him. 'Is there anyone else here?' When Helen silently shook her head he urged her on with his hand.

'The lounge, take me to the lounge,' he demanded and Helen turned and hurried down the hall to the large room. He followed closely behind looking into every room. He indicated with a wave of his hand that she should sit at the landline telephone and with a smirk he told her to call her husband.

'Why do you want to speak to Stuart?' Helen asked, her hand hesitatingly poised over the buttons. 'Who are you and what do you want?'

They both froze as the door chimes rang and Helen automatically stood up only to be pushed back into her seat.

'Who is it?' Kazemi hissed.

'How on earth would I know without going to look?'

'Then do so and remember I am right behind and my gun is aimed at the back of your head.'

Helen walked down the hallway and felt the tall man's presence close behind her. She peeked through the spyhole just as the doorchime rang again.

'It's my friend. She is quite harmless and will go away if I don't answer. Kazemi shoved Helen to one side and peered through the small lens. Despite the distortion he immediately recognized the person outside as the woman who had been held captive by Jahandar in the warehouse.

'I know her, let her in and be careful or she will get hurt,' Kazemi said as he stepped through the kitchen doorway and waited for Helen to open the door. The doctor reluctantly unlocked the door and Reem entered.

'Helen, I just had to come and see you tonight because I have some wonderful news,' the young woman gushed as she embraced her friend. Helen closed the door and Kazemi stepped into the hallway with his gun levelled at Reem.

'So, another piece of the jigsaw that ruined my life,' he said in a threatening manner. 'Back to the lounge and make that call, Mrs Taylor. I'm getting rather impatient to meet your husband. Tell him to come home immediately and to come alone. If I have the slightest suspicion that he has anyone with him I will kill you and your friend. Make sure you tell him that.'

The two women nervously hurried down the hall and once inside the lounge Reem was instructed by a rough push in the back to sit on the settee while Helen went to the small writing bureau to make the call.

'Hello, darling,' Stuart said on answering.

'I've been told to tell you to come home, Stuart,' Helen said, her throat parched from fear.

'What's wrong? Who told you?'

'Major Kazemi says he wants to talk to you. Don't come, darling. He wants to kill you!' Helen leant away from the swinging arm she had detected in her peripheral vision but the gun barrel grazed her forehead and she fell to the floor stunned. Kazemi took the phone that was still clutched in her hand. Reem jumped up to help her friend but he waved her back to the settee with the gun.

'Mr Taylor, it would be wise to do what your wife should have said. Come to the apartment now and I may spare her and the girl,' Kazemi snarled.

'What girl?'

'I overheard your wife calling her Reem and she seems to be a close friend.'

'Major, if anything happens to my wife and Reem I will tear you apart with my own hands,' Stuart roared.

'Do please calm down, Mr Taylor. All you have to do is arrive within thirty minutes. However, any later and I cannot be held responsible for the consequences,' Kazemi said softly and he hung up.

Stuart listened to the low hum of the empty line for a few seconds as he slowly recovered from the shock and then he quickly hung up and dialled his friend.

'Alan, Major Kazemi managed to escape Walid's trap. He wasn't on the Sunseeker when it was being hunted and destroyed. Somehow he had slipped from the boat after it had left Dubaiya Marina and now he's in my apartment holding Helen and Reem hostage.'

Stuart's rapid delivery left Alan as rattled as his friend had been and a few moments passed before he was able to respond. 'My God, Stuart. What does he want?'

'I believe he wants me,' Stuart said calmly. 'And if he doesn't get me he's promised to kill the women.'

'Okay, so what's the plan?' Alan said despairingly.

'No plan yet, pal, other than going straight there and confronting the bastard. Don't worry, we'll get the girls out safely one way or another.'

'You won't be going alone, Stuart. Let's think this through, what would Major Walid do?'

'He'd think of creating a diversion and then surprise the bastard with something completely unpredictable.'

'Right, so while Walid is recovering in hospital you make the bold approach as the diversion while I come up with something unexpected with Captain Dabal.' Alan's spirits rose at the thought of bringing down the man who threatened the girl he loved.

'Right, and as I only have twenty-five minutes left to get to the apartment you will have to bring the captain up to speed as quickly as possible. I suggest you call Dabal and time any action you take for exactly twenty minutes from now. Until then I'll go ahead and see if I can negotiate the girls out of the line of fire.'

'That sounds very dangerous but, as we have to move fast, let's get going.' Alan checked the time as he hung up and then dialled police headquarters.

Two floors below Stuart grabbed his jacket and hurried out of his office giving his secretary a vague excuse for missing his next meeting as he rushed past her desk. His Jeep emerged from the company car park at a dangerous speed, narrowly missing the managing director's Mercedes and he was soon racing through central Manama to the apartment.

Alan quickly explained the situation to Captain Dabal who immediately ordered his SWAT team to surround the building and cordon off the streets. He agreed to pick Alan up from his office on the way and they arrived shortly after Stuart had stepped out of the lift on the twentieth floor and was making his way to his apartment.

'If I position marksmen on the floor they can easily be seen from the spyhole which could cause Major Kazemi to panic and do something desperate,' Dabal said as he conferred with Alan in the lobby.

Yazzan, who had been made SWAT team leader stood close by, listening to every comment before speaking himself: 'I have the best marksmen with night vision equipment in key positions on the roofs of the buildings facing the apartment but the highest they can get will still mean they have to shoot upward. It's an impossible angle but if Major Kazemi comes out onto the balcony and into their line of fire they have been instructed to take him out.' He was armed with a Heckler & Koch machine-gun with the buttstock unfolded and was dressed in full body armour. He handed Kevlar vests to both Captain Dabal and Alan.

'You may need these, sir,' he said unnecessarily.

Alan slipped the heavy vest over his head and then paused, interrupted by a thought inspired by Yazzan's words.

'Balconies.' He said the single word as though he had discovered the Holy Grail.

'Are you thinking what I'm thinking?' Captain Dabal asked cryptically as he suddenly understood the meaning of Alan's remark.

'I'm an extremely experienced climber and to descend from one balcony to another in the dark would be a piece of cake for me,' Alan explained.

'We can't allow a civilian to do what some of my men are trained to do,' Yazzan said but Alan continued as though he hadn't heard the man's objection.

'Give me an automatic and I can be on Stuart's balcony in five minutes at the most.'

'And so can five of my men, sir!' Dabal said.

'I understand what you're saying, Dabal, but I'll ask you this, can your big lads in full combat gear land on that balcony as light as anorexic cats?'

In frustration Yazzan looked to his captain for help but saw that his superior officer was slowly nodding his head.

'I agree with Alan, Yazzan, except I insist that two anorexic cats would be better because I've done quite a bit of rock climbing myself.'

Alan grinned broadly. 'Then let's go, Captain,' and he hurried into the first open lift. Yazzan pushed the button for the twenty-first floor and they went to apartment No. 213, giving the rather attractive German lady who answered the door the shock of her life. After the briefest of apologies the two heavily armed police officers and Dabal hurried through her apartment to the windows that opened out onto the balcony.

Captain Dabal waved down to the marksmen on the roof of the building opposite and received a signal of recognition. The men were at least three floors below the target balcony and the only clear shot would be if Kazemi walked onto the balcony and leant against the guard rail.

Alan looked over the railing to the poorly lit steet below and was surprised at how far it was to the balcony below them. 'About four metres, Dabal,' he whispered. 'We'll need short lengths of rope tied off on this rail with knots every half metre. If they dangle too far down they may be seen by anyone inside the living room who is facing the window.'

Dabal had snatched a look over the railing before returning to Alan. 'If the construction is exactly the same as this apartment then there is a stretch of blank wall to the left of the balcony that cannot be viewed from inside.'

'Well spotted, we'll use that and descend one at a time.'

While the two men had been studying the lower balcony Yazzan had cut and prepared three lengths of rope and he handed two to the captain.

'Sorry, Yazzan,' Dabal said as he took the third piece of rope from the disappointed man's hand. 'I want you to get two of your men and "the big key" and open the front door in precisely five minutes' time. This will create the diversion we need to cover our entry through the balcony windows.'

Yazzan perked up at being ordered to use the steel battering ram on the front door and they synchronized their watches. Saluting smartly he trotted from the apartment, narrowly missing an extremely confused lady who was bringing coffee to the men.

Feigning disappointment, Alan said, 'Danke, mein Fräulein but we've no time to socialize.' He finished tying a bowline at the end of his rope and then double-checked the captain's handiwork. 'That's very good, Dabal. You weren't kidding about knowing something about climbing.'

'I've scaled the Matterhorn and the Jungfrau in summer and in winter,' Dabal whispered back as he hooked a leg over the railing and checked his watch. Seventeen minutes had elapsed since speaking to Stuart and Alan quickly climbed over the rail and lowered himself down, pausing at each knot to steady any sway until he reached the last one and with his arms at full stretch was able to lightly touch the railing of Stuart's balcony with the toes of his shoes. He let his full weight rest on the rail as he placed the flat of one hand against the balcony ceiling before releasing the rope.

Alan lightly jumped down from the railing to land feather-like on the marble floor. He removed the automatic from his pocket and kept watch on the glass double doors as Dabal descended. A foot groping for the railing struck a flowerpot and as it toppled inward Alan quickly bent forward and reached out with one hand to catch it. The earth-filled container drove his hand down to be crushed against the marble tiles and he emitted a low grunt of pain. He steadied the pot before grabbing Dabal's foot with bloodied knuckles to guide it onto the rail.

For a few seconds the two men waited in the dark with their backs against the end wall until it was clear that nothing had been heard inside the apartment. The captain removed the Glock automatic from its holster and then checked his watch once more.

Stuart rang the door chime and there was a short wait before he heard the chain being removed and the locks opening. The door swung open to reveal his wife and behind her with a pistol held to her head was Major Kazemi.

'Do be careful, Mr Taylor. I am very nervous and I don't trust the trigger pressure on this weapon,' he said in a soft disquieting manner.

Stuart entered the apartment and closed the door behind him. 'Are you all right, darling,' Stuart asked concernedly.

'If having a gun held to your head is okay, Stuart, then I suppose it's yes,' she joked with a nervous tremor in her voice as Kazemi slowly pulled her away from the door. After being told to relock the door Stuart followed the couple down the hallway.

They went into the living room and Stuart greeted Reem with a forced smile he hoped would reassure her. 'Hello Reem, I do trust Helen has been entertaining you well.'

'Not as well as this gentleman,' she replied bravely as she pointed to Major Kazemi.

'Shut up or I will shut you up,' the major shouted and they all fell silent. Stuart slowly moved sideways to stand as a shield in front of his wife who had also cleverly put herself before Reem.

At least he hasn't shot me out of hand, Stuart thought. Alan and Dabal may still be on time. He surreptitiously glanced down at his watch and saw that more than nineteen minutes had passed.

'Yes, your time's up,' Kazemi sneered when he noticed Stuart glancing at his watch and he raised the pistol to aim it at the geologist's head. As his forefinger took up the first pressure there was a sudden crash from down the hallway, swiftly followed by a second crash and the splintering of wood.

Kazemi spun around to face the entrance to the living room and Stuart threw himself backwards, knocking both women onto the settee that he had knocked over to provide meagre cover. Helen and Reem tumbled onto the floor as the major turned back, his face as black as thunder.

As Yazzan and a corporal burst into the room the glass doors to the balcony burst inward under the combined impact of two men. Captain Dabal and Alan sprang to their feet with weapons levelled at Kazemi.

The major hesitated between the two groups of men before deciding on taking his revenge. He turned to aim the gun at Stuart who was rising to his feet in front of the settee's protective shield and four weapons roared as one. Kazemi was spun around by the heavy-calibre bullets and collapsed like a puppet with its strings cut, the gun still clutched in his hand. Stuart leapt forward and kicked the weapon from Kazemi's hand before kneeling to assess the damage the bullets had wreaked.

Kazemi had been shot in the chest and stomach and his left arm was almost severed. He was rapidly dying from external and internal bleeding and Stuart stared into the man's eyes without a hint of sympathy.

'Why did you betray your country with drug smuggling?' Captain Dabal said as he also knelt beside the prone man.

Kazemi coughed and fresh drops of blood filled his mouth. 'I was acting under orders,' he gurgled as he began to choke on his own blood.

'Orders? Who can possibly give the police orders to deal in drugs?'

'The Magician—' A fresh bout of coughing cut his words and Captain Dabal shook the man by the shoulders.

'You can't touch Abdullah,' Kazemi managed to say and as he tried to laugh he lapsed into a paroxysm of coughing that splattered the two men with his blood.

'Abdullah who?' Despite the agony wracking his body Kazemi turned his head to stare at Stuart with pure hatred in his eyes.

'Sheikh Al-Tahlawi,' he wheezed. 'He's the number one dealer and pornographer in the Middle East.' Kazemi coughed a gobbet of blood onto Stuart's knee before trying to take air into his shattered lung. 'He sells little girls and boys and uses them himself. He has the protection of other sheikhs and princes, nobody can touch him!' Kazemi wanted to laugh at the horror shown on both men's faces but could only choke as he burst into another bout of coughing that abruptly ended with a long, wheezing exhalation. His head lolled to one side but the dark eyes remained fixed upon Stuart as though daring him to prove his dying statement a lie.

Dabal placed a forefinger on the man's neck and waited a couple of seconds before speaking. 'He's dead.' He stood up and dabbed at the blood spots on his uniform with a tissue. Alan raised Reem to her feet and wrapped his arms around her and the young nurse began to sob with relief.

Stuart and Helen embraced in silence and she pulled back to look at him with tearful eyes. 'How long are you going to keep on rescuing me before it gets through your thick skull that I'd still keep on loving you without all these foolish heroics.' Stuart laughed, then kissed her and drew her close to him again.

'We have a serious situation, gentlemen,' Dabal said gravely. 'Kazemi spoke the truth. Although the majority of the royals are highly respected men Sheikh Abdullah Al-Tahlawi is very close to certain princes and most probably supplies most of them with cocaine and pornography.'

'You mean heroin and innocent children, don't you, Captain?' Helen said softly over Stuart's shoulder.

'You are quite right, Mrs Taylor,' Dabal said sadly. 'If Kazemi's dying words are true then we are powerless to act against this man. He cannot be arrested as we have no evidence and we can only rely on the words of a man we have killed. In the meantime, if it becomes known to the sheikh that we are aware of his activities then you can be sure that all who heard Kazemi's words will one by one either be forced out of the country or made to disappear in the desert.

'Who heard Kazemi mention the sheikh?' Stuart asked as he looked round the room. Yazzan and the corporal slowly nodded as did Captain Dabal, Alan and the two women. 'Then we must all swear to keep our knowledge a secret. This is the only way to protect ourselves and our families. Therefore Kazemi died without saying anything, right?'

'Right,' they chorused as Dabal dialled headquarters and proceeded to report that the renegade police officer had finally been cornered but had refused to surrender and was subsequently killed in an exchange of gunfire.

'His weapon wasn't discharged,' Alan observed after Dabal had finished his call and Stuart went to the weapon lying on the floor. Using his handkerchief he picked it up and with a brief warning to the two women to cover their ears he fired two shots into the settee before tossing the gun back onto the floor.

Captain Dabal smiled broadly. 'Well, that makes my report less complicated to write.' He turned to the grinning young officer: 'Yazzan, gather the men, inform them that they have done an excellent job and return them to headquarters leaving two men to guard the apartment.'

Yazzan saluted and waving to the corporal to join him he briskly left the apartment.

Stuart and Alan were about to lift the settee when Dabal stopped them with a raised hand. 'Forensics will still want to do a routine study.'

Stuart shrugged. 'In which case I suggest we adjourn to a rather nice restaurant near here and fortify the ladies and ourselves after this very unpleasant ordeal.'

'The best idea I've heard for a long time,' Alan chimed in as he took Reem's hand and led the still shaking girl from the room. Stuart offered his arm and Helen curtsied in jest before taking it and waving to the captain to join them.

'I still have to tidy up a few things and await the forensic team but I will join you later, thank you for the invitation,' Dabal said gratefully.

The couple made their way through the small crowd of curious tenants being held back by Yazzan and his squad of SWAT officers to join Alan and Reem at the waiting lift.

As the lift doors closed on the friends Yazzan called a private number.

'*Es salaam alykhum*, cousin. Allah be praised for he has shown us the way to give Esraa everlasting peace in Paradise.'

'Where shall we meet, Yazzan?' Bassam asked.

24

Despite the lateness of the hour the outside temperature was still uncomfortably high and Stuart's shoulder sagged under the weight of an old canvas bag. Helen strode beside him as they entered the hospital and were instantly grateful for the coolness of the marble-floored reception. Alan and Reem were close behind and together they cornered the Night Sister to insist on being allowed to visit Major Walid Safa.

Eventually Helen and Reem were able to assure the sister that they were medical staff and the distraught woman relented and allowed them to visit the major provided they didn't stay for more than ten minutes.

They were shown into a private room and found their old friend comfortably seated in an armchair and fully engrossed in a television news programme. He was wearing a slightly flamboyant dressing gown and apart from leaning to the right to favour his wounded side he appeared to be in fine fettle.

Walid's black eyes sparkled on seeing the two ladies with his friends and he held his hand out to Stuart.

'Stuart, it is so kind of you to come at such a late hour and to bring such beautiful visions with you.'

'Gee, thanks, Walid,' Alan said acting coyly.

The major laughed. 'Obviously you have some news and I insist that you tell me everything that has happened since your return to port,' he said eagerly.

Stuart related all that had taken place without a single interruption from Walid who was clearly fascinated by the turn of events. When he came to quoting the dying words of Major Kazemi he glanced briefly at Alan who nodded and he continued, giving Walid word for word everything that had been said.

'So this is the main man at the end of my long journey,' Walid murmured when Stuart finally ended his report. 'Sheikh Abdullah Al-Tahlawi.' He sighed as though in defeat and sank back into the cushions with a slight grimace of discomfort.

'Is there nothing we can do about him?' Alan asked, knowing too well what the answer would be.

'I'm very sorry, Alan. As much as I would like to arrange his arrest with the Bahraini police and seal off the drug pipeline into Saudi forever there's nothing I can do. He's beyond the law, a power unto himself. He could even have me arrested and jailed by the police authorities on my return to Riyadh and what he might then arrange for me doesn't bear thinking about.'

'What's our best course of action then, Walid?'

'Helen, I would suggest that you all return to the safety of your own countries,' Walid reluctantly admitted. 'He will not bother to send people after you there and I'll write up my report to show that Major Kazemi was the prime dealer and that the drug-smuggling operation has suffered a severe setback.'

'You do know that very soon your task will start all over again,' Stuart said with bitterness in his voice. 'The sheikh will undoubtedly recruit new people in Iran and here in Bahrain to resume his drug-running operations as though nothing had ever happened.'

'And he'll possibly do it with the help of more corrupt police officers,' Alan said.

'I fear you're quite right, my friends. Which means I will have to come back and round up more minor players while being forced to ignore the main attraction—the one man who, if eliminated, could end drug smuggling and child prostitution in this region completely.'

The door opened and the Night Sister crooked her finger at the four visitors. 'It's time to leave and allow Major Walid to get his rest,' she demanded.

Alan grasped the major's hand firmly. 'You take care of yourself and that lovely wife of yours, mate,' he said quickly and turned his head away to hide his sadness at their final parting.

Reem kissed the major on both cheeks and went to stand by Alan as Helen leant over the bluff moustachioed police officer and hugged him. 'I will miss you so much, Walid. You have been our strength when all seemed lost,' she whispered in his ear and then she kissed his stubbly cheek, making the veteran policeman blush.

Stuart took his friend's hand and shook it without saying anything. Then he bent down and lifted up the battered canvas bag he had been carrying. 'This contains the necklaces and jewellery Alan and I recovered from the wreck. What would you like us to do with it?'

Walid smiled and shook his head. 'It's not for me to decide, Stuart. It was your find and although some may claim the cultural origin of the pieces should, by right, place them in the Bahrain National Museum others may argue that the contents were once owned by Portuguese sailors and lost in international waters. That makes them the property of whoever recovered them from the seabed.'

'You mean we can keep them?' Alan asked, his excitement growing.

'Well, the wreck was in international waters so, draw your own conclusions.'

Stuart looked into his friend's mischievous eyes. 'We'll donate three-quarters of their value to the Islamic Relief fund and divide the remainder amongst the six of us.'

'Six? We're only five, Stuart,' Alan corrected, looking around the room.

'There is also Shehhi's family,' Stuart murmured with his eyes fixed on Walid's face.

The major nodded so slowly it was as though he was silently reciting a prayer for his lost comrade. 'Thank you, Stuart, for remembering those so easily forgotten,' he said as he gripped the geologist's arms.

The Night Sister made a shushing noise and beckoned to the group with an annoyed expression. Stuart smiled, picked up the canvas bag and taking Helen by the hand went to the door.

Walid watched the four people he had grown extremely fond of file out of the room under the watchful eyes of the Night Sister and a lump rose in his throat that for some strange reason refused to clear.

They had changed their police uniforms for traditional white cotton *thawbs* and red-checked *smaagh* head coverings to join the protesters and march along Government Avenue. Yazzan and Bassam carried a protest banner that demanded a new constitution and the release of hundreds of Shia men and boys. Like the mass of students and young people surrounding them they were chanting 'neither Sunni nor Shia but Bahraini' as they slowly progressed along the four-lane avenue to make a stand outside the Central Municipal Council building.

The security police, who were largely non-Bahraini Sunni Moslems recruited in Pakistan, Yemen, Syria and Jordan had been tailing the protesters, mercilessly using their long batons to beat those that lagged behind. It soon became evident to the watching media that the protesters were being driven towards a temporary barricade that had been erected across the street by the security police. This was heavily manned by another large force that was armed with batons, teargas rounds and shotguns.

'We're very close,' Yazzan shouted into his cousin's ear and Bassam nodded with a grim determined expression on his face. The two men handed the banner to the two walking in front of them with the excuse that they needed to find a toilet and they then weaved their way to the side of the road where they slipped into a doorway that had been deliberately left open for them by friends sympathetic to their task. Bassam shut and bolted the door and the two men hurried down the hallway with *thawbs* flapping around their ankles to the rear of the building where they emerged into a small courtyard. Bougainvillea was in full riotous colour and the scent of jasmine plants was intoxicating in the enclosed area.

A small wrought-iron gate set in the high wall surrounding the courtyard garden had also been left open and Yazzan peered into the street before quickly ducking back.

'We have another five minutes, are you ready?' he asked as he studied his cousin's face that was drained of all colour.

'I'm ready, Yazzan. For my Esraa I'm more than ready.' He shifted the small bag slung over his shoulder to a more comfortable position and waited for his cousin's signal.

Across the street an opalescent, pink Lamborghini Gallardo glinted in the sun and the large man who guarded the precious vehicle was perspiring heavily.

Yazzan nodded reassuringly at Bassam and then casually stepped through the gateway and crossed the road. The guard quickly turned and watched the strange man approaching with wary eyes.

'*Es salaam alykhum*, do you have the correct time?' Yazzan asked with a smile.

The man glanced down at his wrist and in that split second of distraction Yazzan leapt and grabbed the man by the head. As the impact of the collision drove both men backwards Yazzan gave a violent twist and grunted with satisfaction on hearing the crunch of the top vertebrae snapping. He used the dead man to cushion his fall before rolling to one side and jumping to his feet. Yazzan quickly checked the street in both directions for witnesses before waving to Bassam. The two men swiftly carried the guard back to the courtyard and covered him with empty fertilizer bags that Bassam had found nearby before returning to the gate to resume waiting and watching.

'I feel bad about killing an innocent man,' Bassam groaned despairingly.

'Do not concern yourself about that piece of slime. I had friends check him out and they discovered that he was the one who delivered the children to customers.'

Bassam ran across the courtyard and began kicking the plastic covered body. After a minute of frenzied assault he slowly returned to his cousin with tears streaming down his face.

Yazzan put an arm round his shoulders. 'You will soon have total peace of mind, cousin,' he said softly before looking at his watch and peering round the corner to check on the parked car.

The two cousins had to wait another nine minutes before they saw the sheikh walking towards his Lamborghini. The man paused and looked around with a mixture of anger and puzzlement on discovering that the bodyguard was missing.

He tripped the lock and gave one last look round before lowering himself into the very low sports car and squeezing his massive girth behind the steering wheel.

As the precisely engineered door shut Yazzan touched Bassam on the shoulder. 'Now is the time, quick!'

Bassam left the shelter of the gateway and darted across the street to tap urgently on the driver's window.

Sheikh Abdullah Al-Tahlawi looked up in irritation at the man crouching beside his door and flicked his fingers to indicate that Bassam should go away.

Bassam remained where he was and smiled as he held up a photograph of Esraa. He had taken it on her tenth birthday party and she was dressed in a sugar-starched blue frock and proudly wearing a tinsel crown in her raven locks. Bassam had spent all morning making it for her and she had squealed with delight, proclaiming it her best present. Her innocent eyes were shining with joy as she bent forward to blow out the candles and Bassam had caught that magical moment with his new digital camera.

The sheikh stared at the picture and his wet tongue lasciviously licked his thick lips. There was a soft hum and the window opened giving the man the opportunity to snatch the photograph from Bassam's hand and study it more closely.

Bassam watched the sheikh's small eyes devouring his sister and he surreptitiously slipped his hand inside the satchel to remove the M67 fragmentation grenade. With his eyes still fixed on the man everyone had said was a law unto himself Bassam removed the safety pin.

'I will give you one thousand dollars for this little piece of heaven,' Sheikh Abdullah said as he continued to leer at the picture.

'I'll give you hell and it won't cost you a single *fils*,' Bassam snarled as he dropped the grenade inside the car. He stood up and raced back across the street. The sheikh had immediately recognized the object and he screamed in terror as he tried to reach past his obese body to the floor beneath the foot pedals where the grenade had teasingly rolled. He tried gripping it between his feet and bringing the deadly container to within reach of his scrabbling fingers as the seconds ticked by.

The two cousins, their ears deaf to the screams behind them, closed the courtyard gate and retraced their steps to the front door where they were soon absorbed into the throng of protesters. The original chanting had now turned to cries of pain and distress as the uniformed officers waded into the men and women with flailing batons.

The people began to break up and disperse under the vicious onslaught while shouting promises to each other to meet the following morning. Only the cousins, counting the seconds, were aware of the muffled explosion that came from the street beyond the tall buildings, signalling the Magician's last trick.

'Could we be arrested for joining this protest and disturbing the peace?' Yazzan joked with a grim smile.

'It would make a wonderful alibi, cousin,' Bassam said and the two men linked arms and ran along with the dispersing crowd, laughing.